Jonathan Mantle was born in the north of England, educated in the south and is married and lives in London. He has written a novel and a collection of short stories, and his journalism has been published in the *Sunday Times*, the *Observer* and the *Listener*. *In For A Penny* is his first non-fiction book.

IN FOR A PENNY
*The unauthorised biography
of Jeffrey Archer*

—————

Jonathan Mantle

SPHERE BOOKS LIMITED

SPHERE BOOKS LTD

Published by the Penguin Group
27 Wrights Lane, London w8 5TZ, England
Viking Penguin Inc., 40 West 23rd Street, New York, New York 10010, USA
Penguin Books Australia Ltd, Ringwood, Victoria, Australia
Penguin Books Canada Ltd, 2801 John Street, Markham, Ontario, Canada L3R 1B4
Penguin Books (NZ) Ltd, 182–190 Wairau Road, Auckland 10, New Zealand

Penguin Books Ltd, Registered Offices: Harmondsworth, Middlesex, England

First published in Great Britain by Hamish Hamilton Ltd 1988
Published by Sphere Books Ltd, 1989
1 3 5 7 9 10 8 6 4 2

Printed and bound in Great Britain by
Richard Clay Ltd, Bungay, Suffolk

Contents

List of illustrations

Jeffrey with the Beatles in 1963. Nick Lloyd is second from the left. (*Sunday Times*)

The victorious 1966 Oxford University Athletic Team. Jeffrey as President is seated in the centre of the front row. (John Bryant)

The Director General of the National Birthday Trust in his favourite pose with JFK in the background. (BBC Hulton Picture Library)

Jeffrey with Tim Cobb on their Far Eastern fundraising tour. (Tim Cobb)

The young MP and proprietor of Arrow Enterprises at home in the Boltons. (Times Newspapers)

Mary at Oxford. (Mail Newspapers)

Mary on the day she was awarded her Ph.D. (Times Newspapers)

Jeffrey campaigning in the 1970 General Election in his Louth constituency. (Mrs Philippa Taylor MBE)

Mary on the campaign trail. (Mrs Philippa Taylor MBE)

Jeffrey and Mary in Lincolnshire, 1972. She is expecting their first child. (*Grimsby Evening Telegraph*)

'I've no need to work ever again in my life.' Jeffrey at the time of the Terry Coleman interview in 1973. Disaster was already on the horizon. (*Guardian*)

Jeffrey at the Alembic House apartment – his 'Westminster flat'. (*Observer*)

The 1984 *Grimsby Evening Telegraph* inaugural Literary Luncheon. (*Grimsby Evening Telegraph*)

Chairman of the Conservative Party Norman Tebbit and Deputy Jeffrey Archer, 1985. (Express Newspapers)

The Archers at home in Grantchester, 1985. 'We can use this picture for our Christmas card,' said Jeffrey. 'I think that's rather vulgar,' said Mary. (Express Newspapers)

Jeffrey immediately after his resignation as Deputy Chairman, 26 October, 1986. (Mail Newspapers)

By May, 1987, Jeffrey was unofficially back on the General Election campaign trail, apparently undaunted. (Mail Newspapers)

Jeffrey and Mary after the *Star* libel verdict, 24 July, 1987. (Rex Features)

In for a Penny

'Terry, I want to go out and work sixteen hours a day. Not because I want to make more money. I'm sure that you can see I'm . . .'

'Not on the breadline? No, Jeffrey.'

'No, and I've no need to work ever again in my life. I can now, aged thirty-two, just sit in this room and talk to you for the rest of my life.'

'Yes, Jeffrey.'

'The truth of the matter is I want to work . . . I don't mind how much they tax me as long as I'm allowed to work.'

'Yes, Jeffrey.'

'I can't get out of bed in the morning and say today I'm not going to be ambitious and I'm not going to make a penny. You can't do it. People of course say, "He's ambitious. He's so thrusting." What am I supposed to do? Lie in a cold bath?'

'No, Jeffrey.'

It was July, 1973. Jeffrey Archer realised further protest was futile. Terry Coleman was a good journalist and a 'kind' person, but he worked for the *Guardian*. Jeffrey tended to divide the world into 'kind' and 'unkind' people. This fact is very important to any understanding of his career.

Guardian readers were 'unkind': well-heeled lefties who lived in tasteful affluence in north London. *Guardian* readers were always ready to knock a go-getting free-marketeer like Jeffrey Archer.

He had had more luck with 'Atticus' of the *Sunday Times*. Atticus had not been so unkind, for example, as to question the legend of Jeffrey Archer. Jeffrey Archer, whose father was British Consul in Singapore; who had left Wellington for America via the Panama Canal on a tramp steamer; who had gone up to Oxford, helped raise a million for Oxfam, run for Britain and married the most brilliant girl of her generation; and who gave interviews to journalists at his £170,000 home in The Boltons, South Kensington and at the tastefully furnished offices of Arrow Enterprises in White-hall, a stone's throw from the House of Commons, of which he was the youngest ever member.

A million for Oxfam: 'It's easier now for a young man to make a million than ever before,' he told Atticus. In fact, according to Atticus, he was just about to pull off a coup that would put him well into the millionaire class. Jeffrey had long been in the habit of telling people he wanted to be a millionaire by the time he was thirty. He was thirty-two now, true, but what did that matter? He was already a 'name' at Lloyds; he had been speculating heavily in commodities. 'Expect a fairly sensational announcement,' said Atticus, 'soon.'

Jeffrey neither smoked nor drank to excess, but he was about to make enough money to keep him in Krug champagne and Romeo y Julieta cigars for life. Not to mention the financing of his long-held ambition to be Prime Minister of Great Britain.

Jeffrey was about to make a million pounds, and nothing could stop him.

It was July, 1973.

In Montreal, four men well known to each other checked the market price of a little known stock called Aquablast. All four of them were rich men, and in a few months they would be considerably richer as a result of their labours.

Jeffrey, on the other hand, would be penniless.

Jeffrey Howard Archer was conceived around the time the British Prime Minister, Neville Chamberlain, repeated his pledge to defend Poland. He was thus born a war baby, in the City of London Maternity Hospital, EC1, on 15 April,

1940. Elsewhere on that day, British troops arrived in Norway, and in Berlin another self-made man who had risen from humble origins to high political office contemplated the map of Europe.

His parents differed in age. Lola Cook, at twenty-five, was a few years younger than William Archer. William Archer lived in a boarding house owned by Mrs Rhoda Bowness at 48, Highbury Grove. On Jeffrey's birth certificate he described himself as a journalist, as do many of Highbury's inhabitants to this day. Few traces of William Archer or his work remain, and his one enduring legacy – Jeffrey – would spend most of his life without the benefit of a father.

Lola, by contrast, was a tough, self-taught woman in every respect, and she would outlive William by many years and marry twice more. At sixty-eight she would embark on a programme of formal education – having retired some time earlier from a career, untouched by controversy, in local journalism and the government of one of Britain's best-known seaside resorts.

Lola lived separately across the Thames at 18, Nelson Square, Southwark. Nelson Square lay between Waterloo and London Bridge stations, half a mile south of Blackfriars Bridge. Nearby to the north-east lay the City of London and the Docks. By the time Jeffrey was three months old, British troops had withdrawn from Norway and Dunkirk, and the man in Berlin had declared a war of total annihilation against his enemies. These included William, Lola and Jeffrey. Highbury Grove, Nelson Square and the London Docks were lit up night after night by incendiary bombs. By day, the blue skies over the south of England were criss-crossed with vapour trails as the two airforces fought the Battle of Britain. Winston Churchill, whose recorded war speeches Jeffrey would one day take to the White House, had taken office with the promise of blood, sweat and tears and no surrender. It was not a good time to be in London. William, Lola and Jeffrey, albeit for rather more pressing reasons, did what

3

thousands of Londoners did every summer. They went to the seaside.

Weston-super-Mare was and is the archetypal British holiday resort. London Transport posters of the 1930s included frequent invitations to 'Glorious Weston'. Weston meant esplanades, deckchairs, ice-creams, boarding houses and beach huts. Tucked away beyond the Mendip Hills, 125 miles west of London, it maintained a dignified, English distance on the other side of the Severn from Cardiff. To the west, you could stare across the sands of Bridgwater Bay and out to sea, waiting for the Americans to arrive. Weston was, to some, suffocatingly provincial. But it was safe, and sound, and thus it became, for thousands of evacuees from London, a haven from the unwelcome attentions of the Luftwaffe; and a first proper home for Jeffrey Archer.

If Weston was well behind the lines, the war none the less made itself increasingly felt on the domestic front. Jeffrey was eight months old when German night bombers transformed Bristol into an orange glow only a dozen miles away to the north-east. Three weeks later, just after the festive season of 1940, incendiary bombs destroyed the Guildhall and eight Wren churches in the City of London. In Weston, at least they were alive and learning to cope with shortages.

Jeffrey was a year old when clothes rationing was introduced. Food rationing swiftly followed: milk, eggs and oranges were distributed, with one four pint tin of dried milk per person every two months. The weekly ration of basic foods meant from a shilling to 2s. 2d worth of meat; four to eight ounces of bacon; one to eight ounces of cheese; two to four ounces of tea and eight ounces to a pound of sugar. Everything else was distributed, or withheld, according to a 'points' system. Dried egg became the housewife's main ingredient. Even soap was rationed.

Against this daily onslaught, the decisive events of the war might well have gone unnoticed had it not been for the radio and the newspapers, which Lola read avidly. The Japanese air attack on the US naval base at Pearl Harbor brought the Americans slowly closer to Weston. But the adult non-combatant population, grappling with shortages of every description, human and otherwise, was only temporarily distracted by the news of 1000 bomber raids on Germany or victories in the Western Desert. The adults, to whom pre-war plenty was a memory that would never quite go away, were to suffer physically from six years of the cumulative privations brought on by rationing – especially when they went on long after the war was over. William Archer, never entirely well, would go into postwar decline; baby Jeffrey, brought up on orange juice, halibut liver oil and milk, would grow into a small, thin but healthy child, indifferent to material shortages, having never known plenty.

Jeffrey's fifth birthday was followed by the suicide of the self-made man in his bunker in Berlin. In Weston, as in countless other towns, the freedom from blackout was celebrated by fireworks and bonfires. There was a new Labour government under Attlee, and, closer to Jeffrey's future interests, a new British International Cross Country Team. It seemed appropriate, somehow, that their first concern was to find the 1,816 clothing coupons needed for all their shorts, vests and tracksuits.

William, Lola and Jeffrey Archer never returned to what was left of Nelson Square, Southwark, or Highbury Grove. They stayed in Weston-super-Mare, moving from lodgings to lodgings and finally to a terraced house in Locking Road. William, bent double with back pain, was an increasingly rare sight to the neighbours, who for some reason knew him as 'Captain Archer'. The Archers had hardly any money. Lola did the job of two parents at once. Jeffrey, growing up without brothers or sisters, with a dominant mother and a retiring father, was taking more and more space. Luckily, he was old enough to go to primary school.

Life was now marked for adults by the burdens of a comparatively purposeless peace. The war was over, but few people lit bonfires to celebrate the first anniversary of VE-Day on

8 May 1946, in Weston or elsewhere. The shortages were getting worse rather than better. The winter of 1947 was the worst of the century. Ice floes were sighted off the coast of Norfolk. Ten-foot drifts blocked roads to and from the seaside resort of Weston-super-Mare. Power stations closed down, and the Archers of Locking Road, by emergency government decree, were forbidden from switching on their electric fire between 9 a.m. and midday and 2 p.m. and 4 p.m.

Snow was followed by floods, as is often the case.

The Labour Government got the blame for it all.

Jeffrey, who would go on to castigate a Labour Government as MP for what seemed to him to be one of the coldest constituencies in Britain, was meanwhile making steady if unexciting progress at Christ Church Primary School, Weston-super-Mare.

He also showed precocious signs, perhaps understandably, of being the male breadwinner. In fact, bread, having been short for so long in all its forms, would never again be sufficient for Jeffrey. He joined the Boy Scouts aged eleven and raised the record sum of £3. 17s. 6d in Bob-A-Job Week; the Chief Scout, father to all Boy Scouts, wrote to him personally in gratitude. In the same year, he took his 11-plus at Christ Church Primary School.

The 11-plus examination was the first and most important institutionalised social opportunity for children of the post-war years. It was also uniquely British. Passing it meant that a hard-up but essentially middle-class child could go to grammar school or to one of the many fee-paying hybrids that acted as watersheds in the structure of British society. Failure, by the same token, meant fewer opportunities, fewer choices, fewer chances of succeeding, at least through the usual channels. Jeffrey was about to be given the chance of becoming the beneficiary of a revolution in Britain's education system.

Wellington College, in the Royal County of Berkshire, was

founded by public subscription in memory of the Duke of Wellington, victor of Waterloo, and granted a Royal Charter in 1853. The school buildings stand with robust dignity in some 400 acres of former pinewood estate twenty miles west of London. Wellington College has continued in a distinguished military tradition befitting an institution situated between Caesar's Camp and the rather more modern Royal Military Academy at Sandhurst.

Wellington, as it is better known, has given assistance to a large number of sons of deceased and living army officers and has consequently produced distinguished army officers in further large number. Over 1200 Old Wellingtonians died in the two World Wars and fifteen have won the Victoria Cross for extreme bravery. Wellington, the 'Royal and Religious Foundation' as it is entitled to be called, enjoys a close association with the British Royal Family and each year the school's outstanding scholar is presented with a gold medal struck at the Royal Mint as a personal gift of the Sovereign. Even the appointments of the governors have to be approved by Buckingham Palace. Jeffrey would be gratified in later life to see people nod their immediate approval on his casually mentioning he had been to 'Wellington'.

Wellington School, Somerset, to give it its full name, was and is tucked away between the Quantocks and the Black Down Hills some twenty-five miles south west of 'Glorious Weston'. The school functioned along the conventional boarding house system and its chapel of St Michael and St George was dedicated to old boys who fell in the Great War. The uniform was plain grey and its motto was *'Nisi Dominus Frustra'* which, roughly translated, means 'Unless There's A Boss, All Is Lost'. It is rather a good school, despite its unpretentious image and the fact that the odd old boy such as Jeffrey has allowed it to be confused with its royally recognised and richly endowed namesake. Unkind persons, in later life, would suggest that Jeffrey was sometimes a little tardy in correcting the understandable mistake people made in assuming he had been to a school which did not offer assisted

7

places to the pupils of Christ Church Primary School in Weston-super-Mare.

Jeffrey's success in the 11-plus thrilled Lola and confirmed the Chief Scout's expectations. Henceforth, he would be a vacation visitor to the terraced house in Locking Road. Kitted up in Wellington School grey and ready for rugby, he was still on the small side and managed to look young for his age even at eleven. But as a fit, keen and resourceful only child he was not visibly disturbed at being pitched into the company of the other eleven-year-olds. Churchill was back in No. 10 Downing Street, and at the terraced house in Locking Road William's back was getting worse. In September 1951 Archer, J. H. took up residence in Wellington School's junior boarding house, The Avenue.

He was an intelligent rather than an intellectual boy. His physical slightness led to the inevitable nickname (temperate none the less by public school standards) of 'pune'. He had a wide, flat mouth which was frequently open; when closed, it gave him an unfortunately smug expression. He was also a bit of a loner.

At the end of one term, he was taken by coach to Taunton Station to catch the Bristol train home to Weston. By some mistake, perhaps because he was busy talking to his new friends, he got into the London train instead. Discovering this just as the train was leaving the station, he pulled the emergency communication cord. The train stopped and Jeffrey got off again. It was a lesson he would carry into his adult life.

Wellington School was a sympathetic environment for an energetic self-starter. The Headmaster, 'Bankie Bill' Banks-Williams, was forgiving of academic limitations and appreciative of sporting ability. Jeffrey, with an only child's antipathy to team activities of all kinds, found his particular forte was running. He did so, however, largely by accident.

When he was about fourteen years old, the small boy from Weston had an accident in the school swimming pool. He hit

8

his head on the bottom and hurt his neck. He spent some time in hospital in nearby Taunton undergoing traction, as a result of which he seemed to grow noticeably. After that, his sporting prowess seemed to blossom.

Temperamentally, Jeffrey was a sprinter. He trained himself to beat the school 100- and 220-yard records and became an uncatchable rugby wing three-quarter. The ailing William Archer would sometimes come down and watch him. These were years of uniform austerity and depression, in which post-war gloom was relieved by individually heroic exploits which passed into popular legend. Six weeks after Jeffrey's thirteenth birthday, Hillary and Tensing climbed Everest in time to celebrate the Coronation. Three weeks after Jeffrey's fourteenth, three men on a cinder track in the Iffley Road, Oxford, helped a fourth to make athletic history. Roger Bannister, Oxford man and past President of Oxford University Athletic Club, became the first man in the world to run a mile in under four minutes. One of the three who helped him was another OUAC President and athlete with political ambitions, Christopher Chataway.

That year, Jeffrey went up to the senior house, The Willows, whose housemaster was Bert Nichol. Bankie Bill's reign was coming to a close and a new Headmaster loomed in the form of James Stredder. The chaplain was still a fellow called Lancaster. One day, when William had not been down to see Jeffrey for a while, Lancaster called Jeffrey in for 'a chat'. Thus did Jeffrey learn of his ailing father's death.

James Stredder was not the only one to notice the changes. The new Headmaster had already noticed how young Archer pushed himself to the limit, often without having thought out the consequences. Now the father for whom he had been running had gone; so had 'Bankie Bill', of whom Jeffrey had been visibly fond; and so, it seemed to Stredder, had some of Jeffrey's confidence and judgment.

Years later Stredder, living in dignified retirement near the South Downs, would have his life made a misery by the British tabloid press hounding him in search of a Jeffrey

Archer sex story. What was he like as a schoolboy? Did he wet his bed? Unable to go near a ringing telephone for months afterwards, the retired Headmaster would reflect ruefully on the impetuousness that affected Jeffrey's judgment at an early age, and on the premature death of the father whose own judgment might otherwise have guided him.

Yet, Jeffrey's school career appeared to take off after his father's death. If the child was father to the man, the undersized schoolboy who had pulled the communication cord now showed initiative beyond his tender years.

As well as athletics, he excelled at rugby, tennis and gymnastics. He joined the school cadet corps and became a first-class shot, colour sergeant and drummer in the band. In his last term, the school's physical education instructor fell ill and Jeffrey, as captain of gymnastics, undertook to produce the gymnastic display for the school Speech Day. The prizegiver was Field-Marshal Sir Claude Auchinleck. The climax of the display was for all the participants to collapse, spelling out the word 'AUK', the Field-Marshal's widely-known nickname. The guest of honour was suitably impressed.

Jeffrey became socially and physically more assertive. He adapted and staged one-act plays with himself in the lead and younger boys in supporting roles. He learned how to make his voice carry, on and off stage. He enjoyed reading aloud, and was regularly in the finals of the School Reading Competition. Leonard Isaac, one of his masters, found him academically an enthusiastic low-flier, whose greatest suffering would have been for a teacher to ignore him. But even Isaac, who had attended many such readings over his years at Wellington School, would be moved by Jeffrey's rendition of 'The Burial of Sir John Moore at Corunna'.

He began to push people around for their own good. At the age of seventeen, he was to be seen at the English Schools Athletics Championships, a squat, bulkily powerful, slightly hairy and very loud youth from Somerset. Hardly anybody had ever heard of an athletics team from Somerset. This one was entered for the 4 by 110 yards relay. They had clearly been badgered into forgetting that they were not basically very talented, and believing that they were a great relay team. They believed and they won. Among the hordes of spotty schoolboys looking on was a 220-yards runner from Yorkshire called Adrian Metcalfe. Neither of them knew it, but that day was a forewarning of the most extraordinary acquaintance of Metcalfe's life, and of a most fortuituous friendship for Jeffrey.

In June 1958, Churchill's *bête noire*, the anglophobic Charles de Gaulle, became Prime Minister of France. Jeffrey, who would devote a year of his life to raising funds to campaign for Britain's entry into the EEC, was performing less successfully off the athletics field. A-levels, after the 11-plus, were the second important social opportunity for children of the post-war years. Success meant the chance of a university place and a further widening of choices to achieve earning power and status. Jeffrey's lack of them meant that he left Wellington without a key aid to finding a direction in his young adult life.

The school track hero got a job as a deckchair attendant. He worked in a café for a while, and in an hotel. Weston, glorious Weston, was the same as ever. The summer passed and with it went the tourists and the seasonal jobs. To the west, across the sands of Bridgwater Bay, was America. London was 125 miles to the east, across the Mendips. He had to go somewhere, anywhere, as long as it was away from Weston. But where?

Jeffrey joined the Duke of Wellington's Regiment at its Halifax depot in the summer of 1958, not as a national serviceman but as a would-be regular. He looked good in uniform. He had impressed Field-Marshal Auchinleck. But he had been to the wrong 'Wellington', he did not have the 'right' social background. He remained an NCO, in spite of what contemporaries recognised as his athletic and leadership qualities. He left the army under his own steam.

What was a clean-cut, right-minded young man, of modest qualifications and immodest ambitions, in need of seniors to impress and juniors to badger, to do?

In his dreams, he went to America. In reality there was never any doubt. Jeffrey joined the police force.

The image of the police force, in the later 1950s, was still widely defined in the popular mind by the classic 1949 Ealing film *The Blue Lamp*. In it, a young man joins London's Metropolitan Police force. The fatherly figure who trains him is killed in a shooting, but the killer is apprehended. The training of real-life recruits in Jeffrey's time still had legendary connotations. Peel House, named after the father of the force, in Regency St SW1, was the old RAF officers' training building. After five months there, you were posted to a district.

PC Archer was posted to L Division, in Brixton. Brixton was a tough south London 'manor' with a large West Indian population in the process of colliding with an embittered white working-class. By curious coincidence, the London County Council Member for Brixton at that time was Victor, later Baron, Mishcon, who had distinguished himself as a perceptive and cogent force on the Departmental Committee on Homosexual Offences and Prostitution. Years later, the wise baron would advise the impetuous ex-PC after newspaper allegations had been made concerning Jeffrey and a prostitute called Monica.

L Division was a rather less heroic and captivating story than *The Blue Lamp*. After four weeks, as allowed under the terms of his training agreement, PC Archer resigned from the force.

Nearly thirty years later, the former police constable would publish his fifth international blockbusting novel, entitled *A Matter of Honour*. One passage would stand out in particular:

He should have taken his father's advice and joined the police force.

There were no class barriers there, and he would probably have been a chief superintendent by now.

Jeffrey drifted back to Weston and its deckchairs. He got another job, which was satisfactory solely in that it got him away from that town again. It was at a tiny crammer's school in Hampshire called Vicar's Hill, run by the fearsome Mrs Brewer. Jeffrey did menial tasks and taught PE. The ex-private soldier persuaded the boys to perform elaborate feats of gymnastics and woke up the school with a bugle every morning. He lived in, and when he was not coaching the boys, he trained rigorously at sprinting. Much use was made of new techniques, stop-watches and bits of tape. He had a mentor, a father-figure, called John Steadman, the forty-seven-year-old maths master; he took a shine to Jeffrey, teaching him to play poker and squash.

Jeffrey was now nearly twenty-one years old. Prime Minister Harold Macmillan was making speeches about the 'wind of change'. John F. Kennedy was running for President of the United States. Jeffrey, who would recruit both these names to further his own in the next few years, had already shown he had a talent.

Descartes had summed it up, 300 years earlier: 'I think, therefore I am.' Jeffrey, though he lacked formal training, had evolved his own philosophy of life. In his own way, and via Weston-super-Mare rather than the Sorbonne, he had arrived at the same conclusion. After all, he too was un-convinced by scholastic tradition and theological dogma; he too tried to get back to proving why anything can be said to be true. Modifying Descartes' intentions, Jeffrey had found a fruitful line of thought: 'I believe, therefore it is true.'

Yet now, for the first time in his life, he was in real danger of being left behind on the starting-blocks.

Dover College, Kent, occupied Victorian Gothic buildings on the site of the twelfth-century Priory of St Martin. It does so to this day, flintily bracing itself against the winds

13

from the English Channel, only eight minutes' walk away. Appropriately, the school catered in particular for the sons of absent parents. Dover Castle stood nearby and there was in general an air of solid, ivy-clad authority about the place.

The Headmaster of Dover College was T. H. 'Tim' Cobb. Cobb was ex-Harrow and Cambridge: a fifty-one-year-old crag of a man, whose obvious 'soundness' concealed an unusually open mind. This was perhaps to do with the fact that he was also ex-Secretary of the Uganda Headmasters Association. The Cobbs, Tim and Cecilia, lived with their children in the Headmaster's House. Tim Cobb was faced with the Headmaster's perennial problem, namely lack of staff and funds to pay them. Dover did not have games masters in those days, and the more rugged aspects of the rounding-out process were in the hands of enthusiastic and unpaid amateurs. In keeping, therefore, with Dover's declared aim to provide a secure environment for a rounded boy, he had advertised for a PE master who could teach geography. There were plenty of qualified teachers and he did not have to wait long for replies.

Cobb soon narrowed the field down to four men from their CVs. Three of them had been to Loughborough, the training college distinguished for athletics. One of the Loughborough men had been at a school in the outer London suburb of Raynes Park which was well known to Cobb. Cobb sent for him, and one other.

It was the middle of the summer term.

The Raynes Park and Loughborough man arrived first. He was sound, suburban and utterly suitable in every respect. Cobb's first instinct was to say: 'Well, look here, let's not beat about the bush. You can obviously do the job and I'll offer it to you.'

Instead, some other instinct prevented him, and he found himself saying: 'I can't make my mind up now, because I've got someone else to interview. But when I've interviewed him, I'll let you know.'

The interview over, Cobb and his prospective PE master

14

walked out of the Headmaster's House and down the rather grand steps that led into the Close. As they did so, what appeared to be a teenage boy came up the steps towards them, wearing a tweed jacket and grey flannel trousers.

'Is this the other man?' said the Loughborough man.

'Yes,' said Cobb.

The Loughborough man sniggered. They kept on down the steps and walked right past Jeffrey Archer.

He was very young. He was younger even than the oldest boy in the school, a twenty-one-year-old African. At the interview he spoke to the Headmaster in a way that was both respectful and confiding, almost as if he was addressing a father. Cobb liked that. There was something about Jeffrey that made him feel the boy would be successful.

This was definitely in spite of his better judgment.

'Are you all right on teaching geography?' he ventured.

'No,' said Jeffrey, 'but if I have to teach geography, then I will.'

'I see.'

They went to the gymnasium.

'This,' said Jeffrey, 'is the place where I am *alive*!'

He had that energy; he was obviously athletic; there was also something else there. Cobb could not put his finger on it.

Cobb was also impressed to hear Jeffrey speak so highly of 'Bankie Bill'. 'Bankie Bill' had been a popular junior master when Cobb was at Harrow.

He was very young, though.

'Thank you,' said Cobb, 'I'll get in touch with you.'

Jeffrey said a polite goodbye. He took the train from Dover Priory Station, a few minutes walk away, back to London and Weston-super-Mare. Cobb took himself off to see his Second Master.

The Second Master was a man whose advice he often sought, not least because he did not wait to hear Cobb's opinion before advising him on it.

'Look here,' said Cobb, 'I think this young man is probably what we want. But it's utterly unorthodox and he's never done anything before. There's also a chap I could play safe with and get what we want. What do you think?'

'It's pretty obvious,' said the Second Master, 'you've come to get me to back you up.'

Cobb went away again and sent two letters. One was to the Loughborough man and the other was to J. H. Archer, Esq.

The Loughborough man would be distinctly huffy about this. Jeffrey would be over the moon. Cobb, meanwhile, was having second thoughts.

There was Jeffrey's extreme youth, for a start. He really was a very young twenty.

Then there was the matter of his CV.

Cobb reread it for the nth time:

Wellington.
Army Physical Training Instructor's Course at the Royal Military Academy, Sandhurst.
Member, Duke of Wellington's Regiment basketball team.
Honours Diploma International Federation of Physical Culture, University of Berkeley, California.

Hmm: Cobb decided it would be churlish to inquire further. Instead, he would make a token attempt at contacting a referee. He rang up the proprietress of the school in Hampshire.

Her response was immediate, and distinguished by its succinctness. The Headmaster thanked her and replaced the receiver.

Years later, Jeffrey would tell Tim Cobb: 'When I got your letter it was one of the most exciting things that had ever happened to me.'

Cobb, to whom it was always perfectly obvious when Jeffrey was shooting a line, knew this remark to be genuine. He would make only one future reference to Jeffrey's lack of qualifications, and of the CV there was no further mention. Moreover, nearly thirty action-packed years would pass before the perceptive Headmaster first learned that, while his young protégé's manner was certainly military in origin, it may well also have had something to do with the fact, not mentioned on the CV, that he had recently spent five months in the police force.

Cobb had informed the Loughborough man that his services would not be required. He had offered Jeffrey the job of PE master, with additional geography: 'It's yours,' he had written, 'probably a mad decision, but it's yours.' If Jeffrey had every reason to be grateful, the proprietress of the little school in Hampshire had been equally unequivocal in her response: 'Don't touch him,' she had said. She did not elaborate, and Cobb did not ask her to. If it was the end of her brief dealing with Jeffrey Archer, for him it was just the beginning of a long and extraordinary attachment.

Keen and Able

The declared aim of the founders of Dover College was 'to provide a first-rate education at a moderate cost'. To Cobb, it became quickly apparent that he had acquired a bargain in the form of the new PE master.

This more than compensated for the fact that Jeffrey wasn't terribly good at teaching geography. In fact he was hopeless and the job was swiftly assigned to someone else. Unkind persons with nothing better to do than talk, while others got on with the job, might have raised their eyebrows at this. They would not have lasted ten seconds in one of Jeffrey's training sessions.

Imagine yourself as an introverted, teenage boy, in your first term at Dover. Your parents are both abroad and out of reach, most likely somewhere warm, such as Malaya. Dover is not warm like Malaya. Dover is cold, the salt wind comes tearing at you from the English Channel, the autumn ground is cold and hard. It is early morning and you have left your bed. You have already run six times round the rugby field. Now, with ten other boys with grey sweaters, white faces and blue knees, you are lying on your back in the mud, staring up at a grey sky which is empty except for an occasional seagull.

Then the face comes into view. It is a wide, clenched face and there is a continual stream of speech pouring from it. It is telling you to do things until it hurts. It has to be until it hurts, and when it hurts it is good for you. Raise your legs, three inches. Up, up! Hold it. Hold it! Three inches, not an inch less, not an inch more . . . nonsense, it's good for you. Now down. Now stand up. UP. On the spot, running, thirty seconds, COME ON.

Now do it all over again.

Then it would be six more times round the rugby field,

Jeffrey in his tracksuit, chivvying and harrying. He did not talk, he shouted. He did it all the time. It was very effective. You forgot all about your parents in Malaya. You forgot all about yourself. You forgot about everything. You were conscious only of Mr Archer.

On sports days he would round up everybody to watch. He would not start a race until there was dead silence. Even Cobb lived in fear on these occasions of saying something just as silence was called for, and being called out in front of everyone by Jeffrey.

He would not, especially in the 100 yards, allow any of the spectators to stand level with the finishing tape. 'The judge,' he barked, 'is the only person who should have the best view. Then nobody can argue with him.' It was a prophetic remark, though nobody would have said so at the time.

The younger boys thought he was terrific. If they had not thought so, they would not have performed for him, and they performed for him with a vengeance. The athletics teams believed they could win, and they won. So did the gymnastics teams and the basketball teams. He took charge of everything to do with physical education.

Inevitably, there were dissenters from the general view. One or two of the older boys did not take kindly to this threat to the English public school tradition of 'effortless superiority', in other words, of doing as little hard work as possible. Jeffrey was keen, and keenness was unfashionable. He was therefore suspect.

One or two of the masters had different misgivings. In the early 1960s, Britain was declining rapidly under the archaic conservatism of Harold Macmillan, who insisted on telling the British that they had never had it so good. America was in the ascendant and even the world mile record had been purloined by a New Zealander. The brave new dawn of Wilsonian socialism was on the horizon. Jeffrey, with his visible right-wing attitudes, his emphasis on athletic excellence, his ability to marshal youth and manipulate those of more advanced years, provoked just the tiniest suspicions in the minds of one or two of the more liberal-minded members of staff.

Jeffrey, meanwhile, went on making friends and influencing people. He somehow entered the minds of the boys. He had favourites, like Bruce Dakowski. There was something about Bruce that appealed to Jeffrey. He was lively, wayward and Polish. He did not fit into the establishment. He was intelligent and opportunistic. Dakowski would run down the touchline of a rugger game and find himself being shouted at by Jeffrey: 'Come on Dakowski!' He pronounced it 'DAKOWSKY', like an American. Years later, Bruce would lick envelopes for Jeffrey, while his brother Julian decorated Jeffrey's office. Jeffrey, for his part, would go on to write two blockbusting novels about upwardly mobile Poles (although, in a third, he would have an unnamed young Pole inadvertently expose a servant of Her Majesty's Government to homosexual blackmail).

Having won the hearts and minds of his juniors, he proceeded to cultivate his seniors.

As ever, he was unfailingly polite. He had already justified Cobb's faith in him and he maintained close relations with the Headmaster. He got on well with Edward Bayly, housemaster of St Martin's House. He met various Dover College governors, such as Major-General Sir Gerald Duke.

Duke had himself been educated at Dover College and Cambridge. He had had a distinguished wartime career in the Royal Engineers, being awarded the DSO, and was now approaching retirement as Engineer-in-Chief of the British Army. Like many eminent and distinguished men after years of public service, he did not have a lot of money. He took a keen interest in the welfare of the school and was impressed by its latest recruit, the dynamic, neatly turned-out young PE master.

Another visitor was a former Headmaster of Dover College and Cobb's immediate predecessor, Alexander Peterson. Peterson had already had a fascinating career which swung back and forth from education to propaganda warfare, in which latter capacity he had distinguished himself as Director-General of Information Services during the Malayan Emergency. He had also served on South-East Asian Command with Admiral Lord Louis Mountbatten. Peterson now served as Director of the Institute of Education at Oxford University. He too met and was impressed by the young Jeffrey Archer.

Edward Bayly, housemaster of St Martin's, found himself in need of a new house-tutor. This was the informal job performed by a young man as housemaster's assistant. The house-tutor could make as much or as little of the job as he liked. Jeffrey was offered the job and took it. Soon he was in and out of the house the whole time. He made a great hit with Mrs Bayly, who used to have him and other unattached young men and senior boys to dinner every Tuesday. The Baylys grew fond of Jeffrey and regarded him with a mixture of respect and amusement. He never spoke, though, of his mother or father.

As a bachelor there was no room for him to live in the College, and he lived in lodgings in the town. He did not have to mark books, unlike the other members of staff, so he had time for extra-curricular activities. He acted the part of Puck in an open-air production of *A Midsummer Night's Dream* set in some nearby ruins. It was by all accounts an athletic performance, with Jeffrey spending much of his time standing on his head.

He had ambition and he had ideas. He wanted to make money. It didn't matter what he collected for, as long as he could collect. When Dover College was asked to contribute to a charity campaign in the town, he took a bed out of one of the St Martin's dormitories, put a boy in it, and had him lie in the bed with a begging bowl outside the House on the pavement. Masters threw up their hands in disapproval and passers-by threw in their coins. He sold three-quarters of a shelf-mile of old books and raised another large sum.

He had ambition and he had ideas. He had that energy. There was something about him that made Cobb just know he was going to be a success. But he and Cobb both knew what nobody else did. He didn't have the one seemingly vital ingredient for success in the British social system.

'You've got everything,' Cobb told him, 'except qualifications. Go off and get some.'

And that, in his own controversial fashion, is exactly what Jeffrey did.

Oxford University was at first sight an unlikely choice for an ambitious but insufficiently qualified young man from Weston-super-Mare. In the autumn of 1963, the ancient and august university was generously opening its doors to a new generation of undeserving undergraduates: languid Etonians, practised in the art of effortless superiority; exotic overseas potentates obsessed with cricket; pale, bespectacled grammar boys from the suburbs and shires, beneficiaries of the post-war welfare state who had seized the first two social opportunities of the 11-plus and A-levels, and thereby gained the prized membership to a freemasonry that would last them for life.

The outside world was shaken by national and international developments. The Cuban missile crisis was still fresh in the collective mind; Harold Wilson had been elected leader of the Labour Party; unemployment stood at 878,356, the highest since 1947; and the House of Commons had passed a motion of censure against the Conservative Secretary of State for War, Mr John Profumo, after he had become embroiled with a prostitute.

The new generation of undergraduates lost no time in tackling the issues of the day. They joined the James Bond Club (purpose 'hedonism') founded by old Etonian and future Conservative MP, Jonathan Aitken. They went to the cinema to see *Summer Holiday* starring Cliff Richard, and Brigitte Bardot's *La Vérité*. They welcomed plans for a ten-pin bowling alley. Over 200 of them joined the Communist Club. They went on CND demonstrations. They made a fuss over the Oxford and Cambridge rugby tour of South Africa.

Above all, they made a fuss about women. Were they a good thing? Should they be admitted to the Union? Were they trying to be male? Or were they just trying?

The debate, characterised by what now seems an almost incredibly patronising attitude, rumbled on and on, and like everything else it was picked up and reported in the university's weekly tabloid newspaper, *Cherwell*.

Cherwell also carried photographs of attractive new female undergraduates in their first week at Oxford. One of the beauties brought to popular notice in this way was a stunning, dark-haired chemistry prodigy at St Anne's, called Mary Weeden.

This, then, was the Oxford that was revealed behind the ancient doors of Balliol, Brasenose, Magdalen, Christ Church and Keble. The new generation of undergraduates soon learned to be blasé about which college they were at and what course they were studying. The Oxford of the early '60s was a wonderful pot in which class, background and qualifications simply melted. The conversation had to flag badly before you asked someone what he or she was doing there. Given his relatively humble academic status, this would be a distinct advantage for an ambitious, energetic twenty-three-year-old ex-policeman and PE master, shortly to arrive from the staff of a minor public school in Dover.

The Oxford Institute of Education, as it was then known, occupied a Victorian terraced house in Norham Gardens, a quiet row of similar houses off the Banbury Road. The Institute bordered the lovely University Parks, where the University cricket matches took place and where there were also some beautiful water meadows.

The Institute extended into several other houses and, in distinct contrast to the University, there was a rather temporary feeling about the place. Its exact relationship to the University had always been tenuous; its students always had to be members of a college, but they had never been undergraduates in the strict sense of the word. (There was

23

invariably a moment of slight uncertainty, for example, as to whether an education student was a full member of the University, when it came to renewing his or her Bodleian Library card.) It was quite easy to feel cut off from University life when you were stuck out at Norham Gardens.

The Institute of Education offered a one-year postgraduate course, leading to the award of a Diploma of Education. Its Director, a Balliol man, was the educationalist, propaganda warfare expert – and former Headmaster of Dover College – Alexander Peterson.

Peterson was not a man given to paperwork. When an application arrived on his desk from someone wanting a place on the course, he looked at the man rather than the qualifications. He naturally assumed that the applicant had a first degree. Besides, it was churlish, surely, to ask to see a chap's degree certificate.

Furthermore, in this case he knew the chap in question. Peterson had of course kept up his links with Dover College and on one visit there he had met and been understandably impressed by the dynamic and thrusting young PE master. Nor did it cross Peterson's mind at the time that his successor, the admirable Cobb, would ever appoint someone without very many qualifications. So, without more ado, he had dispatched the offer of a place on the one-year postgraduate course for a Diploma of Education in Geography and PE, to J. H. Archer Esq., c/o The Headmaster, The Headmaster's House, Dover College, Dover, Kent. Then he addressed his mind to other, more important matters.

Jeffrey arrived in Oxford in the autumn of 1963. One of the first things he did was go to the Oxford University Athletic Club ground off the Iffley Road.

The cinder track, that Bannister had laid down as President and on which Brasher and Chataway had helped him run the first sub-four-minute mile, was still there. So was the sacred pavilion. Jeffrey lost no time in getting to know both the ground and the people who frequented it.

In one sense, the Iffley Road ground was a social club where you could turn up after lunch and know you would meet some friends. Whether you did any training, or just wandered about in a tracksuit, it hardly mattered. People would break up into small groups and go off for tea. The autumn dusk would gather; tea would merge into dinner. It was all very undergraduate and amateur and part of the real-life myth of being an eighteen-year-old at Oxford.

On the other hand, there were the serious athletes. The spotty boy from Yorkshire, who six years earlier had marvelled at the way Jeffrey marshalled his winning relay team, was now OUAC President. Adrian Metcalfe, in his last year at Oxford, would run for Britain in the Tokyo Olympics. Mike Hogan, the Secretary, was a world-class hurdler. These were the men of power and influence at Iffley Road and Jeffrey, at twenty-three so much older and more worldly than the eighteen-year-olds, was going to make sure they noticed him.

The Dip. Ed. course was undemanding and he spent all his time down at the track. He was an enthusiastic and highly conspicuous trainer. He was openly ambitious and he had that amazing energy. By the end of the second day of the Michaelmas Term Athletics meeting on that famous cinder track, he had won both the 100 and 220 yard races. The following month, while undergraduates were signing a petition saying they would emigrate if the Conservatives were returned for a fourth term, the future Tory MP and Deputy Chairman was being picked to run for Oxford against Cambridge. Oxford won by a margin of 82 to 53. Jeffrey won the 100 yards and then was hit on the shoulder by a discus thrown by the American Stan Saunders. Saunders went on to set a new freshman's record. Jeffrey, though not badly hurt, was carried off on a stretcher.

It was enough for him to be noticed.

Adrian Metcalfe took a shine to him. As OUAC President, he had a duty to seek out, harness and help athletic talent. As a Yorkshireman, he took a quiet pleasure in differing from the opinion some people in the athletics club formed of Jeffrey Archer. Some people thought he was just a bit too pushy for his own good, and certainly for theirs.

To Metcalfe, however, there was more to Jeffrey than just an *arriviste*. It was the proper beginning of a friendship, first hinted at on a muddy athletics field some six years earlier, that would travel far beyond the politics of Oxford University Athletic Club.

Meanwhile, Jeffrey had also come to the notice of other, less accommodating persons. These were impossible either to ignore or impress, being the anonymous functionaries of the University Registry.

A letter arrived for Peterson, churlishly pointing out that this gentleman on a postgraduate education course did not have a degree. It was all very irregular. Deep waters loomed. Dispensations had to be sought. There was never any doubt they would be granted, though. For one thing, there was an unhealthy precedent to be set by exposing any flaw in the admissions system; for another, the gentleman in question was not one of those troublemakers who went about signing threatening petitions. On the contrary, he was already a stalwart of the Oxford University Athletic Club; and for another thing, he was highly thought of by Sir Noel Hall.

Sir Noel Hall was the Principal of Brasenose College. Brasenose, commonly known as 'BNC', was founded in 1509 and stood in the ancient heart of Oxford. The Bodleian Library and St Mary's Church were a few yards away. The College owed its name to an antique pronunciation of the 'brass nose' or knocker, which hung on the door of the original building and offered sanctuary, since University premises enjoyed the protection of church law at that time, to any member who could reach it. It was thus a fitting place for Jeffrey to find support.

Brasenose had become a college of no mean academic reputation, but it still prided itself on its rugged athletic tradition. Its alumni included Walter Bradford Woodgate (1840–1920), the celebrated oarsman and founder of Vincent's, the University's élite sports club which retained close links with the college. Arnold Nugent Strode-Jackson, winner of the 1500 metres at the 1912 Olympics, was another Brasenose man and Vincent's member. Brasenose still prided itself, in Jeffrey's day, on its cross country team. It was also the college to which Jeffrey, under the rules of the Oxford Institute of Education, had applied to, and through which he had been granted, token University membership.

Sir Noel Hall had been founding head of the Administrative Staff College in Henley. A Brasenose man as an undergraduate, he was thrilled to be back as Principal. He was now sixty years old. Lady Hall, his second wife, was the gutsy New Yorker Elinor Hirschorn Marks. The Halls lived in the charming, richly panelled lodgings in the Old Quad; they also had a house called Homer End, several miles east of Oxford in the beech woods.

Sir Noel had brought a breath of fresh air to Brasenose. Under his twelve-year reign, the college would suffer very little disruption, even in the period of 'student unrest'. He was a businesslike, hospitable man, who prided himself on the fact that his door was always open to undergraduates and other members of Brasenose. The latter rapidly came to include the bumptious young sprinter called Jeffrey Archer.

Hall was immediately bewitched by Jeffrey. He was neither as callow nor as complacent as a normal undergraduate. He spoke to the Principal, as he had done to Cobb, in a way that was both respectful and confiding, almost as if he were addressing a father. Hall liked that. It was not until he met Cobb that Hall realised that Jeffrey made everyone feel that way.

All of which may go some way towards explaining how it came to pass that, one day that autumn, the Head Porter came through the Principal's door. It was nearly the end of the Michaelmas term, 1963; a thirty-six-year-old Tory MP called Humphry Berkeley had been in Oxford speaking on behalf of the United Nations, and the Beatles had just released their second LP. To the Head Porter these events meant little or nothing, but they would have profound significance for Jeffrey.

The Head Porter was in a great state. Someone had delivered a large number of crates which were blocking the entrance to the Lodge. The young gentlemen were consequently unable to get their trunks and suitcases out. It was all very irregular. On inspection, the offending crates were labelled and addressed to a 'Mr Archer'. On closer inspection, they appeared to be full of collecting tins, labelled Oxfam. Did the Principal, sir, have any information, sir, as to what on earth either of these names had to do with Brasenose?

Oxfam had started life twenty-one years earlier as the Oxford Committee for Famine Relief. Until the late 1950s it was a little known organisation of pronouncedly Anglican character. By 1963, however, Oxfam was an internationally known charity, famous for its work with the Congo famine and with refugees from the Algerian civil war. It occupied smart new offices on the Banbury Road, not far from the Oxford Institute of Education. Its Director, Leslie Kirkley, would be knighted for his efforts. Publicity Officer Richard Exley, now twenty-six, had seen his budget rise from £19,000 to over £100,000 a year. It was he who had dreamed up the successful abbreviation, Oxfam.

Kirkley, Exley, Philip Barron and Press Officer Pat Davidson were a successful team. 1963 was Oxfam's 21st birthday year. That summer, they had decided to do something spectacular. Something with high profile, high energy and high results.

In 1963, £1 million was around £10 million by present-day standards. They decided to raise £1 million.

After further brainstorming, the idea was accepted in earnest. All that summer, briefings of regional organisers, gift shop managers and 'pledged gift' fund-raisers took place. A nationwide pub-crawl at Christmas was planned in depth, in which drinkers would be encouraged to contribute to 50,000 Oxfam collecting tins. Advertisements were drafted, leaflets were designed and posters distributed. The Publicity and Public Relations departments went into overdrive. Philip Barron masterminded a massive anniversary rally in Trafalgar Square. ITV networked a one-hour documentary entitled 'The Oxfam Story'. The Oxfam Hunger £Million campaign was well under way. Oxfam, in other words, were steaming ahead with every means at their disposal.

This included, on 11 November 1963, a modest advertisement in *Cherwell*.

Not long after this, Exley was visited in his office by an ebullient youth with a loud voice and a tweed jacket. This in itself was not unusual; there were after all some 5000 freshmen in Oxford. But this one was different. For a start, he looked about nineteen, but he was obviously older.

'Right,' he said, 'I've come to get you organised.'

Exley, the former Stockport Grammar School boy and Manchester University graduate, was not immediately impressed. So he decided just to look at him.

'For a start,' said Jeffrey, 'I'll need 3000 collecting tins.'

He had a definite charisma. He gave you the impression that, even if he did not make it all the way, he would go far.

'3000. I'm going to get Oxford University organised. These students are well-heeled, Richard. Think of the Christmas vacation.'

Exley pointed out that, at that moment, there were probably 200 tins left in the basement. Possibly 300. Certainly no more.

'Well, get them then!'

Exley saw he had energy, but there was also something else there. Exley couldn't put his finger on it. The Oxfam campaign had encouraged lots of members of the public to volunteer their services. As a matter of routine, these volunteers were vetted. In Jeffrey's case, the task fell to the Press Officer, Pat Davidson.

Davidson had a brief interview with the young man in question. He told her he had been at Berkeley, California on a sports scholarship, and was now at Brasenose. Pat Davidson and Richard Exley discussed it with their colleagues in the routine fashion. Exley found him 300 collecting tins.

A few days later, he came back.

'The publicity isn't going fast enough, Richard. What we need is some real youth involvement. I'm going to get the Beatles.'

'Fine,' laughed Exley, and off he charged again.

It was then that Jeffrey made his vital visit to the offices of *Cherwell*.

Cherwell sold about 4000 copies a week and its offices were in what looked like a prefabricated shack, behind the Oxford Union. Its editor was a St Edmund Hall man, Nick Lloyd.

Lloyd was a smart operator. An instinctive journalist, he was already supplying student stories to the *Daily Mail*. As *Cherwell* editor, he would send undergraduates out with the exhortation to 'get some real stories'. The undergraduates would accordingly do so, and come back with tales of the most horrific and lurid goings-on amongst their contemporaries.

Lloyd would appear horrified.

'I can't print that,' he would say, 'this is a family newspaper.'

The undergraduate would look crestfallen.

'Look,' Lloyd would go on, 'here's a fiver . . . go out and get another story.'

Then, when the undergraduate had gone, Lloyd would pick up his phone: 'Is that the *Mail*? Get me Copy.'

Lloyd was one of the richer undergraduates in Oxford. But for sheer effrontery, even he would be outdone by Jeffrey Archer.

Jeffrey bounded in, in his usual style. The editor listened while Jeffrey launched into how he was working with Oxfam. He wanted every student in Britain to go out with a collecting tin that Christmas. They were going to raise a million pounds.

Lloyd admitted it looked like a story. But initially he was sceptical. After all, it was a million pounds. It was also a bit do-goody. It was a story they might, under normal circumstances, have run on an inside page. On the other hand, they were short of a lead story that week. On 30 November 1963 *Cherwell* would show that it, too, had a social conscience.

'Roll up, roll up . . .' The banner headline exhorted the 4000 *Cherwell* readers to go out and collect for Oxfam. It is not known if they included Leslie Kirkley, Richard Exley, Philip Barron and Pat Davidson, all of whom were rather busy at the time. They would no doubt have been surprised to learn that the Oxford end of Oxfam's 21st anniversary campaign to raise £1 million was being masterminded by Jeffrey Archer.

'This,' Jeffrey was quoted as saying, *'will sort out the doers from the talkers.'*

Then he started thinking about the Beatles.

The Beatles, that autumn of 1963, were in the process of becoming the biggest names in the history of popular music. They performed at the Royal Command Performance. They were making a film. Their second album *With The Beatles* had received 250,000 advance orders. The *Daily Mirror* had coined a phrase for what was happening. They called it 'Beatlemania':

YEAH! YEAH! YEAH!

You have to be a real sour square not to love the nutty, noisy, happy, handsome Beatles.

If they don't sweep your blues away – brother, you're a lost cause. If they don't put a beat in your feet – sister, you're not living.

How refreshing to see these rumbustious young Beatles take a middle-aged Royal Variety performance by the scruff of their necks and have them Beatling like teenagers.

Fact is that Beatle People are everywhere. From Wapping to Windsor. Aged seven to seventy. And it's plain to see why these four cheeky, energetic lads from Liverpool go down so big.

They're young, new. They're high-spirited, cheerful. What a change from the self-pitying moaners, crooning their lovelorn tunes from the tortured shallows of lukewarm hearts.

The Beatles are whacky. They wear their hair like a mop – but it's
WASHED, *it's super clean. So is their fresh young act. They don't*
have to rely on off-colour jokes about homos for their fun.

The *Daily Mirror* and its chief rival the *Daily Mail* found
themselves waging hype wars over the Beatles. The idea of
them endorsing a charity campaign for anybody was laugh-
able. Richard Exley had laughed goodnaturedly at Jeffrey
for this very reason. Jeffrey, the dynamic ball of energy, the
doer and not just the talker, was in danger of getting wiped
out in the crossfire.

Jeffrey would tell Exley that he had approached Brian
Epstein, the Beatles' extremely possessive manager (who
would himself later become the butt of 'off-colour' jokes).
He said he wanted the Beatles to endorse the Oxfam Hunger
£Million campaign. Epstein's alleged response may politely
be described as 'Jeffrey who?'

Jeffrey told Exley that he then said to Epstein: 'Do you
really want to go down in history as the man who wouldn't
help starving children?'

To Nick Lloyd, Jeffrey would tell a slightly different
story. He said it appeared that the Beatles had 'forgotten' the
'undertaking' they had given him.

Neither of these stories was true. The truth was that he
was alone in the belief that the Beatles wanted to help him.

The *Cherwell* piece had made little impact. The Oxford
undergraduates were taking little notice either of him or his
collecting tins. The Christmas vacation was looming and
something clearly had to be done. Something sensational that
would make everyone sit up and take notice.

The *Daily Mail*'s universities correspondent, Geoffrey
Parkhouse, was coming down to Oxford on a routine news-
gathering visit. He would be meeting Nick Lloyd as usual at
the Oxford Union. Jeffrey took himself along.

He bombarded Parkhouse with his notion: Varsity Oxfam
drive . . . Oxfam Hunger £Million . . . all backed up by the

Beatles. Would the *Mail* really turn down an opportunity to sponsor the whole thing with a big publicity drive?

Parkhouse made some notes and returned to Fleet Street with his usual bag of Nick Lloyd undergraduate stories. His deputy editor was Derek Ingram. Parkhouse put up a memo, which Ingram passed on to editor Mike Randall. Randall was keen on campaigns. A conference took place; and a decision came back down the line to Jeffrey.

The *Daily Mail* liked the idea. It would give it serious consideration . . . *if* and *when* there was firm evidence of the Beatles' support.

Jeffrey then took his begging bowl to Epstein's friend Brian Sommerville, the ex-naval officer turned Fleet Street journalist, who was in the process of becoming the Beatles' PR man. Sommerville had been entrusted with the Beatles' winter tour while Brian Epstein was in America. For six weeks, the Beatles would perform one-night stands at cinemas across Britain. In Liverpool they were going to do a TV show as well as a concert. Sommerville, too, told Jeffrey to get lost. But he did subsequently indicate that, if Jeffrey were to present himself at the Empire Theatre, he might just get their autographs.

Nick Lloyd went with him on the train.

The two young hopefuls took some Oxfam collecting tins and a big Oxfam poster. 'WANTED,' it said, '£1,000,000,' and there was a picture of a starving child.

Lloyd felt he was beginning to know Jeffrey a little better now. He still did not know what Jeffrey was studying, though he assumed he was an undergraduate. He had incredibly short hair and reminded Lloyd of a young army officer. The *Cherwell* editor and St Edmund Hall man, by contrast, affected a distinctly Beatle-ish look.

The train droned on to Liverpool. Lloyd and Jeffrey made their way to the Liverpool Empire, along, it seemed, with the entire pubescent female population of Great Britain. The Beatles had arrived by limousine and were closeted backstage in a tiny, lavatorial dressing room. They were surrounded by hangers-on and looked distinctly bored. 'They didn't know who we were,' Lloyd would say, later, 'from a bar of soap'.

Jeffrey produced the Oxfam collecting tins, which the Beatles made jokes about and held up in the air. John Lennon and Paul McCartney stood next to the Oxfam poster. Everyone had their photographs taken; Lloyd looking like a Beatle; Jeffrey looking like a young army officer; the Beatles looking like every other photograph of them taken at that time.

Then Archer and Lloyd took the train back to Oxford.

At Oxfam's headquarters in the Banbury Road, Richard Exley was busier than ever. But even he stopped what he was doing when he saw the magic photographs of the Beatles apparently endorsing Oxfam.

Jeffrey meanwhile was pacing up and down the office.

'Well, we've got the Beatles. What we need now is a bit of class . . . seniority.'

He went on pacing, thinking aloud.

'Harold Macmillan . . . that's it.'

He seemed to be dreaming it up as he went along.

'Grand old man of politics . . . we'll get him.'

Harold Macmillan, 'Supermac', had recently resigned as Prime Minister and been replaced by Sir Alec Douglas-Home. He was also Chancellor of Oxford University and therefore not unrelated to the idea of 3000 students going round with collecting tins.

'We'll get him,' said Jeffrey.

And he picked up Exley's telephone.

Exley then watched and listened in growing amazement as Jeffrey obtained and rang the number of the Macmillans. Lady Dorothy Macmillan answered the call. She actually pulled Macmillan in from the croquet lawn or the tomato bed, and there and then Jeffrey told him what he was doing: Oxfam, the Beatles, 3000 students, etc. Would he please help?

'Yes,' said Macmillan. After all, there was not a lot else he could say.

Jeffrey put down the telephone.

Exley, not a man given to hyperbole, was even more impressed. By now he too, like Nick Lloyd, felt he was beginning to know Jeffrey a little better. He admired his brash enthusiasm. He never saw him socially, though. He never met any of his friends or family or even knew if he had any.

Later when the story spread that Jeffrey had 'got' the Beatles and helped raise £1 million for Oxfam, Exley would keep his own counsel. Exley personally knew many of the thousands of people who raised that Oxfam Hunger £Million. He knew that Jeffrey's undergraduates raised a modest proportion of the £136,000 that went into Oxfam's collecting tins. Jeffrey's real contribution to that campaign, in Exley's opinion, was to create the 'buzz' factor among the undergraduates.

He knew, too, that this would never be enough for Jeffrey. Of their nine or ten meetings at the Banbury Road offices, the memory of one in particular would remain forever in his mind.

There was a lull in the offices. Exley, in a casual sort of way, asked him what he was going to do with his life.

'I'm going to be Prime Minister,' said Jeffrey.

'Which party?'

'Don't be so damned naïve, Richard . . . which party has been in power for most of this century?'

'It's as simple as that?'

'If you want to get on, why join the losers?'

Exley, having established what he was going to do with his life, asked him how he was going to achieve it.

'You get an Oxford Blue. I'll get one.'

Then he said, 'You make a name for yourself in charity, which I am in the process of doing.'

'And then?'

'You've got to unseat somebody in a pretty spectacular by-election.'

'And then?'

'You've got to get yourself noticed as Private Secretary to a rising young Cabinet minister.'

'And then?'

'And then it's in the bag.'

Oxfam Press Officer Pat Davidson already had the restless young man marked down as a less than happy person. To her he seemed to be a loner, driven by some inner obsession of his own. He told her, too, that he wanted to be Prime Minister. More interestingly, he told her where he had got the idea. His idol and role model, he said, was Christopher Chataway.

Chataway had first come to popular notice in 1954, when he helped Roger Bannister run that first sub-four-minute mile on Iffley Road's sacred cinder track. Jeffrey was then fourteen. Chataway had been President of OUAC. He had been launched by his work with World Refugee Year in 1959, got onto the Greater London Council, become a Tory MP and was now hotly tipped, with the young Michael Heseltine, as a future Prime Minister.

Jeffrey told Pat Davidson he had studied carefully what Chataway had done. He had already joined OUAC, as far as she could see, by sheer singlemindedness. Now he was being launched with Oxfam: 'I'm going to be President of OUAC,' he said, 'like Chataway.'

Richard Exley would leave Oxfam shortly afterwards, to work for better conditions in the so-called 'homelands' of South Africa. A couple of years later he would walk into a newsagent's there and pick up his English newspaper. The headline read: 'YOUNGEST EVER TORY UNSEATS SIR WILLIAM'. The story told how the leader of the Greater London Council had lost his seat to the dynamic ball of energy, Jeffrey Archer.

Exley rushed home to his wife, Helen.

'My God!' he said. 'It's happening! He *is* going to be Prime Minister!'

A year or two later, Exley was still in South Africa when he bought another English newspaper. This time it told how Jeffrey had become Private Secretary to a rising young Tory.

Exley by this time knew what to expect. He might still have been surprised, however, had he known what Jeffrey had told Pat Davidson. The rising young Tory in question was none other than Christopher Chataway.

Back at the Oxfam offices in the Banbury Road, that autumn of 1963, Exley told Davidson that Jeffrey had 'got' the Beatles and had wonderful photographs to prove it. Jeffrey was going to show them to the *Daily Mail*. It would be interesting to see what the *Mail* did with them.

They always knew this would be a hazardous undertaking. In 1962 when Oxfam had been desperately trying to alert media attention to the Congo famine, they seemed to get nowhere. On Christmas Eve the famine finally 'broke' as a newspaper story. The *Daily Mail* dispatched its man with his toothbrush to Brazzaville. On Boxing Day, the first dramatic stories came back.

Oxfam, greatly relieved after all their efforts, telephoned the *Daily Mail* and said they were cabling £10,000 and emergency food and blankets to the Congo. The following day, the *Daily Mail* acknowledged this with the banner headline: 'BRITISH CHARITY RESPONDS TO DAILY MAIL INITIATIVE'.

On 4 December 1963, the *Daily Mail* carried the following headline by its universities correspondent, Geoffrey Parkhouse: 'BEATLES BOOST FOR VARSITY OXFAM CAMPAIGN', it blared, and told of how Britain's hottest showbusiness attraction had agreed to endorse the Oxfam Hunger £Million campaign: 'An Oxfam spokesman announced last night . . .'

There was just one problem. In their haste to secure a 'youth' story over their rivals, the *Daily Mail* had overlooked one thing. The Beatles had not actually agreed to support Oxfam at all.

Parkhouse could be forgiven for thinking otherwise, in view of the photographs; as could the mysterious 'Oxfam spokesman'.

But whoever this was, it was not Pat Davidson. In the

Oxfam offices on the Banbury Road, Davidson's telephone had not stopped ringing since the *Daily Mail* exclusively revealed that the Beatles were going to help Oxfam. How had they managed to succeed where a hundred other charities had failed? What exactly were the Beatles going to do for them? Would there be concerts? Did she have their autographs? She suddenly found herself in the nightmarish position of being unable either to confirm or deny the story. She stalled while she tried frantically to find out exactly what had happened.

She remembered Jeffrey had told Exley that the Beatles had 'agreed' to help Oxfam. Exley, for his part, had seen the photographs Jeffrey had brought back to the Oxfam offices. But neither they nor anyone else at the Banbury Road offices, or elsewhere, had ever received any official confirmation whatsoever that the Beatles had agreed to endorse the Oxfam Hunger £Million campaign.

Jeffrey was suddenly hard to contact; eventually, he crept into Davidson's office. What followed, she found nothing less than horrific. Had he, Jeffrey Archer, she asked, actually persuaded the Beatles, and more importantly their manager Brian Epstein, to agree to support Oxfam?

No, he admitted, he had not.

Had he got hold of Epstein?

No, he had not. He had been trying desperately to do so. But there was no way.

Jeffrey by now looked a sickly white.

Pat Davidson tried hard to concentrate and not think about the awful possibilities. For a start, Oxfam's credibility as a charity was about to go down the drain.

Not to mention hers, as its Press Officer.

'Pat,' Jeffrey said, 'you've got to clear this up.'

'How, Jeffrey?'

The dynamic ball of energy said nothing. As Davidson later recalled, he was 'unbelievably embarrassed'.

For two terrible days and nights, Pat Davidson tried to succeed where Jeffrey had failed. NEMS refused to speak to anyone from Oxfam. So she tried to get hold of Brian Epstein's ex-directory telephone number.

Eventually, through interminable and remote showbusiness contacts, she did it: it was Belgravia 8714. In the climate of Beatlemania, this alone was a remarkable achievement. She was trembling by this time, with the strain of carrying Jeffrey's secret. To make matters worse, the news had gone out in Oxfam's broadsheet. Now regional organisers were demanding to know more.

Epstein was trembling with fury.

'There's no chance,' he said, 'no chance. If the Beatles align themselves with one charity, we'll have them all after us. It's an impossible situation.'

Davidson wisely agreed. A renegade element claiming to speak for Oxfam had acted out of line, she said. In no sense would the public attach any responsibility to Epstein or the Beatles. The question was, how could they contain the damage?

Epstein and Davidson came to a deal: she would draft a press statement denying the Beatles had ever agreed to support the Oxfam Hunger £Million. She would call him back to approve the wording.

Less than an hour later, she was still puzzling over it when the telephone rang. It was Epstein.

'Look,' he said, 'I've talked to the boys. We don't need stories saying we won't support charity. Whatever the circumstances. They'll do it.'

Davidson was numb by now. All she could think of to say, was: 'I'm sorry it had to happen this way.'

'So am I, Pat. So am I. Tell me the minimum we have to do and we'll take it from there.'

A meeting was hastily set up at the *Daily Mail* for 9 December and Exley and Davidson were asked to attend. Amazingly, the *Mail* agreed to run a front-page story every day for twenty-one days. It would lead to the completion of Kirkley, Exley and Davidson's dream of £1 million being raised in three months for Oxfam. It would lead to an increase in the *Daily Mail*'s circulation. It would lead to a career in Fleet Street for the enterprising Nick Lloyd. Last, but by no means least, it would lead to the first major national newspaper story featuring Jeffrey Archer. On 12 December 1963 the *Daily Mail* machine ground into action, sweeping all before it. The paper kicked off with Oxfam, the *Daily Mail* and the Beatles united in an unholy trinity.

Every day there was a new celebrity, a new angle, a new conference.

Davidson found herself seconded to the *Mail* newsroom: 'What have we got for tomorrow?' the *Mail* kept asking. She and Parkhouse stage-managed events with the *Mail* promotions department: as well as the Beatles, singer Harry Secombe drove a stagecoach down Fleet Street, actress Susannah York looked concerned, footballer Jimmy Greaves, jockey Josh Gifford and many others lent their time and their names. Every day, the *Mail* ran a two-and-sixpenny coupon. On 31 December, the last day, the *Mail* ran a coupon on every single page; above each one was a clearly recognisable logo of the Beatles. Volunteers were photographed counting cash at Oxfam's Banbury Road offices. Up and down the land, thousands of people rattled their collecting tins. Exley and Davidson organised a carol concert in Trafalgar Square. Davidson and Nick Lloyd, now also seconded to the *Mail*, co-ordinated the razzmatazz of the *Mail*'s publicity.

Lloyd's carefully cultivated contacts with the *Mail* were beginning to pay off in a big way; this was better than recycling undergraduate gossip. But even he was taken aback when the *Daily Mail* published the following piece by Vincent Mulchrone on Tuesday 17 December:

THE MAN BEHIND BRITAIN'S BIGGEST PUB CRAWL
He's 23 and far from being a nut case, but judge for yourself.

Jeffrey Archer, you probably won't be surprised to learn, but 3 of his friends at Oxford describe him as a nut case, a pain in the neck and a ball of fire . . . and all mean the same thing.

He is a stocky 23 year old student of Brasenose, reading Education, he can do 100 yards in 9.9 and has a passion for amateur dramatics and people. It is his passion for people which has brought Archer to the fore.

It is because of him that 3,500 undergraduates from Oxford and other universities will spend most of their time from now until New Year rattling tins around most of Britain's 72,000 pubs to try and raise £500,000 for Oxfam.

And as the first of the three friends quoted above put it: 'Only a nut case could persuade Oxford men to do that.'

The second said: 'He's a pain in the neck because he won't stop talking until you agree to do something for some starving kid in Dehra Dun. You say yes, and he stops.'

The first two agree with the third. I agree with all three. Jeffrey Archer is a ball of fire.

He talks in short sharp bursts like an intelligent machine gun. That's how Oxfam first met him:

'He came in' said a pillar of Oxfam who is now a disciple, 'and said he wanted 10,000 collecting tins. We just looked at him.'

THINKING BIG

The fact is that Jeffrey Archer now has 12,000 collecting tins and worries in case there won't be enough to go round.

'The thing is that people come along to do the dreary boring jobs because they care. They care like hell. Kennedy cared. He was so incredibly vital. He may have been a man of your generation, but he was also a man of our age.

'Every age has something to conquer. Everest hadn't been conquered when you were a young man. The worst thing young people today can say is there's nothing left to do. There's so much left to do.

'My generation has to do different things. We have to strive for unity through peace. But first we have to rescue the starving. Sounds corny, but it's the most exciting challenge we've got.

'3,500 undergraduates think so, anyway. It's a feeling with young people all over the world. We're not different . . . we're typical . . . and isn't that exciting?'

41

Yes, Mr Archer. Nut case or not, and I think not, that I find exciting.

Nick Lloyd could have been forgiven for casting his mind back in amazement to the first time he met Jeffrey. It was less than a month, after all, since he had first bounced into the *Cherwell* offices: 'I was a bit mortified,' he admitted later, 'it was very nice for Jeffrey, but I thought: "I did all this work." I'm sure Oxfam would sympathise with that.'

Richard Exley, the 'pillar of Oxfam who is now a disciple', was not at all surprised that neither his nor Pat Davidson's were names mentioned in any of the *Daily Mail* pieces. Neither of them would have wanted it. Besides, Oxfam had got their million, so what did it matter?

'Basically,' Exley would say later, 'the guy muscled in and made a lot of money, and in my view slightly exaggerated things. He did definitely get loads of students to be very active. The Beatles did blow-all . . . all they actually did was hold up a poster and say: "Great thing, guys."

'My criticism is that he tends to put abroad the idea that he raised £1 million for Oxfam. In a sense, it is accurate that he helped Oxfam raise £1 million. But there were one hell of a lot of people from John O'Groats to Lands End who were also helping raise that £1 million.'

Exley, Davidson and Nick Lloyd would keep quiet for twenty-five years while the story spread that Jeffrey had 'got' the Beatles to support Oxfam. Why did they do it? In Nick Lloyd's case, Jeffrey was to become a useful source of stories.

Pat Davidson, however, was never beholden to him. 'I just didn't care,' she would say later, 'I still don't. It depends, anyway, on how you define "getting" the Beatles. In a sense it was Jeffrey who got them, wasn't it? I just picked up the pieces.'

President Kennedy, having been assassinated three weeks earlier, was unavailable for comment. Years later, his widow would resign her publishing job apparently in protest at the publication of a novel in which Jeffrey would attempt to assassinate another of her close relations. By that time, however, Jeffrey would have given up charity fundraising and gone into the storytelling business full-time.

The Hilary term began, and with it resumed the quest for news in the prefabricated shack behind the Union.

Oxford, in truth, did suddenly seem rather parochial. The film *Lawrence of Arabia* arrived. The Oxford University Chess Club was refused half-Blue status by the committee of the élite sporting club, Vincent's. A Miss Edwina White was involved in a controversy over whether she should wear her hair up or down at the Union. An undergraduate got three years' probation for smuggling Indian hemp, and had to undergo 'treatment' for his 'psychiatric trouble'.

Things picked up a little in February of that year, when *Cherwell* carried a student riot supplement. The editors went to Paris and interviewed some pretty girls, including one of the dancers at the Lido. They followed up with a termly pull-out on careers, with lots of jobs in industry and the Civil Service, and a report on the Oxford and Cambridge tiddlywinks match.

In March there was yet another sex rustication. Quite coincidentally, St Hugh's, Lady Margaret Hall and St Hilda's, all women's colleges, extended their visiting hours from 7 p.m. to 10 p.m.

Jeffrey, needless to say, had not been idle during this time. For one thing, he took his new Iffley Road friends to meet Françoise Hardy.

The *Daily Mail* naturally wanted to thank itself for coming to the relief of Oxfam. It had accordingly arranged a lunch at the Westbury Hotel in London, and called it Oxfab. Jeffrey, as the dynamic ball of fire who had captured the Beatles, was naturally invited. So were the Beatles. They didn't turn up, of course. The *Mail*, however, managed to book the then popular French singer, Françoise Hardy.

Thus it was that President Adrian Metcalfe and Secretary

Mike Hogan found themselves sitting next to the bewitching French chanteuse. The reaction of the post-existential heroine to finding herself in the midst of a lot of clean-limbed track heroes was not recorded.

The week after, they all had their photograph in *Cherwell*.

Jeffrey was actually living with Metcalfe and Hogan now, at their digs in the Iffley Road. The landlord, a vet, was a great sports enthusiast. He and his wife had grown-up children who had left home, and the three noisy young men in the three rooms upstairs brought a breath of undergraduate life into the house. They helped with the shopping and generally behaved like a second family.

Metcalfe felt he was beginning to know Jeffrey a little better by now. But he still knew very little about him. There was the obscurity surrounding his course, for a start. They did not know where that took place. Then there was the obscurity surrounding his past. He never mentioned his father, or mother, or what he had been doing before Oxford. He did not seem a lot older than anybody else, but he was much smarter and more worldly. Metcalfe could never come to terms with two indisputable facts about Jeffrey: his amazing energy, and his ability within seconds to decide where to apply it.

Which was how, one day in early March 1964, Metcalfe found himself clambering out of bed, where he had been incapacitated with influenza, to go and meet the Beatles.

The Beatles had not been idle, either, since that night at the Liverpool Empire.

At Christmas, while hordes of people carolled in Trafalgar Square for Oxfam, they performed their own Christmas show at the Finsbury Park Astoria. Their new album *With The Beatles* had sold almost a million copies. Their new single 'I Wanna Hold Your Hand' had reached Number One in the Top Twenty. After a messy and violent trip to Paris they had gone on to New York and Washington. Beatlemania was everywhere they went. They had overstayed in America and missed a number of British engagements. One of them was that Oxfab lunch. It was unlikely they even remembered the short-haired figure in the tweed jacket who had persuaded them to pose for Oxfam.

One of the prizes of the *Mail*'s Christmas Beatle drive was an autographed poster for the schoolchild who had raised the most money for Oxfam. This was to have been presented by the Beatles at a dinner in London. Harold Macmillan was going to be present. Now, the Beatles' extended stay in America meant that this, too, had to be cancelled. But Brian Epstein had given a reluctant undertaking to Pat Davidson. The Beatles would present the poster. But where?

Pat Davidson had given the job of finding an alternative venue to Jeffrey.

The hastily arranged alternative was to be a bizarre encounter, even by Beatle standards. The unlikely saviour on this occasion was none other than the obliging Principal of Brasenose, Sir Noel Hall.

The former business school head had long ago forgiven Jeffrey for blocking up his gateway with crates of collecting tins. Why not, he suggested, have the prizegiving dinner in the Brasenose Lodgings?

Preparations went ahead in conditions of the utmost secrecy. The Oxford police were terrified of Beatlemania. The Fab Four and their entourage were filming *A Hard Day's Night* 'somewhere in Oxfordshire' and would motor to Brasenose. Lady Hall was in America at the time; Sir Noel, for some reason best known to himself, decided a suitable hostess for the occasion would be Louise, their thirteen-year-old daughter.

A telephone call was put through to her Headmistress and a special dispensation obtained for the schoolgirl to host a party 'for some American friends'. Even Louise Hall would have no idea who was really coming, until she turned round on the stairs of the Lodgings and found the four lovable moptops charging up them behind her.

First, however, the Beatles went for drinks at Vincent's,

the élite sporting club whose main rooms looked over The High onto Brasenose. Vincent's would assume great significance for Jeffrey; but on this particular cold day in spring, with its dingy entrance and tiny second-floor bar, it was an alien and hostile landscape to four already confused and exhausted proletarians from Liverpool.

It began to spill over, as it were, in the second-floor urinal. George Harrison and John Lennon were in their Beatle suits and winklepickers. Between them, in his Harris tweed jacket and flannels, stood Adrian Metcalfe.

'What the fock's goin' on 'ere, eh?' they asked him. 'What's all this about, then? What are you doin' 'ere?'

Other undergraduates crowded in, and nudged each other. It was then that George Harrison, who hated publicity most of the four, made his immortal remark: 'Why don't you go and get a bottle?' He turned and indicated his penis. 'Bottle this, and sell it for Oxfam.'

They adjourned across the road to the Brasenose Lodgings. Jeffrey ushered them into the wood-panelled drawing room with its chintzy sofas.

'This,' he said, 'is the hive of the life of the College.'

One of the Beatles said, 'Do you mean Dover College?'

It was a truly bizarre encounter. The Beatles; Brian Epstein; Pat Davidson; Sir Noel Hall and his thirteen-year-old daughter; Nick Lloyd; Michael O'Flaherty of the *Daily Mail*; the prizewinning schoolgirl and her Headmistress; Tim Cobb; Alexander Peterson; and Jeffrey. Jeffrey lorded it around; he had not invited Richard Exley. He had reluctantly invited Pat Davidson. Davidson had had newspapers ringing up from all over the country. She had been forced to make an agreement with Brasenose that only the *Daily Mail* would be there.

The *Oxford Mail* had been very upset by this. How, they enquired, did she expect them to help Oxfam in the future? Davidson had told them what time to loiter in the shadows, outside the main gate of Brasenose College.

White-coated college servants stood in readiness by the

buffet. One of them offered Paul McCartney champagne in a silver goblet.

'I'd rather have milk,' he said, and he meant it. McCartney would play his usual role, the charming PR man who chatted to everybody. George Harrison, inspired by his Vincent's performance, beckoned to one of the eager scouts.

'Have you got any jam butties?' he said. 'I'll trade you an autograph for a jam butty.'

John Lennon stood in the corner most of the time with Ringo, being himself. 'What the fockin' 'ell am I doin' 'ere?' was the evening's litany from the composer of *Help!*

Tim Cobb had received his invitation in the strictest secrecy. He managed to procure the Beatles' autographs; the next day, back at Dover College, the Headmaster would sit at lunch with them in his pocket. But the opportunity to show them to the boys somehow never arrived.

There was absolutely nothing he could think of to say. 'It was like trying to talk to royalty, only worse, because they were not trained to make conversation. They just sat on the sofas in their suits and winklepickers and never offered anyone a seat.' Cobb was riveted.

Peterson, too, was fascinated. He hardly ever saw Jeffrey, after all. On his way to this most secret of destinations, he had been accosted by half a dozen girls outside the front gates.

'They're 'ere, sir, aren't they? They're 'ere!'

The old psychological warfare specialist had played a straight bat, however; and he too was rewarded with a signed record which became his daughter's most precious possession.

The *Daily Mail* congratulated itself in a vast picture spread and a story across three columns. The *Oxford Mail* got their photographs (and sold them for vast sums). Sir Noel Hall received letters of protest from Brasenose men from all corners of the Empire. The lucky little girl was handed her autographed poster.

'It was an odd evening,' Nick Lloyd would say later, 'they didn't stay long. I should think they needed it like a hole in the head. It was a publicity stunt for them. Macmillan wasn't there. That's a myth.'

'Kind' people, however, people in search of good copy, would not be so churlish as to say so.

Thus Valerie Grove, then Jenkins, would write of Jeffrey in the *Evening Standard* on 4 November 1970: 'It was he who got the Beatles to have dinner with Mr Macmillan and the Principal of Brasenose, Sir Noel Hall, in aid of Oxfam . . .' Of such stuff were the early Archer dreams made.

'So they came,' Mrs Grove went on, 'and another Oxford man who found himself, during the lunch, next to Ringo in the Gents, reports that Ringo muttered, of Jeffrey Archer: "That man, he'd probably bottle my pee and sell it for £5."'

Meanwhile, Jeffrey bounced around as usual. In April, he produced a sports column for *Cherwell*.

The column was called 'With The Blues'. In it he introduced the first of the many fictional characters of his career. This one appears to have performed the function of 'a little bird tells me'. She was called 'The Grand Duchess': 'The Grand Duchess hears . . .' he would start off, or 'The Grand Duchess visited . . . today'.

Unlike many of his later characters, however, she was not visibly based on persons of Jeffrey's acquaintance. Nor, in spite of her title, did she use her wealth and power to gain even more of the same.

Jeffrey, for his part, was now faced with the likelihood of being written out altogether. As a member of the University, but not an undergraduate, his one-year course at the Institute of Education was almost over. Qualifications loomed, and with them the prospect of leaving Norham Gardens, Iffley Road and Brasenose forever. Even more dreadful was the prospect of having to go back to teaching. Chataway never had this problem; he never knew how lucky he was. What was to be done?

Once again, the saviour on this occasion was the Principal of Brasenose, Sir Noel Hall.

Hall's admiration for the young athlete and entrepreneur had gone from strength to strength as a result of that bizarre night at the Lodgings. Jeffrey was unfailingly polite and always called him 'Sir'. To Lady Hall, the energetic Elinor, he represented anything but the stuffy side of Oxford. But he never talked to the native New Yorker about Berkeley or any other part of America. But he was always in and out of the Lodgings. He gave their son a set of blocks and taught him how to sprint.

Hall contacted the Director of the Institute of Education, Alexander Peterson. His tone was urbane and businesslike. Brasenose, he said, needed more first-rate athletes on its books. If Peterson was not violently opposed to the idea, how about letting young Archer stay on at the Institute and do some research?

Peterson was initially sceptical. What postgraduate degree was he going to work for? A B.Litt.? A D.Phil.? An M.A.? Sir Noel was extremely understanding. 'Oh,' he said, 'I just want him to do some research. Surely you've got someone in the Institute who has something to do with Physical Education?'

Peterson then recalled that there was indeed such a person; that his name was Burrows; that his ostensible subject was geography, and that he was something of an athlete.

'Splendid! That's settled then.'

So it was settled. Jeffrey would do 'research' into physical education for the obliging Mr Burrows. The research did not involve assiduous attendance at the Institute; it was open-ended and not directed at any specific degree. Nor did it carry a grant, although there were college funds and other bursaries available. No more was said on the subject, and the tedious formality of paperwork was bypassed. Peterson, to whom it was already quite obvious that Jeffrey's métier was as a public relations man, continued to see as little of him as ever. Jeffrey would remain in Oxford.

That summer, he became the new Secretary of the Oxford University Athletic Club, in the footsteps of his distinguished flatmates Adrian Metcalfe and Mike Hogan. In June, he arranged the inter-college finals well enough to be noticed by the *Oxford Mail*. 'Unlike many of his predecessors, he had gathered round him a large number of helpers,' it reported, 'and his tight schedule . . . was carried through efficiently.' He also met that stunningly beautiful young chemistry prodigy from St Anne's, Mary Weeden.

Mary Doreen Weeden was born and brought up in Surrey. Her father, Harold Weeden, was a slightly irascible chartered accountant. She was one of three children, with a younger brother, David, and an older sister, Janet. Home was a big, safe Anglican household full of dogs and children; in the attic was Harold's elaborate model railway layout.

Mary had gone to St Christopher's School, Epsom, and then to the genteel and formidable Cheltenham Ladies' College. While Jeffrey marshalled his relay teams in the mud of the athletics field, she was developing her ability to sing and play the piano; above all, she was showing an outstanding ability in chemistry.

At sixteen, she won a Nuffield Science Scholarship to Oxford. She spent a year in Austria learning German to help her read scientific treatises. At Oxford, where the ratio of males to females was seven to one, there was no shortage of admirers. A lot of girls were written about as beauties: Mary Weeden was certainly one. She was also bright, and she had steel. She had been photographed by *Cherwell*. She partied with the likes of Nick Lloyd, Patrick Marnham and Jonathan Aitken.

To Lloyd, she was rather quiet and self-contained, a 'nice' girl. Adrian Metcalfe found her 'extraordinarily dispassionate. Very cool . . . one always had the feeling that Mary would live her own life and reach her own goals.'

Lady Hall found her 'beautiful, but schoolmistressy. Mind you, he was schoolmasterly; he used to boss her around. When she was his fiancée, and he brought her to the Lodgings, I would say: "Would you like a drink?" and she would say: "Do you have a whisky and soda that doesn't look like one?" One of the things Jeffrey was schoolmasterly about was drinking . . .

'She's a private person . . . a very private person. I've known Mary, but don't know Mary. I've known Jeffrey, but I don't know Mary.'

There was never any doubt that she would get a First; but she worked extremely hard, as if there was only the slightest chance she would do so. She was intellectually precocious and, by her own admission, socially blinkered. She was also five years younger than Jeffrey.

Jeffrey would later describe how he wrote to her boyfriend, asking to take her out. He would say that standards of chivalry had declined. Mary would say, in a rare candid moment: 'He likes to clear the decks as he goes along.'

Adrian Metcalfe would say later: 'I think Jeffrey had made his mind up that she was the catch of her generation.'

Nick Lloyd thought so, too: 'She wasn't an extrovert or a femme fatale. He was extrovert and pushy and very much on the run. If he met a girl like Mary and found her attractive he would probably pursue her; she would probably find him rather attractive, and the image of what a go-getting young man ought to be.'

Mary Weeden, Adrian Metcalfe and Nick Lloyd came to know Jeffrey better than anybody. All three, too, in their own ways, would develop a degree of detachment in their relations with him. 'One then remembers,' Lloyd would say, 'this grand romance blossoming. It was very passionate and it went on from there.'

Michaelmas term, Oxford, 1964: Harold Wilson was Prime Minister, and the ex-policeman, former PE master, sometime Dip.Ed. student and future Deputy Chairman of the Conservative Party, was Secretary of OUAC.

One new arrival at the sacred cinders of Iffley Road was an introverted distance runner from an obscure Somerset grammar school, called John Bryant: 'I was aware of these Olympians, like Adrian Metcalfe, and Jeffrey. He was jumping around like a jumping bean. He was not the best sprinter who used to hang around Iffley Road, by any means. He was unbelievably ambitious, though. He would talk about being very ambitious. I formed a friendship with him almost straight away.'

This was partly based on the fact that Bryant came from Somerset. 'We're two Somerset boys,' Jeffrey would tell Bryant, 'in the same team.'

Bryant had hardly been out of Somerset at the time. His accent was so broad that people used to stop him in Queen's College and say: 'Say something.' Jeffrey, born in the City Road of London and a migrant to Weston-super-Mare, had cultivated a clipped, militaristic accent in which he used to bark orders at the sprinters. In later years, he would also become well known for his ability to put on a broad Somerset accent.

Years later, Bryant, who was to become a successful newspaperman, would stand Jeffrey a meal when he was down on his luck. He never had any illusions about him, which was probably why they stayed friends.

'The thing about Jeffrey was that he was hellish ambitious. I think he had a vision of a sort of schoolboy-annual type of hero. He would be a Double Blue, get a First and be President of the Union. Academically, he didn't get off the starting blocks. I never had any impression of him working academically at all.'

Bryant was interested by the contrast between Jeffrey's and Mary's academic styles: 'I only ever saw him with Mary. She was very, very pretty, and very, very quiet. She spent a lot of time singing and was a hardworking academic. She was so quiet, compared with Jeffrey. Jeffrey was just a nonstop talker. He was so funny and enthusiastic.'

Jeffrey proposed Bryant for membership of Vincent's.

The Vincent's hardcore were rowing, cricket and rugby Blues; the OUAC men spent a lot of time there.

Vincent's came to occupy a position of great importance in Jeffrey's life. In itself, it was neither great nor grand, but it reeked of the authentic Oxford. As its founder, W. B. Woodgate, a Brasenose man, wrote: 'The theory of this club was that it should consist of the picked hundred of the University, selected for all round qualities; social, physical and intellectual qualities being duly considered.' Woodgate's photograph hung over the fireplace in the second-floor bar, the nerve-centre of the club. It was a small space, about three paces across. A hurdler could cover it in one bound. Wherever you sat, you were close to the fire. Vincent's was effectively a 'late drinking club'. One of its specialities was the 'Pink Panther': this consisted of six measures of gin with a touch of grenadine and a dash of orange. The record for consuming these was ten in one hour. There was a group of old boys who came in from time to time, called the 'Geriatric Club'. One of them was a bishop, who came in in full regalia, ordered his pint and downed it with the rest of them.

Vincent's had a clubroom, next to the bar, with dark brown sofas, tables and writing paper. It looked directly onto The High and Brasenose. There were more photographs here too, including, by 1964, one of Jeffrey.

The stairs up from the second floor were dominated by an amateur portrait of Lieutenant-Colonel Arnold Nugent Strode-Jackson, of the King's Rifles. A Brasenose and Vincent's man, he had won the Olympic 1500 metres Gold Medal in Stockholm, in 1912. He was the youngest colonel of World War One, in which he was heavily decorated. After the Great War he had gone to America, where he had made a lot of money in commodities.

Strode-Jackson used to hold court in Vincent's in Jeffrey's day. Clad in a cloak and deerstalker, with a slight American accent, he was a commanding figure in the bar. 'You fellows,' he would drawl, 'are running yourselves into a tizzy!' He was universally known as 'Jackers'.

Jeffrey worshipped him. Years later, having himself had a modest military background and invested heavily in commodities, he would describe for the benefit of one interviewer a father who was a colonel in the Somerset Light Infantry. When John Bryant saw him on television, discussing the relative merits of Roger Bannister and Sebastian Coe, Jeffrey was wearing his Vincent's tie.

That Christmas Jeffrey was university organiser for Oxfam. Seventy per cent of the undergraduates would give up some of their vacation to help. Nick Lloyd was on the *Daily Mail* by now and the plan was to hold another carol concert and an auction. The carol concert was a great success; the auction, as Lloyd would later recall, was an absolute and unmitigated disaster.

The idea was that people should donate interesting and valuable items which would then be auctioned. Jeffrey, who, it may be remembered, had been an evacuee, obtained a recording of Winston Churchill's war speeches, with a view also to obtaining Churchill's autograph on them. Sir Winston, alas, was too infirm to do so. What was to be done?

Jeffrey telephoned Sir Noel Hall. He had, he said, just been talking to the White House. LBJ, who had succeeded the 'incredibly vital' John Kennedy, had agreed to autograph the speeches in Churchill's place. Could Sir Noel lend him the aeroplane fare to go and see the President of the United States?

Hall, who had no money to speak of, said, 'Yes.'

The next day, Jeffrey telephoned again. 'It's all right,' he said, 'I've got the *Daily Mail* to sponsor me.'

'Fine,' said Hall. Nothing Jeffrey said surprised him any more.

Jeffrey did indeed then fly, through the good offices of the American Embassy in London, all the way to Washington. The White House sent a car to the airport. It was the first and not the last time that Jeffrey would meet an American

President. History does not record the substance of their conversation. LBJ and Jeffrey had their photograph taken together; the tough-talking Texan signed Winston Churchill's war speeches. He was much preoccupied with blood, sweat and tears in Vietnam at the time. The car took Jeffrey for a drive around Washington, and then took him back to the airport.

The auction at the Mansion House was an anti-climax; it was nobody's fault. It was snowing heavily and hardly anybody turned up. Possibly, too, the British public did not want to spend money on Harold Wilson's old raincoat.

The *Mail* drew a discreet veil over the whole affair. Nick Lloyd had accompanied the big-time reporters on the way to the Mansion House; on the way back, they mysteriously melted away: 'Right, then, Nick, okay? We can leave it to you . . .' Lloyd learned another lesson that night about Fleet Street. Jeffrey, of course, got his photograph with LBJ splashed all over *Cherwell*.

At Iffley Road and Vincent's, he bounced around making friends with people who were going to be useful to him. He was also becoming potentially useful to others. The Oxford Union, aware like everybody else of his fund-raising exploits, appointed him to boost its undergraduate membership. It was not a successful appointment, however. Elsewhere, too, his efforts were suddenly not paying off; at least, not without 'unkind' voices first being raised in opposition.

His nomination for President of OUAC, which should have been automatic, was opposed. This was highly unusual and all very unfair on the dynamic ball of energy. Chataway never had this problem. Metcalfe and Hogan voted for Jeffrey as President. Fellow sprinter and St Catherine's man Andy Ronay voted against; Ronay was always quicker on the track and their rivalry extended off it. So did OUAC President and 880 yards man, Hugh Pullan.

Jeffrey, having said he would not stand if opposed, now changed his mind. The two ex-Presidents had their way. In

May 1965, the twenty-five-year-old Jeffrey Archer became President of Oxford University Athletic Club.

The new OUAC President spent part of his summer vacation as a deckchair attendant at the Winter Gardens, Weston-super-Mare. In October, he was invited to give the prizes at Northway School, Oxford. He was quoted as saying: 'Perhaps, after all, the safest advice is to try and keep the Ten Commandments. As a start, one could always treat them like an examination and only attempt eight.'

Shortly afterwards, he and Mary announced their engagement.

But it was at Iffley Road that his energies found their full expression. Once or twice a week he would have mass training sessions, with everyone jogging to the parks. A lot of OUAC members had their own ideas on training and thought it was a waste of time. But even they could not fault his enthusiasm. Oxford, after all, was still pervaded with the tradition of being seen to succeed without trying. Jeffrey was certainly trying.

He used to bounce around the Iffley Road ground, saying: 'We've got to work like hell to beat the 'Tabs!'*

Oxford life elsewhere followed a less than dynamic pattern echoed in the pages of *Cherwell*. Should colleges be allowed to control their undergraduates' morals? Women undergraduates: were they stupid, slovenly or simply unoriginal? Should undergraduates have parking rights?

Jeffrey, who by now had acquired a vintage car of his own, was too busy to take notice of this; except for the job applications. After all, there would be no future here even for him, once he had been President of OUAC. In staying for three years and no longer, even he would resemble an ordinary Oxford undergraduate.

He applied for and was shortlisted for the post of Director of the National Birthday Trust. There were 120 applicants for the job, which was based in London and involved fund-raising to make childbirth safer. He approached it in his usual style.

* Cambridge team (from '*Cantab*').

Adrian Metcalfe would recall: 'Anyone with an interview coming up would try and do some research. But he was absolutely in a different class to anybody you've ever met in your life.

'He and Mary sat down and said: "How are we going to crack this?" He came up with about 100 ideas for raising funds. Chart after chart of programmes for the next ten years . . . he was quite brilliant.'

Jeffrey, the youngest of the 120 applicants by ten years, got the job. Like Chataway, Jeffrey had taken the next step on the way to becoming Prime Minister.

The day dawned of the Inter-Varsity Athletics Match. It was to be Jeffrey's finest hour.

In those days the Inter-Varsity used to be held at London's White City stadium. The Oxford University Athletic Club teams were accustomed to catching the train to London on the Saturday morning and competing on the same day.

Jeffrey decided otherwise. On the Friday night, the team went up to London and stayed at an unsalubrious hotel on the North Circular Road. Jeffrey subjected them to a 'team talk', to which some members took exception. John Bryant, the distance runner from Somerset, thought it was rather amusing.

'People were ambivalent about him then, as I think they always have been throughout his career. They would be open-mouthed with horror at what he was doing and yet they would go along with it.

'He used to chide people for not being ambitious enough. "Are you going to win, John?" he would say. "Are you going to run a new record?" In a way, he was more honest.

'I'd never seen university sport before, and for all I knew he was the sort of person they would usually have as President. It was only subsequently I began to realise that he wasn't quite the norm.'

On Saturday, the Oxford University Athletic Club team took to the field of combat. The 'Tabs never had a chance.

By the end of the day's proceedings, Oxford had won by a record margin.

Almost immediately, Cambridge lodged a complaint.

'That man Archer,' they said, 'is a professional. He's not an undergraduate. He's not a graduate. He's not a post-graduate. What is he?'

It was a good question; but once again, older, wiser counsels prevailed. Arthur Selwyn, Senior Treasurer of OUAC, like Sir Noel Hall, Tim Cobb and 'Bankie Bill' before him, had always had a soft spot for Jeffrey. Besides, possession was nine-tenths of the law; and Oxford, by 87 points to 66, were very much in possession.

The OUAC 1966 team photograph taken back at Iffley Road tells the story. Jeffrey never let anything happen by accident, and would undoubtedly have orchestrated the seating plan. Here, to the left, was Andy Ronay, the sprinter whom Jeffrey had good reason to fear and who had opposed his Presidency, seated in the front row but at a safe distance; here, closer in was Tim Jones, the Secretary, who went on to become Bursar of Bristol University; in the centre, J. H. Archer (BNC), 100 yards and 220 yards hurdles, the President; to his right, Tim Taylor (St Peter's), the 880 yards man and Jeffrey's successor, later Headmaster of Bromsgrove School; John Bryant (Queens), the 3000 metres steeplechase man from Somerset; Hugh Pullan, another 880 yards man, the previous President who had also opposed Archer's Presidency. Behind them, in the serried ranks, Henk Altmann (New College), the brilliant South African 3 miler, invariably debarred from international success by his nationality.

Years later, when Jeffrey had made a broadcast on the popular BBC radio programme *Desert Island Discs* (which included the tune 'Oh Lord, It's Hard To Be Humble When You're Perfect In Every Way'), one of the men in the photograph telephoned another of his contemporaries in the front row.

'Tell me,' he said, 'which eight stories would you tell on your desert island?'

Jeffrey sits centre-stage, with that wide, flat mouth and the dark blue track suit bearing the inverted laurels of OUAC. He would still be wearing it to referee rugby matches, twenty years later.

That summer, he would finally win his full British vest for running against Sweden in Stockholm. On 16 September, he was in the winning 4 by 400 metres relay team. The day after, he was third in the 200 metres in 22.3 seconds. He became a member of Achilles, then the élite athletics club to end all clubs. Achilles was entirely composed of ex-Oxford and Cambridge men.

The ethos of Achilles was very much like that of the popular film *Chariots of Fire*. They too used the inverted laurel wreath, but it was in gold on a white background. Achilles men were usually on the verge of internationalism. Twenty-one years later, the morning after he had won half a million pounds in damages against a newspaper which claimed he had had sex with a prostitute, the ex-President of OUAC could be seen on television jogging with his son, William. He was wearing his long, white Achilles club sweater.

'Jeffrey,' John Bryant would later say, 'doesn't put on a sweater without carefully choosing it. The Achilles Club really embodied all the things he aspired to. That's how much he was in love with Achilles.'

However, even Achilles had his weak points.

Jeffrey Howard Archer (Dip.Ed.) and Mary Doreen Weeden (B.Sc. (Hons) First Class) were married in the University Church of St Mary the Virgin, Oxford, on 11 July 1966.

It was a lovely, sunny day. The University Church was decorated with flowers and the presence of notables. Sir Noel and Lady Hall had made the short walk from the Brasenose Lodgings to witness the nuptials of surely the most unconventional member of the University they would ever meet. The chaplain of Brasenose, Leslie Styler, officiated. Lola was making her first appearance to many of her son's Oxford acquaintances. Lola's foster-daughter, Elizabeth Fullerton, was one of the two turquoise-clad bridesmaids; the other was Mary's sister, Janet. Jeffrey was resplendent in morning dress and top hat. Mary, who had chosen the music for the occasion, looked radiant in her white organza dress and veil.

The *de facto* guard of honour consisted of OUAC men, past and present. Adrian Metcalfe, Olympian flatmate and object of worship, was prominent. John Bryant, the Somerset distance runner, was now captain of cross country. He would remember the wedding as a good day, if a little peculiar in one respect.

It happened at the reception, which was held in Brasenose. Bryant was filing past the bride and groom, with the usual small talk and shaking of hands. As Bryant reached the groom, the latter beamed, as might be expected.

'Ah, John,' said Jeffrey, 'good to see you.'

Bryant reciprocated and started to move on; but then, to his astonishment, the groom went on: 'Phone this number,' he said, 'you ought to be running for BUSF.'

'And indeed,' Bryant said later, 'I did ring up and they did say, "We want you to run the steeplechase for British Universities Sports Federation." But it was a strange thing to say at his own wedding reception.'

The reception over, Mr and Mrs Jeffrey Archer went away in Jeffrey's 1924 Morris. Part of the honeymoon would be spent on Dartmoor, in the cottage belonging to Jeffrey's senior colleague at Dover College, Edward Bayly. The rest of it took place in Ireland. Then in the established manner of young people going places, they moved to London.

Charity Begins at Home

Mr and Mrs Archer took up residence in their first home in a rented flat at 87 Cadogan Place, London SW1. Mary, still only twenty-one, pursued her doctoral thesis at Imperial College in heterogeneous catalysis in solutions. Jeffrey, now twenty-six, also occupied himself full-time with solutions; in this case, to the problem of how to raise large sums of money.

He did not altogether abandon his own academic career. That autumn, in a move worthy of Evelyn Waugh's *Decline and Fall*, he was appointed a governor of Dover College. Thus was the former PE master elevated alongside such eminent figures as Sir William Oliver and Sir Gerald Duke. Needless to say, this was effected through the good intentions of Tim Cobb, and would lead to further adventures for himself and Jeffrey.

Meanwhile, Jeffrey threw himself into his new job with characteristic energy. As Director of the National Birthday Trust (salary £2000), he offered money for the other halves of Shell 'Make Money' tokens. Then he embarked on a campaign to persuade Mary Wilson, the shy, poetry-loving wife of the then Labour Prime Minister, to sponsor a fund-raising dinner in aid of the little-known National Birthday Trust at No. 10, Downing Street.

Tim Cobb was one of the first to visit him in his new offices at 57 Lower Belgrave Street, London SW1. The board-room was lined with portraits of elderly dowagers; bene-factors of yesteryear. Behind his desk was a photograph of John F. Kennedy. Jeffrey usually posed with it for his own photographs.

Jeffrey was telephoning more or less non-stop and his ex-employer had plenty of time to take in the scene. This included Jeffrey's secretary, an attractive young woman called Rosie.

Cobb exchanged pleasantries with Jeffrey and went on his way. Twenty years and numerous encounters with him later, Cobb was attending a cousin's eightieth birthday celebrations. The party was hosted by his cousin's son, at a house near Guildford. He had six children, and an attractive wife.

Cobb walked into the house, and the wife said; 'I've seen you before.'

It was Rosie. 'Tell me,' she said, 'do you still see Jeffrey Archer?'

'Occasionally,' Cobb replied.

'He'll drop you, of course,' she muttered.

Cobb did not reply.

Childbirth, safe or otherwise, was not yet on the agenda in the Archer household; but that did not prevent Jeffrey and Mary from having babysitters in mind.

The idea was simple. Nurses did not have enough money to go out, so they sat at home and watched TV. Why should they sit at home and watch TV alone, when they could go out and watch it with the children of rich parents sleeping in the next room? And, moreover, be paid for it? Mary and Jeffrey picked up the telephone, made some calls, and made themselves some money. They called it 'Babysitters Unlimited'.

That summer, Prime Minister Harold Wilson had announced a six-month freeze in prices, wages and salaries. But Jeffrey and Mary Archer were not only getting by, they were going up. The unpopular policies of the Wilson government would also have cataclysmic effects at the local government level, and not the least of them would be the first major political opportunity to be noticed and seized by Jeffrey Archer.

The Greater London Council, or GLC, was the traditional repository of aspiring politicians and anti-government sentiment. It was based in County Hall, on the opposite side of

Westminster Bridge from the Houses of Parliament. During Jeffrey's later adventures as Deputy Chairman of the Conservative Party, when he had recourse to his Achilles sweater, its anti-government sentiments would spell final dissolution for the left-wing GLC. But in the winter of 1966 and spring of 1967, County Hall was the goal of all aspiring Tory politicians. These had of course included the Conservative Member of Parliament, until very recently, for Lewisham North, and Vincent's and Achilles man, Christopher Chataway.

Chataway had lost his Lewisham seat and was looking to re-establish his political base. As the Conservatives accrued more and more capital at the local political level, it became clear that the GLC elections on 13 April 1967 were going to constitute a massive vote of no confidence in the Wilson government.

Jeffrey, who of course had wasted no time in cultivating friends like the athletic Chataway among the motley denizens of County Hall, found himself in a position to do exactly what he had promised Richard Exley nearly four years earlier. The dynamic ball of fire, educated at Wellington and Oxford, who had helped raise a million for Oxfam, was standing for the Havering council seat of none other than Sir William Fiske, the Labour leader of the GLC.

It was the age of the opportunist, the whizzkid, the man who was going places. Most important, it was the beginning of an anti-Labour swing. Jeffrey was qualified by virtue of his youth, if nothing else. He neither ventured any policy statements, nor was he asked to do so. He had little or no experience of campaigning in anything other than favourable political conditions. Nevertheless, he did win – not simply by being there, of course; but in the sense that he was the quintessential opportunist whizzkid who was going places and who knew a bandwagon when he saw one.

Furthermore, founded on *Cherwell* and developed on the *Daily Mail*, there was the Archer publicity machine.

The *Evening News* of 16 April 1967 profiled the new Tory

GLC member and youngest-ever councillor at twenty-seven. Jeffrey, it was reported, had studied engineering in California; he had also been elected, in his very first term at Oxford, to the élite sporting club known as Vincent's. 'Only Sir Alec Douglas-Home,' it said, 'has equalled that feat in the present century.'

King Edward the Eighth, who alone in fact had achieved this feat, presumably rotated athletically in his resting place. No one else was eligible until his second year; once and once only was the rule which barred membership to freshmen broken. But what did the membership rules of an obscure Oxford drinking club matter to the readers of the *Evening News*? And what place did the *Evening News* occupy in the priorities of the drinkers at that tiny, august bar?

The answer was the same in both cases; and besides, the colour of an old school tie (or old club tie, in Vincent's case) as worn by Harold Macmillan and Sir Alec Douglas-Home, or Jeffrey Archer, or any tie, for that matter, no longer signified so much in the London of the mid '60s. Jeffrey, whose own ties would get wider and more ebullient with age and money, was the man of the moment.

The subliminal message was clearer, though, to those few to whom Jeffrey had confided his dearest ambition. If Sir Alec, a Vincent's man, could reach No. 10, Downing Street, then so too, surely, could Jeffrey Archer.

A few days later, while Richard Exley was buying his newspaper in South Africa and goggling over the headline 'YOUNGEST EVER TORY UNSEATS SIR WILLIAM', the youngest ever Tory in question was leaving, in his other capacity as a governor of Dover College, for the steamy climes of the Orient.

It had been Tim Cobb's idea for Jeffrey to become a governor. After all, he had breathed new life into the school as its PE teacher. Cobb and Sir Gerald Duke, then Chairman of the board of governors, had engineered it between them. Jeffrey of course did not take much persuading.

This was not without a degree of opposition from certain other members of the board, who felt that Jeffrey did not always defer to them to the extent they felt their advanced age and seniority demanded.

Cobb's plan, approved by Sir Gerald Duke and the other governors, was that he should visit Hong Kong in the Easter holidays. Hong Kong was the home of numerous and wealthy parents of Dover boys, from whom much-needed funds could be painlessly extracted. Cobb then intended to travel from Hong Kong to Singapore and Kuala Lumpur. A wealthy parent had already guaranteed his air fares.

Cobb did, however, have two small problems, both of which he confided to Sir Gerald. 'Look here,' said Cobb, 'I've lost all my tropical kit and I must have some sort of suit for Hong Kong.'

As ever, the obliging ex-sapper backed him up.

The governors quite rightly allotted the Headmaster £100 for such expenses.

Cobb then had another idea. 'Look here,' he said, 'I've never tried raising money before, and he's rather good at it. Can I take Jeffrey with me?'

Once again, his suggestion was accepted. Cobb, in a quite unwearable suit, departed for the Far East. Jeffrey followed a few days later, having put in for his £100 expenses.

The two men were reunited in Hong Kong. They were then taken to Macao, to see the notorious gambling hells. Jeffrey, mindful of the fact that he was a governor, and perhaps flushed by his recent local electoral success, somehow gained the impression that he would be 'allowed' to win by the croupiers. Cobb, his discomfort already exacerbated by his ill-fitting tropical suit, looked on as Jeffrey proceeded to lose practically the whole of his 'expenses' in half an hour.

Then they went on to Singapore.

Their host there was a Chinese doctor of whom Cobb was very fond. The doctor was less smitten with Jeffrey. Jeffrey banged his knee on a concrete slab at the airport and for some reason made a most un-Oriental fuss.

The Chinese doctor was not impressed. 'Your Jeffrey,' he said, 'has a very low pain threshhold.'

Then they went on to Kuala Lumpur. Jeffrey made a speech at dinner; 'I'm so glad,' he said, 'to be back with you people of Singapore.'

Then they went back to London, and more familiar territory.

The new GLC councillor and his wife invited his old Headmaster and Mrs Cobb to the theatre. Jeffrey, who, it may be remembered, had once starred as Puck in *A Midsummer Night's Dream* in the Dover ruins, had booked a box at the Old Vic for a performance of Molière's *Tartuffe*.

Mary collected Cobb, whose wife was coming later, at Charing Cross. As she was driving them to the Archers' flat, Cobb could not help but be struck once again by this woman whose extreme youth was only equalled by her apparent aplomb. 'Here am I,' he thought, 'being driven about by a slip of a girl who got the most brilliant First in Chemistry since the War. Stop wishing you could take hold of her leg and change gear with it!'

During the interval Jeffrey, who had managed to get onto a GLC committee concerned with arts and leisure, led the way into the theatre manager's office, where a number of smoked salmon sandwiches were available. Mary and the Cobbs dutifully trooped after him. There was not a lot to do in the theatre's manager's office, apart from eat the smoked salmon sandwiches. But when a member of the theatre staff put his head round the door and informed them that the curtain was about to go up, he was left in no doubt as to who the real audience was that night.

'Give us another five minutes,' Jeffrey told him; and that is exactly what they did.

Cobb would later seek to excuse this display of youthful hubris on the part of his protégé. The theatre audience, in truth, would have been ignorant of the cause of the delay. It probably gave them more time to down their own interval drinks. Mary's feelings, as has so often been the case, went unrecorded. The truth is, she was much preoccupied with heterogeneous catalysis in solutions.

A recollection of Adrian Metcalfe's may offer some empirical evidence to support this.

Mary and Jeffrey stayed one night at the Metcalfe home in Twickenham. There was a ball to be attended, and Mary was pressing her dress with a steam iron. The Metcalfes went out and left them to it.

A few hours later, Metcalfe and his wife returned home. There was a smell of burning in the air.

Mary had left the steam iron on, flat down on the asbestos pad. The water had dripped into the pad, completely ruining it.

'It was a liberating thought,' Metcalfe said later, 'here was a woman who had got a Congratulatory First at Oxford; who was beautiful and intelligent and academic and donnish; and very intimidating; and she'd left the iron on.'

In his quest for publicity, the new GLC councillor had telephoned Pat Davidson. The former Oxfam Press Officer went along to the Junior Carlton Club imagining this was to be a purely social occasion. Jeffrey had long promised her 'lunch at my club'.

She was surprised, however, to find herself being bombarded with a stream of anecdotes which she was expected to take down, about Jeffrey the Rising GLC Councillor and Jeffrey the Founder of Babysitters Unlimited. She was further expected to go away and 'place' them with 'kind friends' in the media.

Davidson decided to humour him, and did not mention that as she now had a baby son and daughter, she was concentrating these days on writing children's stories under the name of Anne Digby. In fact, she was being rather successful at it. But then Jeffrey had not even asked her what she was doing at the time.

*

Jeffrey's well-publicised success as local politician and fund-raiser naturally enough brought him to the attention of Conservative Central Office, and of the Chairman of the Conservative Party, a true Somerset man, the formidable Edward du Cann.

There was little chance, though, of his fund-raising skills being employed by the Opposition Conservative Party of the time. Among the mandarins of Smith Square, where there was already an established fund-raising procedure, it was felt that the employment of hirelings, however able, would be inappropriate.

Besides, there was also the not inconsiderable matter of *gravitas*, or lack of it, in the case of the ebullient youngest ever councillor.

But this early, pre-Thatcher encounter was nevertheless the beginning of a relationship between Jeffrey and Conservative Central Office that was to divide the Party mandarins, fascinate the Tory faithful, satisfy the press and lead to monumental misunderstandings on all sides for the next two decades.

He also met powerful and influential individuals, many of them dinner guests of Chataway. He had a winning way with older men, as he had already shown. He met the Leader of the Opposition, Edward Heath; the Leader of the Conservative Party delegation to the Council of Europe, Geoffrey Rippon; the Opposition Deputy Chief Whip and Conservative liaison with the GLC, the art-loving Brian Batsford; and, most significantly, the former young Turk of the Tory Party, who had spoken on behalf of the UN at Oxford in Jeffrey's day and who was now Chairman of the United Nations Association: the ambitious and thrusting forty-one-year-old bachelor, Humphry Berkeley.

The United Nations Association's brief was to secure support for the United Nations in Britain. The UN was of course a worldwide organisation; a fact reflected in the credentials of the Association's highly-experienced Director, John Ennals.

Ennals had joined the UN's precursor, the League of Nations, as a schoolboy in 1932. During the Second World War he had worked closely with the Yugoslav partisans. He had been Secretary General for ten years of the World Federation of United Nations Associations in Geneva. Before becoming Director of the United Nations Association in London he had been General Secretary of Ruskin College, Oxford. He had twice stood as a Labour Parliamentary candidate and was active in the anti-apartheid movement. He was now forty-nine years old.

The London headquarters of the UNA consisted of Director, Secretary, Finance Officer, Press and Information Officer, Student Section, International Service Department and all the usual panoply of an international fund-raising charity. They were housed on the seventh and eight floors of a windy, modern tower marooned on the Albert Embankment. Other floors consisted of luxury apartments with stunning views of the River Thames, the Tate Gallery and the Houses of Parliament. The ninth floor was occupied by none other than the hero of the Oxford University James Bond Society, Sean Connery. The building was called Alembic House.

The UNA's members tended to be either Liberal or Labour, and a Conservative was therefore usually sought as Chairman. The leaders of the three main British political parties were joint presidents of the Association. The kind of Conservative interested in the United Nations and international affairs in general was by definition a rather unusual person. Nigel Nicolson, the previous Chairman, had not alway agreed with his party over foreign affairs. Nor had the present Chairman and former MP, Humphry Berkeley.

There had been some hesitation over the appointment of Berkeley as Chairman of the UNA. The position was unpaid and effectively honorary. Traditionally, the Chairman had come into the offices once a month or so to chair the Executive; he was a person to whom Ennals, the full-time paid Director, could go and say, 'We're having a deputation to the

Foreign Office. Can you spare the time?' The Chairman would add his weight selectively, at important meetings.

Berkeley, however, decided otherwise.

The new UNA Chairman had not long ago lost his seat as MP for Lancaster. Like Chataway, with whom he was on close terms, he was casting around for a base on which to re-establish his political career.

As John Ennals would later recall: 'He'd started making "wind-of-change" type statements about Africa which made him popular with some people. I remember he kept on talking about Kenneth Kaunda. He loved to be close to the famous. That's a very important thing to understand.'

It is in truth hard to imagine two temperamentally less compatible people than John Ennals and Humphry Berkeley. Physically, socially, intellectually and politically they were and are diametrically opposed to each other. The stage was already set for the power struggle which would lead to both men's resignation.

Berkeley moved into Alembic House and took an office as Chairman. As Chairman, he appointed a personal assistant and brought in a Press Officer. The Chairman of the Finance Committee at the time was the Labour MP for Sheffield (Heeley), Frank Hooley.

Hooley was not entirely happy about Berkeley's new broom: 'Don't worry,' said Berkeley, 'I'll raise the money.'

It was in order to raise funds, and on the recommendation of his good friend Christopher Chataway, that Berkeley engaged the services of a professional fund-raiser.

He had chosen a personable young man, a successful athlete, who had already helped raise a million pounds for Oxfam; who had done such a good job at the National Birthday Trust, and become the GLC's youngest ever councillor.

For Ennals, it was the first time he had even heard of Jeffrey Archer.

Jeffrey joined the United Nations Association as fund-raiser on 1 July 1967. John Ennals, as Director, would remember his arrival at Alembic House. He was pleasant, courteous and bright. Ennals would also remember that Berkeley made it clear that Jeffrey was responsible directly to the Chairman, that he would take orders directly from the Chairman and that he would report back directly to the Chairman.

Jeffrey was given an office and he immediately set to work doing what he did best, which was raise money. During the year that followed, he was perceived as a hard working and popular employee of the UNA. He was also rumoured to be the highest paid, on a salary of £3500 per annum. His main achievement was to arrange another fund-raising dinner at the address with which he appeared obsessed: No. 10, Downing Street.

Prime Minister Harold Wilson, on whose shy, poetry-loving wife Mary, Jeffrey had already made such an impression, was a sympathetic UNA joint-president. Wilson was persuaded to host the dinner. The guests were persuaded to contribute handsomely for their places at the table.

'Archer,' Ennals would recall, 'had an extraordinary capacity for finding, identifying and chatting up businessmen who were on their way up, but who wouldn't otherwise have reached the dizzy heights of Downing Street.'

He found, identified and chatted up the directors of rising building companies like Sunley. Olav Kier, chairman of another rising building firm, was likewise prevailed upon to open his wallet in return for a place at the dinner table. Kier would be prevailed upon by the charming young fund-raiser to invest in another project in the near future. A dinner for fifty at No. 10, meanwhile, did everyone some good.

Wilson sat in the middle, with Berkeley on his immediate right. Ennals was there as UNA Director; Kier and Sunley met Ted Heath and Jeremy Thorpe; and Jeffrey met Michael Sobell, father-in-law of Lord Weinstock, and Lord Harlech, former ambassador to the USA and, with Geoffrey Rippon, one of the keenest advocates of Britain's entry into Europe. By the end of pudding, some interesting new acquaintances

71

had been made, as well as £250,000 for the United Nations Association.

Jeffrey had done it again. As Ennals would recall, 'Some people of course said: "This is not the way to raise money. We usually go around selling flags in the street." Well, money is money. It was legally gained and Jeffrey Archer was obviously an absolute ace at it.'

Berkeley, too, was delighted for obvious reasons. If he had merely been himself, chairing meetings and making statements to the press, his position would have been less secure. As it was, he had produced a young man who in turn had produced a quarter of a million pounds, when the rest of the country (under Harold Wilson) was going through a period of severe economic restraint.

Ennals, for his part, went on trying to run the United Nations Association despite his differences with Humphry Berkeley.

Jeffrey, meanwhile, was getting to the stage where he no longer needed the UNA.

Arrow Enterprises, a business partnership, was formed on 29 April 1968 in the names of Jeffrey Archer and Humphry Berkeley. Ennals was told that, on renewal of Jeffrey's yearly contract in July 1968, the UNA would henceforth be employing Arrow Enterprises rather than plain Jeffrey Archer.

'We were told,' he said, later, 'that it had been arranged by Humphry. We supposed it was more convenient taxwise for Jeffrey to be paid through his company. Not that I ever saw how much he was paid. We didn't know Humphry and Jeffrey had set up this company together.'

Humphry Berkeley would never reveal the exact circumstances surrounding the formation of his business partnership with Jeffrey Archer. Whatever the details, the partnership was dissolved on 9 December, 1968.

The truth of the origins of Arrow after so many years is of little interest. But the circumstances surrounding the formation of any partnership are not without significance. Furthermore, by the time of the dissolution of the partnership the two men had fallen out. The dispute was over Jeffrey's expenses.

In July 1968, as well as renewing his contract of employment with the UNA, Jeffrey had submitted his first year's expenses claim. Needless to say, they were considerable, given the highly sociable nature of the job he was doing. Certain persons, however, most notably in the form of the satirical magazine *Private Eye*, would use the dispute over Jeffrey's expenses as ammunition in their campaigns against him for years to come.

Private Eye, then in its heyday, was largely dependent for copy on its receipt of stories which for one reason or another, usually legal, the major newspapers were unwilling to publish. In this respect, like the bird on the back of the crocodile, it performed a valid and useful function in the British press.

It was, moreover, immune to the demands of advertisers, compared with the likes of *The Times* and the *Daily Mail*. It had access to only limited funds and welcomed the threat of litigation. The saga of Jeffrey Archer, Humphry Berkeley, John Ennals and the United Nations Association would become one of its most celebrated and obscure obsessions.

Jeffrey, so the *Eye* would later report, had claimed personal expenses regarded as 'generous' by an organisation which depended on voluntary funds. (The magazine omitted however to credit him as the main source of the same funds.) For the period 1 July 1967 to 1 July 1968, he had claimed more than £1700. An inquiry launched by Mr Harold Jowitt, the UNA's Deputy Honorary Treasurer, found some claims to have been made in error. For instance, the magazine said, there was the lunch at the Savoy on 28 March 1968; the £24 18s. 7d claimed back by Jeffrey had already in fact been paid by his lunch companion, the Honorary Treasurer of the UNA, Lord Luke. Two other innocent beneficiaries of Jeffrey's lunchtime largesse, the magazine reported, were fellow Dover College governors Sir Gerald Duke and Sir William Oliver.

As a consequence, the magazine continued, Jeffrey repaid the grand sum of £82 17s. 4d to the United Nations Association, which he agreed had been improperly charged. This was less than the sum he had lost in the gambling hells of Macao a year or so earlier. The problem of expenses would, however, dog Jeffrey long after he had left the UNA.

John Ennals, meanwhile, had too many of his own problems with Berkeley to worry about any feud between Berkeley and Jeffrey Archer. 'I knew,' he would say, later, 'that the Blessed Jeffrey had now become a rather nasty word. He'd dropped out of the canon of saints. Humphry never made any secret of his likes and dislikes. I got the strong impression that Jeffrey was no longer Humphry's favourite person.

'I never knew what led to any disagreement; it was just suddenly clear that there had been one.'

Jeffrey continued to toil away at the UNA and to cultivate friends in high places. Mary, missing the structure and calm of Oxford, became the youngest ever research fellow of St Hilda's. The Archers worked hard at their separate lives, but they were recognisably a couple.

That October, Jeffrey made a number of appearances in his capacity as assistant to Christopher Chataway, then head of the Inner London Education Authority. It was the time of violent demonstrations against American involvement in Vietnam. One of these appearances was at Westminster City School. The youngest ever GLC councillor and governor of Dover College launched straight into his theme.

'I want to show my colleagues,' he said, 'that not all young people are layabouts and hooligans. So I want you to get up a petition supporting police restraint, and take it round the streets. The boy who gets the most signatures will spend a day at Scotland Yard.'

Jeffrey had been lunching with major-generals and was perhaps unaware that some of the school's senior pupils had helped organise the demonstrations in question. Furthermore, in spite of the radical flavour of the times, the pupils had been told that they would not be allowed to form a socialist society, since politics had no place in school life.

Jeffrey was rather taken aback when his speech was greeted with uproar. Perhaps, though of course it will never be known, they even sensed this was something of a recruiting talk on the part of an ex-policeman who, had he stayed on the force, might well have become the youngest ever Chief Superintendent.

Jeffrey left the United Nations Association in February 1969. In doing so, he inevitably weakened the position of his ex-patron and partner, Humphry Berkeley.

Berkeley's main preoccupation was now with John Ennals.

Jeffrey found himself driven into a defensive alliance with the distinguished libertarian.

'I think we were both attacked by Berkeley,' Ennals recalled, 'and that put us in the same situation. There was certainly never an "Ennals-Archer entente", as the newspapers would have it. I respected Jeffrey and I think he respected me, though he wouldn't have dared mention anything favourable about me to Berkeley.

'During the last few weeks he was here, he would look into my office and say, "I want to run a fund-raising do up in the north-east; who do I talk to?" Or: "We want to do something in Wales. They seem a pretty dozy lot down there . . ." and I'd tell him who to talk to.

'My impression of Jeffrey was that he was extremely good at his fund-raising. He may not even have had a secretary, and it takes a different kind of person to go round and chat up businessmen and get £50,000 out of them, than it does to go back home and write up your bus fares.

'I liked him. Our politics were different: I'm Labour Party and always have been, and he's Conservative and I would say on the right wing of the Conservative Party, but it never affected our working relationship.

'I've never seen any reason to change that view.'

Ennals also perceived something else about Jeffrey. Though they had little in common and never met socially, he noticed how important it was for him to talk about Mary. 'She was a constant thing to hang on to,' he said. 'He was very proud of her.'

The differences between Ennals and Berkeley brought the United Nations Association to the brink of collapse. Eventually, it was decided that the only way to prevent total ruin was for both men to resign. Ennals and Berkeley would depart in opposite directions. Berkeley would never be seen in the United Nations Association again. Ennals would be back a few weeks later as a volunteer.

Jeffrey Archer, who played no more than a bit part in their drama, would also return to the windy, modern tower marooned on the Albert Embankment. A few years and many adventures later, he would take up residence in Alembic House, in one of the luxury flats above what had once been the offices of the United Nations Association. Its previous occupant, the James Bond film composer John Barry, had left the country, and the flat was offered for sale.

Jeffrey, meanwhile, wasted no time at all in getting his career as a full-time professional fund-raiser off the ground. He set about this with his by now well-known combination of energy, networking genius and sheer nerve.

His first office consisted of a couple of rooms in Lincoln's Inn Fields. He acquired a secretary called Noreen: 'You can't work for me with a name like Noreen,' he told her. So she changed it to Natalie.

It was one of the things about him that did not strike her as odd at the time. He told her about his army days, but glossed over the rest. 'He was completely ruthless,' she would recall, 'and everything was always in the interest of politics.'

He was a good employer. When she left, he gave her an expensive vanity case which she still had twenty years later. She was still called Natalie, then, too.

Meanwhile, Jeffrey continued to seek ways of capitalising on his contacts. No sooner had he left the United Nations Association, for example, than a letter arrived on the desk of Finance Committee Chairman, Frank Hooley. The letter came from Arrow Enterprises, prop. J. Archer. Arrow, it said, would undertake to raise funds for the UNA.

Hooley declined the offer. A few months later, the UNA got another letter from Arrow Enterprises; this time, bizarrely, addressed to Humphry Berkeley.

In the second letter, Jeffrey tendered for the UN dinner that was to take place the following year, chaired by the Duke of Edinburgh. He suggested speakers such as Alec Douglas-Home and American Vice-President Hubert Humphrey.

Berkeley, it should come as no surprise to hear, gave his erstwhile golden boy a dusty answer.

The UNA connection would continue to be a mixed blessing. He had rather better luck, for example, with Lord Harlech, former ambassador to the United States, and Geoffrey Rippon, both powerful and well-connected advocates of Britain's long-delayed entry into the European Common Market. Lord Harlech had been a guest at that highly successful dinner at No. 10 Downing Street. Arrow Enterprises became official fund-raisers for the pro-EEC ginger group, the European Movement.

Arrow's target was a fund-raising banquet at London's Guildhall on 29 July 1969. A glittering cast of dignitaries had to be assembled for the occasion. The cause was not a charitable one and therefore even more attention than usual had to be taken with the preparations. Above all, the banquet had to have what its youthful organiser conspicuously lacked: *gravitas*.

Jeffrey's solution to this problem perfectly illustrated his talent for refining gold from the disparate elements of a past which he spent so much of his time embroidering. Once again, he found the solution in the magic circle of Archer supporters who would stand by him through thick and thin, and with a steadfastness, it must be said, that was not always reciprocated.

Jeffrey rang up the distinguished former chief sapper, Major-General Sir Gerald Duke. Sir Gerald, a paternal and honourable man, had always enjoyed the drive and flair of the young PE master-turned-Dover College governor, whom he had sent to Hong Kong with Tim Cobb. The two of them had lunch.

Sir Gerald had now retired from the army and was with a firm of civil engineering contractors. After a lifetime of public service, he had a knighthood and very little money. Both were to become important factors in his relationship with Jeffrey Archer.

Sir Gerald had already been helping Jeffrey on a casual basis while the latter was still at the UNA. When the engineering firm which employed him went bust, he became a partner and full-time worker at Arrow Enterprises. Sir Gerald, with his friend and fellow Dover College governor, Sir William Oliver, brought with them military precision, honourable intentions, a mass of contacts and respect. Above all, they brought *gravitas*.

As Jeffrey, whose energy they so perfectly complemented, would tell Nick Lloyd, 'We do the trumpets, the red carpets, the timing, the lot. But if I ring up the Palace and say, "This is Jeffrey Archer of Arrow Enterprises," I don't get through. If they ring up and say, "This is Major-General So-and-so," they get through to anyone. They're brass hats.'

They were brass hats, furthermore, who were grateful for only modest remuneration for their services.

The Guildhall dinner for the British Council of the European Movement absolutely reeked of *gravitas*. Lord Harlech's oration on the desirability of Britain's entry into Europe was applauded by the Archbishop of Canterbury, the Prime Minister, the Lord Mayor of London, the Leaders of the Opposition and of the Liberal Parties and Lord Mountbatten of Burma. £750,000 was made, and again a number of interesting new acquaintances. The *Evening News* reported the following day that Lord Mountbatten had been 'delighted' with the function and added that he had asked the dynamic ball of energy Jeffrey Archer to meet him to consider 'an idea for a project'.

Two years later, Harold Wilson, no longer Prime Minister, produced his memoirs. A brief passage concerning the Guildhall banquet described for the first time how a last-minute hiccup had narrowly been averted. 'I had heard,' Wilson wrote, 'that the fund-raising firm, Arrow Enterprises, which was in charge of the fund-raising activity, had been promised ten per cent of the proceeds. I revolted against this form of professionalism.'

Wilson and Liberal leader Jeremy Thorpe (who would become the next Chairman of the UNA) refused to speak at the banquet until reassured that Arrow Enterprises would receive a flat fee instead. Under the original arrangement, Arrow stood to gain £75,000 for arranging the evening. The eventual flat fee went unnamed in Wilson's memoirs.

The controversy over Jeffrey's alleged policy of taking a percentage of the funds raised would rumble on in those quarters of the press where oppositon lay to the irresistible rise of Jeffrey Archer. The concept of fund-raising for a percentage profit was a fine moral point that was not lost on the expense-fiddlers of Fleet Street. The truth was of course less simple. Was Jeffrey Archer merely a pioneer of American-style fund-raising techniques that would later become less distasteful to the British? He would remain distinctly sensitive about press comment on the subject. The *Sun*, in an article on 18 November 1970, would carry an article about Jeffrey entitled 'Mr Four and a Half Percent'. Jeffrey would claim the journalist in question was 'nearly sacked' for his presumption. In fact there was no sacking, near or otherwise, and in any case the news editor at the time was none other than the man who had given Jeffrey his first big break, ex-*Cherwell* editor Nick Lloyd.

Sir Gerald Duke would maintain later: 'I noticed an article

in which someone was getting a bit snide about him in a London Sunday paper, which said he was one of these chaps who always took a percentage. That's absolutely untrue. We felt as fund-raisers it was a very unethical thing to take a percentage, so we said to the organisations: "This is going to cost you £5,000 or £10,000 or whatever." A flat rate and that was our fee. We never took a percentage.'

Jeffrey and his new friends lunched each other assiduously and there was no shortage of sympathetic older ears for the ideas of the dynamic young fund-raiser. Among the Conservative MPs he had encountered, it may be remembered, was the Conservative Chief Whip and liaison with the GLC, the art-loving member for Ealing, Brian Batsford.

Batsford's own earlier life had been remarkable. He had painted under the name of Brian Cook, before becoming a successful publisher. He was on close terms with Chief Whip William Whitelaw and Party Leader Edward Heath. He had first met Jeffrey in County Hall and he, too, regarded him as a 'whizzkid'.

Batsford, who had run an art gallery before the war, had lunch with Jeffrey one day, and afterwards the conversation quite naturally turned to making money out of pictures.

Batsford had the idea of a picture shop. 'If you walk down the Bayswater Road on a Saturday or Sunday,' he told Jeffrey, 'you'll find enough pictures to put in a small gallery each week and make quite a lot of money. I spend lots of time in junk shops and I often find things by quite well-known artists.'

'What a good idea,' said Jeffrey, 'let's start a picture gallery. Leave everything to me!'

'I visualised a small shop,' Batsford recalled, later, 'in a back street off Kensington High Street or somewhere. But his idea of a picture gallery was very different from mine.'

Batsford did not see Jeffrey again for a while. Jeffrey's next port of call was the up-and-coming builder, Olav Kier. Kier, it may be remembered, had been a satisfied guest at the United Nations Association dinner at No. 10, Downing Street. Was he, Jeffrey now asked in his inimitable way, remotely interested in getting in on the ground floor of an all-too-rare new opportunity in the highly lucrative world of international art?

Mrs Kier had 5000 shares and Mr Peter Fawcett, a Director of Kiers, had 2500. Jeffrey had 15,000 shares as Managing Director. The Chairman was the satisfied pro-Common Marketeer and Shadow Minister of Defence, Geoffrey Rippon. The Archer Gallery Ltd, 23 Grafton Street, London W1, registered on 25 August 1969, with a capital of £25,000, was in business.

Jeffrey then went back to Brian Batsford. 'I refused to be involved financially,' Batsford would recall, later, 'but as it had been partly my idea and I knew a bit about pictures, I was brought in. And to give him his due, he did get hold of some remarkable paintings and sculpture by Leon Underwood. Jeffrey definitely put him on the map.'

That October, the Archer Gallery opened on its plum West End site between Bond Street and Mayfair. The Conservative Party Leader Edward Heath officially opened it at a glittering party.

Arts and Antiques Weekly described the occasion as 'A tribal confrontation of Tory art lovers'. Mr Heath was quoted as saying, 'I spend all my time in art galleries.' Brian Batsford would later say, 'There was the most fearful scrum and the Gallery was launched.'

Tim Cobb, who later bought a rather nice little Norfolk landscape, would recall, 'I said to Jeffrey: "What on earth are you doing running a picture gallery? You know nothing whatever about art." And he said: "I did it purely for the address on the writing paper."'

The Archers already had one good address by now, a home of their own, at 18 Lancaster Mews, London W2. In the mornings they would set off in opposite directions, as they so often would do throughout their married life. Mary first to Paddington Station five convenient minutes away, to Oxford, and thence by bicycle to St Hilda's, and Jeffrey to 23 Grafton Street in his bronze MGB. At St Hilda's, Mary taught clever girls about electro-chemistry, and in the new Arrow offices above the Archer Gallery, Jeffrey and his loyal staff grappled with the solutions to different equations:

Arrow Enterprises specialises . . .
. . . in the organisation of large functions and social events. Our clients include professional institutes, charities, trade associations and other organisations who wish to run a major event but who have neither the staff nor time to devote to it, nor the experience required to ensure a success.

The partnership offers a complete service, from the preliminary planning stage right through to the detailed organisation of the function itself. Our staff is small, but expert in this particular field. Events for which we have been responsible include banquets, charity concerts, the opening of new buildings, and fiftieth anniversary celebrations: the experience gained in all these activities is at your disposal.

The service we offer to clients begins with the preliminary planning of the event. At this stage there are many decisions to make; what type of function, where and when to hold it, selection of guests and financial arrangements. In discussions of these and other planning problems, our advice is freely given.

Should we be engaged to organise and fund a function we will, in close co-operation with the client, take the whole of the detailed management off his shoulders. This includes co-ordinating invitation lists, drafting and dispatching letters of invitation and formal invitation cards, dealing with acceptances and refusals, preparation of seating plans and all aspects of catering, including design of souvenir programmes. We can also arrange for photography and advertising, and liaison with the press and television companies where appropriate.

ARROW ENTERPRISES

23 Grafton Street, London W1X 3LD   01-499 9746

Jeffrey Archer MP
Sir Gerald Duke
Sir William Oliver
Sir Noel Hall
Robin Leach

Jeffrey's photograph in the brochure shows him scrubbed, combed and ready to place himself at your disposal; he also looks thinner and has a faintly vulpine air. Sir Gerald Duke and Sir William Oliver, his small but expert staff, radiate benign capability. This was the team that had so delighted and impressed Lord Louis Mountbatten; that was now deep in discussion with him over a major new fund-raising project.

Jeffrey had come a long way from City Road and glorious Weston. He had come a long way from the cinder tracks and the playing fields and the deckchairs. He had come a long way in a short time, but now he was only nine months from his thirtieth birthday. 'I *must* be a millionaire by the time I am thirty,' he had said to Sir Gerald Duke and others.

To both Richard Exley and Pat Davidson, he had said he was going to be Prime Minister. To Davidson he had confided that he was going to follow in the footsteps of Christopher Chataway. And, although, it was becoming clear that Chataway would never quite live up to his early promise, the small step of Jeffrey becoming an MP, however, still had to be made.

The saga of how Jeffrey managed to do so, and thereby crown the most extraordinary year of his life, would involve one or two old faces and an entirely new set of characters. These were the people who sat down, in the autumn of that year, to make the next move in the snakes and ladders of the political career of Jeffrey Archer.

The process had begun some time before the Archer Gallery opening night. The glittering constellation of guests like

Edward Heath, Geoffrey Rippon and Brian Batsford marked approval of the dynamic ball of energy's suitability as a Conservative candidate at senior Party level. The grass roots aspects, such as submitting a CV to Conservative Central Office, being placed on the list of candidates, finding a seat to contest and then being successfully adopted, were well in hand by this time. Instrumental in this process was a less well-known but equally important guest at the Archer gallery opening night, Major Reginald Clixby Lloyd Fitzwilliams.

Major Fitzwilliams was a Justice of the Peace and County Councillor for Lindsey, which was then one of the three historic 'Parts' of the county of Lincolnshire. He was a Lincolnshire and Cambridge man, a 'Tab' as Jeffrey might irreverently have put it (which of course he never did to the Major). After a wartime career in the Welsh Guards, he became a chartered accountant and Chairman of the Vitacress Group of Companies, a wholesale fruit and vegetable business. Major Fitzwilliams lived near Grimsby with his lively and forthright American wife, Pauline. He was also on the committee that was trying to choose a shortlist of candidates from which to select the successor to the recently deceased MP for Louth, Lincolnshire, Sir Cyril Osborne.

Sir Cyril Osborne had died after twenty years as MP for Louth, during which entire time he resolutely lived in his home county of Leicestershire. He was a self-made man, a knitwear king, politically extremely right-wing, a fact which made absolutely no difference whatsoever to the bulk of the Louth electorate.

Louth was and is an extremely independently-minded area, one of the last bastions of English rural resistance to the process of political centralisation begun by the Normans; for which resistance it would be punished by the 1974 boundary changes. The Louth electorate voted for the man and not the party, a factor, therefore, which should not be under-estimated in the rise of Jeffrey Archer.

Major Fitzwilliams and his colleagues on the committee had been grappling with a shortlist of 108 names, which they reduced to around twenty. The Major had been assisted in this by the Conservative Party Vice-Chairman Richard Sharples, with whom had had been at prep school.

The Chairman of Major Fitzwilliams' small committee was another self-made man, fish-finger magnate Jack Vincent. Vincent was the genius behind the Ross group, which from the 1930s dominated the Grimsby fishing industry. Vincent was a tough customer, hard as a frozen cod, whose judgment was widely respected in Lincolnshire political circles. Vincent, Fitzwilliams, and local farmer Henry Sharpley were now instrumental in reducing the shortlist to just three candidates.

The first of them was John Davies. Davies was a former managing director of Shell and had a big following in the City of London. Edward Heath, too, had made no secret that he wanted Davies in his Cabinet. The National Farmers' Union reckoned he was the right man to represent an agricultural constituency in Westminster.

Second was David Walder. Walder was an experienced ex-MP who had lost his seat at the last election and was brought in as the middle way.

Third was Jeffrey Archer. As Major Fitzwilliams would recall, later, 'We knew very little about him in advance. We had the usual CV from Central Office. We knew about his Blue at Oxford and his work for Oxfam and that he was on the GLC, having stood and won against the Chairman of the Council. It was quite clear, though, that the committee felt strongly that here was somebody young and full of vigour.'

Major Fitzwilliams, a young and vigorous fifty-five, did not demur, even though he himself had once been regarded as possible heir apparent to this safe seat by the colourful Sir Cyril Osborne.

Jeffrey, naturally, had very little idea either of the Louth constituency or of its inhabitants. He accordingly left nothing to chance or to the imagination. The Archer publicity machine shot into action for this first and crucial client meeting.

His confirmation that he would be available for the shortlist came by cable from New York. The day before the interviews, Major Fitzwilliams and his committee of self-made men and women were informed that he would be flying from America into Heathrow on the overnight plane, and then by helicopter up to Cleethorpes Beach, where he would be available for interview at 10.30 a.m.

However, the advance publicity served to obscure the actual facts of the matter. He went up to Grimsby by train, and spent the journey reading how his rival John Davies was highly regarded by Conservative Party Leader Edward Heath. At Grimsby he kept them waiting because there was no taxi to greet him.

That night the three candidates took their turn trying to impress the small committee with their qualifications for the job. The next day, Monday 6 October, Jeffrey had the first of what turned out to be many lunches at the Fitzwilliams' home. That afternoon, Major Fitzwilliams took him round Immingham, an urban and predominantly Labour area, and the factories on the windy banks of the Humber.

That evening there was a meeting of the full Executive Council of the Louth Conservative Association. It took place in Louth Town Hall, and the streets of the elegant little market town were cluttered with the Land Rovers and saloon cars of the farmers and their formidable wives who traditionally settled the fate of parliamentary candidates in this independently-minded rural constituency.

The Chairman, the tough-minded fish-finger magnate Jack Vincent, had already arranged a press release revealing the three shortlisted candidates. Now they had fifteen minutes each to speak to the audience in Louth Town Hall. There were something like 120 people there from eighty-nine villages and the three urban centres of Immingham, Louth and Cleethorpes. There were ten minutes for questions from the floor, the Chairman would sum up, and then the wives would be invited onto the platform one after the other. They were expected to smile and say they were supporting their husbands in this venture.

John Davies, favourite of Edward Heath and the National Farmers' Union, was first on the platform. As he had done with the small committee the previous night, he now revealed to the audience his global economic overview, his mastery of statistics and his close relationship with Ted Heath.

'When,' asked the women, 'will you have time to look after our interests?'

Mrs Davies, although evidently at home with Ted Heath and the global economic overview, also seemed a little ill at ease in such a rural setting.

Then came David Walder. He gave a near-perfect rendition of the Conservative manifesto. He answered all the questions perfectly, whether he felt strongly about them or not. He was the perfect middle-of-the-way candidate. Elspeth Walder, too, was a pleasant and polished performer who knew the technique and smiled warmly at the wives.

Then came Jeffrey.

The dynamic ball of energy hit them like a bolt from the blue. He did not work to notes. He had thought out his speech extraordinarily well. For a start, it was different from the one he had given to the small committee. Heads on the platform started nodding in approval.

He had, too, already summed up the audience he was addressing. When the owner of one of the mud-spattered Land Rovers asked him an agricultural question, he was brilliantly candid.

'No,' he said, 'I'm coming to Lincolnshire and you farmers have got to teach me what the problems are.'

Mary, too, charmed the predominantly female audience. She spoke with her unique blend of touching conciseness, about how she supported her husband now as she had done during his career on the Greater London Council; how she had her own career, grappling with scientific solutions; how she might not be able to come to the constituency as often as she wanted; and how they both, unlike Sir Cyril and Lady Osborne, intended to make their home there.

Then they came to the vote.

The candidates and their wives retired and there was a discussion during which the Chairman welcomed questions. The voting was close from the start. On the first vote, it became clear that the senior section of Louth Conservatives was pro-Davies. A timely telegram from Henry Plumb of the National Farmers' Union attempted to round up dissenters among the Land Rover owners.

The first vote had Davies and Archer neck and neck. Walder dropped out and there was a second ballot.

The second time around, there was one vote in it. It belonged to Trevor Knight of the Immingham Young Conservatives. The gap that had opened between the farmers and the young Tory Turks of Immingham had widened during the last days of Sir Cyril Osborne. After two hours of counts and recounts, it was about to become a yawning gulf. Knight was about to make one of the most extraordinary decisions of British domestic politics.

The vote went to Jeffrey Archer.

Afterwards, one of the pro-Jeffrey members of that small committee would say: 'I think a lot of us walked out of that room thinking it was Mary Archer who had won it over Mrs Davies!'

Elsewhere, there was not quite unanimity of response at the news that Jeffrey Archer had been elected prospective Conservative candidate for Louth, subject to his formal adoption by the membership of the Association. The news was particularly badly received, for example, by the Chairman of the United Nations Association, Humphry Berkeley.

Berkeley, it should be recalled, was locked in mortal combat with his Director, John Ennals. Having lost his own seat within recent memory, the news of Jeffrey's selection to stand for a safe one now appears to have enraged Jeffrey's former friend and mentor. Berkeley wrote the very next day to Conservative Party Chairman Anthony Barber.

His theme was a familiar one: the question of Jeffrey's UNA expenses.

Barber put the matter to Jeffrey, who replied to Barber's satisfaction, but not of course to Berkeley's. There then began the tradition of a new and unexpected item being added to the agenda of Conservative Party Conferences: namely, a Jeffrey Archer Crisis.

The Sunday after the election, and only a couple of days before the formal adoption was due to take place, Major Fitzwilliams received a telephone call from Louth Conservative Chairman, Jack Vincent. Vincent told the Major he was telephoning because he felt that of all the local people, the Major knew the person in question better than anyone. Lady Osborne, Vincent went on, was very worried about what was being said at the Conservative Party Conference in Brighton. What did the Major think they should do?

Major Fitzwilliams thought he should telephone his old prep school colleague, Conservative Party Vice-Chairman Richard Sharples. At his Hampshire home, hoping for a quiet Sunday, Sharples told the Major that the matter was to be investigated at 11 a.m. on the following day, Monday 13 October, by the Chairman of the Party, Anthony Barber.

This was only two days before the formal adoption was due to take place in Louth. Speculation about the dynamic ball of energy's suitability as a Conservative candidate was now spreading beyond Lincolnshire.

Clearly, something had to be done. On the afternoon of the fateful Monday 13 in question, the Major received another telephone call. This time it was from Conservative Party Chairman, Anthony Barber. Barber came straight to the point. Central Office, he said, had investigated the allegations against Jeffrey Archer and was satisfied with his suitability as a candidate. But the final decision, said Barber, had to be made by the local branch. Where was Jack Vincent? What, in what was by now becoming a familiar refrain, did the Major think they should do?

Major Fitzwilliams thought that Jeffrey should catch the

16.30 train from King's Cross to Grimsby. He rounded up the other members of the committee and arranged for them all to meet at the Yarborough Hotel at 7.30 p.m. that evening. The adoption meeting was now little more than twenty-four hours away.

Jeffrey arrived at 7.45 p.m., closely followed by Jack Vincent.

Dinner was eaten, and the little party withdrew to the hotel lounge for a private discussion. The members of the committee then questioned Jeffrey closely about the rumours that were in danger of discrediting his candidature and their judgment. The Major had the impression that the committee was still concerned.

Major Fitzwilliams then made his final offer. He would go to London the next morning with Jeffrey. If he was satisfied that Jeffrey was vindicated then he would return with him in time for the adoption meeting.

Vincent and the others told him to go to it.

The following morning, the Major and his youthful protégé went to the House of Commons. It was the day of the adoption meeting. They were met by the Labour MP for Sheffield (Heeley), Frank Hooley. Mr Hooley, it should be remembered, was United Nations Association Finance Officer. Hooley showed Major Fitzwilliams correspondence which proved that the expenses under dispute had been repaid by Jeffrey. Furthermore, as far as the UNA was concerned, Jeffrey had done a wonderful job.

Major Fitzwilliams was then joined by the Shadow Minister of Defence, pro-Marketeer and Chairman of the Directors of the Archer Gallery, Geoffrey Rippon. Rippon explained that he had already spoken to Berkeley and had arranged to meet him in person that afternoon. Rippon assured the Major that the whole matter was 'a storm in a teacup'.

Fitzwilliams and Jeffrey were then visited by Anthony Barber and Richard Sharples, both of whom assured them of their support and echoed Rippon's view. At 4 p.m. Major

Fitzwilliams and Jeffrey left the House of Commons without seeing Rippon again, to catch the train for Louth and the adoption meeting. They were met at Louth station by Major Fitzwilliams' wife, Pauline.

Mrs Fitzwilliams, too, had had a busy day.

A short time before she left to go to the station, she had received a telephone call from Geoffrey Rippon. Rippon had assured her of his confidence in Jeffrey Archer. He also assured her that Humphry Berkeley would not pursue the question of Jeffrey's expenses. When Mrs Fitzwilliams asked Rippon if he had an assurance from Berkeley in writing, Rippon said he had not, but that a verbal assurance was quite enough.

This was only the latest in a line of telephone conversations that had kept her busy that day. Earlier, she had been privileged to hear from none other than Jeffrey's erstwhile role model, Christopher Chataway. Chataway asked her to tell her husband that he had every confidence in Jeffrey.

The Chairman of the Tory Party, Anthony Barber, had also been on the line. He, too, told Mrs Fitzwilliams that the whole affair was nothing more than 'a storm in a teacup'. She retorted that it might seem so in London, but it did not seem that way to them, and particularly to Jack Vincent, who that evening had to face around 400 people at Jeffrey's adoption meeting.

'Politics is a dirty business,' Barber told her.

'Then I'm glad,' she replied, 'that my husband is involved no higher than at county council level.'

Mrs Fitzwilliams then took Jeffrey to the adoption meeting. The Major went straight off to see Jack Vincent.

'We got over that hurdle,' Major Fitzwilliams would recall, later, 'but it was a bit hairy, because none of the UNA business had come out in the selection interviews.

'Jeffrey rode it completely. He was perfectly frank that he had done a job for them and that this was nitpicking over expenses. I satisfied myself, and was able to tell the Chairman.'

Such, then, were the circumstances surrounding Jeffrey Archer's formal adoption that night as Conservative Parliamentary candidate for Louth, Lincolnshire.

The *Grimsby Evening Telegraph* photograph, taken against the background of a Union Jack, showed Jeffrey shaking hands with Lady Osborne. Mary stood between them, beaming. To the right hovered the hard man, frozen-fish magnate Jack Vincent:

I'll gain a 10,000 majority, says Tory

Taking the theme of Mr Edward Heath's speech last weekend, the Conservative candidate for the Louth Division, Mr Jeffrey Archer, said last night he would fight the Labour Government on its record – and gain a 10,000 majority in the constituency.

He was speaking to about 400 members of the Louth Conservative Association at his adoption meeting at the Town Hall, Louth.

Following on from Mr Heath's speech at the Conservative Party conference, he said the record of the Government was one of record taxation, record unemployment and record debt.

'Key marginal'

He said this compared with a record rise in the standard of living, a record increase in social spending, combined with a record reduction in taxation while the Conservatives were in power.

Outlining his coming campaign in the by-election, caused by the death of Sir Cyril Osborne, he said the eyes of the nation would be focussed on the people of Louth.

'We must fight this seat as a key marginal and we must not be satisfied with a slight change in the poll or a slight swing our way,' he said.

'Harold Wilson will look to every sign and every by-election for a glimmer of hope, and if he sees it anywhere he may well go for a quick election. Louth must not be that glimmer of hope, it must be the stepping stone for victory at the next General Election.'

Incentive needed

He said Conservatives must bring back incentive to industry and keep ownership in the hands of people and not the state. The party should fight for a better country in which every citizen had the chance to create a better life for himself.

'We want a country that reaps the rewards of hard work rather than taxing it to a standstill. We want a country of which we can be proud, not a country of which we are ashamed,' said Mr Archer.

He paid tribute to Sir Cyril for all the work he had put into serving the constituency. 'It will be immensely hard to follow,' he added.

There were still six weeks to go, though, before the actual by-election. If a week was a long time in politics, they must have begun to seem like an eternity to the likes of Anthony Barber, who now received the following communication from Humphry Berkeley:

I was disturbed [wrote Berkeley] to hear from Mr Vincent that Mr John Ennals had telephoned him to inform him of Mr Archer's innocence in the matters which I have raised. Mr Ennals, as Mr Archer well knows, is a suspected member of the Communist Party and is viewed by the Foreign Office as a security risk. ... Mr Ennals and his left-wing supporters will use any efforts that they can to dislodge me from the chairmanship of the UNA and thus turn UNA into a fellow-traveller organisation.

Vincent in fact rang Ennals at the UNA offices from a telephone box in Grimsby.

Ennals knew by this time that the only way to prevent mortal damage to the UNA was for both himself and Berkeley to go. He would resist Jeffrey's plea for help in a libel action against Berkeley. 'I was sympathetic to Jeffrey, but I didn't want to get involved. That's not my scene. I don't like being nasty to people. If I'd know that Berkeley was going to be Chairman, I'd have gone on being General Secretary of Ruskin College, Oxford.'

The next UNA Chairman would be Jeremy Thorpe.

On 16 November, three weeks before the by-election, things took a turn for the worse:

Tory row over election candidate [read the *Observer*]
A row has broken out in the Conservative Party over the Tory candidate chosen for the Louth, Lincolnshire, by-election to be held in three weeks' time. Nominations officially close a week tomorrow.

The man at the centre of the storm is 30-year-old Jeffrey Archer, a highly energetic public relations man who, contrary to all expectations, was chosen by the local association in preference to the nationally known John Davies, former Director-General of the Confederation of British Industry.

The by-election is caused by the death of Tory MP Sir Cyril Osborne. He had a 4,092 majority at the 1966 General Election. The constituency has thus chosen not just a candidate but in effect the next member of Parliament.

Postponement sought
A few hours before the writs were issued in the Commons party leaders received urgent representations both from former Conservative MP Mr Humphry Berkeley, chairman of the United Nations Association executive, who had previously employed Mr Archer as a fund raiser, and Mr Berkeley's friend and business partner Mr Edward du Cann MP, previously party chairman. Both suggested it would be wise to postpone the by-election.

More and more MPs came to hear of the dispute [the *Observer* went on], *at the weekend one Tory member travelling with a Tory candidate and a member of the Central Office found they talked of nothing else during the journey.*

Fear has been expressed that Labour MPs and peers connected with the United Nations Association might pass on details of the dispute to the Prime Minister and that Labour might use this incident to its own electoral advantage. . . .

The following day, the *Daily Telegraph* kindly blasted back:

Complaints against candidate 'smear' says Tory chief
Complaints against Mr Jeffrey Archer, 30, Conservative candidate in the Louth by-election, were dismissed yesterday as 'smear without substance' by Mr J. Vincent, chairman of Louth Conservative Association.
Conservative party executives maintained a diplomatic silence on the

row over Mr Archer's candidature which has developed since Mr Humphry Berkeley, chairman of the United Nations Association, and former Conservative MP for Lancaster, criticised the selection . . .

At his home yesterday Mr Vincent said: 'I listened carefully to Mr Berkeley for a couple of hours. I regarded it as of no moment. We have every confidence in Mr Archer.

'It is smear and innuendo. Nothing that worries me at all. It all happened a year ago. We have no objection to Mr Berkeley making it public.'

'No comment'

What were the remarks Mr Berkeley made to Mr Vincent? 'I would rather not comment,' Mr Berkeley said. 'It is nothing to do with me.'

Mr Vincent discussed the conversation with Mr Anthony Barber, chairman of the party. They decided to take no action. Mr Barber refused to comment yesterday.

Mr Archer, a public relations consultant, is in touch with his legal advisers. 'It is a great non-story,' he said. 'I am not concerned about it. Beyond that I have nothing to say.'

In London, in the Arrow offices, the small but expert staff toiled away above the Archer Gallery. They were working on a project for Lord Mountbatten. Mary continued to journey from the pretty mews house to Paddington and the bright girls of St Hilda's. Meanwhile, Jeffrey bounced round the constituency predicting he would raise his majority to over 10,000 – assuming, that is, he was still the candidate on by-election day.

One of the first new people he met and cultivated was a young reporter then on the *Immingham News*, Pat Otter.

Otter was immediately both sceptical and impressed, and would remain so throughout the years of his acquaintance with Jeffrey Archer. 'There was a stereotyped version of a Conservative politician abroad at the time. Cyril Osborne fitted that stereotype to a tee. This man was a breath of fresh air. I thought something was happening in politics. I still couldn't vote for him, though.

'Basically he knew how to manipulate people; this was his great skill. He knew how to manipulate me and I knew I was being manipulated and I got a lot of good stories out of him.'

Jeffrey's encounters with other reporters were not so successful, however. *The Times*, not to be outdone by its rivals, sent their men to interview him about the row. After several broken appointments, the Conservative candidate for Louth was tracked down to the waiting room of Louth station at 7 a.m., where he was hiding behind a newspaper. (History does not recall if it was a copy of *The Times*.)

Over breakfast on the train back to London, *The Times* reporter asked him about what Berkeley was saying. To the reporter's intense embarrassment, the would-be MP, who had once played the part of Puck in the ruins of Dover Priory, put on the most amazing performance. Tears welled up in his eyes. His good name, his family, his friends were all at risk, he said. He was only asking for a little back of what he spent his whole life giving; namely, charity.

The Times reporter struggled and just managed to keep a grip on himself. He gamely pursued his line of questioning. In the taxi at the other end, the would-be MP went through another amazing transformation. Puck gave way to the barking PE master. 'You'll be hearing,' snapped Jeffrey, 'from my solicitors!'

The Times did indeed hear very shortly from Mr Anthony Rentoul of Rentoul & Co., Readymix House, Feltham, Middlesex. In a letter to the paper dated 18 November, Rentoul & Co. let it be known that if any of the contents of Berkeley's letters were published in *The Times*, a writ would be issued for libel. Jeffrey's own writ against Berkeley, meanwhile, would in the short term successfully muffle the latter's volubility on the subject of petty cash and his erstwhile protégé. In the long term, however, it would cost Jeffrey quite a lot more than £82 17s. 4d.

Jeffrey slogged round the constituency, its eighty-nine

villages and its three urban centres of Louth, Immingham and Cleethorpes. The independently-minded electorate, some of whose more rural members appeared unaware that Sir Cyril was no longer with them, paid due notice to the energetic and personable young man whose wife had made such a hit with the Tory women.

Sir Cyril's majority at the last election had been 4092. Bruce Riggs, the Labour candidate, a lecturer in electrical engineering from Huddersfield, and John Adams, the Liberal language lecturer also from Huddersfield, were no doubt doing their best to reduce it still further. But on Friday 5 December, the Louth by-election result must have made them glad they had jobs to which they could return.

Jeffrey's share of the 44 per cent turn-out gave him a 10,727 majority and fulfilled his adoption meeting promise. He went back to the Fitzwilliams' house near Grimsby. The Major announced the new MP to all and sundry. 'I shall do all in my power,' Jeffrey was shouting excitedly. 'I shall do my best!'

Mrs Fitzwilliams' elderly mother was staying with them at the time. 'That young man,' she was heard to say, 'is altogether too brash. I shall have to go and lie down.'

The new MP for Louth spent the weekend resting and opening congratulatory telegrams at his mews home with Mary. The following Tuesday, 9 December, watched by various constituents, he took his seat in the House of Commons.

There was an established procedure for doing this, which Jeffrey and his two sponsors, Chief Whip William Whitelaw and Deputy Chief Whip and Archer Gallery Director Brian Batsford, had rehearsed in the passage outside the Chief Whip's Office. The Speaker said, 'Members desirous to take the oath', and the new member and his sponsors took several paces forward. From there, the new member proceeded on his own to sign the Test Roll and be introduced to the Speaker. This Jeffrey duly did and thus took his rightful seat in the Mother of Parliaments.

The Class of '69

The youngest MP and the young Ph.D. continued to pursue their separate careers in Lincolnshire and Oxford. Neither had time nor inclination to interfere with the other's busy schedule, and his visits to the university city were consequently even rarer than hers to Louth on market day.

'Mary is a very private person,' Mrs Fitzwilliams would recall later, echoing Lady Hall, 'and it was not easy for her to be an MP's wife. She is a complete academic, and as Jeffrey has said on many occasions she has got far more brains than he has.

'She would probably have been quite happy to stay in the academic atmosphere and never get married. He was quite surprised that she said she would.'

Mary Archer was also a strong-minded woman, capable of leaving dinner parties to check on the progress of her experiments in the laboratory. By the same token she was also capable of gritting her teeth and leaving her experiments to attend a Louth Ladies' Committee celebration tea party.

Their joint appearances in his constituency coincided with important occasions, such as the selection meeting, and the business of thanking everyone who had been involved in a Conservative by-election victory.

Three weeks after the by-election victory, Jeffrey and Mary spent two days and 300 miles thanking the people who had helped him accomplish the next step on his way to becoming Prime Minister. After meeting at the Cleethorpes Conservative Ladies' Luncheon Club, they journeyed back to Louth via Waltham, Holton-le-Clay and North Thoresby.

At Louth, they attended the dedication of the Louth Borough Council Christmas Crib, and sat in for a short time at a meeting of the Louth Borough Council. Jeffrey then called at the New Clee Constitutional Club, Cleethorpes, the Immingham Conservative Club and the Immingham Men's Conservative Association. The athletic new MP rounded off the evening by talking to members of the Committee of Immingham Football Club.

The following afternoon he witnessed the Christmas rush at Louth Post Office, before being reunited with Mary at the Louth Ladies' tea party.

Then they went back to London. Jeffrey was due at the Commons for a debate on prices and incomes, two subjects in which he had always taken a keen personal interest.

At Westminster, the new young MP quickly adapted to his new surroundings, as witnessed by this anonymous tribute from one of his less dynamic and enterprising colleagues: 'Archer was absolutely appalling. He had one of the longest tongues for sycophancy I've ever seen. He congratulated everyone on whatever they were doing. He was quite clearly destined for higher things.'

To another backbench colleague he did not seem to have changed much since Oxford. He was a rather good heckler, from the furthest back bench in a loud voice that carried. He was quick, but he lacked *gravitas*. He started telling people he wanted to be Minister for Sport.

Two of the first people he entertained at the Carlton Club, of which he was now a member, were Sir Gerald Duke and Tim Cobb. The energetic new member gave them lunch and was thrilled when Cobb pointed to a table patronised by Cabinet members and told him he would be there one day.

Jeffrey would reciprocate by returning to Dover College in his capacity as governor and MP, and inflicting a political sermon on the other dinner guests, who included the Abbot of Ampleforth.

His maiden speech was in the debate on the Second Reading of the Government's Misuse of Drugs Bill. He had already arranged to be photographed conducting some first-hand research in London's Piccadilly Circus:

WELCOME [the *Daily Mirror* kindly blared]: THE YOUNG MP REALLY DOING HIS HOMEWORK

Mary, for her part, was featured in a stunning portrait in the *Sunday Times*. The occasion was the award of her Ph.D:

MRS MARY ARCHER, 25 [the caption read], *wife of the Tory MP for Louth, received her Ph.D. at London University on Friday. Here she is, tricorn hat and all. In a party that ponders long on the suitability of a candidate's wife, Jeffrey Archer must have been grateful to her when he was securing the safe seat Sir Cyril Osborne vacated last year: not just beautiful and young, a Fellow of St Hilda's College, Oxford, too.*

That same month of March 1970, the grateful Tory MP for Louth received a letter from a Mr C. G. Dickens. Mr Dickens was now Finance Officer of the United Nations Association and claimed again that Jeffrey allegedly still owed a certain amount of money in expenses.

Could he, wrote Mr Dickens, please see his way towards sending them £159 1s. 10d.?

Jeffrey agreed that he could.

It was all very irritating for the dynamic young entrepreneur who had told Mrs Fitzwilliams that he had to be a millionaire by the time he was thirty. Now his thirtieth birthday had passed, and he was still being pestered over sums that seemed ridiculous.

He had successfully muffled Humphrey Berkeley's noises long enough for him to win the by-election. He even tried unsuccessfully to beard Berkeley in his UNA den, backed up by Major-General Sir Gerald Duke.

Sir Gerald, meanwhile, was still hard at work with his great friend and colleague, Sir William Oliver at Arrow Enterprises. The two bluff ex-soldiers with straight backs and spotless records helped steady the boundless ball of energy, who used to rush in with wonderful ideas and then rush off again in his bronze-coloured MGB sports car, registration ANY 1.

'We'd think about his latest idea,' Sir Gerald recalled, later, 'and if it worked we'd do something about it. If it didn't, we'd persuade him it wasn't practical.'

Sir William Oliver had been a successful soldier and then worked at the Colonial Office before becoming High Commissioner of Australia. He had commanded the British effort at EXPO 67 in Canada, where he met a press officer who became another Arrow employee, Judy Horlington.

Sir William and Miss Horlington had returned to Europe and worked for Viyella for a while. Miss Horlington was working for *The Times* when Sir William suggested she join the small but expert team above the Archer Gallery at 23 Grafton Street.

One of the first things Judy and the generals worked on was the opening of the new Hall for the Institute of Chartered Accountants. True to form, it was organised by Sir William with military precision.

The Institute of Chartered Accountants had heard of Arrow Enterprises, and their Secretary came round to see Sir Gerald Duke. Sir Gerald listened while the Secretary explained how they wanted to open their new headquarters with a flourish.

'I see,' he said, 'well, who do you have in mind?'

'We rather thought the Queen.'

'I see,' said Sir Gerald.

After he had explained that the Royal calendar did not quite work that way, and that perhaps they might be aiming just a little too high, the resourceful ex-sapper came up with another idea.

'I know,' he said. 'What about the Queen Mother?'

'Good gracious! Do you think you could get her?'

'No problem, old boy.' This time the voice was that of Sir Gerald's distinguished colleague, Sir William Oliver. Sir William shared the office with Sir Gerald and Judy Horlington, and had been listening.

The former High Commissioner was on close terms with the Royal household. There and then, with the others looking on, he picked up the telephone and dialled the Queen Mother's Private Secretary.

'Do you think,' he said. 'Her Majesty would be prepared to open a very influential new Institute in the City?'

'Well, old boy,' said the voice on the other end, 'I'll certainly pencil it in.'

Sir William replaced the receiver.

The man from the Institute of Chartered Accountants was understandably impressed.

The Arrow machine went into top gear. Guest lists were discussed and finalised, artwork designed, invitations went out, replies collected and liaison kept with the Institute. Speakers were confirmed, toasts agreed and caterers briefed. On 6 May 1970 the red carpet was rolled out at the new Chartered Accountants' Hall, Moorgate Place, London EC2 and Her Majesty Queen Elizabeth the Queen Mother turned up right on cue.

Arrow went from strength to strength.

'I've never been so surprised,' Alexander Peterson would recall, later, 'as I was at a United World Colleges meeting, when I was told that "our new consultants Arrow Enterprises are coming" . . . and then the team marched in, with my old friend Jeffrey Archer at the front and Sir William Oliver tagging along behind!'

The United World Colleges was an idealistic and at that time little-known venture, that had begun with the founding of Atlantic College in Wales. The ethos arose from the belief of a number of people, including industrialists and politicians as well as ex-Heads of Dover College and the Oxford Department of Education like Peterson, that one way to prevent World War Three was to bring young people from different countries together. The UWC had been short of funds; at one point Peterson and his colleagues had guaranteed the next month's staff salaries. Now, they were looking for new ways to raise funds.

Peterson had had little or no contact with his ex-student since the days of Oxfam and the Beatles. The UWC contract was the 'idea for a project', then, which Jeffrey had been invited to discuss with Mountbatten, the new UWC President, after the Earl had been so impressed with his management of the Guildhall European dinner a year or so earlier.

Mountbatten was only the latest in the succession of older men whom the personable and fatherless young athlete had impressed with his charm. Major Fitzwilliams, Edward Heath, Christopher Chataway, Sir Noel Hall, Sir Gerald Duke, Tim Cobb, 'Bankie Bill': there was a distinguished cast of predecessors in the role.

Mountbatten was a legendary and formidable operator, with a lifetime's experience of successfully manipulating other people into fulfilling his own stratospheric ambitions. Jeffrey would of course suggest he held some sway with his new acquaintance, as well as enjoy retailing stories about his weekends at the palatial mid-Georgian Mountbatten home, Broadlands. But Alexander Peterson had served on Mountbatten's staff during the war, before he got to know Jeffrey Archer and the shrewd old psychological warfare specialist and propaganda expert was therefore uniquely qualified to pass judgment in this particular instance.

'I would say,' Peterson recalled later, 'that the relationship between Jeffrey and Mountbatten was not a close personal one. But Mountbatten had a very strong appreciation of Jeffrey's skills as a publicity man.'

The independently-minded electors of Louth neither knew nor cared greatly about these things. But that June they received another barnstorming visit from their recently-elected young MP, after Prime Minister Harold Wilson had had the temerity to call a General Election.

Jeffrey stayed with his friends the Fitzwilliams. As usual, he rushed around charming everyone, including the domestic staff.

Freda Fox had worked for the Major and his wife for forty years, but she had never met anyone like Jeffrey. 'He was very nice, he always treated us. He always gave us a pound. One day, he couldn't change any money, so he said,

"I'll go to Freda. She can change some money, she's always got plenty!" He always came through the kitchen and spoke to us. He was very likeable, very excitable. We always found him very nice.'

Margery Hurst had cooked for the Fitzwilliams for almost as long. 'He liked his home food. He said, "I've been guessing on the way up what you've been cooking for dinner, Mrs Hurst."'

Jeffrey's election posters read:

Vote
ARCHER
ARCHER
ARCHER
———> *X*

Thus armed, the young pretender went forth to do battle. Detailed to drive him around the constituency, and keep an eye on him, was the son of the Deputy Chairman of the Louth Conservative Association, Roger Sharpley.

Sharpley's farmer father, Henry, was not one of Jeffrey's biggest fans. In fact, he was profoundly suspicious of the whizzkid who had got himself elected in the place of the farmer's favourite, John Davies.

Henry Sharpley had told Jeffrey straight on election night: 'I didn't vote for you,' he said. 'I think you're fairly skin deep. Show us what you can do.'

Jeffrey promptly obliged.

With eighteen-year-old Roger Sharpley at the wheel, they set off in the mornings on an electioneering tour of the rural, windswept constituency. They drove round in a minivan with open back, '*ARCHER*' placards and a microphone connected to loudspeakers. Jeffrey made effective use of that. Roger had been working on a Grimsby trawler for three or four weeks beforehand; he was waiting to go up to Cambridge; he had refused to go into farming. He was relatively sophisticated, in Lincolnshire terms; but he had never met anyone like Jeffrey Archer.

'I remember the sensation when Jeffrey got in at the by-election. I know that some of the traditional Conservative hierarchy were anti-Archer. There were Conservatives in the constituency who wouldn't give him the time of day. But they hadn't lifted a finger for years.

'He was very lively, very fit and an amazingly hard worker. He really put his all into it.'

Sharpley drove Jeffrey for miles and miles around the constituency he had been elected to represent only six months earlier. They went to the Labour stronghold of Immingham; to the snooker halls of Cleethorpes; to every one of the eighty-nine villages. Jeffrey slid down the banisters of Cleethorpes Town Hall with a *Grimsby Evening Telegraph* photographer and the two of them were chased out of the building like naughty schoolboys. He spoke at two or three venues a night, charming the women and winning over the younger Conservatives. Even the older ones, like Roger Sharpley's father, Henry, were converted.

'Mary was very rarely there,' Roger Sharpley would recall later, 'but she was a great asset. I don't think this was something she took to, but she was a very attractive lady. A lot of academics can't talk to people, and Mary could. She would go to the tea parties and meet the Women's Institute. I'm sure she didn't like it, but she did it.'

Towards the end of the election campaign, Mary was always in the local press. On polling day, Jeffrey made sure he drove round Louth with Mary.

Mary stood on the steps of Louth Town Hall holding an '*ARCHER*' rosette. Jeffrey posed for an informal snapshot, almost blocking out the wife who had helped him to victory.

Jeffrey retained his seat with a reduced majority of 9256. But Henry Sharpley and the farmers were impressed. On a national level, Edward Heath, who had opened the Archer Gallery, had won a famous electoral victory and was now Prime Minister.

*

The Archer Gallery, by contrast, was not performing quite as well as some people had expected.

That year it was reputed to be losing some £1800 a month. Brian Batsford had kept a safe distance; but Olav Kier was losing his patience. Sir Gerald Duke, who was Company Secretary, grappled manfully with the books, even though he had never done accounts in his life except in the army. The Gallery held another exhibition, a percentage of whose takings went to the British Empire Cancer Relief Fund. The Duchess of St Albans opened the exhibition and there was some talk of amalgamating with her gallery. The Archer Gallery continued to be a good address and a bad investment.

Preparations for the United World Colleges fund-raising event meanwhile were well under way at the offices of Arrow Enterprises above the Archer Gallery.

The idea was Jeffrey's and it was a good one. Needless to say, it was also ambitious and spectacular, with an international cast of millionaires and royalty, and a last-minute twist in the plot.

Jeffrey sold Mountbatten the idea of having two celebrity concerts in two world-famous venues on one spectacular night. It would be so spectacular, they would call it the 'Night of Nights'.

Jeffrey had already encountered fierce opposition to this idea from United World Colleges Deputy Chairman, Sir George Schuster. Schuster, a hard-headed City man, was for some reason opposed to Arrow having anything to do with the United World Colleges.

He had reckoned without Jeffrey's ability to appeal to higher authority in these cases.

'All right,' said Mountbatten, 'who should we get? It's got to be really big and it's got to have worldwide television rights, otherwise it's no good at all.'

'Frank Sinatra,' Jeffrey replied, 'Bob Hope and Noël Coward . . . all on the same stage.'

'Nonsense,' said Mountbatten, 'ridiculous, rubbish. They're far too old. We want someone young.'

Jeffrey may have feared, for one dreadful moment, that the Admiral of the Fleet was about to order him to get hold of the Beatles.

The moment passed. Mountbatten reputedly then telephoned showbusiness impresario, Bernard Delfont. 'Who in the world would be the biggest draw for this thing?' he asked Delfont.

'Frank Sinatra,' Delfont replied, 'Bob Hope and Noël Coward.'

Arrow Enterprises were in business.

It was decided to hire the Albert Hall and the Royal Festival Hall on the same night, and have Bob Hope in one and Frank Sinatra in the other. Sinatra would do the first half in one and Hope in the other, and then they would swap round. The logistical problems inherent in this immediately occurred to the ex-chief of the Royal Engineers, Sir Gerald Duke.

'Jeffrey had blarneyed Dickie Mountbatten into this scheme,' Sir Gerald would later recall, 'and I was the staff officer, as it were. Now, I realised it would be very dicey indeed, in the length of a theatre interval, to move Frank Sinatra with a back-up orchestra and all the trappings from the Albert Hall to the Royal Festival Hall at nine o'clock on a busy Monday evening.

'It simply,' concluded Sir Gerald with admirable military conciseness, 'wasn't on.'

They settled for the one concert with Sir Noël Coward introducing the two artists at the Royal Festival Hall. Sir Gerald and Sir William set to work with Judy Horlington. The postbag from people who wanted tickets to hear Frank Sinatra was phenomenal. Help was drafted in to deal with it in the form of Jeffrey's athletic favourite from Dover College, Bruce Dakowski. Vast sums of cash began to flow into the Arrow offices.

Then came the last-minute twist. Sir Noël Coward was taken ill.

'Who are we going to get?' said Mountbatten to Jeffrey. 'I could get David Frost, I suppose.'

'*I* could get David Frost,' Jeffrey is reputed to have said, 'you've got to get someone who would come for no one but you.'

Mountbatten telephoned Princess Grace of Monaco, who as the Hollywood film star Grace Kelly had appeared with Frank Sinatra in *High Society*. Kelly, coincidentally, had also been the name of the Admiral's favourite wartime command. Prince Rainier had insisted his beautiful bride give up acting after they married. But Mountbatten was not an easy man to say no to, even if you were a reigning Prince, albeit of the Ruritanian variety.

Thus it was that Judy Horlington found herself telephoning the Royal Palace in Monte Carlo. 'I was amazed. I got through, and I said. "Could I speak to Princess Grace, please?" And she said: "Speaking."'

Princess Grace, dressed in white and making her first stage appearance since her marriage, was beautiful and superb. Princess Alexandra was present at the first half, with Jeffrey hovering at a respectful and attentive distance. The second half was attended by the Prince of Wales and Princess Anne. Bob Hope clowned and Frank Sinatra sang. The 200-page programme was packed with glossy sponsors. The 'Night of Nights' on 16 November 1970 raised around £150,000 for the United World Colleges.

After the concert, there was a reception at St James's Palace beginning at 1.45 a.m. The Prince of Wales and Princess Anne were there and guests paid thousands of pounds for tickets.

Jeffrey had done it again.

Two days later, the *Sun*, whose news editor was Nick Lloyd, published an article entitled 'Mr Four and a Half Percent', alleging that he took that percentage from his charity work. 'You must have someone of immense status working for you,' Jeffrey was quoted as saying, 'A man like Lord Mountbatten or Lord Harlech . . . I can supply the ideas, but it needs someone like Lord Mountbatten to carry them out.'

Jeffrey's revenge was to cast Lloyd in his first novel as an alcoholic scandal-seeker. Sir Gerald Duke also later denied that Arrow ever took a percentage.

The *Sunday Express*, too, took an unkind line the weekend after Jeffrey's successful extravaganza:

PRINCESS GRACE, Bob Hope and Frank Sinatra raised some £150,000 for charity at a Festival Hall concert.

BUT THE real winner that night seems to have been Mr Jeffrey Archer, MP. The stars gave their services free but Mr Archer, whose firm organised the show, is reported to have made £8000 out of it. Modestly he denies that, saying that the fee charged would more likely bring him £4000 out of the charity money. 'Hardly extortionate,' he insists. But quite nice all the same.

It raises again the old problem of how much of the money contributed to charities is actually spent on the purpose for which it is given, and how much goes to those who organise or administer the charities.

WHY NOT compel every charity to state on its notepaper how much of what it raises actually gets through to the work for which it was donated?

To take any newspaper article about oneself too seriously is not only to confer on the articles in question, their overpaid authors, their overweight editors and their overdrawn proprietors a degree of moral sincerity and concern which is both alien and abhorrent to the British press; it is also to confer on oneself an excessive degree of importance. The fact that Jeffrey took such articles seriously testifies to his growing *hubris*. It was an attitude on his part that was to lead to comic results. In the mid-1980s, for example, he would even deny to *The Times* Diary that he had once been a policeman.

In January 1971, ownership of the Archer Gallery was transferred to Watches of Switzerland Ltd, of Aylesbury, Buckinghamshire; 24,998 shares were transferred in this way and Jeffrey and Rippon kept one share each.

Arrow Enterprises then moved lock, stock and barrel to

27/31, Whitehall. Jeffrey, Sir Gerald, Sir William, Judy Horlington and co. had two floors of a rather narrow four-storey building opposite the Whitehall Theatre. Downstairs was the British Sugar Corporation. Down the road was No. 10, Downing Street.

Jeffrey, characteristically, managed to get the whole building renamed Arrow House. His office overlooked the Whitehall Theatre, which showed such hits as *Pyjama Tops*. He had it redecorated by Bruce Dakowski's brother, Julian, in the modern style. There was a black leather three-piece suite, a big glass desk, an arc-shaped lamp and strange, cloudy, viscous effects on the walls.

Sir Gerald, Sir William and Judy Horlington were on the top floor. They were working on a second fund-raising scheme for the United World Colleges. Leonard Bernstein was to conduct the Vienna Philharmonic Orchestra at the Royal Albert Hall, in the presence of the Queen Mother and others.

Arrow, too, had changed its legal structure. It was reconstituted from a partnership into a limited liability company. Jeffrey was Chairman; Sir Gerald was Director and Company Secretary; and Sir William was Director.

Jeffrey's own appearance, always neat and tidy, now began to reflect the increase in grandeur evidenced by his surroundings. The Chairman of Arrow Enterprises commuted from his Bayswater mews house in his bronze MG, ANY 1, to his Whitehall offices and thence to the Houses of Parliament. He had started wearing rather smarter suits, pinstripes, with matching shirts and patent leather shoes. If journalists appeared unlikely to mention this, he would ensure that they did by cleverly suggesting it would be both predictable of them to do so and unobservant of them not to.

That February, he travelled in great secrecy to Las Vegas. His mission was to persuade another self-made man, Elvis Presley, to perform for the first time ever in Britain.

The *Sunday Express*, however, seem to have caught him unawares. The newspaper which had said such unkind things about him tracked him down to the International Hotel, Las Vegas.

'What makes you think I have been seeing Mr Presley?' the voice said a little petulantly over the transatlantic telephone. Then, amazingly, he continued in what sounded like an American accent: 'I think you have got the wrong Mr Archer. I am not the person you think I am. You must have got me muddled with someone else.'

The International Hotel later confirmed to the *Sunday Express*, which in turn passed it on to its readers, that there was only one Jeffrey Archer staying there.

Elvis Presley never made it to Britain. The right Mr Archer returned from Memphis with his usual clipped, crypto-military accent and carried on with business as usual.

The Leonard Bernstein concert was a great success. Jeffrey was summoned a short walk away to No. 10, Downing Street, where he was congratulated by Mr Heath. Not long afterwards, he found another kind journalist, albeit for the lowly magazine *Reveille*. She interviewed him, if that is the correct term, at Westminster:

JEFFREY ARCHER, Tory MP for Louth, is only 30. He has been an international athlete, a radio broadcaster, and was the youngest man ever to serve on the Greater London Council.

He is an Oxford graduate and his beautiful wife Mary is a brilliant scientist.

His life so far could form the basis of a pocket book manual on 'How To Be A Success'.

Yet his real talent is for raising money for charity. He estimates that he has raised between 'two and three million pounds'.

Charities almost queue outside the door of his company, Arrow Enterprises . . .

'No,' Sir Gerald Duke would say later, 'I don't think we ever turned anyone away.'

While still a student at Oxford he arranged an extraordinary dinner party with the Beatles and Harold Macmillan as guests. . . .

At the moment, however, Mr Archer is not even rich by his definition. He has not made his first £100,000 yet.

By his present age, he points out, Aristotle Onassis and Paul Getty were already millionaires. . . .

Once again, that successful UNA dinner at No. 10, Downing Street three years before brought in business. This time, the satisfied customer who came back for more was one of the richest men in England, Michael Sobell.

Sobell would be knighted shortly afterwards for his services to numerous worthy causes, not least the Conservative & Unionist Party of Great Britain. He was also President of the National Society for Cancer Relief.

The Society had sponsored the Lillian Board Appeal for funds to aid cancer research, in memory of the popular British sprinter who had died tragically young of the disease at the controversial Issels clinic. Jeffrey, once a sprinter and always in rude health, enthusiastically set a target of £1 million for the appeal at which Arrow would aim. He also organised some fund-raising social activities for members of the Board family and Lillian's former fiancé (who subsequently married her twin sister).

Having disposed of the Archer Gallery and acquired the Whitehall offices, the young MP now found himself being taken at his word and acquiring a country property:

Mr Archer is planning to take a house at Swinhope, near Binbrook, following his announced intention of having a home in the constituency if he was elected.

Thus read the *Grimsby Evening Telegraph*, over a year earlier. Mary's speech, too, had stressed the fact that unlike the feudal Sir Cyril Osborne, they were going to have a house in the constituency. A year and a half later, they still did not have one.

'Well,' Roger Sharpley would recall his father, Henry,

saying to Jeffrey, 'you did say you were going to get a house in the constituency, so do it!'

On 31 July 1971, Mary Archer was writing her name and Jeffrey's in the Fitzwilliams' visitors' book. She had just started to write 18 Lancaster Mews, W2, when she changed it. The new address, so new that Mary had forgotten it, was Church Farm, Church Lane, Brigsley, Grimsby.

Church Farm was a pretty, eighteenth-century house in a quiet village; so quiet, in fact, that it had no post office, no public house and no street lighting. To this day, Church Farm is known locally as Jeffrey Archer's house. Local legend has it that it was here, pale and resolute, he wrote his first book; a letter arrived here for him as late as 1987. The house stood beyond the village church; a photograph on one of the walls showed a family from the nineteenth century who had lived there and were buried next door. The garden was lined with apple trees. There was off-street parking for the bronze MG.

Jeffrey and Mary held a couple of drinks parties, and invited the Fitzwilliams, the Sharpleys and the younger Conservatives. Pat Otter, now on the *Grimsby Evening Telegraph*, went to one of them with his wife, Eva.

'Mary was totally different,' Otter would recall later. 'I never saw them together as a couple at that party, but as two individuals, and as two individuals they worked very well. She provided the intellectual side of the marriage and he provided all the bull and pzazz . . . an astonishing man.'

That summer and autumn, the Member for Louth busied himself with local and national political matters. In August, Sir Cyril Osborne's successor and former policeman wrote to *The Times* after the murder of a Blackpool police superintendent, echoing the national mood and demanding an end to the 'hollow sham of life imprisonment'. In September, the fund-raising mastermind for the European Movement could be heard giving his opinions on Britain's entry to the Common Market: 'I must confess,' he told the *Grimsby Evening Telegraph*, 'temperamentally I have been pro-EEC for many years. However, early on in the Great Debate I decided it would be unconscionable blindly to pursue my beliefs if there was any possibility that my constituents would suffer thereby ... I held public meetings in Immingham, Cleethorpes and Louth ... I now feel that with under a month to the crucial vote, I should give my considered decision. I have decided to vote for entry, as everything I have seen in all my soundings in the constituency suggests that we will all benefit from the Common Market.'

In November, the *Grimsby Evening Telegraph* was able to report that as a result of his efforts the RAF bombing range at Theddlethorpe was being moved to Donna Nook. Jeffrey's political preoccupations, though unspectacular by comparison with his personal ones, were well-researched, well-aired and made him increasingly popular in the constituency. At the Commons, he was good value to lobby correspondents and journalists such as the *Sunday Express*'s 'Crossbencher' Robin Oakley. He showed judgment in his choice of researchers: David Mellor would go on to achieve high office, and Richard Ryder would run Margaret Thatcher's office before he too became MP for a safe rural constituency.

At Arrow House, though, business was at a crossroads. The aim was still to raise funds. The question was, for whom?

The Lillian Board Appeal for cancer research, which Jeffrey had so enthusiastically taken up, had raised only a fraction of its £1 million target. The National Society for Cancer Relief informed Arrow Enterprises that its services were no longer required.

Judy Horlington, who had worked for Arrow since the Grafton Street days, wanted to go on raising funds and organising functions for charities. The latter no longer seemed to be beating a path to Arrow House's door. In February 1972 she began to apply for other jobs, but would remain at Arrow for another year, before departing with Sir William Oliver.

A photograph of Jeffrey and Mary, taken in March of that year, showed the couple in his Lincolnshire constituency.

It was a cold day and they were both wrapped up, Mary in Zhivago-esque fur and Jeffrey in a less tasteful sheepskin number that would have done justice to a used-car salesman. His ties had got wider and both his shirt collars and his hair were longer, after the fashion of the time. His face was heavily lined for a thirty-two-year-old. Not the tallest of men, he nevertheless loomed over the twenty-seven-year-old woman who had been one of the brightest and most beautiful undergraduates of her generation. She was still beautiful and bright; she was also pregnant.

Mary's lecturing at Oxford went on, but she also had a job in London now, just around the corner from the old Archer Gallery at the Royal Institution, Albemarle Street. She made a great impression on the Director there, Sir George Porter. Both the Archers would continue to impress dignified and successful older men: headmasters, major-generals, politicians and judges.

William Archer was born nine weeks prematurely in Guy's Hospital that June. Mary was lecturing in Oxford when she began to feel 'unwell'. She knew she was pregnant, of course. She went to the library to look up what to do next. The book appears to have recommended a short course of cycling, for she then mounted her bicycle, rode to the station and boarded the London train. She reached the hospital, with her husband's help, just in time.

In a sense of course, it was a rebirth, given that this was the name of Jeffrey's long-lost father. The christening took place in the chapel of the crypt of the House of Commons. Tim Cobb was among the guests.

Afterwards, there was a party at 24a The Boltons. The little house at 18 Lancaster Mews had given way to a slightly bigger one in this most salubrious part of South Kensington. 24a, as its number suggests, was not one of the big houses which characterised The Boltons; in fact it was tacked on to the side of one of them, like the servants' quarters which it probably once was. But it shared that prestigious address.

Fine paintings adorned the walls, souvenirs of the Archer

Gallery. An elegantly furnished drawing room ran through to the garden, which was patrolled by a large cat called Sir Percy (after Rugg, the ex-Tory leader of the GLC). Elizabeth Fullerton, Jeffrey's foster-sister who had been bridesmaid at the wedding, was recruited as live-in nanny. The bronze MG, ANY 1, had given way to a more grandiose Daimler bearing the same registration.

The money for the European Movement kept on coming. Sir Michael Sobell alone was rumoured to have donated more than £600,000 via Arrow Enterprises. Other contributors included another up-and-coming firm related to the construction industry, JCB.

JCB made earthmoving machinery; its name was based on the initials of its fifty-six-year-old founder and Chairman, Joseph Cyril Bamford. Bamford's twenty-seven-year-old son, Anthony, had launched the company's French operations and received a Young Exporter of the Year Award. Both Bamford Senior and Bamford Junior were obviously pro-European. Young Anthony got on particularly well with the like-minded entrepreneurial, squash-playing young fund-raiser, Jeffrey Archer.

Two years and more had passed since his thirtieth birthday. He was a father, but still nowhere near being a millionaire. Apart from the small but expert staff, all sorts of people were now to be seen going in and out of Arrow House. Two of them were Yvonne Haesendonck and Adrian Metcalfe. Yvonne Haesendonck had been temping when her agency said a very important client needed secretarial help. Haesendonck had wanted the day off but the agency insisted, so she went along. Jeffrey said, 'Come and work for me.'

'No,' she said, 'I don't want to work for you full-time.' They started talking about the theatre. Jeffrey mentioned the actor Donald Sinden. Noticing her interest, he said, 'If I get Donald Sinden here for tea tomorrow, will you work for me?'

'Yes,' she said.

By the end of the next day she had met Donald Sinden,

agreed to work for Jeffrey Archer and had her name changed. Just as Noreen had become Natalie, so Yvonne Haesendonck now became Jo Haesen: 'I didn't mind,' she would recall later. 'I hated the way everyone called me E-vonne.'

Jo Haesen went to work on the Marlene Dietrich concert Jeffrey was promoting for MIND, the mental health charity. She found Jeffrey extremely organised and hardworking. Judy and the generals meanwhile were still toiling away upstairs.

Metcalfe had just left ITV and was working for an American producer. Jeffrey lent him office space. The two sometimes went to the House of Commons for lunch.

'He was pushing very fast,' Metcalfe recalled later, 'his political career was launched and he knew that to be a successful politician he had to be 100 percent free of money worries.

'Jeffrey was the smartest guy and yet like all of us he was easily seduced by a personality. By the feeling that here were the people moving in megabuck territory. He loved to be seen around with them and have lunch at the Savoy Grill.

'His desk never had more than one piece of paper on it. One piece of paper, with six things written on it.' For example:

> Nigeria
>
> Gold
>
> Haircut
>
> Summer Show
>
> Lenny Bernstein
>
> Aquablast

Aquablast Inc. was headquartered in Scarborough, Ontario. How the name of this obscure Canadian company came to be on a piece of paper on the glass desk in the Whitehall office of Jeffrey Archer MP, and what happened as a result, is a textbook story of gullibility that would have sent Sir Noel

Hall screaming all the way back to his business school in Henley.

Aquablast, as its name suggests, was a registered company at one time intended to market a device for cleaning buildings with high-pressure water jets. But the only thing it ever properly took to the cleaners was J. H. Archer Esq.

By mid-1972, Aquablast was already known to business journalists in Canada as a distinctly dodgy proposition. It was registered in Montreal, which was the least policed of Canadian stock exchanges. Montreal was also a major Mafia port of entry, and there is some reason to believe that illicit money-laundering facilities of an Italian nature were at the disposal of the guilty parties in what became the Aquablast stock-promotion.

Stock-promotion, or share-pushing, involves buying up a large number of shares in a company at distressed prices – say, 5 or 10 cents – injecting an element of real money into the company, and then releasing the stock at a starting price of, say, $5 a share. The consequences are as obvious as the intentions: a large number of foolish investors are defrauded of large sums of money by a handful of brilliant criminal specialists.

The Aquablast stock-pushers were among the most experienced in the business and, in this respect if in no other, Jeffrey could truly claim to have been taken by experts.

One of the reasons why they were experts, of course, is that they could spot a likely victim when they saw one. The Canadian stock-pushers, working out of Monte Carlo, Amsterdam, Geneva, Munich and London, were among the best of the best. They included Emanuel 'Manny The Snake' Silverman. Silverman and his associates had already achieved phase one of the Aquablast stock-promotion. They had acquired large numbers of shares at distressed prices, and printed even greater numbers of an unregistered variety. Phase two was the injection of some real money – and therefore temporary credibility – into the company. Silverman did this by means of the Wyman Idler Adjuster Valve.

The Wyman valve was the invention of a Munich engineer, Curt Wyman. It was supposed to reduce lead pollution in car engines and was therefore in theory of immense commercial potential.

In practice, it did not work. Wyman would later claim that he had been paid only a token sum of money for the invention which would subsequently be revealed as a worthless gadget.

Silverman, of course, let it be known that Aquablast had paid a large sum for the world rights to an invention which would make very rich men of its shareholders. To this end, against worthless Aquablast shares and debentures, he had actually managed to extract £181,250 from the London branch of the Bank of Boston.

Phase two was complete. Phase three was simple: now find your foolish investors.

The cast of characters in the Aquablast stock-promotion included men sinister beyond belief. Men whom you might expect to look at you in a sinister way did just that. These were men who would look bored and somewhat impatient at the fact that you were consuming some of their share of the oxygen in the room. But these were not the men who appeared in your office, wrote you a letter or even spoke to you on the telephone.

The chain of men who led Jeffrey to become a foolish investor may have begun in Montreal with notorious share-pushers with access to Mafia venture capital. But by the time it reached London, the Aquablast investment had a totally innocent face; in this case, that of the Assistant Vice-President of the First Bank of Boston, Michael Altman.

The First Bank of Boston had already invested £181,250 in Aquablast through its London branch. Altman appeared one day in the Arrow offices. Jeffrey, who may well already have received telephone calls and letters from a bogus British 'subsidiary' of Aquablast, listened to what he had to say.

Was Jeffrey, Altman enquired, remotely interested in getting in on the ground floor of a revolutionary new device that was going to make a fortune for its investors?

It should be stressed that there was absolutely no reason to suppose that Altman was doing anything more than passing on inside gossip of the sort that prompts a thousand shrewd investments. By the same token, there is no reason to suppose that Jeffrey was doing anything more than listening, as any self-styled shrewd investor would do.

However, there is equally no reason to deny that he then broke the first basic rule of business. Namely, there is no such thing as a free lunch.

Here was his chance: his chance to make good the claim he had made to Sir Gerald Duke, Mrs Fitzwilliams, Judy Horlington and dozens of others; that he had to become a millionaire by the time he was thirty.

Here was his chance to be 100 percent free of money worries and concentrate on a career in politics.

Here was his chance.

Did Jeffrey try to ascertain the soundness of a company that was registered on the notoriously lax Montreal stock exchange? A company that had been known to be in the hands of suspected share-pushers since 1970? A company whose product would obviously make so much money for its shareholders, that it would be churlish for them to make a few standard enquiries? Let alone ask themselves why they were being offered such a privileged opportunity in the first place?

'*I must be a millionaire by the time I am thirty.*'

A Canadian-based financial expert, who knew many of the guilty parties, would later offer the following scenario:

'*If the initial letter was intriguing enough, if it was followed by a clever enough phone call, and if any meeting that subsequently took place was sufficiently intriguing, a potential investor could have reacted in two ways. One, he could have borrowed all he could get his hands on in order to get 100 percent of the action. Two, he might be a little bit nervous, and want to try it out on a friend.*'

History would show that Jeffrey was susceptible to cleverly worded phone calls.

'In fairness, if I were on the receiving end of one of those phone calls, it would take all my expertise to get off the phone. They're brilliant, they really are. It's not just one man who will phone you up. They have a tester, who will first try the water and see if you are right. Then someone will come in like a warm-up man on the second phone call. Finally, the man who is really going to do it to you will come on. He will only be given those calls where the hook is going to go into the mouth. Because his time is too precious, his talent is too rare.

'These guys are worth hundreds of thousands of dollars. They are great salesmen. It would be hard to resist them. Especially if you have already been losing money.

'There you have a fish absolutely ready to be landed.'

The first batch of Aquablast shares cost Jeffrey £100,000. He borrowed the entire sum from Williams and Glyns. After all, if the bank approved, it must be a good investment. A second mortgage on the Boltons home stood surety.

'Where would the money go? There would not necessarily be Aquablast bank accounts in Aquablast names. For a start, there could be a broker in between. There were dubious stockbrokers who were members of the Montreal stock exchange. There are Mafia-controlled brokerages to this day in Montreal and New York. So there would be no problem: a straightforward and totally legitimate series of transactions. You send your cheque and your letter of instruction and you get back an acknowledgement. You could have been buying Royal Bank of Canada through the same procedures.'

Would Jeffrey ever have been able to creep upstairs and take out his Aquablast shares and say, 'I've been a clever boy'?

'Quite possibly; because although they like to spin out the procedure in order to keep selling, if the punter starts to get suspicious or doubtful, one of the best ways is to produce lots of beautifully engraved paper. It doesn't cost a lot to get printed.

It's not in itself a fraudulent document, either. They may be real shares in a real company. Real value, zero or two cents a share, cost, $5, $10, $15, $20 a share.'

'Two, he might be a little bit nervous, and want to try it out on a friend.'

In November 1972, while the Arrow staff worked away at the preparations for the European Movement banquet at Hampton Court Palace, Jeffrey approached his squash-playing friend and pro-European, Anthony Bamford.

Was he, enquired Jeffrey, remotely interested in getting in on the ground floor of a revolutionary new device that was going to make a fortune for its investors?

'You need to keep your major investors content. They do indeed want to take out their investment and admire it. Any signs of nervousness, such as the punter calling in and saying, "How's it going?" and they'll tell him something good. Or, they'll say, "Jeffrey, we'd love to tell you, because there is something rather special about to happen. But you know that will appear in the quarterly report, and the regulatory authorities forbid us from giving out advance information. That's insider trading, you know; we can't do that."

'Or, they might sell him some more: "Jeffrey, at the end of this phone call, I want you to forget having spoken to me, but have I got some good news for you. That interesting development we thought was not going to happen until the end of November looks like it's going to come off next week or the week after next. And because you're such a big shareholder . . ."'

Anthony Bamford lent Jeffrey £172,162 to buy a further 50,000 shares in Aquablast. The deal was that Jeffrey would sell the shares by Christmas and give Bamford thirty percent of the profits. Jeffrey had now invested £270,000 of other people's money, plus interest, in a company whose share price was already falling rapidly.

'Any signs of nervousness, such as the punter calling in and

saying, "How's it going?" and they'll tell him something good. Or, they'll say, "Jeffrey, we'd love to tell you, because there is something rather special about to happen."'

As the Aquablast share price fell further, Jeffrey was visited a number of times by Aquablast President and former Chief Executive Officer of Chrysler in Geneva, Robert S. Mitchell. Both Mitchell and 'Manny The Snake' Silverman would shortly be urgently sought after by the Royal Canadian Mounted Police.

On 1 January 1973 Britain entered the European Economic Community. The following night, the British Council of the European Movement held its celebratory banquet at Hampton Court Palace, organised as usual with military precision and showbusiness flair by Arrow Enterprises. The Archbishop of Canterbury said Grace before dinner. The menu was tactfully in French.

The seating plan, too, was worthy of note. Of the 350 guests, at the top table sat the Prime Minister, the Archbishop of Canterbury, Lord Harlech and the various ambassadors and chargés d'affaires. At Table B, Anthony Bamford sat next to financier Jim Slater. Jeffrey sat next to rock music impresario Robert Stigwood on Table C. On Table D, Mr Bamford Sr sat opposite Lord Melchett. The evening was a great success. In the midst of it all, and in spite of the growing Aquablast problem, Jeffrey still found time to write personal thank-you letters to his small but expert staff at Arrow Enterprises.

Not long afterwards, the Young Exporter of the Year who had sat next to Jim Slater raised the little matter of the loan he had made to Jeffrey 'until Christmas'.

Jeffrey told Bamford that the Aquablast share price had indeed fallen; but that the Bank of Boston, who had also invested in the company, would ensure that the price would rise again. His 30 percent profit plus interest was in safe hands. Bamford, who had borrowed the money to lend to Jeffrey, and who appeared unaware that the dynamic ball of energy had already borrowed elsewhere to invest in the venture, agreed to hold his fire. He was further assured that successful property schemes then in the offing would provide Jeffrey with the wherewithal to pay him his money back.

That spring, Jeffrey also had to contend with Humphry Berkeley again. The ex-Chairman of the UNA had a long memory when it came to old scores. These included the libel suit taken out against him by his erstwhile protégé. Jeffrey had sued Berkeley after certain of his letters had been leaked to *The Times* and other newspapers. It was thought a court case would be messy for the Conservative Party, but the confrontation had long since reached a stalemate. Then a go-between came forward in the form of the Old Etonian founder of the Oxford University James Bond Club, Jonathan Aitken.

Aitken, then employed on the *Evening Standard*, had not succumbed to Aquablast's blandishments, in spite of his Canadian connections. He knew and had some regard for both Jeffrey Archer and Humphry Berkeley. As he was shortly to become Conservative candidate for a safe seat in the Home Counties, he was happy to oblige in the role.

The case of Archer and Berkeley was finally resolved at the last moment. There was no mention of Berkeley paying any damages or making any apology. Jeffrey withdrew his libel writ. It would be correct to assume that he also had to pay substantial costs as a result of his ultimately unsuccessful action against the former Chairman of the United Nations Association.

Lincolnshire now represented one of the few areas of stability in Jeffrey's life. They were rapidly decreasing in number. The white Daimler ANY 1 could still be seen parked by the pretty eighteenth-century cottage in Brigsley. Its owner still rushed around his constituency, congratulating successful Conservative councillors, calling for law and order and prophesying that there would be an election the following year. He was secure here, in his safe seat, with the farmers on his side, and the press grateful for good stories.

Some of these were also a little worrying.

The *Sunday Times* of 3 June, 1973, for example, carried a profile in which Jeffrey inferred that he was all but a millionaire; his parliamentary salary, he said, went to charity. Even Atticus, it seemed, would never be so unkind as to question the legend of Jeffrey Archer:

Tycoon at work

I hear that Jeffrey Archer MP, now well into the property game, is about to pull off a spectacular coup. Even his best friends admit he's a pushy man and nobody ever doubted that he would make himself a very rich man. The deal he is now working on so secretly will certainly, from all reports, put him well into the millionaire class.

All his enterprises he has approached with enormous energy. At Oxford he persuaded the Beatles to help raise £250,000 for Oxfam . . .

Today Jeffrey Archer, 33, has given up fund-raising ('not enough money in it') and become something of a financial wizard. 'It's easier now for a young man to make a million than ever before,' he told us at his Whitehall office, opposite Paul Raymond's revue, Pyjama Tops. *'I started with £10,000 lent by a friend and repaid it five months later. People now approach me for money.'*

This much was certainly true: his friend Bamford had indeed been approaching him for the £172,162 he had lent him.

'My company mainly finances films, plays and TV shows, as well as property. I employ 14 people, one more than John Bentley. I bought this block, Arrow House, a few years back and now Lord Campbell of Eskan (the Socialist sugar magnate) is my tenant. I donate all my parliamentary salary to charity.'

He has given up buying shares and invests heavily in sugar, cocoa and copper options on the commodity market. . . . Despite his classless accent and identikit clothes he comes from a fairly Establishment background. He went to Wellington and his late father was British Consul in Singapore. . . .

A cupboard-full of jigsaw puzzles helps him relax. 'I've not slept for a month because of this deal. I creep downstairs and play in the middle of the night.'

Expect a fairly sensational announcement

said Atticus, '*soon*'.

The 'spectacular coup' that Jeffrey was reported as being about to pull off was the 'successful property scheme in the offing' with which he had managed to stall Bamford. Jeffrey had in fact been trying to rent and sub-let the notoriously empty 388-foot glass skyscraper in Tottenham Court Road called Centre Point.

In his mind, he towered over everybody; as his plans collapsed, his interviews took on an air of perfectly serene unreality. The apotheosis took place in that interview with Terry Coleman in the *Guardian* of 21 July, 1973:

Archer's score

JEFFREY ARCHER is a success. He is 32. He is a Conservative MP with a seat so safe that, unless he should stab the Prime Minister in circumstances of the greatest publicity, he will hold it for the next 30 years. . . .

Over cornflakes, Mr Archer talked about his early days. He was brought up mostly in Somerset. His father was in the Royal Engineers and then in the diplomatic service, and was once British Consul in Singapore. . . .

After leaving Wellington he sailed to California via Scotland and the Panama Canal on a tramp steamer. On his return he went up to Oxford where he read education, gained blues in athletics and gymnastics, met his wife, and showed the first signs of genius. This genius was for money. Various reports say he raised anything from £250,000 to £1 million for Oxfam. What should the figure be?

He said that Oxfam, on the occasion of its twenty-first anniversary, was trying to raise £1 million, but with six weeks to go had only £150,000. Archer went to Oxfam and said he had an idea, they told him to go ahead, he went ahead, somehow persuading the Beatles to lend their name to the campaign and somehow persuading the Daily

Mail *to lend its publicity. The million was raised. Macmillan, as Chancellor of the University, dined at Brasenose College with the Beatles. . . .*

'I want to go out and work sixteen hours a day. Not because I want to make more money. I'm sure (indicating the splendidly furnished room with a wave of his hand) that you can see I'm . . .'

Not on the breadline? – 'No, and I've no need to work ever again in my life. I can now, aged, thirty-two, just sit in this room and talk to you for the rest of my life. . . .'

'We thought he had gone a bit crazy,' Judy Horlington would recall.

'But he'd made no secret of the fact that he wanted to be a millionaire. We were very sorry for him.'

A year would pass before Jeffrey's true situation was made public in a newspaper. By that time the situation would have worsened, bit by bit, until the Gordian knot he had tied for himself would have to be cut by others.

Anthony Bamford continued to press him for repayment. The property schemes came to nothing. Mitchell, the Aquablast President who had visited Arrow House a number of times to assure him all was well, resigned. The Aquablast share price fell from £3.20 to 30 pence; Bamford stepped up the pressure. 'Manny The Snake' Silverman and his sinister associates tiptoed away to New York, Amsterdam, Geneva. So did many of the other fair-weather friends who had been glimpsed going in and out of Arrow House.

Jo Haesen came to dread it, every time Jeffrey came in. 'He kept saying: "We need another chart of what they are doing", and another great tranche of Aquablast would have gone.

'My heart was going down to my boots. It was all so very personal. In the office you were aware that something was going vitally wrong.'

Eventually she would leave to work for Adrian Metcalfe. By that time it was a question of reducing costs in every way possible, to avoid Jeffrey being made bankrupt.

Judy Horlington went, too, as she had come, with Sir William Oliver. Horlington, who liked raising money for charities, found a job with the United World Colleges. Sir William followed. She would stay there for three years, but the honourable ex-soldier lasted only six months on an irregular basis. He was left with his puny military pension and retired to Crowborough. Until the day he died he kept in touch with Miss Horlington. The collapse of Arrow dealt a great blow to a man trained to follow orders and believe in his commanding officers; even if they were half his age and had not been to Sandhurst.

Sir Gerald Duke, too, was left with little more than his army pension. He fortunately also had an interest in an Essex marina. The former Chief Royal Engineer and Dover College governor had seen the warning lights flashing long before Arrow became a limited company. Sir Gerald became Chairman of the company that built the marina, and retired, still active, to Kent.

Bamford kept up the pressure for repayment of the loan, interest on which was mounting rapidly.

It was perhaps in such a cost-conscious frame of mind that the founder of the Archer Gallery abstained, that autumn, from a Commons debate on museum and gallery charges.

That winter, the whole of Britain was experiencing an economic crisis. The Bank Rate went up to thirteen percent and the speed limit went down to fifty m.p.h. to save fuel. The three-day week was announced. It was the beginning of the end for Prime Minister Edward Heath.

The end, too, was now in sight for the dynamic ball of energy whose art gallery had been opened by the same Prime Minister. That January, while the miners prepared for their ballot, Jeffrey had another meeting with Anthony Bamford.

This time, Bamford brought his solicitor. Jeffrey was told that unless he repaid the money in the immediate future, legal proceedings would be taken to regain it. Jeffrey, according to Bamford as it was later reported, then suggested that this would be the end of his career. His home was mortgaged, he said. He hinted that there was a possibility the shares might still be saleable. He managed to persuade Bamford to give him more time.

Apart from the parties concerned, like Bamford, his solicitor, Jeffrey, Mary and a handful of others, like Judy Horlington and Jo Haesen, there was still no public knowledge of Jeffrey's worsening economic crisis. The full extent of it would shock many people, including Mary.

A couple of weeks later, the miners voted by eighty-one percent to call a strike. Mr Heath called a General Election. Jeffrey had won a further reprieve from his creditors.

Jeffrey campaigned with an energy that seems almost incredible under the circumstances, up and down his unsuspecting constituency. Mary, who was pregnant again, took time off from the Royal Institution to join him at various stages. One of these was a visit to Immingham Dock.

The idea, which was Pat Otter's, was to take the various MPs to environments in which they would not be particularly at home.

The young Conservative MP as usual amazed Otter, this time by the way he got on with the dockers. He bounded about in his sheepskin jacket and chatted with the lorry drivers. He captured traditional Labour voters. Very few Tory MPs would even have shown their faces here. When the Immingham dockers drank at the Conservative Club, it was only because it was right next to the entrance of the docks.

Mary impressed them too, albeit for different reasons. Unacquainted with her intellectual qualities, the dockers took one look at the young Ph.D. standing by the white Daimler ANY 1, and wolf-whistled their approval.

'She took it very well,' Otter would recall, 'she just stood there with Jean Blackbourn. She's still very attractive; but in 1974, she was a stunner. After all, you don't see many people like that down Immingham Dock . . . on the Mineral Quay.'

*

Jean Blackbourn was the Conservative agent for Louth. Miss Blackbourn had come to the constituency two years earlier from Bletchley, where she had worked for the local Conservative party. Her family came from Lincolnshire.

Being an agent was a paid, full-time job. It was also a lonely job, made less so by a good relationship with the MP in question. Miss Blackbourn was a dedicated, businesslike professional, one of the many such women who would spend part of their lives trying to keep Jeffrey Archer to a schedule.

Jeffrey would drive up alone from London on a Friday night and stay at the Brigsley house or with the Fitzwilliams or Sharpleys. On the Saturday morning he would hold his 'surgeries' in the usual manner of a constituency MP. Miss Blackbourn would arrange the appointments and one by one the constituents would troop in through the office door in the Louth parish churchyard.

'You would be amazed at the variety of things they wanted to talk about,' Miss Blackbourn would recall later, 'pensions, tax, houses, family squabbles. They'd come from far and wide and they were all ages. He'd see them, I'd record what they were about and his secretary in London would follow them up.'

Miss Blackbourn was well prepared for a General Election. Edward Heath was clearly in doubtful shape and there was a Liberal threat in the constituency. She planned the campaign at the Louth offices with a map that stretched from below Louth to Fetherthorpe, Binbrook, Immingham and Cleethorpes. No area could be missed, large or small.

With a driver and timetable, to which she tried to keep him, Jeffrey bounded forth each day to do battle with the Liberals.

'He never walked anywhere,' Miss Blackbourn said, 'he had them all running and used to tire the old ladies out.'

He covered hundreds of miles and spoke at dozens of meetings. Not once did he give a real impression that the rest of his professional life was far less secure than his seat here in Lincolnshire.

'He was at all the surgeries and functions,' Miss Blackbourn would recall, 'he never let that slip in any way. There was no reason to think he was in the trouble that he was.

'He said ready cash was a bit of a problem. But I had no idea that it was to *that* extent.

'I was his agent. I spent more time with him than anybody else. And I didn't know.'

Jeffrey increased his majority by 452 to 9718. The result was: J. Archer (C) 25,158; J. Sellick (Lib) 15,440; A. Dowson (Lab) 15,148. On a national scale, however, the election had resulted in no clear majority. On 4 March Prime Minister Edward Heath resigned and a minority Labour government took office. There was obviously going to be another General Election.

A week later, a writ was issued on behalf of Anthony Bamford. Bamford wanted his money back: £172,162, plus ten percent interest. At the date of issue, that meant a further £23,017. Jeffrey did not respond. Bamford did not go away.

Judgment was entered against him in default of an appearance. Jeffrey did, however, appear at Louth Town Hall around that time, where judgment was very much in his favour. He was unanimously reselected as the Conservative prospective parliamentary candidate. In his speech to the Annual Meeting of the Louth Conservative Association, a week after his thirty-fourth birthday, he predicted an October election and thanked everyone who had helped him win that February. He also presented the Association's quota of membership trophies: the challenge shield for general efficiency to the Welton-le-Wold and South Elkington branch, the membership trophy to Grimoldby and Manby, the efficiency cup to South Reston and District and the Challenge shield for membership to Theddlethorpe.

Mr Sharpley and Miss Blackbourn were photographed

looking delighted; Jeffrey was well-dressed as ever, but looked tired and wan. One or two people noticed this, but nobody knew or asked why.

'He didn't seem the same,' Pat Otter would recall, 'there was a change in his demeanour. He'd lost a bit of his bounce.'

Four weeks later, with Mary now seven months pregnant and still working away at the Royal Institution, Jeffrey telephoned Bamford again. He would produce documentary assurances, he said, contracts to prove that the money would soon be paid.

The bankruptcy notice against him was again held off. Three days later, Bamford was told by his solicitor that no such assurances had been forthcoming. On 23 May 1974 a notice of bankruptcy was served on Bamford's behalf against Mr Jeffrey Archer of 24a The Boltons, South Kensington, London SW10.

Six days later, Aquablast was suspended from trading on the Montreal Stock Exchange. Its last share dealings in Britain were at 9 pence, 'if you could sell them', as one official put it.

Jeffrey then told two people rather more about his situation than they knew before. One was Mary; the other was Victor Mishcon.

Mary, so legend has it, was making jelly for William's second birthday party. 'I felt weak at the knees,' the accountant's daughter would later recall, 'but there was nothing else to do except carry on with the party. When you are told something like that, a sense of unreality takes over, and you are carried along in a state of shock which preserves you from the worst anxiety.'

Shock does not last for ever. It wears off. What follows is pain. A disfiguring rash was the first sign. Sleeplessness followed, and instead of taking a month off as planned after the experience of her first baby, she tried to prolong the anaesthetic by working. Her second son, Jamie, was born in the second week of June.

Victor Mishcon took the news rather better, as was only to

be expected. He was Jeffrey's new solicitor. Mishcon, it may also be recalled, had been LCC member for Brixton during PC Archer's brief posting there fifteen years earlier.

It was unlikely that there was time to compare reminiscences. Mishcon appealed on Jeffrey's behalf against the judgment. On 16 July the appeal was rejected. Jeffrey then appealed again against the decision to a judge. But Bamford's patience had finally run out. The Gordian knot was about to be cut. 'Challenge by MP over £172,000 loan ruling,' read the front page of *The Times*:

Mr Jeffrey Archer, Conservative MP for Louth, has conceded that he owes a company director more than £170,000. Legal proceedings over the debt resulted in the issue of a bankruptcy notice. . . .

Mishcon issued a statement that afternoon, denying that at that precise moment Jeffrey owed Bamford any money. That night, the statement appeared in the *Grimsby Evening Telegraph*. Needless to say, it caused some consternation in Lincolnshire.

Miss Blackbourn, Jeffrey's agent, had gone home for a funeral. Her aunt and brother had died on the same day. It was already one she would remember for the rest of her life, when the telephone rang at her mother's home in Scunthorpe.

'Jean? I'm terribly sorry.' It was Henry Sharpley, Chairman of the Louth Conservatives. 'I know you won't have read the papers, under the circumstances. But we have to have a meeting. Jeffrey is in financial trouble and it's got into the press.'

Already in a state of shock, Miss Blackbourn rushed back to Louth. That same day, she had to circulate the following notice to the Executive members:

LOUTH CONSERVATIVE ASSOCIATION

Member Of Parliament: Jeffrey Archer, M.P.

27th July, 1974

Dear Sir/Madam

EXECUTIVE COUNCIL

In view of recent reports in the Press concerning Mr. Archer and his financial position, the Chairman is calling a meeting of the Executive Committee of the Association where its members may be fully informed of the facts and consider the Association's position.

This meeting will take place at –

6 UPGATE, LOUTH

on Tuesday, 30th July, 1974

at 7.00 p.m.

and the above matter will be the only item on the Agenda.

Yours sincerely,

J. M. Blackbourn
Secretary and Agent

The Committee decided to set up a panel under the Chairmanship of Henry Sharpley. The panel then requested the company of their MP at an extraordinary meeting.

'People were absolutely stunned,' Jean Blackbourn would recall, 'when they heard the story. After all, this was after we'd successfully fought an election. So we were thinking, when the next one came, we should be all right.

'Poor Jeffrey. He was naturally very subdued. He could only say he was very sorry. What could he say? I don't think it had sunk in on him at that meeting.'

Henry Sharpley was equally desperate. The Chairman was being hounded by the press and by the anti-Archer faction who, unlike him, had not come to appreciate the job he had done in the constituency.

Roger Sharpley, who had driven Jeffrey during his General Election campaign, was now driving a pea lorry at night to earn some extra money. 'The Conservative traditionalists had seen the numerous newspaper articles about "Is he a millionaire or isn't he?" That upset some people because they felt that there was no need to say it. When Aquablast happened, they were all able to come out and say, "We told you he was riding for a fall."'

While the Committee pondered what to do, with the election looming, there were many long and anguished conversations. Jeffrey told Major Fitzwilliams that he and Bamford had gone into the venture jointly. Now he was in danger of being made bankrupt for the full amount. A bankrupt could not stand for Parliament. What, he asked, did the Major think he should do?

Major Fitzwilliams went to see the former Chairman, the tough-minded fish-finger magnate Jack Vincent.

Vincent was adamant. 'Clixby, unless you can bring Jeffrey to me and say there is no chance of him being sued for bankruptcy, we don't want him for our candidate.'

The Major regretfully then told Jeffrey what he should do. He should not resign, but neither should he put his name forward for re-election.

'Yes,' the Major would recall, 'it was traumatic.'

'I feel very bitter about it,' Mrs Fitzwilliams would recall, 'I'm sure there was no way out. But this was the opportunity for some people who considered him to be a whizzkid, to say "enough is enough".'

The Committee officially voted to notify Jeffrey of its 'concern'. A couple of days later, Henry Sharpley received a letter. Jeffrey confirmed that he would not be seeking re-election as MP for Louth.

Sharpley wrote back:

Your decision to give the resolution of these difficulties your undivided attention is one I understand and admire.

Your work for the constituency since you were first elected as Member of Parliament for Louth has been outstanding and many people in many places have reason to remember your efforts with gratitude.

This, and the courage with which you have followed your own convictions, has set a standard which will be hard for your successor to follow.

I hope that in the future, when your current problems are behind you, you may be able to resume the political career you have pursued with such diligence.

Jean Blackbourn was devastated. 'It was not my brightest moment. My whole *raison d'être* was gone. I was absolutely shattered, because everything had seemed to be going so well.

'Had the election not been imminent, we might have said, "Don't resign now, leave it." But there wasn't time for that. It had to be a quick decision.'

Pat Otter was not a Conservative, but the beer was cheap in Immingham Conservative Club. The *Grimsby Evening Telegraph* man had already heard the rumours that all was not right with Jeffrey Archer.

Otter was on holiday the week it happened. He was decorating his house, when the news editor telephoned. 'There's some problem with Jeffrey Archer,' his colleague said. 'Have you got any phone numbers for him?'

Otter gave him the numbers. But when the paper telephoned him, Jeffrey was not available for comment. The news editor called Otter back, and asked him to try.

Otter telephoned him at The Boltons. Mary answered and they had a short conversation. Eventually, she said, 'Give him ten minutes.'

Ten minutes later, Otter's telephone rang. 'Pat? This is Jeffrey. I'm giving you this interview because I trust you. I have been a fool . . .'

*I HAVE BEEN A FOOL, THIS IS A PERSONAL TRAGEDY –
ARCHER*

They did the whole interview on the telephone. The next day, Friday 23 August 1974, it was splashed with photographs of Jeffrey, Mary and the Brigsley house, across the entire front page of the *Grimsby Evening Telegraph*:

LOUTH MP MR. JEFFREY ARCHER WHO, IN A SHOCK ANNOUNCEMENT LATE YESTERDAY, SAID HE INTENDS TO STAND DOWN AT THE NEXT ELECTION, TOLD THE EVENING TELEGRAPH LAST NIGHT: 'I HAVE BEEN A FOOL . . . THIS IS A PERSONAL TRAGEDY.' IN AN EXCLUSIVE INTERVIEW WITH PAT OTTER, HE SAID: 'THIS WHOLE BUSINESS IS A TRAGEDY AND, NATURALLY, I AM VERY SORRY FOR LETTING DOWN ALL MY CONSTITUENTS.'

'I don't think I'm angry,' Jean Blackbourn would say, thirteen years later, 'very upset, more than anything else. It was so sudden. Being an agent is your life. I'm not married and I haven't any children. When you've worked very closely with someone for two years and thought everything was going well, it's a disaster, really. . . .

'He said he wanted to be a millionaire. He had done well at Oxford and then got this plum seat. He didn't think anything could go wrong.

'He could always make you feel that you were the one person he was talking to.'

Pat Otter was not quite as surprised. 'I think the extent of it surprised me. But suspicion cushioned some of my surprise. As a publicist he was brilliant . . . brilliant. I've met a lot of very able politicians, but as a publicist I don't think I've met anyone like Jeffrey Archer. I won't say as good as Jeffrey Archer. I won't say as bad as Jeffrey Archer. But I've never met anyone like him.

'This was in the '70s when it was trendy to have a young MP with an attractive wife. He seemed to symbolise the age we were all living in. The age of the opportunist, the age of

137

the get-rich-quick person. People looked up to whizzkids . . . in those days.'

They both put a brave face on it. Mary posed uneasily at home with the children and said she was 'just not given to despair'.

'One thing I can say,' she added. 'Life with Jeffrey has never been dull.'

A week later, Jeffrey opened the Immingham Conservative Association's Fête and told people he had received 500 letters of support. He could not believe yet, perhaps, that he really would not be allowed to stand for re-election. Three days later, the pretty eighteenth-century house by the church in Brigsley went up for sale. The estate agent's advertisement stressed 'early possession'.

The Crash of '74

The white Daimler gave way to an old Mini. The millionaire who never was, now set about building a new legend on the ruins of the old. It was hard going.

In the next few stressful years, the best publicist ever interviewed by the *Grimsby Evening Telegraph* would reveal that he may have lost his money, but he had not lost his touch. Just how much money he had lost, in fact, would be increasingly open to question. Five years later, journalists would wrongly describe Jeffrey as having made, lost and remade a million. Jeffrey would refrain from correcting them. As the figure grew with repetition and distortion, so, by inference, did the achievement of the man who had made, lost and remade it.

Meanwhile, the shock of realising he really would not be standing for re-election that October had begun to wear off. In a letter on House of Commons writing paper to the Fitz-williams, he wrote in desperation:

Many thanks for your letter. I was particularly touched by your comments about Freda: it is one of the few times I have felt like crying when I have read a letter.

I have been overwhelmed [he went on] by the amount of letters from the Constituency, Cabinet Ministers, Shadow Cabinet Ministers, distinguished people in the Arts and other worlds, most of whom have said my decision was wrong and that I should have stayed still. Had I known the contents of my post bag I would never have stood down, but having made an honourable agreement with Henry I shall naturally keep to it.

Those particular Lincolnshire Tories would stay friendly with Jeffrey, even though another ten years would pass before the prodigal son would revisit his adopted parents. But the prodigal son would soon discover that other friendships were less enduring. He was surprised and hurt by the number of people whom he had taken to the Savoy and who now dropped him the moment he was no longer the bright young MP.

One of the less sympathetic listeners was Mr Justice Lawson. Jeffrey's appeal against the judgment was again dismissed, and this time there was only the Court of Appeal to which he could now take his case. He was fighting an increasingly rearguard action against Bamford and his JCBs.

On 10 October Labour won a majority of three in the General Election. Jeffrey's safe seat was now irrevocably in the hands of the new Conservative MP, Michael Brotherton. That day he wrote again to the Fitzwilliams on House of Commons writing paper; one of the last times he did so. Already, it no longer bore the legend 'From Jeffrey Archer, MP':

Dear Pauline,

I wonder if you could help me on two matters.

One, I have quite a bit of 'good junk' which I would like to give to the WRVS and, therefore, will need it collected from Brigsley and secondly, I have a little bit of furniture that I would like to store for the time being as I have sold the house. I wondered if you might have any ideas where I could put it? It consists of a three piece suite and a bed.

Hope all goes well with you.

The following day it was announced that he had withdrawn his appeal to the Court of Appeal.

Mary embarked on a lecture tour of America to make some money. She had hoped to have a third child, perhaps a daughter; now it would be impossible. Jeffrey, who had once been the proprietor of 'Babysitters Unlimited' for wealthy folk from areas like The Boltons, now minded his own children. As he had done so many times before, the thirty-four-year-old ex-dynamic ball of energy rang up Sir Noel

Hall. Could he bring the children down for the day? The Halls still had their country place, Homer End, seven miles from Oxford in the beech woods. As they had done so many times before, they obliged.

In London, he was to be spotted trudging the pavements, a pedestrian, no longer the proud possessor of the Daimler ANY 1. Henry Taylor, another of the Louth Tories, met him in Trafalgar Square.

'Let's have a drink at the office,' said Jeffrey. Arrow House was partly let out to a property developer; the rest was deserted. The property market had crashed and the lease was worth nothing.

'Things'll never get better,' the ex-MP told his former constituent.

Roger Sharpley, too, remembered bumping into Jeffrey during this period. 'His appearance was quite a lot different from what it had been. He wasn't as well dressed . . . it had knocked it out of him.' Sharpley was to hear from Jeffrey again, and be rewarded in an unusual way for his loyalty.

John Bryant, the distance runner whom he had met at OUAC, took him out for a square meal during these hard times. So did Adrian Metcalfe. So did Nick Lloyd. Metcalfe lent him his life savings. Metcalfe had never done business with Jeffrey and had no doubt that he was going to survive.

Others who had done business with him were less charitable at the time, though the bad memories would fade and charitable thoughts return. Jeffrey was rather reluctant to stand down as a governor of Dover College. Sir Gerald Duke, none the less, thought it was 'the right thing'.

'Dear Pauline,' he wrote, on an old piece of Arrow Enterprises writing-paper,

Would you be kind enough to ask the WRVS van to come to Church Farm House on either Friday November 8th after 3 o'clock, or Saturday morning to collect some objects.

Hope all goes well with you.

He cut out adverts for jobs as a dishwasher. Mary's sense of humour, never explicit, now deserted her. The brave face in public, for the benefit of a press she feared and despised, could not be privately maintained. She took it hard.

Clearly, desperate measures had to be taken.

As he so often did during these hard times, the former OUAC and Vincent's man found encouragement in the little band of friends from Oxford. On this occasion, he was in a car with Adrian Metcalfe.

It was a suitably unlikely beginning to one of the most extraordinary literary success stories of their time. The two men were driving up to Scotland for the marriage of Hogan the hurdler. Metcalfe, who was Jamie Archer's godfather, was at the wheel. Jeffrey was an unhappy passenger:

'I know I can get a job for £20,000 or £30,000 a year,' he was saying, 'there's no question I can earn, and I can do anything. But I can't, can't raise £400,000 through work, Adrian. I can't do it!'

Metcalfe nodded and concentrated on driving. 'I've tried property,' Jeffrey went on, 'and that didn't work. I've tried shares and that didn't work. I've tried all the things that everyone else has tried and they didn't work.'

Metcalfe listened sympathetically.

'The only thing I can think of is to write a bestseller.'

Metcalfe nearly drove off the road.

'A bestseller,' Jeffrey went on, 'which turns into a movie. That's the only way of making enough money to sort out my problems.'

'Jeffrey,' said Metcalfe, 'you can't write!'

'Don't be ridiculous, Adrian. It's nothing to do with writing, I'll *produce* a bestseller. I can tell a good story. I'm convinced of it.'

'Don't tell anyone' – the best publicist Pat Otter ever met was uncharacteristically embarrassed – 'but that's what I'm going to have to do.'

The car droned on towards Scotland and Hogan the

hurdler. On the drive back, the two men talked more about the idea of a book. Almost exactly a decade later, the near-bankrupt former sprinter in the passenger seat would appear, in his capacity as internationally best-selling master story-teller, as guest of honour at the *Grimsby Evening Telegraph*'s inaugural Literary Luncheon. By that time, however, Metcalfe would long ago have been repaid his life savings, and Jeffrey, the first man ever to be President of OUAC without being an undergraduate, would have proved that producing a bestseller was not just to do with writing.

Not long after that, the telephone rang in Homer End, Sir Noel and Lady Hall's house in the beech woods. Lady Hall answered it.

'How's my favourite woman?'

'What do you want, Jeffrey?'

There was something he had to do, he told her, which was impossible in London. The telephone kept ringing there and the children were always in and out. Mary had insisted on a nanny, if she was to support them. He wanted to borrow Little End, the cottage attached to the Halls' house.

Lady Hall told him she had installed her Filipino help there. Would he, she added, like the guest room in the main house?

Jeffrey accepted with alacrity.

His routine followed a pattern. He would arrive from The Boltons on Sunday nights at about 10 p.m. The following morning he would get up and immediately go for a run, usually to the View, a beauty spot a mile or so away through the beech woods. He would forgo breakfast and go upstairs to work. At about 12.30 p.m., he would go out to lunch at one of the local pubs, come back at about 1.45 and work until six. If the Halls were there, he would show them something of what he was up to. He would have dinner with them on some nights, and on others he would go into Oxford. On Friday afternoons, at about five, he went back to London.

His room was always tidy. He never asked for anything. There was little or no noise, least of all the sound of a typewriter. Jeffrey would never learn to type. He was writing it all in longhand.

Several weeks later, he showed it to Adrian Metcalfe.

Metcalfe read the handwritten manuscript in its entirety and made various comments. One of them concerned the need for a working title, which Metcalfe promptly came up with.

'Why don't you call it "Not A Penny More, Not A Penny Less",' he said, 'until we think of something better?'

Roger Sharpley, whose name would appear in the book attached to a fictional character, was living in Elvaston Place when he too was telephoned.

'I'd like you to come round,' said Jeffrey, 'and read this film script I've written.' Sharpley went round to The Boltons and found Jeffrey surrounded by numerous pieces of paper. ('No,' Sharpley would say later, 'he had not previously struck me as a master storyteller. But he could quote quite long chunks of plays he had seen.')

'I'd like you,' said Jeffrey, 'as a complete layman to read this. I've shown it to a few people and they think it's pretty good. Can you spare a couple of hours?'

Sharpley obliged, as did others. He invited them round, he rang them up, he read them the first chapter in cheap restaurants. Many of these names would appear attached to fictional characters. Nick Lloyd would find his character a little too fictional for his liking.

Jeffrey rang him up. 'I've written a book,' he told the ex-*Cherwell* editor, now on the *News of the World*. Lloyd was sceptical, being of course familiar with Jeffrey's previous attempts at writing. 'I've written a book,' said Jeffrey, 'and you're in it.'

He proceeded to read an extract over the telephone. It described Nick Lloyd, hack supreme, on his third triple gin and tonic and hunting for scandal:

'If you had any bloody money, I'd sue you for that,

Jeffrey with the Beatles in 1963. Nick Lloyd is second
from the left. (*Sunday Times*)

The victorious 1966 Oxford University Athletic Team.
Jeffrey as President is seated in the centre of the front
row. (John Bryant)

The Director General of the National Birthday Trust
in his favourite pose with JFK in the background.
(BBC Hulton Picture Library)

Jeffrey with Tim Cobb on their
Far Eastern fundraising tour.
(Tim Cobb)

The young MP and proprietor
of Arrow Enterprises at home in
the Boltons. (Times Newspapers)

Mary at Oxford. (Mail Newspapers)

Mary on the day she was awarded her Ph.D. (Times Newspapers)

Jeffrey campaigning in the 1970 General Election in his Louth Constituency. (Mrs Philippa Taylor MBE)

Mary on the campaign trail. (Mrs Philippa Taylor MBE)

Jeffrey and Mary in Lincolnshire, 1972. She is expecting their first child. (*Grimsby Evening Telegraph*)

'I've no need to work ever again in my life.' Jeffrey at
the time of the Terry Coleman interview in 1973.
Disaster was already on the horizon. (*Guardian*)

Jeffrey at the Alembic House apartment – his
'Westminster flat'. (*Observer*)

The 1984 *Grimsby Evening Telegraph* inaugural
Literary Luncheon. (*Grimsby Evening Telegraph*)

Chairman of the Conservative Party Norman Tebbit
and Deputy Jeffrey Archer, 1985. (Express
Newspapers)

The Archers at home in Grantchester, 1985. 'We can use this picture for our Christmas card,' said Jeffrey. 'I think that's rather vulgar,' said Mary. (Express Newspapers)

Jeffrey immediately after his resignation as Deputy Chairman, 26 October, 1986. (Mail Newspapers)

By May, 1987, Jeffrey was unofficially back on the
General Election campaign trail, apparently undaunted.
(Mail Newspapers)

Jeffrey and Mary after the *Star* libel verdict, July 24,
1987. (Rex Features)

Archer' – Lloyd was not totally amused – 'not that you'll ever see it printed, ha, ha.'

Even Lloyd presumably could not have predicted that the book that used his name would be printed in hundreds of thousands; or that, quite coincidentally, and under different editorship, over a decade later the *News of the World* would help put an end to the political comeback of the master storyteller.

That spring Mrs Margaret Thatcher became Leader of the Opposition Conservative Party. Jeffrey, whose interest in politics had not diminished one whit in spite of what he told other reporters, had followed her career closely through his continued contact with lobby correspondents. The slow upturn in fortunes of the Conservative Party would coincide with the recovery of its youngest ex-MP. The latter would not go unnoticed either by Mrs Thatcher or certain elder statesmen of the Tory Party.

Meanwhile, the dog-eared manuscript written in longhand passed through numerous processes of refinement. Jo Haesen, who had kept in touch since she left in the last days of Arrow to work for Adrian Metcalfe, was responsible for some stupendous bursts of typing. Mary, when she was not lecturing abroad or looking for a job, helped remove the hanging participles. The would-be author did what he did best; he stirred up publicity for his unpublished novel in the newspapers.

Then someone told him about Deborah Owen.

Deborah Owen was then best-known for being married to Dr David Owen, Labour MP for Plymouth, Devonport, future Foreign Secretary and rising young star of the Labour Party. Mrs Owen was also a literary agent, with a small but lucrative list of clients including cookery writer Delia Smith and the estate of the romantic novelist, Georgette Heyer.

The last thing on earth Deborah Owen might have wanted were the scribblings of an *arriviste* ex-Tory MP, when she was trying to secure the future of a potential Leader of the

Labour Party. As it turned out, the earnings from the neatly-typed manuscript which landed on her desk, and the ones that followed, were to help keep her husband through the political wilderness in a style which even the confident Mrs Owen could not have predicted.

Not A Penny More, Not A Penny Less told a straight-forward, well-organised tale of four men who discover they have been swindled out of their money in a share-pushing fraud. They decide to band together to recover the exact sum lost. They recover the money by means of various adventures in London, Monte Carlo and Ascot. There is a neat twist in the end.

Deborah Owen read the manuscript and liked it. Some confusion exists over why she did. Legend would have it that Dr Owen himself read the manuscript in bed and laughed so much that he attracted his wife's attention. Jeffrey's own widely-publicised real-life experiences of stock-pushing gave the story that extra whiff of authenticity. It was also potentially filmable, as Jeffrey kept telling the newspapers.

The manuscript furthermore contained a number of idiosyncrasies worthy of biographical interest. The names Roger Sharpley and Henry Sharpley both appeared, attached to fictional characters; as, of course, did Nick Lloyd. Detective Inspector Clifford Smith was the name of the real-life Fraud Squad member who had investigated Aquablast; his assistant Detective Sergeant Ryder was named after one of Jeffrey's researchers at the Commons. Michael Stacpoole would later achieve brief fame as an Archer retainer. Lord Brigsley of Louth was another character; the villains included Bernie Silverman a.k.a. 'Manny The Snake' Silverman.

To make matters more confusing for the biographer, a number of real people appeared under their real names as themselves. These included the photographer Patrick Lichfield, gossip columnist Richard Compton-Miller, Jeffrey's favourite painter, Leon Underwood, and Williams and Glyn's Bank, Birchin Lane Branch, who would shortly sue Jeffrey for the large sum of money which he had so unwisely borrowed from them.

Finally, there was the hero's wife, *Mary*:

Robin was relieved to be let off the hook until the morning. He clambered in beside his fragrant silk-clad wife and ran his finger hopefully down her vertebral column to her coccyx.

'You'll be lucky, at this time of night,' she mumbled.

The idiosyncrasies and ironies of the manuscript in all its forms were not what sold it to Deborah Owen. What sold it to her, simply, was the fact that it really was quite good. A myth would inevitably grow, however, as it did with everything connected with Jeffrey: that the number of publishers who turned it down in Britain somehow conferred upon it 'misunderstood greatness'.

The truth was more prosaic, if no less honourable. Deborah Owen offered it, negotiated and sold it to the American publishers Doubleday for a modest sum. The book would appear in due course to modest reviews and continue in print. It was certainly not an instant, worldwide bestseller.

Meanwhile, the real-life characters in Jeffrey's life were behaving as if they had minds of their own.

Mary took a lectureship in inorganic chemistry at Newnham College, Cambridge. Jeffrey had settled with Bamford and the bankruptcy notice was withdrawn; but this and the action brought by Williams and Glyn's meant they would have to leave the house in The Boltons. While Mary and the children were in Cambridge, Jeffrey scraped along in London, living in a rented flat off Lowndes Square. The faithful little band of friends continued to take him out for lunches.

Meanwhile, Deborah Owen continued her efforts to improve Jeffrey's cash-flow and hers. The seventh or eighth publisher she approached was Tom Maschler.

Maschler, then forty-two, had been something of a publishing *wunderkind*. At twenty-five he had become a fiction editor at Penguin Books; two years later he became Editorial Director at Jonathan Cape. Maschler was undoubtedly a brilliant salesman. Cape, of which he was now Managing Director, was approaching the height of its prestige as one of London's few money-making literary publishing houses. Cape meant Patrick White, Kurt Vonnegut, William Styron, Gabriel Garcia Marquez. Cape also published a small number of less literary thrillers, a fact naturally known to Deborah Owen.

Thus it was that, while its author languished in his borrowed flat, *Not A Penny More, Not A Penny Less* landed on the doormat of Cape's elegant Bedford Square offices.

Maschler's readers perused it once, twice, and were still unable to return a verdict. So they passed it on to him.

Maschler rather liked it. 'I found it really very engaging,' he recalled later, 'the idea of someone writing a book about a con he was involved in, and also writing it in order to make a lot of money. It wasn't great literature, but it was entertaining, it was original, it was a lot of fun.'

Maschler paid Jeffrey around £2500 for *Not A Penny More, Not A Penny Less*. He then turned his mind back to Patrick White, Kurt Vonnegut and weightier matters.

Jeffrey's life continued on its own erratic way. That autumn, he was contacted by the Royal Canadian Mounted Police. Four of the alleged perpetrators of the Aquablast stock-pushing fraud were to be put on trial and witnesses were required. Was he at all interested, they enquired innocently, in a trip to Canada?

Jeffrey lost little time in replying, and in contacting the *Sunday Express*. 'I would be delighted to go,' he told them, 'they will fly me there first-class, put me up at the best hotel and pay all my expenses for about two weeks. It will be a nice break for me,' he told them, adding, somewhat tactlessly, 'I have not been able to get away anywhere this year. My wife Mary has. She went on a speaking tour of American universities.'

Needless to say, the *Sunday Express* in turn contacted the

Royal Canadian Mounted Police, who in turn confirmed that they may have got their man, but he was flying economy like everyone else.

Deborah Owen worked valiantly to sell rights to Jeffrey's first novel. But Williams and Glyn's, Birchin Lane Branch, were closing in. The bank already held his paintings as surety.

That spring and summer of 1976, the inimitable Archer publicity machine went into overdrive. 'All my financial problems are behind me,' he told the *Daily Express*, 'I don't owe a bean to anyone. This book should see me making another fortune.' *Not A Penny More, Not A Penny Less*, he declared, had sold 25,000 copies in three weeks in America. Warners had bought the film rights. Billy Wilder was going to direct the film, which would 'possibly' star Rod Steiger and Dustin Hoffman.

Writing was hard work, he blithely told the *Guardian*'s Lesley Adamson: 'I never realised you could make a million just by writing a book,' added the ex-MP who less than two years earlier, as Adamson pointed out, had told reporters he would rather help old-age pensioners in his constituency than be on a yacht in the South of France. 'You could say I have changed my attitudes about money.

'When I was in public life,' he went on, apparently straight-faced, 'I found the British people very critical of anyone who goes out to make money. In any other country you are helped and supported.'

Jeffrey would never quite be able to accept that there was no anti-Archer conspiracy among the *Guardian*-reading lefties of Highgate.

That September, *Not A Penny More, Not A Penny Less* was published in Britain by Jonathan Cape Ltd, price £3.50. *The Times* review called it 'a neat job', a verdict that would not be among those quoted in subsequent paperback editions.

'Delightfully old-fashioned crook-adventure story' said the

Observer. *The Times Literary Supplement* was closer to the mark: 'Jeffrey Archer's ingenious plot, with its echoes of Edgar Wallace and vintage Sexton Blake, is the sort to take the public fancy. The novel has a curious racy innocence all its own.'

But it was the *New Zealand Times*, of all reviews, which said what Jeffrey and Deborah Owen most wanted to hear: 'It's fun to read and would be fun to see.'

The book was dedicated 'To Mary and the fat men', the latter being William and Jamie, now four and two respectively. Acknowledgements included Sir Noel and Lady Hall, Adrian Metcalfe, Mary's doctor brother David who had supplied certain surgical information, and Jo Haesen.

Sir Gerald Duke in Kent received a copy. So did Lady Hall, of course, in Oxfordshire. Hers was inscribed: 'To Eli . . . the only other girl in my life'.

So did Miss Blackbourn, in Cleethorpes: 'I think the book came out too soon for me,' she said, later. 'I was picturing Jeffrey all the time I was reading it, and it didn't seem like him to me. I kept thinking "Jeffrey wouldn't say that" and "That's not like Jeffrey"'.

Tom Maschler, by contrast, was pleasantly surprised. 'It got nice little reviews and it sold for a first thriller extremely well,' Maschler would recall. Cape even sold the British paperback rights for around £10,000 to Coronet, who were owned by Hodder and Stoughton.

Jeffrey bounced around, avoiding the *Guardian* and cooking up stories for journalists like Nigel Dempster of the *Daily Mail*.

Dempster, the doyen of his profession, would eventually punish Jeffrey for placing his trust in Fleet Street gossip columnists. But for the time being, he was the very soul of kindness. This was exemplified in The Telephone Call That Never Was.

Jeffrey, so *Mail* readers were informed, had recently received a telephone call in New York from an American toy manufacturer. Had he, the company enquired, sold the title of his novel *Not A Penny More, Not A Penny Less* (soon to be a major motion picture) to any other toy company?

Jeffrey replied that he had not. The company in question then revealed that it intended to produce a million games based on that title, to the considerable enrichment, of course, of the author.

The author, in this exclusive story in the *Daily Mail*, then told Dempster, 'Yes, it is true. The call came out of the blue and I was rather flabbergasted.'

'Already [Dempster whispered] I hear, he has made £220,000 from the book and film, with royalties continuing to pour in.'

Dempster had 'heard' this from Jeffrey. There had of course been no such telephone call, nor game, nor sum in royalties. But the effect of such a notion appearing in print, however, was to give all these things credibility. The old publicist had not lost his touch since the days of the 'Wrong Mr Archer', a fact not lost on Deborah Owen.

Mrs Owen had not found it necessary to steer her new client in the right direction. He seemed to know his way there in the dark. His agent merely kept him on the right tracks, made appointments for him to meet the right people. The purpose of all these ploys, of course, was to achieve *bankability*.

This is the goal of the modern-day, *Pygmalion*-like process in which the author is merely a part of the machinery that designs, manufactures and markets a bestseller. This is what Jeffrey had grasped, during that car ride with Adrian Metcalfe.

The basic requirements of bankability are simple:

– A straightforward imagination unfettered by excessive literacy
– A deeply-felt desire to achieve wealth and fame on a colossal scale
– A plot lavishly tailored to flatter and titillate the American mass market
– A willingness and ability to promote the finished product

on radio, television and street-corners, from Boise, Idaho to Blackburn, Lancashire.

As a job description, it could have been written for Jeffrey Archer.

Tom Maschler was not surprised when the next manuscript from Deborah Owen and Jeffrey Archer landed on the doormat of Cape's elegant Bedford Square offices. The standard second book option was in the terms of the first contract. The readers' reports were again unable to return a verdict. This time Maschler, too, was uncertain.

'It wasn't special the way I thought *Not A Penny More, Not A Penny Less* was a really nice little book,' Maschler would recall. 'If it had been the first I'd read, I might not have taken it. I don't know . . . I wasn't over the moon about it.'

Maschler's reservations concerned the fact that, if anything, this particular book was a little *too* lifelike. It lacked imagination, charm. These were literary attributes which the Managing Director was accustomed to finding, even in Cape's small thriller list.

The manuscript was entitled *Shall We Tell The President?* The story, like that of the first book, was simple. Five men know of a plot to assassinate the President of the United States. Four of them are killed. The fifth has six days in which to prevent the assassination.

The plot resembled that of Frederick Forsyth's brilliant international bestseller, *The Day Of The Jackal.* Forsyth's book had furthermore been successfully filmed. Although both readers of the book and watchers of the film knew that in reality the intended victim, President de Gaulle, had survived, the dramatic skills of the author and director ensured that they forgot this fact.

Shall We Tell The President? resembled Forsyth's book in that Jeffrey's intended victim, too, was a real-life person. He was Senator Edward Kennedy. Jeffrey had made him President for the purpose of murdering him.

Maschler effectively came to the conclusion that the book was not bad enough to turn down. Cape paid £5000 for the British volume rights to *Shall We Tell The President?* and again sold the paperback rights to Coronet.

By this time Maschler was getting on quite well with Jeffrey and thought he had got to know him a little better. 'When you encounter an author,' Maschler would say later, 'who is as determined to succeed as Jeffrey, they will. There's no stopping them. The talent he had shown in the first book and to a lesser extent in the second one, plus his amazing drive, energy, restlessness and so on. . . . He's not going to fail, he's going to be a big deal author. It's absolutely clear.'

Maschler would always remember one conversation in particular. Jeffrey told him he had read John Fowles' literary bestseller, *The French Lieutenant's Woman*, not once, but three times.

'Tom,' he went on, 'if I read this book another five times, do you think I will have a chance at the Nobel Prize?'

Maschler struggled to maintain his composure. What Jeffrey was really asking, he realised, was that if he put enough energy, craft and intelligence into writing, could he become a great writer?

Maschler spoke as his friend and publisher. 'Jeffrey,' he said, 'you are amazingly good at what you are doing. But in my experience, Nobel Prizewinners have tended to start off as such.

'Jeffrey, I think the odds are stacked against you.'

The would-be Nobel Prizewinner slogged away, none the less. He was rewarded, and his bankability proven, when the telephone call came through from New York. This time it was true. The resourceful Mrs Owen had auctioned the American hardback rights to *Shall We Tell The President?* to the Viking Press for $250,000.

It was just over two years since that car journey with Adrian Metcalfe.

Not long afterwards, Metcalfe's telephone rang. It was

Jeffrey. Did he by any chance want to come and look at a flat?

Thus it was that the former employee of the United Nations Association came to return to the windy modern tower marooned on the Albert Embankment. The UNA was no longer at Alembic House, of course, but the luxury flat of John Barry was still on the tenth floor. Barry was not, however, and a speedy sale was required.

Jeffrey and Metcalfe unlocked the door of the abandoned apartment and came upon a scene straight out of the 1960s. There were rocking chairs and *objets trouvés* and thousands of records. They opened the dressing-room doors and found twenty St Laurent silk safari suits.

The apartment had two bedrooms, two bathrooms and a vast L-shaped living room. It could hardly have been described as a *pied-à-terre*; it literally towered over everything around it. It was better than Arrow House. It was better than the top floor of Centre Point. It overlooked the Tate Gallery on the north side of the Thames; and further up, so near and yet so far, the Houses of Parliament.

Jeffrey particularly liked that.

The hall would be hung with posters advertising his books. Jeffrey, who had gradually managed to reclaim his paintings from the bank, hung them on the walls and bought a Henry Moore and a large coffee table. Julian Dakowski obliged with Chinese silk wall hangings and hand-woven rugs.

The apartment was not somewhere that Mary and the children, now five and three, would ever call home. They were safely in Cambridge with the nanny. But it was the perfect base for Jeffrey from which to launch his forays into transatlantic bankability, to entertain the little band of friends who had supported him, and to pester his publishers. He took to holding monthly all-male parties; guest-lists would be circulated in advance and the guests were from a deliberate mixture of the worlds of sport, politics, showbusiness, commerce and the arts, and old friends like John Bryant, Nick Lloyd and Adrian Metcalfe.

Above all, though, it was the perfect place to entertain journalists.

The irrepressible ex-dynamic ball of energy, ex-MP and would-be Nobel Prizewinner now made up for lost time at every opportunity. Immediately before the British publication of *Shall We Tell The President?* he was to be seen ostentatiously 'correcting' the proofs. One journalist spotted the following, scribbled in the margin:

He unziped [sic] her skirt and caressed her gently. She began to move her hand up his leg.

He told others that if the Conservatives did not win an election soon, he would have to go to Ireland as a tax exile. He no longer had any parliamentary ambitions, he said. Even the sight of an MP leaving for a ten o'clock vote was no match for the sight of himself leaving for America or Barbados. There was nothing sadder than the sight of an ex-MP hanging around the Houses of Parliament.

His admiration for Mary knew no bounds, he told them. He could never put her through such traumas again. He hoped he had grown up; there was no one he wanted to beat any more.

Mary, meanwhile, worked and lived in Cambridge with William, Jamie, the nanny and Sir Percival Rugg. Mary did not 'approve' of journalists. She was frightened of their power and horrified by their salaries. Even Jeffrey's acquaintances among the serious, political correspondents found getting to know her a lengthy process.

She had been superseded, though, in one respect. As his *de facto* editor, she had played a large part in bringing order to the handwritten mass which threatened to swamp the idea of his first book. But Deborah Owen was taking no chances with the bankability process. Jeffrey had been placed under the tutelage of veteran New York editor Corlies M. 'Cork' Smith, for the drafting of *Shall We Tell The President?*

Cork Smith was a publishing legend. He had known Steinbeck and Hemingway, both Nobel Laureates. Now he reconciled himself for a suitable fee to the prospect of further educating the would-be Nobel Prizewinner sent to him by Deborah Owen.

As Professor Higgins to Jeffrey's Doolittle, Smith left his protégé in no doubt as to who was the boss in the process of getting Jeffrey into the members' enclosure. 'Am I allowed to tell you what I think of this book,' Smith is reputed to have boomed, 'or do I have to be polite to you for the next three damn weeks?'

Thus began one of the least-publicised and most lucrative partnerships in modern mass-market fiction. Smith's knowledge and experience were endless, and they were both up for sale.

He gave good value. One of the things he told Jeffrey about was 'Horse under the picture'.

'Jeffrey,' Smith would point to an offending passage, 'here is a picture of a horse, okay? And here is a caption underneath it. What does the caption say? "A Horse."'

Smith was teaching him not to state the obvious. 'Horse under the picture, Jeffrey. Horse under the picture!' Smith would say, striking out the offending passage in question.

That autumn, Viking published *Shall We Tell The President?* in America. The advertisements carried the magic hand-signal to book-buyers of all descriptions. 'Brilliant,' the ads declared. And then, in a nod and a wink to the cognoscenti: *bankable*.

Shall We Tell The President? was published in America on 10 October 1977. The first reviews were dreadful: 'Clumsily plotted, indifferently written, wantonly silly', said the *New York Times*, adding that it had 'nothing on its mind but money – for Jeffrey Archer and for the publisher'. The last line of that review was rather enigmatic. It would also, in true Archer style, lead to an apparently unexpected publicity bonanza: 'Anybody associated with its publication,' the *New*

York Times mysteriously concluded, 'should be ashamed of herself.'

Jeffrey, meanwhile, had flown into New York the previous weekend. The would-be Nobel Laureate slept badly and went to see *Star Wars*. On the Monday morning he presented himself at the Viking Press offices on Madison Avenue.

Viking were depressed about the *New York Times* review. This was perhaps understandable, in the circumstances. But the circumstances were not what they appeared to be. A piece of information which may be relevant at this point is that one of Viking's consulting editors was Mrs Jacqueline Kennedy Onassis.

Mrs Onassis had worked for Viking for two years, during which time she had edited a book of Russian costumes and décor called *In the Russian Style*. She was now working on a second book about Russian fairy tales. As widow of the late assassinated President she had been, of course, sister-in-law to Senator Edward Kennedy.

Jeffrey spent the day promoting his book on local radio shows. That night he had dinner at the 21 Club with Viking President Thomas Guinzburg. The following morning, the author of *Shall We Tell The President?* set off on a twenty-four-day coast-to-coast promotional tour under the standard terms of his part in the Archer–Owen–Smith–Guinzburg bankability machine.

Three days later, he had done three television shows, eight radio shows and four newspaper interviews in Pittsburgh, Cleveland and Los Angeles, when a message arrived for him to telephone the *Boston Globe*. Did he, they enquired, have any comment to make on the fact that Edward Kennedy's brother-in-law, Stephen Smith, had voiced criticisms of *Shall We Tell The President?*

Jeffrey naturally replied that he had, and made appropriate noises. Smith was not much of a name to conjure with; but it was a start.

That night he had dinner with one of the many Hollywood

types who would take out a film option on *Not A Penny More, Not A Penny Less*. (The book possibly made more money this way than it would have done if any of them had actually filmed it.)

Early the next morning, the telephone rang. This time it was the *New York Times*, whose unkind review had appeared to cause such depression a few days earlier in the Viking offices. Did Jeffrey, they enquired, have any comment to make on the fact that Mrs Jacqueline Kennedy Onassis had resigned from the Viking Press?

Jeffrey would claim later that even he was lost for words. Shortly afterwards, however, he found them again. This was a publicist's dream: a real-life Kennedy apparently resigning in protest at the publication of a novel about the attempted assassination of her brother-in-law. The fact that she actually resigned because the *New York Times* had been rude about her was conveniently ignored for the time being. So was the fact that Guinzburg, a friend of Mrs Onassis, had consulted her before buying it. The potent Kennedy legend and the myth of Mrs Onassis's resignation took off together into the mass-media stratosphere, pulling Jeffrey and his 'clumsily plotted, indifferently written, wantonly silly novel' happily along behind.

Sixteen cities later, the Viking Press took a half-page advertisement in the *New York Times* quoting reviews from all the way across the nation. Jeffrey, meanwhile, straight-facedly confessed to the *New York Daily News* that he was 'distressed' over the feeling the book had caused, especially in those people who churlishly had not yet bothered to read it.

Back in England, he described the American tour in an article for the *Sunday Express*. It was an amusing and masterly example of what Mary called his 'gift for inaccurate précis'. Having softened up the reader with tales of his two small sons saying goodbye to their father, who was afraid of flying, he cast himself in the role of an innocent abroad, to whom successively wonderful things happened and whose main concern was that the quality of his book should not go unnoticed amid all this silly fuss about Jackie Kennedy.

Mary's reaction to this, as to so many things, was not recorded. Nor was she available for comment three weeks later, when Jeffrey gave her £100,000 to become a Lloyd's underwriter. Just in case his generosity was not sufficiently appreciated, he told the *Daily Mail*.

Since it appeared that the *Mail* was for some reason interested, he took the opportunity to refresh readers' memories of some of his other achievements. He had lost exactly £427,727 in that bad investment, he said. Now his first two books had earned, yes, over a million pounds. Faced with the dreadful prospect of tax exile, he had discussed it with Mary, whose view surprisingly was that there was no place like home.

As a final carrot to Dempster's readers, he let drop that he was off to Barbados to write his third book. The plot of it was known to only four people, including his agent, the Foreign Secretary's wife Deborah Owen.

He did not say if he himself was one of the four. Nor did he say if they included his publisher, Tom Maschler.

Maschler saw Jeffrey from time to time when the latter was not grappling with his new novel in Barbados, promoting the previous one in Tokyo, or removing horses from beneath the picture in New York with Cork Smith. He was, not unnaturally, pleased at the way the first two books had sold, and was looking forward to the third.

So it was with some excitement, late in 1978, that he unwrapped the new 500-page slab of manuscript from Deborah Owen via Cork Smith and Jeffrey Archer.

'Jeffrey,' Deborah told Maschler, 'wants a lot of money for this one.'

Maschler noted the title: *Kane and Abel*.

At home, he started reading.

Kane and Abel was not a thriller. Nor, on the other hand, was it by any stretch of the imagination a 'literary' work. But neither was it as charmless as *Shall We Tell The President?* Maschler read on until the truth dawned on him.

This was a saga.

'I am not,' Maschler said to himself, 'into sagas.'

He kept reading, though, and he finished it.

'Now,' he would recall later, 'there is absolutely no doubt in my mind that had *Kane and Abel* come to me as a first novel, I would have turned it down. Not because I would not have recognised it was saleable. I would just have said: "This is not our writer. This is not a Jonathan Cape book."

'However, for the first time without exception in my life, I find I have discovered a "commercial" writer. Furthermore, he's one whom eight other buggers who publish "commercial" writers didn't have the nous to take.

'What am I going to do?'

Maschler was in a dilemma. Having stumbled upon this page-turning blockbuster, was he to forgo it in the sure knowledge that someone else would make an enormous success? He decided to show it to Cape's Managing Director, Graham C. Greene, and Publicity Director, Tony Colwell.

They thought the same as Maschler: (a) it was clearly a blockbuster, and (b) it was clearly not a Jonathan Cape book.

'*Jeffrey wants a lot of money for this one.*'

Maschler decided to grasp the nettle. 'She says he wants a lot of money,' he told Greene and Colwell, 'there are only one or two things she can have in her head. £25,000, or £50,000.

'I think we should not mess about with £25,000. I think we should offer £50,000. Because then we are really going to feel we've got to get behind this book. We have got to do a major campaign, we've got to do what the commercial boys do, which we can do just as well as they can. Any twerp can do that. Agreed?'

They agreed.

Maschler picked up the receiver and dialled Deborah Owen's telephone number.

'Deborah? It's Tom. Jeffrey's book is extraordinary. It's fantastic. It's terrific. We're going to offer you £50,000.'

'Oh,' said Mrs Owen.

Maschler was temporarily speechless:

'Wait a minute, Deborah,' he said, 'you don't mean to say you were thinking of more than that?'

'No,' she said, 'no, it's not that. But I must talk to Jeffrey about this.'

'Deborah,' Maschler said, 'aren't you pleased? This is Jonathan Cape! 50,000 quid, Deborah! The book is amazing, but you can't tell me you were expecting £100,000!'

Slowly, but surely, a terrible fear was beginning to dawn on Maschler. Deborah Owen had assumed he would offer well below what he had. That way, having already decided with Jeffrey, she could take the book elsewhere.

Maschler tried to keep up the momentum. 'Okay, Deborah,' he said, 'you do that. You talk to him. Get back to me tomorrow, would you, or the day after?'

A couple of days later, his telephone rang. It was Deborah Owen. 'Of course,' she said, 'Jeffrey's very pleased. But he wants to know how you *really* feel about this book. How do you *really* feel?'

Maschler lost his patience. 'Deborah,' he said, 'this is going too f—ing far! I mean, steady, will you? If you want me to tell you or to tell Jeffrey that this is a great book or a major work of literature, I'm not prepared to do that. It's absurd. I've told you, I think he's done it wonderfully, it's fabulous, it's a wonderful read, it's great stuff, but FOR GOD'S SAKE LET'S GET THIS INTO PROPORTION!'

He was quite upset. After all, an author whom he had discovered was now turning down an advance twenty times that paid for his first book. His second book, too, had been published for a modest sum under the standard second book option. The third book reeked of paydirt. Now it was slipping away, and there was nothing Maschler could do about it.

'I don't think Jeffrey thought "I can't run this guy the way I can run those guys",' Maschler said later. 'I think the reason he left is that he really wanted to be admired. And he wasn't going to get it from me. I wasn't prepared to say: "Jeffrey, I publish all these people, but Jeffrey, you are the greatest."'

Deborah Owen sold *Kane and Abel* for £50,000 to Hodder and Stoughton. Hodder and Stoughton of course owned Coronet, who already published Jeffrey in paperback. Jeffrey seemed pleased: he would dedicate his sixth book to Coronet's Managing and Sales Directors. Maschler and Jeffrey remained on friendly terms for the time being. Jeffrey particularly enjoyed suggesting to Maschler that his own turnover was now greater than that of Jonathan Cape. Considerable sums of money would continue to flow into Jonathan Cape from the sales of the first two books. But, after the affair of the third, Maschler did no more business with Deborah Owen.

In fact, it would be fair to say that relations between them were never quite the same. 'I said to her at the time and I would say to her now,' he would maintain, 'what you should have done was write to me, saying: "Listen Tom, we're terribly grateful for what you have done. But Jeffrey is now going in another direction and it isn't for you. He's not going to feel at ease with you and you're not going to feel at ease with him."

'That's what she should have done.'

A few years later, Jeffrey's ex-publisher was interviewed about his long and distinguished career in publishing. Among other interesting tales, he not unnaturally retailed the story of himself, Jeffrey Archer and the Nobel Prize. Jeffrey, by then a million-selling international blockbuster and the very epitome of bankability, was not amused. Nor was Mrs Owen, who chided Maschler for being so unkind about her protégé. Perhaps she had forgotten that hell had no fury like a publisher scorned.

Maschler did not see Jeffrey thereafter. But reminders of what might have been continued to haunt him. One day on

Reading station, he found the entire bookstall display apparently given over to one book: the new Jeffrey Archer. As a salesman, the latter's ex-publisher could not resist asking the bookstall attendant how such a single-minded display had come about. It transpired that Jeffrey had visited the windswept platform personally, and taken the bookstall attendant out to lunch.

Maschler had sold a lot of books in his time. But even he knew when he was beaten. 'I mean, how on earth,' he said, later, 'can you argue with a guy who is prepared to go *that* far to achieve his ambitions?'

Tom Maschler would go on waiting for his letter from Deborah Owen. A few years later, after Jonathan Cape had been through financial difficulties, the company was bought up and Maschler himself received around £6 million. This at least brought his personal turnover a fraction closer to Jeffrey's.

For Jeffrey had paid off most of his old debts. The Conservatives had not won an election, but he did not go into tax exile. Nor did he slacken his contact with certain lobby correspondents. He stopped telling people, though, that there was nothing sadder than the sight of an ex-MP hanging around Westminster. Instead, he started to tell them that success was nothing to be ashamed of. The country, he said, was lying on its back because of its negative attitude, when it should be getting up and doing something about it.

It was a broadside worthy of the late Sir Cyril Osborne. Such thoroughly sound statements would not go unnoticed forever, surely; least of all by another self-made product of Lincolnshire, the Leader of the Opposition Conservative Party and soon-to-be Prime Minister, Mrs Margaret Thatcher.

The Commercial Traveller

Kane and Abel was published in Britain on 9 September 1979. Jeffrey told people he had rewritten the opening lines at least a hundred times. Now at last it seemed he had got them right:

She only stopped screaming when she died. It was then that he started to scream.

Thus began the saga on which the Archer-Owen-Smith-Hodder team rested their hopes. *Kane and Abel* is the story of two men born on the same day in 1906. One is an illegitimate and impoverished Pole, the other the privileged and wealthy child of a Boston banking family. The illegitimate and impoverished Pole escapes from a Russian labour camp to America where he sets up a hotel chain. The privileged and wealthy Bostonian builds up his family banking empire. The two megalomaniacs cross swords with each other for the next forty-five years and die. Their children outlive them, as children are wont to do.

The book, it need hardly be added, was pitched squarely at the American mass market. Deborah Owen's hard sell had targeted the paperback book-buyers of New York, Pittsburgh, Cleveland, Los Angeles, Minneapolis, Milwaukee, Chicago, Atlanta, Nashville: the path trodden by her protégé on his previous promotional tour of the United States. In New York, Cork Smith and Jeffrey had worked hard at removing the horses under the picture, so hard, in fact, that in spite of its length, Jeffrey was instantly suspicious of anyone who suggested it might be shorter.

Jeffrey's admiration for Cork Smith knew no bounds. The would-be Nobel Laureate even started telling people that

Smith edited him the way Maxwell Perkins had edited Scott Fitzgerald. 'Cork is a great man,' Jeffrey would say, 'it makes your book better to have a man of that calibre look at it.'

After they had finished *Kane and Abel*, Smith asked him what more he wanted out of life. Jeffrey said he wanted to write one book which gained him respect all over the world as a writer.

Smith said, 'You'll never do it, Jeffrey.'

Jeffrey appeared genuinely upset. So Smith, perhaps taking pity on him, said, 'But of all the men I have ever worked with, you are the greatest storyteller.'

This in itself was no mean compliment, coming from a man of Smith's standing. But it was not enough for Jeffrey. As Tom Maschler had already suspected, Jeffrey really wanted to be admired as a great *writer*. So he had recourse, once more, to his gift for inaccurate précis.

'I wept,' he would say. 'It was one of the greatest moments of my life. He knew Steinbeck, Hemingway, knew them all; and he acknowledged me above all the great giants.'

Whenever he telephoned the Hodder and Stoughton offices, he refused to speak to anyone but his editor in person, even to arrange a squash match. The atmosphere created in the Hodder offices by a telephone call from Jeffrey was electric as people dropped what they were doing.

The *Kane and Abel* publication party was held at Alembic House. Journalists and other guests were greeted by blown-up photographs of the bestseller lists with Jeffrey's name prominent. Inside the tenth-floor apartment, among the Leon Underwoods, the Russell Flints and the Graham Sutherlands, the scrum included Hollywood director Otto Preminger (himself shortly to experience cash-flow problems) and Mary. Mary's distrust of journalists did not seem to have softened on closer contact with the overpaid merchants of fear. She returned shortly afterwards to Cambridge. Jeffrey bounced around as usual, but this was one of the few occasions that his wife would be sighted at such a gathering.

Kane and Abel would be a success, of course, not just

because it was marketed as one but because of what Cork Smith recognised as Jeffrey's talent for remorseless self-promotion. The legend of Jeffrey's chequered past, of millions made, lost and remade, went down well with radio and TV interviewers from Boise, Idaho, to Blackburn, Lancashire. Authors in general were not good popular copy, but this one was different. Even his books were marketed as examples of the good, old-fashioned tradition of storytelling. 'You can only do what you can do,' he would later tell one interviewer, 'and if I had to write sex scenes with violence and bad language, I wouldn't be able to do it – I'm a storyteller, a rather gentle storyteller.'

Perhaps it was appropriate that the interviewer was from the National Westminster Bank's *Moneycare* magazine. Someone, in the cause of bankability, had certainly been able to write just those sorts of scenes into *Kane and Abel*.

Kane and Abel makes interesting reading for those willing to indulge in some good old-fashioned literary criticism. It is after all a book about missing parents and fortunes lost and found, written by a fatherless one-time near-bankrupt. The men in it are all unbridled over-reachers; the female characters are one-dimensional and unconvincing.

The sex scenes, violence and bad language bear the hallmarks of a calculated come-on to a jaded mass-fiction market. The beginning of the 550-page book, over which Jeffrey laboured so lovingly, is followed within sixty pages by a three-page description of a teenage virgin being gang-raped to death in the presence of her adopted brother. Fifty pages later, there is a two-page judicial amputation scene; the word 'fuck' appears in various places; two teenagers have sex in a lifeboat; a schoolboy is seduced by his housemaster's wife; Abel goes to a prostitute; he has sex on a Persian carpet.

These scenes are counterbalanced by an odd and at times touching naïveté when it comes to good old storytelling. An attractive woman either has a business qualification or she has long hair falling loose and wayward to her shoulders.

Undergraduate life is characterised by a cheery, pipe-smoking bonhomie and a camaraderie that lasts forever. In spite of Cork Smith's labours there are still some horses under the picture, which Mary would once have removed free, gratis and for nothing.

Kane and Abel was sold for paperback in America for half a million dollars.

Jeffrey had not been idle in the period between finishing the manuscript and the publication party. As well as possessing a good eye for a painting, he was still a keen theatregoer. The former policeman who had played Puck took himself off to the Old Bailey, where he was researching a courtroom drama. Characteristically, he sent a manuscript of it to Otto Preminger and the producer of the West End's longest-running play, *The Mousetrap*.

He was also house-hunting again. But he had no intention of selling the Alembic House apartment with its views of the Tate Gallery, National Theatre and especially the Houses of Parliament. The Houses of Parliament were creeping more and more into the background of photographs of Jeffrey.

That winter, he told a journalist how he had woken up one morning to find himself over £400,000 in debt. It was the good, old-fashioned story he liked to tell; how a bank statement had fluttered through the letterbox of The Boltons one day that said he was £427,727 overdrawn. It hadn't been his fault, he said. He had had no doubt as to the proper course of action.

'I didn't dare go bankrupt,' he told the journalist. 'My father was a colonel in the Somerset Light Infantry and he would have killed me.'

By curious coincidence, a Somerset Light Infantry sergeant called William Archer did win a Distinguished Conduct Medal in the First World War; a few years later his grandson would send photographs of him to the regimental archives. The regimental secretary, himself a lieutenant-colonel, would subsequently report that there was no connection between the valiant sergeant and the late William Archer, journalist, who had courted Lola Cook in wartime London.

Jeffrey seemed obsessed with finding a past with which he could be happy. Now that he was rich, far richer than he had ever claimed to be in the Arrow days, he took great pains to prevent the politically damaging image of the bankrupt from resurfacing. When the *Sunday People* inadvertently described him as having been one in an otherwise highly flattering article, he forced them to publish a retraction. Even recent rejection was rewritten to achieve bankability. When Preminger showed no interest in either his play or the film rights to *Kane and Abel*, Jeffrey lost no time in telling journalists that Preminger's offer of 'half a million dollars' was just not worth thinking about. Mrs Owen, too, played along when the rights were eventually sold, as a TV 'mini' series.

'I think we've decided to go for quality and stick with London Weekend,' she told reporters loftily, 'although there's obviously less money,' she added.

The house the Archers eventually settled on came with a literary legend of its own as well as vacant possession. The Old Vicarage, Grantchester, was a couple of miles from Cambridge and reachable by punt. The owners were Lola and Peter Ward, whose father, Dudley, had briefly accommodated the First World War poet Rupert Brooke as a lodger. Thus had arisen the legend of 'Rupert Brooke's house' behind the pretty village church whose clock he immortalised in his poetry. Brooke himself had succumbed to his own Byronic legend, dying not of wounds heroically sustained but from a mosquito bite on a hospital ship off Gallipoli.

The house was of seventeenth-century origin, and apart from the legend came complete with three and a half acres of garden and Victorian folly. Jeffrey set up an office there. Outside it he erected a souvenir: a sign that read 'Rural District of Louth'. Inside, he installed a secretary and a powerful Olivetti Super ETS 1010 word-processor. The house and garden were Mary's domain; she once said they were the third child she never had. Mary worked hard at belonging in the village, some of whose inhabitants initially found her precise and clinical approach a little disconcerting. As a musically-minded Anglican, she would blossom as the local choirmistress.

The Archers spent much of that year apart both at home and abroad while the two boys, now eight and six, stayed at home with a nanny. Mary lectured and attended conferences and Jeffrey went about his own business. He researched his new novel, *The Prodigal Daughter*. He revised *Not A Penny More, Not A Penny Less* with Cork Smith, removing horses under the picture; he would do the same a few years later (though not with Smith) with *Shall We Tell The President?*

He also revised his CV, carefully building the politically more acceptable image of himself as an honest investor who had paid the price of wisdom rather than folly.

'My parents,' he told one journalist, 'had set certain standards for me and I not only lived by them, but believed everyone else lived by them, too.

'At first, losing my career hit me harder than losing the money. I loved the House of Commons but, faced with bankruptcy, I had to resign. It was the only decent course.'

The press, he said, had created this whizzkid image: 'They believed that everything I touched was bound to do well. My friends believed it. And I began to believe it.

'In one day I lost £427,727 . . .'

He rewrote his entry in *Who's Who*: he changed 'Author and has-been politician' to 'Author and politician'.

Mrs Thatcher, whose own '*Who's Who*' entry now read 'Prime Minister', took note.

A Quiver Full Of Arrows was Jeffrey's first collection of short stories. He dedicated it to Robin and Carolyn Oakley. Oakley, a political columnist, later on *The Times*, had been a friend and regular dinner companion since his House of Commons days as a newsworthy young MP. His name was attached to one of the heroes in the rewritten version of *Not*

A Penny More, Not A Penny Less. Now, in Jeffrey's new short story collection, he became Secretary of Cambridge University Cricket Club.

The stories were the closest Jeffrey had come so far to the good old-fashioned storytelling of which he professed to be an exponent. They did not attempt to be bankable in so far as they contained neither the callous sex scenes, violence nor bad language of *Kane and Abel*. They frequently took place in a square-jawed, adventurous past, reminiscent of John Buchan and Percy F. Westerman. They were fractionally more plausible than the novels, but constrained by the device of the pay-off. In their way, they also said quite a lot about Jeffrey.

'Old Love' tells of a marriage made in Oxford. Husband and wife are rival academics in the same field, both assured by themselves and others that they are the stars of their year. She plays the spinet, as in real life did Mary. She is also by far the more formidable of the two, if the male trepidation unwittingly betrayed in the narrative is anything to go by. In spite of this, and the stilted dialogue, they manage to survive half a century of marriage. When she dies, he kills himself.

'The Century', too, has an idealised Oxford background. The anonymous narrator retells a cricketing yarn told in the hearty, all-male environment of Vincent's. This is not the Vincent's of George Harrison's urine for sale, but the Vincent's of Wisden, Bradman, Hobbs and the beating the ''Tabs'. The latter come from a place, we are informed, 'cartographically described on the map [sic] as Cambridge'.

'One Night Stand' deals with marital infidelity as an in-joke between two married men who have been friends since schooldays. The woman in question is divorced, but only available when one of her two married admirers comes to New York. There is an implausibility the size of the Empire State Building in the idea of an unhappily divorced woman happily having an affair with a happily married man. But this is no ordinary happily married man, either.

'Why would any man want to divorce you, Debbie?'

'Oh, nothing very original, I'm afraid. He fell in love with a twenty-two-year-old blonde and left his thirty-two-year-old wife.'

'Silly man. He should have had an affair with the twenty-two-year-old blonde and remained faithful to his thirty-two-year-old wife.'

'Isn't that a contradiction in terms?'

'Oh, no, I don't think so. I've never thought it unnatural to desire someone else. After all, it's a long life to go through and be expected never to want another woman.'

'I'm not so sure I agree with you,' said Debbie thoughtfully, 'I would like to have remained faithful to one man.'

Oh hell, thought Michael, not a very auspicious philosophy.

'He's not good at writing about women,' Mary would say, in a rare interview, 'he's never been terribly interested in women as characters. He likes doing things – running, jumping, politics, whatever it might be.'

Another journalist asked for her views on marital infidelity. 'It can be tolerated,' said Mary, 'more than indifference. That is the absolute killer for any marriage.'

The Vincent's man, who had married one of the brightest girls of her year, went to the Bahamas. He was trying to finish *The Prodigal Daughter*.

He was also profiled in the popular British TV programme, *This Is Your Life*. The programme traditionally began with the subject apparently being taken by surprise. The former OUAC President and ex-MP was taken by surprise jogging across Westminster Bridge. On the equally popular BBC radio programme, *Desert Island Discs*, Jeffrey told the good, old-fashioned story of how the bank statement had landed on the doormat of The Boltons house reading £427,727 o/d. The seventh record he chose to be played on the programme was Mac Davis's 'Oh Lord, It's Hard To Be Humble (When You're Perfect In Every Way)'.

*

The Prodigal Daughter was published in Britain on 5 July 1982. Jeffrey made no comment this time about how many times he had rewritten the opening lines:

'PRESIDENT OF THE UNITED STATES,' she replied.

'I can think of more rewarding ways of bankrupting myself,' said her father, as he removed the spectacles from the end of his nose and peered at his daughter over the top of his newspaper.

'Don't be frivolous, papa. President Roosevelt proved to us that there can be no greater calling than public service.'

At this point, most fathers would have put an eleven-year-old daughter who spoke like this over their knees and given her a lesson in *realpolitik*. Jeffrey, who had no daughter or sisters and whose inability to portray women as convincing characters had been noted by his wife and others, allows his eleven-year-old to go on to become President of the United States.

In a shrewd marketing move, he had already rewritten his Presidential assassination thriller *Shall We Tell The President?* with the obnoxious eleven-year-old (grown up a little) in the starring role. Not content with this, however, he also presented the first half of *The Prodigal Daughter* as a rehash of *Kane and Abel*.

The result was worthy of that review the *New York Times* had given *Shall We Tell The President?* Unfortunately, this time President Reagan churlishly refused to resign in protest at being replaced by a woman so lacking in substance. Florentyna Rosnovski made even him look like a deep political thinker.

Even the Archer buff is hard-pressed to find items of interest in this book, which extends the frontiers of pro-American sycophancy to new and hitherto unknown limits. The frosty little girl's governess is named after Mary's Headmistress at Cheltenham Ladies' College; the telephone number given for the Bank of America is in fact one of Jeffrey's; and there are some passages which appear to have escaped even the combined intellect of the Archer-Owen-Smith-Hodder fiction factory:

Florentyna Rosnovski never referred to the conversation again for twenty-two years . . .

Jeffrey meanwhile set about the real business of selling.

Kind journalists converged on the tenth floor of the windy, modern tower on the south bank of the Thames. Enthralled, as if for the first time, they listened and went back to their cuttings libraries for the good, old-fashioned stories of how Jeffrey had helped raise a million first for Oxfam and then for himself; how one day, suddenly, the fateful bank statement had dropped through the letterbox of a magnificent house in The Boltons.

The author of these and other tales was on the road again; only this time, the whole country was his constituency. Directors of Hodder and Stoughton and Coronet had replaced the constituency workers for his cause. Sales representatives, bookstall attendants, radio interviewers, television make-up artists and cameramen had to be bludgeoned and flattered. It was a portrait of the artist as a salesman.

Mary pursued her own solitary path through the groves of academe. The boys were away at prep school, but there was still so much to do: her work at Newnham and Trinity and her research into the photo conversion of solar energy, her own book which was much-awaited; the scrubbed and spotless Vicarage with its ten rooms, three bathrooms and housekeeper to maintain; the church choir to train; and the garden. The garden was becoming more and more an object of absorption for Mary. Having come to Grantchester with little experience of horticulture, she had educated herself on the subject with the same systematic sense of order she brought to everything and everyone else in her life.

The garden was also the scene once a year for a summer party to celebrate Jeffrey and Mary's wedding anniversary. There were plenty of familiar faces at these gatherings amidst the Krug champagne, the Pimms and the waitresses. Sir Gerald Duke, the Fitzwilliams, Roger Sharpley, Nick Lloyd, David and Deborah Owen all congregated at one time or another on the lawn where Rupert Brooke had once read his poetry to D. H. Lawrence.

Jeffrey, for his part, was still trying to put his own wilderness behind him. This was the period of the first Conservative government under Mrs Thatcher, and the ex-MP was broadcasting to her on any frequency he could commandeer for the purpose.

'I'm often accused of being an opportunist,' he informed one journalist, 'but as I see it that's a good thing – if you see something you want, go for it. As a country we should be more opportunist.'

He knew the only way he was going to climb back into politics was by slogging unpaid round the village halls of Britain, impressing the constituency parties with his buccaneering style and No. 10, Downing Street and Conservative Central Office with his workload. He had this on good authority from the political correspondents with whom he had deliberately kept in touch since his days as a newsworthy young MP. He had also kept a close watch, with their help, on the irresistible rise of Margaret Thatcher. The Prime Minister, in turn, did not conceal her approval of the unsubsidised, enterprising manner in which the personable ex-MP had slogged his way out of his own personal recession. The fact that he was now wandering the shires in the cause of a leaner, fitter Britain began to be noticed at Central Office.

Westminster began to dominate his thoughts in the way that it did the view from the tenth-floor apartment. He referred to it as his 'Westminster flat', even though it was on the other side of the Thames in Lambeth. He had been filmed jogging over Westminster Bridge for *This Is Your Life*. He was invariably photographed against the background of the Palace of Westminster.

Twenty years earlier, in the Oxfam offices on the Banbury Road, the publicity-hungry young education student had told

Richard Exley and Pat Davidson how he was going to become Prime Minister. Now, in his rented villa in the Bahamas, and in the folly at the bottom of Mary's garden, the forty-three-year-old millionaire turned his mind to another good, old-fashioned story. This one would begin with the young Conservative victor of a by-election taking his seat in the House of Commons. One of its less elegant lines would assume ironic significance for Jeffrey. Even as he and others laboured manfully over the manuscript, other voices were beginning to make themselves heard: 'Fleet Street', the line went, 'are not quite the bunch of shits everyone imagines them to be.'

In the case of *Private Eye*, however, an editor might well have removed the 'not' from the above sentence. The magazine had been a dedicated seeker and source of Archer gossip since the days of Berkeley and the UNA. In a gripping new series entitled 'Great Bestsellers of the World', it was inevitable that the liverish *Eye* should turn its gaze on Hodder and Stoughton's most bankable author.

The *Eye*'s erratic report reserved its full scorn for the Archer-Owen-Hodder creative team. It singled out Jeffrey's editor at Hodder, Richard Cohen.

Persons outside the book trade gave the story little thought, and those inside had heard it all before. Jeffrey, so scurrilous and uninformed sources within the trade whispered, relied heavily on his editor.

Graham Greene never had so much trouble.

As the next Archer novel neared the printers, its author wandered the shires in the hope of a telephone call from Margaret Thatcher: 'I think I'm frustrated,' Jeffrey told a journalist on the eve of publication of his new novel. 'I actively want to return to public life, though not as a Member of Parliament.

'But I want to do something worthwhile for my country, for Margaret Thatcher. I've been working very hard earning my spurs and there are rumours,' he added, 'that Margaret is going to offer me something.'

So far, with the exception of the rumour he himself had just started, these rumours had been confined exclusively to No. 10, Downing Street and the corridors and tea urns of Conservative Central Office. There had been speculation about Jeffrey for some time at 32 Smith Square, SW1, the home of the permanent civil service of the Conservative Party. He was, after all, rich, he was ideologically sound, he was ambitious and he was keen to make a contribution. What were they waiting for?

One of the things they were waiting for was the departure of John Selwyn Gummer.

Gummer was Chairman of the Conservative Party. But he was a peace-time appointment and the Conservative Government was gradually approaching its mid-life crisis. The recruitment of extra personnel to deal with the run-up to the next election was becoming a matter of some interest in some sections of Central Office. Another thing they were waiting for, then, was the first smell, the first sighting, of a General Election.

Jeffrey would have to wait a little longer for the telephone call from Downing Street. He continued to rush around the village halls and give interviews. In his imagination, though, the stage was set for his return. His new novel revealed once and for all the world Jeffrey missed most and from which he could not bear to face the prospect of being barred forever. It was the world of the Central Lobby, the Speaker's windows, the committee rooms, the back benches and Annie's Bar: a real world that cannot be forgotten by anyone who has entered it; and that no one has ever quite managed to recreate in fiction.

First Among Equals was published in Great Britain on 2 July 1984. 'Every detail in this one,' Jeffrey told the *Mail on Sunday*'s *YOU* magazine, 'has to be 100 percent accurate.'

The *Mail on Sunday* agreed. In a bold move, it had just paid him £90,000 for the right to reproduce the entire novel in four successive issues, and spent £500,000 on a TV advertising campaign. Hodder and Stoughton had already received advance orders for 100,000 copies. The Archer-Owen-Cohen team seemed to have found a formula that enabled them to print money.

Jeffrey, meanwhile, did not deny rumours that he had sold the television rights to Granada TV for the sum of £1. 'They will have to pay extra when it is produced,' he added, 'but if they give me a production like *Brideshead Revisited* or the *Raj Quartet*, something I'll be really proud of, I won't be too interested in the money.'

First Among Equals tells the story of four ambitious MPs over three decades and culminates in one of their number becoming Prime Minister. The questions of who does it, and how, are adroitly posed and answered against a rich Westminster background. It was no coincidence that Jeffrey's two most readable books would stem from his own experience. Nor, since his experience was of foiled ambition, was it surprising that the one-time near-bankrupt ex-MP who wanted to be Prime Minister should come up with what *The Times*'s Nicholas Shrimpton memorably described as a 'mechanical but deeply-felt fantasy'.

For amidst all the hype and publicity, the interweaving of real and imaginary figures, the burden of trying to be 100 percent accurate, there is a good old-fashioned story trying to be told. But it would be a mistake to look for political ideas. *First Among Equals* is in some respects Jeffrey's fictional autobiography.

If his characters behave according to the demands of plot rather than human nature, they still have a flicker of life in them. This is because they have been cajoled into forgetting they are basically fictional stereotypes, and into believing they are front-runners in the race for No. 10, Downing Street. Jeffrey has done to them what he did to his schoolboy relay teams.

Nor does it matter that his notion of No. 10, Downing Street and the Houses of Parliament was formed by his adolescent fantasies, and by his relatively brief career as a back-bench MP. The effects of being out of politics for a long time would make themselves known to him only in real life. Jeffrey's new fiction, meanwhile, was well received, and not only by the obscure provincial newspapers whose reviews Coronet were so fond of reproducing inside the cover of his paperback editions.

The book also charts the domestic vicissitudes of the characters. Simon Kerslake, a career Conservative, marries a doctor who distrusts the media and detests politicians. He also remortgages the house without telling her, to disastrous effect. She comes to support him, but he does not end up as Prime Minister.

Andrew Fraser, the Tory's son who becomes a Labour member, was described as 'puny' at school until he took up body-building. He and his wife adopt a child of mixed-race, as Lola had adopted Elizabeth Fullerton.

Raymond Gould, the grammar school boy who marries too early, is blackmailed by a prostitute. He consults his lawyer, refuses to hand over the money and ends up as Prime Minister.

The Press are remarkably taciturn. As he said in the line that would become famous: 'Fleet Street are not quite the bunch of shits everyone imagines them to be.'

Fleet Street were then directing their unkind attentions at the growing number of peccadilloes, banana skins and blatant cover-ups mandatory to any mid-term government. This government, however, seemed particularly accident-prone. Mrs Thatcher and her Press Secretary Bernard Ingham faced a barrage of awkward questions about the sinking of the Argentine battleship *Belgrano*, worsening unemployment, Northern Ireland and other ticklish matters.

Home Secretary Leon Brittan had been a friend of Jeffrey's since his time as a young lawyer in the days of Archer *v.* Berkeley. Jeffrey had made one of the earliest speeches of his comeback campaign in Brittan's old Cleveland and Whitby constituency. Eighteen months later Brittan, the youngest Home Secretary in living memory and a personal protégé of the Prime Minister, would fall on yet another banana skin after the controversy concerning the Westland helicopter company. But for the time being, Brittan had the ear of the First Among Equals.

At around this time, a visiting journalist to the Alembic House apartment found himself witness to a conversation concerning No. 10, Downing Street.

A telephone rang in the middle of the interview and Jeffrey was handed the receiver. The journalist admired the paintings for a few moments, while an apologetic Jeffrey dealt with whoever was calling. But the journalist soon found his attention being directed back from the Underwoods, Sutherlands and Vuillards.

The conversation appeared to be a rather interesting one: 'Yes BERNARD. I should be delighted of course. No, BERNARD. No, of course I won't tell anybody . . . and please do give MARGARET my regards. I look forward to seeing MARGARET . . . MARGARET . . . at NUMBER 10, tomorrow. Goodbye, BERNARD.'

The Times diarist also came to hear rumours of the impending lunch between Mrs Thatcher and the best PR man ever interviewed by the *Grimsby Evening Telegraph*. When they published the story *The Times* received a telephone call from the irate author:

'Totally untrue!' he yelled down the receiver. 'I won't just be taking you to the Press Council for this. I'll be taking you to the highest court in the land!

'Furthermore,' he concluded, 'you have personally ruined my lunch with MARGARET tomorrow!'

Jeffrey's lunch with Margaret was not ruined of course, although the exact nature of it would go undisclosed until the Prime Minister's memoirs. The consequences would be revealed somewhat sooner. Jeffrey, meanwhile, brushed up his CV and got on with his new novel.

The new novel was provisionally called 'The Czar's Crown'. As usual, Jeffrey had laboured lovingly over the opening lines:

'It's a fake,' said the Russian leader, staring down at the small exquisite painting he held in his hands.

'That isn't possible,' replied his Politburo colleague. 'The Tsar's icon of St George and the Dragon has been in the Winter Palace at Leningrad under heavy guard for over fifty years.'

That September, the former MP for Louth went back to his old constituency, reshaped in the hated boundary changes and renamed Brigg and Cleethorpes. It was his first visit for ten years. He had left under a cloud, but returned as the prodigal son to his faithful admirers, and a new generation who knew little of the real events of that fateful summer of '74.

The occasion was the *Grimsby Evening Telegraph* inaugural Literary Luncheon. The idea of inviting Jeffrey was an inspired one, and though credit was unclaimed, it may reasonably be awarded at least in part to Pat Otter.

The Luncheon was advertised for Friday 21 September 1984, at the Winter Gardens, Cleethorpes. Within three days, all 320 tickets had been sold and could have been sold again three times over.

Jeffrey bounded around, saying hello to everyone in his usual way, including Pat Otter. Otter had lost contact if not sight of Jeffrey since the days when the latter used to pull up in his white Daimler ANY 1 outside the *Telegraph* offices on the Cleethorpes Road. But he still remembered that time he and his wife, Eva, went to the Brigsley house for Sunday lunchtime drinks with the independent-minded Archers. It was one of only two occasions on which his wife ever met Jeffrey.

But Otter was always being amazed by him, and ten years on he would not be disappointed. 'Great to see you, Pat,' said Jeffrey, and then, quick as a flash, 'how's Eva?'

Jean Blackbourn was there; she was still Conservative agent for Brigg and Cleethorpes. So was Mrs Fitzwilliams. So were the Mayors and Mayoresses of Grimsby and Cleethorpes. Major Fitzwilliams was in the Chair. The organist, Jack Lawton, played 'Who Wants To Be A Millionaire?' as Jeffrey entered the packed ballroom. There were copies of his books everywhere. Even the menus were bound in the covers of his novels. He stared from the back of them in a photograph taken by former Labour Defence Secretary Denis Healey. The Houses of Parliament stood ghostlike in the background.

The Bishop of Grimsby said Grace, and everyone tucked into their Melon Benedictine, Sole Véronique and Chocolate Savarin. Major Fitzwilliams toasted the Queen, and paid tribute to the *Telegraph*'s noble attempt to enrich the cultural life of the area.

Then he turned to Jeffrey. 'My Lords, Ladies and Gentlemen,' he declaimed. 'Your Grace. Our guest is one of the world's best storytellers. Jeffrey Archer . . .'

Jeffrey was already on his feet. Microphone in hand, he launched straight into the good, old-fashioned story he had been telling since the early days of his four-year comeback, from a village hall in Cleveland and Whitby to No. 10, Downing Street. He was unstoppable. In five seconds he had them in the palm of his hand, and within ten he could have been reciting the Grimsby telephone directory. He spoke in his clipped, alternately hilarious and sepulchral tones, as one observer noted, that had the effect of prompting the audience into laughter for which he then proceeded to scold them. As more and more pairs of eyes, especially female ones, turned in the direction of the trim, presentable figure in the blazer and flannels, so more and more folk fell under the spell of one of the world's best storytellers: '*Exactly £427,727 overdrawn . . . 142 years to pay that off on a House of Commons salary . . . Not A Penny More, Not A Penny Less . . . 1,172,000 copies sold . . . You can throw aside a 9 to 5 job if you have to . . . Look at me, I did. . . .*'

'I have never fully recovered from the fact that I no longer represent you,' he added. 'But today, it is wonderful to come home.'

The *Telegraph*'s editor proposed the vote of thanks and announced that Jeffrey would be autographing copies of his books that afternoon; proceeds would go to the local lifeboat fund.

The next day, the *Telegraph* carried the full story. By that time, the prodigal son had come and gone again. But his friends in Lincolnshire would continue to have a little-known and far-reaching influence on the political career of Jeffrey Archer.

That autumn the peccadilloes, banana skins and cover-ups continued to trouble the second Thatcher government. The scandal of Cecil Parkinson and Sara Keays still haunted Conservative Central Office, where people referred to Parkinson's Chairmanship as a golden age. Cecil was professional, he was adored by all the women in flowery hats and he had a nice way with the cleaners. John Selwyn Gummer enjoyed a warm relationship with his staff, but he was not in the same league as Parkinson, whose subsequent political rehabilitation was never in doubt.

Neither Parkinson nor Gummer would have begrudged Jeffrey praise for his toiling in the shires; but nor would they have credited him with altruistic motives. Jeffrey had clearly gained in stature among the Conservative Associations and in the eyes of the Prime Minister; but neither Parkinson nor Gummer, again, would very likely have encouraged the rumour that 'Margaret is soon going to offer me something.' It took an event that was both unexpected and tragic to bring Jeffrey closer in from the cold.

In November 1984, the week of the Conservative Party Conference, a massive bomb planted by the Provisional IRA exploded on an upper floor of the Grand Hotel, Brighton.

A number of people were killed. They included Roberta Wakeham, wife of the Government Chief Whip, John Wakeham. Many more were injured, some critically. These included Mrs Margaret Tebbit, wife of the Trade and Industry Secretary Norman Tebbit, who was also seriously injured and had to be dug out of the rubble by firemen. The Prime Minister miraculously escaped without injury.

The Brighton bomb, as it became known, would bring to

an end the active political career of Tebbit, who had become one of Mrs Thatcher's most trusted and ruthless operators. Although he would continue as Trade and Industry Secretary for a time, his own injuries and the paralysis suffered by his wife which resulted in her being confined to hospital, meant that his talents would have to be put to different use.

The appointment of Tebbit as Chairman of the Conservative Party nearly a year later, with a very sick wife and his own injuries still troubling him, would necessitate the unusual recruitment of a temporary surrogate to take on the more physically demanding tasks normally performed by the Chairman. These included toiling in the shires, rallying the Party faithful and selling the Party line.

It was not a policy-making job. Indeed, it was tailor-made for a committed Conservative of independent means and uncomplicated ideology. The right candidate might even end up with a seat in the Lords, if he kept his nose clean and the Conservative government was re-elected. But who, in these troubled times, possessed such unusual, almost old-fashioned qualities?

Jeffrey bounced around the country, selling his books and his brand of free-market revivalism to ever-increasing audiences. At the Conservative Women's Conference in London, there was near-adoration on the faces of the faithful. All he had to do was wave his arms about and speak in those clipped, alternately hilarious and sepulchral tones. It was Archermania. The stewards at the front included Jean Blackbourn. Miss Blackbourn thought it would have been nice to meet Jeffrey again. But she was not the sort of person to battle through crowds just to gaze at someone, whoever they might be.

In Lincolnshire, Mrs Fitzwilliams was given a direct order by her husband in her capacity as secretary. Major Fitzwilliams, as Chairman of the Brigg and Cleethorpes Conservative Association, asked her to take a letter. It was to the Prime Minister.

Was she aware, Major Fitzwilliams respectfully enquired, how much sterling work Jeffrey Archer was doing for the Party? Did she appreciate his flair for publicity and his sheer enthusiasm? Had she by any chance considered finding some post for him in these troubled times?

The MP for Brigg and Cleethorpes, now Michael Brown, was not impressed. But nor, it should be made clear, was Major Fitzwilliams' letter by any means the only one of its kind to arrive at No. 10, Downing Street. That, though, was surely the point. Moreover, Jeffrey's Lincolnshire friends had known him for a long time, an additional factor not lost on the most famous alumna of Kesteven and Grantham Girls' School. Mrs Thatcher was now facing her mid-term crisis with her customary ironclad certainty; and with an undiminished capacity for listening to presentable, self-made men with the future of the Party at heart.

Shortly afterwards, Mary and Jeffrey were invited for the weekend to Chequers, the Prime Minister's country residence. Mary still distrusted media people and politicians, but ultimately lined up with the Party faithful. She respected Mrs Thatcher as a political leader and a professional woman, while not necessarily sharing Jeffrey's apparently boundless enthusiasm for the First Among Equals. But for sheer *gravitas*, Chequers, like Jeffrey, was hard to ignore.

Such was the messy coalition of ambition and circumstance that led to one of the most flamboyant and controversial appointments in recent British politics. Wiser counsels than Mrs Thatcher would fail to prevail. Willie Whitelaw, Deputy Prime Minister and a man of tremendous influence over Party and Prime Minister, would be reported as regarding Jeffrey as 'an accident waiting to happen'. Former Prime Minister Edward Heath, who had opened the ill-fated Archer Gallery sixteen years earlier, made little secret of his opposition to her on this as on other matters.

But Whitelaw was ignored and Heath's status may be measured by the fact that anything he said against Jeffrey would immediately have enhanced the latter in the eyes of the Prime Minister. On Monday 2 September 1985, Leon Brittan became Trade and Industry Secretary, and a still far from healthy Norman Tebbit replaced John Selwyn Gummer as Chairman of the Conservative Party. This was a wartime appointment; the General Election was now officially in sight. That night, one of the world's best storytellers received a telephone call from the Prime Minister.

This time there was no need to drop heavy-handed hints to journalists. By the following evening, the whole of Fleet Street knew he was the new Deputy Chairman of the Conservative Party. Mary was still unaware of the latest news; she was lecturing at a conference somewhere near Naples. Jeffrey telephoned her and the boys in a state of excitement that was high even by his standards. After towering over them for so long in his imagination and in his penthouse on the tenth floor, the prodigal son had now truly returned to the real Houses of Parliament. And Deborah Owen was telling people that Jeffrey should be Prime Minister.

The Prodigal Son

The appointment of Jeffrey Archer as Deputy Chairman of the Conservative Party was variously hailed as an inspired piece of casting, an act of criminal lunacy, a last-ditch attempt to achieve credibility by a discredited government, and a piece of showbusiness gimmickry. As usual with Jeffrey, there were few neutral opinions on the matter. Labour Deputy Leader Roy Hattersley, in his own way a writer of a somewhat less bankable variety than Jeffrey, called the appointment 'gimmick made flesh'. At Conservative Central Office, too, there was a certain amount of scorn at the fact that 'the novelist' was back.

But Jeffrey had no plans to write any more novels while he was in his new job. Every detail in this new, real-life story had to be 100 percent accurate. Shortly after his appointment, he went on a progress around the offices with Mary. It was the only time she was conspicuously present at Smith Square.

He then set about arranging his office on the first floor, next to that of the Chairman. This, first and foremost, meant that some of the Vice-Chairmen had to give way, a fact that did not particularly please them. Such was the bold, innovative nature of the appointment, there had not been a Deputy Chairman for some time. A game of musical offices thus began, in which most people except Norman Tebbit moved round and Jeffrey moved in. It caused some amusement, mainly among those who had not been compelled to move, that the new Deputy Chairman kitted out his office with expensive furniture that far outdid everyone else's, including the Chairman's.

The Chairman, Norman Tebbit, made all the right noises. 'He will bring a touch of dash and style to the Party,' Tebbit told journalists, 'a rather different dash and a rather different style,' he added, 'from my own.'

Tebbit and Jeffrey did in fact get on quite well in the beginning. While Tebbit felt that he should have appointed his own Deputy, the reasons for this particular one being appointed, no matter by whom, were obvious. The Chairman was himself in bad physical condition after the Brighton bomb. While Margaret Tebbit was in Stoke Mandeville Hospital he was living in lodgings. His domestic life lacked both organisation and anchor, and was characterised by pain both physical and emotional; apart from his own injuries, there was the knowledge of what his career had done to his wife.

Tebbit wanted to be near his wife; he also wanted to stay in the Smith Square offices thinking up policies. He did not want to fulfil the traditional role of Party Chairman, which was to be out in the shires, rallying the faithful and diverting the flak from the Leader. He realised the advantages inherent in having a Deputy who was a rich man, who would not be a drain on Party funds and who did not appear to mind being apart from *his* wife for much of the time. Nor was Jeffrey a total political nonentity; in short, not only did he get on quite well with Jeffrey, he realised he needed him.

That was how the situation was perceived by Norman Tebbit.

Jeffrey would rapidly arrive at a different interpretation.

That autumn, the new Deputy Chairman seemed to have become his old self again. The General Election, in which several hundred constituencies and approximately thirty million people would determine the ideological colour of a nation, soon paled into insignificance compared with the return to prominence of the man who wanted to be its Prime Minister. The ruling Conservative Party, which had been in power for most of the century, as he once told Richard Exley, would surely benefit from a few home truths from its prodigal son.

'Naughty, naughty,' he told a journalist who asked his opinion on the claim of the Minister for the Arts that he could not live in London on £33,000 a year, 'what a bunch of wallies some of those Ministers are.'

He was right, of course. But it was a strange thing for a Conservative Party official to say to a journalist in the run-up to a General Election. Nor did he stop there.

'You wouldn't buy a used car from this government,' he told another straight-faced representative of Fleet Street.

David Faber was the latest recruit to Alembic House. Faber was a grandson of the former Tory Prime Minister Harold Macmillan. He was a personable young man with political ambitions and had already worked for Keith Best, the Conservative MP later prosecuted for taking Mrs Thatcher's exhortations to popular capitalism too far by making illegal multiple share applications. At Oxford, Faber had been a member of the Assassins' Club, the main purpose of which was to fulfil adolescent fantasies. He was not to be disappointed in his brief spell as right-hand man to Jeffrey Archer.

Three weeks or so after he was appointed, the new Deputy Chairman launched his own manifesto in none other than Nick Lloyd's *Daily Express*. The photograph showed Mrs Thatcher staring bravely into the future, flanked by her own loyal personal assistants, Norman and Jeffrey.

Jeffrey's message was a familiar one, in that he reiterated the Conservative manifesto, 1985-style, with the same, simple effectiveness that he had done the manifestos of 1974 and 1970. The ideological character of an era had always stuck to Jeffrey like fly-paper; the eleven years he had spent out of politics did not seem to have diminished his ability in this respect. But if the mouth from Louth was working as well as ever, the political nose would shortly reveal itself to be in need of tuning.

Two weeks later, Jeffrey was interviewed on the influential BBC Radio programme, *The World This Weekend*. He had just returned from a fact-finding trip to the unemployment black spots of the Midlands.

The interview, which lasted twenty minutes, began with the interviewer predictably asking about the present unemployment figures. What did the Deputy Chairman think of them?

Jeffrey said, 'I don't think there is a palatable way of bluffing these figures,' and then appeared to prove exactly that, by trying to do so. After a brief reference to the new Employment Secretary Lord Young, he proceeded to quote the example of his recent visit to the Midlands. In remarks which the embarrassed local councillors of Wellingborough would later demonstrate were not based on fact, he suggested that young people did not want to take the opportunities given to them. In short, they were work-shy.

As usual with Jeffrey, any point was worth making rather than none. The interviewer, perhaps sensing this, did not press too hard. Downstairs, the telephone switchboard at Broadcasting House was already over-heating.

The interviewer then gently raised the issue of youth demoralised by the prospect of long-term unemployment. Did he, the interviewer asked, think that this was a problem for the government?

Jeffrey did, but appeared to do so for unusual reasons. 'A lot of the reason they believe that,' he rapped, 'is because they are taught it in schools. There's a large group of schoolmasters and mistresses who take great pleasure in telling them to prepare for no job, that they have a right to claim every state benefit there is; there is a right to claim every advantage.

'You try telling the old that,' thundered the good old-fashioned storyteller, 'who fought for us in the last war, who are now collecting their old-age pensions.'

Somewhere in the circle of Hell reserved for right-wing knitwear manufacturers, the ghost of Sir Cyril Osborne raised his port glass in approval. Downstairs at Broadcasting House, the switchboard began to smoke.

Jeffrey thundered on, oblivious to the fact that he was now being allowed to do just that. 'The truth is,' he snarled, 'that many of the young are quite unwilling to move from their own areas. They are quite unwilling to put in a day's work ... I was unemployed with debts of £400,000 ... I know what unemployment is like ... getting off your backside ... no use saying that the figures are really three million ... make sure you don't cut this ...'

The interviewer gave him one last chance. Did he not agree, all the same, that there were tens of thousands of energetic, intelligent young people who had no prospect because there were no jobs for them?

Jeffrey said that he did, then immediately threw back the lifebuoy by returning to the 'example' of Wellingborough. He even asked the interviewer to 'explain' it.

The interviewer had thus far been under the naïve impression that he was speaking to the Deputy Chairman of the Conservative Party, and therefore to a man whose job it was to 'explain' matters pertaining to unemployment, about which he, the interviewer, was paid to ask questions. Now, it seemed, he was wrong. He had all along been speaking to a political animal of the kind he thought was extinct. He was becoming a little fed up. 'It's for you,' he said, 'to give me an explanation, surely.'

Jeffrey did not disappoint him. 'Now that's very interesting,' he snapped. 'That's a typical BBC reporter attitude. I can come out here, I hope you put this on the air, and interview this man. I can ask him for all his views. I wouldn't actually put up any ideas myself ...'

Listeners to *The World This Weekend* were not amused. They included Jean Blackbourn, then recovering from a stroke in hospital. Everyone else on the ward who listened to the radio knew she had been Jeffrey's agent.

'They all said to me,' she recalled, later, 'what is he going to say next? He was our MP, wasn't he? Did you know him well? And all I could tell them was: "He always was an excitable boy."'

The next day, the newspapers were full of the millionaire who mocked mass unemployment as a sponger's myth. In the Commons, both Tory and Labour MPs condemned Jeffrey's remarks. The new Minister of State for Employment, Kenneth Clarke, remarked, 'Jeffrey can be a bit dramatic.' Lord Young, the Employment Secretary, confirmed that he would not have used such language.

At Central Office, the anti-Archer faction rubbed their hands in their downgraded offices. In his own quarters on the first floor, a more than usually grim-faced Norman Tebbit tried to repair some of the damage by talking to reporters. But there was no doubt that, added to the injuries he had suffered in the blast, he was now experiencing a new and equally painful sensation in the region of his neck.

Jeffrey was let off after Tebbit had given him a blistering reprimand, and an order to enrol himself on a crash-course on elementary Government policy.

The Conservative Party Conference in Blackpool that October was undoubtedly a success for the Deputy Chairman. If Jeffrey spoke with maximum dramatic effect, his silences were equally impressive. Journalists could not help noticing how he appeared to have mastered the art of platform stagecraft: the visible listening to other speakers, the statesmanlike nod and the dignified handclap. He had even got rid of the unstatesmanlike car registration, ANY 1. Was he, at forty-five, at last acquiring *gravitas*?

He even appeared with Mary at a number of functions. The Tory old guard, who could never quite understand why she had married such a pushy *arriviste* in the first place, were charmed by the cool, elegant wife and mother who chatted on about her life in Cambridge. Furthermore, she seemed not only immune to Jeffrey's 'dramatic' tendencies, but possessed of the power to make them go away altogether. Was there not some way that this rare talent could be used to the good of the Party?

Alas, just as it had done with the voters of Louth sixteen

years earlier, the vision from the Old Vicarage appeared and, having done its job, evaporated, rarely to return.

Jeffrey bounced around, autographing everything he could, particularly the copies of his books which were conveniently on sale at the Conservative Political Centre Bookshop and the Imperial Hotel kiosk. Home Secretary Douglas Hurd was also the author of several political thrillers, but did not appear to have followed Jeffrey's example; perhaps he was unaware of the principles of modern marketing. Perhaps it was because, unlike Jeffrey, he did not have Deborah Owen as his agent. Or perhaps it was because he felt his own books looked better coming immediately after Graham Greene's on the shelves of bookshops.

Hurd's latest was called *A Palace of Enchantments*. In it, a psychiatrist accuses the central character of being 'dried up': 'I recommend a course of intellectual hydration [he says], say a Harold Robbins or a Jeffrey Archer twice a month. When you have read them all, start again – you won't notice.'

The rehydrated Deputy Chairman, fresh from his Conference triumph, launched himself once more on the shires and provinces. The faithful queued up to shake his hand and hear his speech and buy his books. What did it matter that it was sometimes difficult to decide if he was selling himself or the Conservative Party? They were one and the same, after all. What did matter was that Jeffrey did not come across like some grandee who had descended from Central Office as if it were Mount Olympus.

Then came the fateful decision to visit another part of the realm. In retrospect, it was an explosive mixture. The ingredients were Northern Ireland, the BBC and Jeffrey Archer.

Jeffrey had never had much luck, it seemed, with the BBC. Now, on Radio Ulster's *Inside Politics*, he waded straight into the Irish quagmire.

They were talking about the somewhat delicate subject of a united Ireland. 'If the North were to join the South,' Jeffrey innocently declared, 'I would not be surprised to find that nine out of the next ten Prime Ministers come from the

North. I wonder,' the Deputy Chairman of the Conservative Party went on amiably, 'if Ian Paisley would like to become Prime Minister of all-Ireland?'

Again, the switchboard began to smoulder. Outside, Catholic and Protestant unsheathed the ancient weapons with which they fought their bloody battles on both sides of the border. Catholic politician Seamus Mallon politely disagreed with Jeffrey's 'fertile imagination'. Ian Paisley, Protestant leader, Catholic hate-figure and thorn in the flesh of Her Majesty's Government, put it more succinctly.

'Archer,' he snarled, 'should see a psychiatrist.' (He did not say if he could recommend one.)

Back at Smith Square, the Chairman urgently requested the company of his Deputy.

Tebbit's own life had already been changed forever by the atrocious face of Irish politics. Now, he had somehow to administer a second reprimand without losing control altogether and simply throttling his subordinate. Jeffrey was henceforth ordered not to give any more interviews without Tebbit's permission and before being briefed on the subject by Central Office.

For the time being, however, the future looked rosy. The next novel was on schedule for publication in June 1986. The real-life saga of Jeffrey's relations with Downing Street was also much more romantic than unkind newspapers would have their readers believe.

Jeffrey's brief as Deputy Chairman was not just to go forth and rally the troops, something he was singularly good at. A lesser-known, but equally important aspect of his job was to report back what the troops were grumbling about. While relations between Jeffrey and Norman Tebbit went up and down, Jeffrey was going in and out of No. 10, Downing Street. The First Among Equals may publicly have kept her distance, but privately she set a high store on Jeffrey's ability to report independently on what she was fed by Conservative Central Office.

He slogged away in the shires, unpaid as ever, shaking hands, signing books, making the same speech to the same popular reaction. 'I'm a Deputy,' he told audiences in a Wild West drawl, 'now I'm going to make all you deputies go out and capture votes.'

The more fastidious Tory MPs may have winced, but they knew a super-salesman when they saw one, and they wanted him in their constituencies. Even Jeffrey probably did not realise just how good at it he was: *'Exactly £427,727 over-drawn . . . 142 years to pay that off on a House of Commons salary . . . Not A Penny More, Not A Penny Less . . . 1,172,000 copies sold . . . You can throw aside a 9 to 5 job if you have to . . . Look at me, I did . . .'*

Ruined men queued to shake the hand of the man who had come back from the brink of bankruptcy. Conservative women mobbed the athletic, self-made man so highly thought of by Mrs Thatcher. Even the liverish, long-term inmates of Central Office discovered an irritating, contradictory truth about Jeffrey: he was human.

One full-time Central Office employee who worked closely with him was James Goodsman. Goodsman came from the north of Scotland. One day he heard from Angie Peppiatt, Jeffrey's assistant. Jeffrey, she said, was going away on tour to Inverness, Moray, Banff, etc.

'What sort of brief has he had from our Edinburgh office?' asked Goodsman.

'Nothing,' said Peppiatt.

'I come from there,' said Goodsman. 'I know the local constituencies. If he thinks it will help, I'll gladly talk to him for five minutes so that he doesn't drop any clangers.'

Goodsman duly appeared in Jeffrey's office and initiated him into the mysteries of North Scottish Conservative politics. As he left, Goodsman made a jocular reference to the fact that his own father and mother would probably be at the lunch in Elgin Town Hall.

Goodsman then turned his mind to other, more pressing matters. Later, he heard that his advice had been put to good use; also, that Jeffrey had not forgotten his parting remarks.

As soon as Jeffrey had arrived in the Town Hall at Elgin, he had Goodsman's mother and father found in the crowd. He made a great fuss of Mrs Goodsman, saying what a splendid job her son was doing and how he was a vital part of the team. He made her feel 'very nice' and he was equally kind to Mr Goodsman Sr, who was quite elderly and had arthritis. Goodsman Jr never forgot this.

'He didn't need to do that,' he recalled later, 'there was nothing in it for him. It has become very fashionable to disparage Jeffrey Archer and write him off, but he did those little things that made people feel important. You don't forget them.

'It would be the easiest thing in the world,' Goodsman concluded eloquently, 'to say "Archer's a complete shit". But he isn't.'

Fleet Street, meanwhile, continued to demonstrate their unawareness of this fact. A perfectly healthy bout of xenophobia on Jeffrey's part quoted in *Cosmopolitan* magazine was now used in evidence against him by the *Sunday People*, a newspaper that made even Jeffrey's writing look, well, like Graham Greene's:

'The bloody Japanese are out there, the French are out there – and they'll cheat at anything – and the Americans, who think they're better than we are.

'If we crawl around saying: "We really don't want to beat the Japanese – lovely little people – or the Germans, we're now friends with them . . ." Balls! I want to beat them all.'

When he made a speech suggesting that pinstriped City fraudsters were not even investigated unless more than £10 million were involved, the *Daily Mail* blared '*ARCHER DOES IT AGAIN!*' Even Sir David English, a knight of the realm, could not be relied upon, it seemed. But Jeffrey's tub-thumping talent continued to be recognised in Downing

Street and Smith Square. As long as he kept out of the latter, he was welcome in the former. Even Bernard Ingham, Mrs Thatcher's powerful Press Secretary, was heard to remark that at last Jeffrey was becoming predictable.

That Christmas, the Deputy Chairman returned to Grantchester and his wife and sons, the eldest of whom, William, had just finished his first term at Rugby. It started as a quiet family affair – just Jeffrey, Mary, William, Jamie, and half the Cabinet. Mary's pre-Christmas champagne and shepherd's pie parties were becoming as celebrated as the summer gatherings in the garden.

The New Year was traditionally a quiet time in politics. Tebbit was still suffering from the effects of the injuries he had received in the Brighton bomb. Now, he decided, was a good time to go back to hospital for what he bravely described as a 'wash and brush-up'. Even more bravely, he left Jeffrey in charge in his absence.

Twenty-four hours later, Defence Secretary Michael Heseltine had resigned over the controversy concerning the Westland helicopter company. Trade and Industry Secretary Leon Brittan soon followed him onto the back benches. Brittan was one of Jeffrey's oldest political friends. Heseltine would bounce back, but the end of Brittan's ill-starred tenure as one of Mrs Thatcher's golden boys meant a diminution of Jeffrey's power base within the Cabinet.

In May, 1986, the latest opinion polls suggested that the government was doing badly in its attempt to be re-elected. In the light of the Westland affair and British co-operation with the American air raid on Libya, this was hardly front-page news. The papers looked around for someone else to blame, and one or two of them came up with Jeffrey. Needless to say, he did not agree with them. Nor did Mrs Thatcher and the 150 Conservative Associations he had visited, including those in the West Country. Insofar as anything was certain in politics, Jeffrey's future seemed assured.

That June, his new novel was published in Britain. The title had been changed from 'The Czar's Crown' to *A Matter Of Honour*.

Hodder and Stoughton had printed 125,000 copies of the latest product of the Archer–Owen–Cohen creative team. Jeffrey took shares in the ailing *Today* newspaper in lieu of £125,000 worth of serial rights. Saatchi & Saatchi, advertising agents to the Conservative government, shot a thirty-second television commercial for it at a London greyhound stadium. In the USA, Simon and Schuster printed 300,000 copies and Steven Spielberg bought the film rights for a reputed $1 million.

Jeffrey celebrated by going to the Foyles Literary Luncheon. He had been expected to turn up with Mary. With Nigel Dempster's man from the *Mail* hovering and poised to shoot, Jeffrey told him that his wife had had to go to Paris for a lecture.

'We have just celebrated our twentieth wedding anniversary,' he added. 'I gave her an antique walnut table.'

Dempster published the story anyway; but it was a far cry from the heady days when Jeffrey used to ring up the *Mail* and tell them he had just given her £100,000 to become a Lloyd's underwriter.

A Matter Of Honour is the story of a son who sets out to redeem his late father's ruined reputation. Colonel Gerald Scott, DSO, OBE, MC, leaves a letter to be opened after his death. His son Adam opens and reads it. As the tale of his father's disgrace unfolds, it widens to encompass the fates of father, son and – naturally – the balance of power between America and the Soviet Union.

The father-figure suggests an amalgam of two people. One is the real-life Major-General Sir Gerald Duke, KBE, CB, DSO, the distinguished ex-sapper and Chairman of Dover College governors, whom the youthful Jeffrey had employed at Arrow Enterprises. The other is the imaginary father he had claimed for himself, the 'colonel in The Somerset Light Infantry'.

Adam, the son, has gone to Wellington College and the Royal Military Academy, Sandhurst. His own military career, however, has been under-rewarded. This is in spite of the fact that he has 'distinguished himself in the Malayan jungle in hand-to-hand fighting against the never-ending waves [sic] of Chinese soldiers'.

While this in itself is no mean feat, it is perhaps all the more so in the light of the fact that the Malayan Emergency was a classic guerrilla war, with few opportunities for never-ending waves of soldiers. Perhaps Jeffrey was thinking of Korea. Adam is awarded an MC and a job at the Foreign Office. Then he opens his late father's letter . . .

A Matter Of Honour is clearly written to be filmed, with its James Bond-like set-pieces that range from the Kremlin to London, Paris and Geneva. As fiction it is consequently rootless, but it contains one or two insights into the author's own past: 'He should have taken his father's advice and joined the police force,' one passage reads. 'There were no class barriers there, and he would probably have been a chief superintendent by now.'

The book is less successful in its attempts at verisimilitude. Sir Maurice Oldfield, sometime head of the real-life Secret Intelligence Service, becomes Sir Morris Youngfield. A ludicrous sequence describes how six SAS men attempt to rescue Adam from the Russians at an airfield in France, while 'correctly dressed in SAS battle kit' – a naïveté unworthy even of someone with Jeffrey's limited military experience.

The efforts at bankability, too, are somewhat below par. The trail of mangled and abused bodies includes twenty pages of a naked man being tortured and a scene of homosexual prostitution. After the twenty pages of torture, Adam conveniently escapes.

At the end of the book, we are back at Dover Priory Station. Captain Adam Scott, MC, ex-Sandhurst, sits on the train having resisted torture by reciting the names of the plays of Shakespeare; he does not, however, look up and see the ruins of the priory, where, so long ago, the part of Puck was played by a young PE master.

In August, Jeffrey looked back on his first year as Deputy Chairman in an article for the *Sunday Times*. It was an amusing, anecdotal article, the sort that made full use of his gift for storytelling. Having summed up his first year as Deputy Chairman in terms of the number of ham salads and bottles of mineral water he had consumed, he went on to characterise anti-government demonstrators as Jeffrey Archer autograph hunters.

Jeffrey dismissed the rumours that all was not well between Mrs Thatcher and Norman Tebbit. Nor did he suggest that relations between himself and the Chairman were anything other than friendly. He was even restrained in hinting that he would not object to another year as Deputy.

In fact, he seemed altogether older and wiser. After a year of Westland, Libya, Militant Tendency and the dispute within the SDP, he realised one thing: nothing was certain in politics.

He looked forward to another year as Deputy Chairman. Who knows? Perhaps even he would be more predictable.

Privately, he hinted that the Prime Minister would soon be coming to dinner. After all, the First Among Equals had survived the resignation of Cecil Parkinson, the Brighton bomb, the Westland affair, the resignations of Michael Heseltine and Leon Brittan, the Libyan raid controversy and a year of having Jeffrey as her Deputy Chairman. Surely the least she deserved was a candlelit dinner for her and Denis with Jeffrey and Mary at the Old Vicarage, Grantchester.

Predictably, it was not to be.

On the night of Monday 8 September 1986, the Deputy Chairman had dinner at Le Caprice, the fashionable restaurant much loved by the grander members of the publishing trade. He was there in his capacity as one of the world's greatest storytellers, and his fellow diners were Richard and Caroline Cohen.

Cohen was now Editorial Director of Century Hutchinson, but he had remained on close terms with the author in whose work he had always taken such a keen editorial interest. Caroline was eight months pregnant.

At around 10.45 p.m., the Cohens were seen to get up and leave. Jeffrey for his part would stay behind and engage in conversation with other parties. The next few hours were to involve them and others in one of the most bizarre political scandals of the decade.

Jeffrey was about to make the biggest error of judgment since he invested in Aquablast. The result would be equally ruinous for Mary. Instead of refilling Denis Thatcher's glass over intelligent talk at her dinner table, she would shortly find herself handing out mugs of tea to the last people she wanted on her doorstep: the powerful and overpaid fear-merchants of Fleet Street.

Le Caprice lies just south of the good end of Piccadilly, in Arlington Street, a smart backwater adjacent to Green Park. Less than a mile due south is Buckingham Palace, and beyond the Palace is Victoria station.

Here, the environment flakes and peels, as it does around all big urban railway stations, and reveals the old wallpaper and linoleum beneath the smart surface of things. The streets and squares around Victoria do not have the leafy opulence of, say, The Boltons. They have an atmosphere of expiring leases and temporary tenants; of moonlight flits by unlicensed minicab. By night, the shadow of the big station is a twilight world of shunting yards; and in its fringes are the scenes of other, sadder couplings.

The Albion Hotel, Gillingham Street, was just such a setting. A sign on the door of the four-storey Victorian terraced house said 'Founded in 1914'. An old map of London was stuck to the wall. Opposite and on either side, similar hotels offered 'Hot and Cold Water'. There was a minicab office, a Chinese takeaway restaurant and a pub called the Warwick Arms. If its name seemed like an ironic tribute to another Britain, so did many of its clients. Occasionally, they would include an unwary foreign tourist booked in by a fly-by-night travel agent. More often, the bills were paid by the Department of Health and Social Security. Day and night, the Albion's fourteen bedrooms were for hire, as were its most regular patrons, the prostitutes from Mayfair's Shepherd Market.

One of the Albion's regulars was a thirty-five-year-old single mother called Monica Coghlan. Monica had been born into a devout working-class Catholic family in Manchester. Her father left home when she was five, and Monica left school at fifteen. She drifted in and out of jobs, took to shoplifting, claimed to have been sexually assaulted, and inevitably ended up as a prostitute.

Now she commuted by British Rail from her two-bedroomed bungalow in Rochdale, Lancashire, to Shepherd Market. She already had forty-seven convictions for soliciting. But a weekend's work there could earn her up to £1500, most of which she put into her savings account with the Halifax Building Society. She was, in a sad way, doing exactly what both Norman Tebbit and Jeffrey Archer had told the inhabitants of unemployment blackspots like Rochdale to do. She was getting off her backside, on her bike, and going to work. Ironically, it was now to be alleged that one of her clients was Deputy Chairman of the Conservative Party.

Monica usually called herself by the work name of 'Debbie'. She had a key to Room 6a of the Albion Hotel. On the night of Monday the 8th, while Jeffrey was saying goodbye to Richard and Caroline Cohen at Le Caprice, she was saying hello to customers less than half a mile away, in Shepherd Market. One of them was a wealthy Pakistani solicitor and entrepreneur, Aziz Kurtha.

Kurtha had come a long way to Shepherd Market, certainly

much further than Rochdale. A childhood immigrant to Britain, he had written, produced and starred in his own good, old-fashioned success story. He went to the London School of Economics in the '60s and espoused Labour Party ideals of the moderate old school. In the '70s he went back to Pakistan, from where he successfully built up business connections with Dubai, traditionally the free-market capital of the Arabian Gulf.

By 1981, Kurtha was also travelling regularly to London as presenter of a TV programme called *Eastern Eye*. As the boom years of the Gulf came to an end, he invested in London property. He had married well to an heiress called Nadira, with whom he had two children. They lived in an opulent home in Kew. Like Jeffrey's, it was stuffed with paintings.

But there were other sides to Kurtha. He retained his good, old-fashioned socialist leanings. He stood as Labour candidate in Kew to humiliatingly little effect. Paradoxically, he failed by trying to appear exactly what a successful politician like Jeffrey was not; a good, old-fashioned English gentleman. Like Jeffrey, he too flirted with the press, albeit in a more amateurish fashion. For several years, he had regularly fed anonymous stories, usually about business in the Arabian Gulf, to Jeffrey's longest-standing enemy in journalism, the magazine *Private Eye*.

He liked to take visiting Pakistani friends on adventurous tours of the capital. He was a gambler. He was a regular patron of the prostitutes in Shepherd Market. One of them was 'Debbie', the woman in the tight white jumper, black wet-look mini-skirt and fishnet stockings, whose real name was Monica Coghlan.

At about the time Richard and Caroline Cohen were leaving Le Caprice, Kurtha was leaving the Park Lane Casino. He got into his dark-blue Mercedes and drove the short distance to Shepherd Market.

There, he met Monica. She would later allege that she had already been approached by another would-be client, to whom she said she had a room at the Albion Hotel, Victoria. The other man did not want to go there by taxi, so he went to fetch his own car. He had still not returned, however, when Kurtha arrived.

Kurtha, for his part, may have been in the company of friends he was trying to impress. Whatever the truth, one thing was certain. Kurtha and Monica agreed a price, and he drove her to the Albion Hotel, Gillingham Street.

Monica let them into Room 6a, with her key.

The first-floor bedroom was equipped like all the others. There was a sink and a double bed. Kurtha and possibly others had sex there with Monica. Afterwards, she asked him to drive her back to Shepherd Market. He agreed.

Monica locked the door and they went downstairs, past the old map of London and onto the pavement of Gillingham Street. Kurtha's Mercedes was parked nearby. It was after midnight and there was a light drizzle. Both Kurtha and Monica later alleged that this was what happened next.

As Kurtha came down the steps with her, he saw a dark-coloured Daimler saloon parked near his Mercedes. The driver sounded his horn and flashed his headlights. Then he got out of the car.

Monica would claim later that she recognised him as the man who had failed to return with his car to Shepherd Market a little earlier. Now, it seemed, he had remembered the address she had given him and followed her here. How long had he been there? Had he seen her go off with Kurtha? Who was he? None of these things mattered much to Monica, whose main preoccupation was with increasing the contents of her account at the Halifax Building Society.

But Kurtha was exultant. He called her over. 'You've hit the jackpot, this time!' he told her. 'That's Jeffrey Archer!' he alleged.

As the driver of the Daimler escorted Monica back towards the Albion Hotel, Kurtha melted away. Why did he not stay, perhaps in the safety of his own car, to see what happened next? In the light of his subsequent behaviour, the journalistic instincts which he had many times demonstrated to *Private Eye* seem strangely to have deserted him. Perhaps he had not been alone with her in the room, and felt compelled to depart either with, or in hot pursuit of, his associates. Monica would claim later that she took the man upstairs and unlocked the door of Room 6a. They had sex and he told her he was a used-car salesman. He hoped she didn't mind his having followed her from Shepherd Market. He admired her nipples. Then he became nervous again and left. She took a taxi back to Shepherd Market.

Kurtha, meanwhile, had left Gillingham Street with a face and the first three letters of a car registration number. He would claim it was a dark-coloured Daimler, like Jeffrey's. The first three letters, he alleged, were CUU, the same as those on Jeffrey's number-plate. If the face was unfamiliar to Monica, it was all too familiar as far as Kurtha was concerned. To the conspiratorially-minded international business-man and *Private Eye* secret agent, this was a story to tickle the most jaded of palates.

The next day, Kurtha contacted a *Private Eye* journalist, Paul Halloran. Halloran found himself reading the draft of another of Kurtha's anonymous contributions, only this one was a bizarre variation on the author's usual Middle Eastern business theme:

A Matter of Dishonour

Irrefutable new evidence indicates that Jeffrey Archer's prurient position as vice-chairman of the Tory Party is entirely appropriate and not merely fortuitous.

In the wee hours of Tuesday, 9 September, the morally uptight Mr Archer was spotted waiting in his green Jaguar car (number CUU . . .) in Gillingham Street, Victoria SW.

An Arab-looking gentleman was seen emerging from the seedy Albion Hotel at No. 6 with a woman in the usual leatherette black skirt, white blouse and fishnet stockings. She walked towards the Arab's car.

The impetuous Mr Archer then moved into action. He hooted his horn and the woman looking at the occupant of the Jaguar car (re-

gistration no. CUU . . .) gave a knowing smile and walked towards him.

The rich Arab customer, now feeling like a lump/can of meat on a conveyor belt, looked up and walked towards Monica as she approached the redoubtable vice-chairman who then turned his face away.

The Arab spoke furtively to the woman but whatever was said caused her to look round in quiet astonishment towards Archer.

She recognised him and said: 'Cor blimey. I've hit the jackpot.'

Halloran read the article and passed it on to *Eye* Editor Richard Ingrams. But although the *Eye* had plagued Jeffrey since time immemorial with unkind stories, to Kurtha's surprise, Ingrams did not find anything very newsworthy about a story alleging that Jeffrey had been seen hanging around Shepherd Market.

The article would remain unpublished until ten months later, when Kurtha found himself reading it aloud in the witness box of a packed Court No. 13, in the High Court. Even then it would not be well-reviewed.

The Judge, Mr Justice Caulfield, would take a dim view of the literary efforts of the Pakistani solicitor.

'You didn't put "Once upon a time" at the top, did you?' he said scornfully, and looked at the jury. In a libel hearing that was in so many ways to be a battle of good, old-fashioned storytellers, Kurtha was simply not in the running.

Meanwhile, though perhaps himself unconvinced of its literary merit, Halloran passed on the gist of the story to Eddie Jones, of the *News of the World*.

Jones was the investigations editor of the Murdoch-owned tabloid whose masthead boasted 'BRITAIN'S BIGGEST SALE' and whose nickname was the 'News of the Screws'.

Jones and his editor David Montgomery knew a potential politician-in-sex-scandal story when they saw one. While *News of the World* hacks frantically tried to locate Monica, Jones casually invited Kurtha for a drink at the Fleet Street watering-hole, the Wine Press.

Kurtha told Jones what he had told Halloran. Jones played

it sceptically at first, but there was no need to do so. Kurtha, the print-struck businessman who prided himself on knowing his way around the souks and bazaars, was an innocent abroad when it came to dealing with Fleet Street.

Kurtha did not want any money, at least for himself. He said he wanted to 'get Archer'. He appeared to believe he had a mission to inform the public about what he saw was the hypocrisy of the Tory Party. He wanted two things from Jones. First, Kurtha wanted a payment of £10,000 to be made on his behalf to a friend, Arif Ali. Ali, who was the editor of the *Caribbean Times*, would distribute it to various Pakistani charities.

Second, Kurtha wanted an indemnity clause written into his contract with the *News of the World*. If the paper broke its word and revealed his name, it would be liable for any professional loss he suffered as a result.

Jones listened to all this patiently. Away from the Wine Press, his men were closing in on Monica. As soon as they had secured from her a sworn affidavit allegedly identifying Jeffrey as the man in question, and bought her exclusive story by means of a payment to the Halifax Building Society, they would let Kurtha go. There was never any question of their paying him any money.

Jones and Montgomery would eventually tell Kurtha there was no deal. In the story that they printed, there would be no mention of the fact that Kurtha had wanted the money to be paid to charity:

He offered to pay Monica for her help [the *News of the World* would declare with sublime hypocrisy] *but she refused. He then contacted the* News of the World. *We declined to enter any financial arrangement with him.*

Long after the libel hearing that ruined all of them, Kurtha would reserve for the *News of the World* his special loathing: 'Those people,' he told this biographer, 'are worms.'

Meanwhile, he went off to see Paul Foot at the *Daily Mirror*.

Foot, a leading left-wing journalist and *Private Eye* stalwart, was no fan of the Conservative Party Deputy Chairman, or of Mrs Thatcher. But without Monica, whose silence had now been bought by the *News of the World*, there was little he could do except sound sympathetic.

But Kurtha made the mistake of thinking that by giving them his story, he had secured a deal with the *Mirror*. While Kurtha was boasting that he had done a deal with a major newspaper, the news of the story spread like a rumour of free alcohol through the watering-holes of Fleet Street.

Jeffrey was blissfully ignorant of these rumours. He was getting ready for the Conservative Party Conference in Bournemouth. It was to be his second Conference as Deputy Chairman. Soon, too, the Prime Minister was coming to dinner. In the not so distant future, the prospect of a peerage, too, was surely coming closer: 'Lord Archer of Brigsley' . . . no, perhaps not . . . 'Lord Archer of Wellington . . . Sir Jeffrey and Lady Archer . . . services to the Party and the Nation'.

The prospect that he had less than seven weeks left as Deputy Chairman could not possibly have crossed his mind. To have come so far only to be brought down by such an undramatic, banal little tale . . . it was implausible . . . unbankable . . . unthinkable.

Such things didn't happen in real life. But to Jeffrey, the man who had once believed he was a millionaire when he was on the point of bankruptcy, and whose fiction had to be 100 percent accurate, real life had never been much more than a good idea. The remade man who, at forty-six, at last appeared to have *gravitas* within his grasp, was about to be taught an embarrassingly public lesson in the ways of the world by none other than the good, old-fashioned storytellers of Fleet Street.

That week, the week that had begun with his visit to her and his alleged sighting of Jeffrey, Kurtha tried to get in touch with Monica. He left messages for her at the Albion Hotel.

Back in Rochdale, she telephoned the hotel to make a booking for the following weekend. They told her about the gentleman who had been telephoning every day, and gave her a number. She dialled it, and was put through to Kurtha by his secretary.

She told him she was coming back to London that weekend. He arranged to telephone her there. But on the Saturday night in question, he turned up in person.

Monica later claimed that she thought he was there as a client again. But this time, he had a different proposition in mind. He was offering her money and anonymity to talk about the man who had followed her in the big car from Shepherd Market.

Monica was not yet under contract to the *News of the World*. Later, under their control, she would claim Kurtha had frightened her. She would describe how she went back to Rochdale on 16 September after a weekend of avoiding his telephone calls. He continued to telephone the Albion Hotel in her absence. He was in fact trying to find out what the *News of the World* was doing. Monica would claim in a newspaper article, that his 'harassment' 'compelled' her to telephone Jeffrey for help.

The newspaper article in question would be somewhat selective; after all, it appeared in the *News of the World*. It did not, for example, tell the story of their negotiations with her.

Monica was approached at the Piccadilly Hotel, Manchester, by the *News of the World*'s John Lisners. Lisners told her he knew what had happened on the night of 8–9 September. He told her the story was already circulating in Fleet Street. He was trying her out in the role of victim in need of protection in the big bad world of Aziz Kurtha and Jeffrey Archer. Lisners was satisfied, and it was arranged for her to meet Eddie Jones in London.

As he had done with Kurtha, Jones had treated her sceptically at first. Within a few seconds she had threatened to walk out, thereby convincing the *News of the World* team of what they already believed.

The *News of the World* started paying her £500 a week to compensate for 'loss of earnings'. But they did not have the talkative Kurtha. The other papers were on the trail. Nor did they yet have a story: 'VICE CHAIRMAN AND VICE GIRL', or something like that.

The first thing they did was tell Monica that she should not ask Jeffrey for money. That way, she could be prosecuted for blackmail. The second thing they did was give her his telephone number.

On Thursday 25 September 1986, a little more than two weeks after Kurtha claimed to have seen her go with him into the Albion Hotel, Monica telephoned Jeffrey at the Alembic House apartment. The *News of the World* recorded the entire conversation.

The Conservative Party Conference in Bournemouth was now imminent, and the Deputy Chairman had little else in mind:

Monica: I don't know if you remember me, this is Debbie here . . .
Jeffrey: Who . . .?
Monica: Debbie.
Jeffrey: No, I'm sorry, have you got the right number?
Monica: Well, I met you in Shepherd Market a few weeks ago and we went back to Victoria, there was a gentleman there when we was leaving. He's giving me a lot of hassle.
  He's telling me who you are and he's been offering me money. I don't want anything to do with this, I just want this guy off my back. I've got a two-year-old son, you know, I live up North.

As the tape turned, so did the screw. She kept him talking.

Monica: Well, he told me who you were, right, and he put a propo-sition to me about money but I don't, I don't want to know about any of this, I just want this guy off my back.
Jeffrey: Well, I'm awfully sorry but I don't know who you are and I don't know who he is, but, of course, if he was saying that I would tell the police straight away.

> *Monica: You would tell the police . . .?*
> *Jeffrey: Of course I would, because it's not true and I don't even
> know who you are. I'm awfully sorry, but I've never met you and
> I don't know who you are.*

Jeffrey still did not put down the receiver. With the *News of
the World* tape still running, she dangled the bait:

> *Monica: He said he recognised you, right?*
> *Jeffrey: What's his name?*
> *Monica: It's like a foreign name, Kurtha, or something like that. He
> said that he thinks you recognised him. He just won't leave me
> alone. I'm really frightened.*

Each time Jeffrey repeated his suggestion that she go to the
police, she repeated her suggestion that both she and Kurtha
had recognised him that night in question. Still, Jeffrey did
not put down the receiver. Nor did he telephone the police,
Central Office or even his solicitor. He certainly did not
telephone Mary. Instead, he asked her for Kurtha's telephone
number.

Monica said she had 'left it at home'.

Where was she calling from? She said she would call again
with the number.

Eventually, they both put down the receiver, and the tape
stopped running.

Later, much later, a legal opponent in the shape of Mr
Michael Hill, QC, would suggest that Jeffrey had told one or
two good, old-fashioned stories about how and when he first
found out about the rumours sweeping Fleet Street.

Jeffrey, however, insisted that he had absolutely no knowledge of Monica or the rumours, until he first had wind of
what was happening via Michael Dobbs, seconded from
Saatchi & Saatchi to run Central Office's advertising campaign, and Peter Jay.

Dobbs was a friend of Norman Tebbit. Jay was a former

wunderkind and British ambassador to Washington, a period of his life marked by the fact that his wife Margaret had run off with Watergate hack Carl Bernstein. He was now an executive on the *Daily Mirror*. The *Mirror*, it may be remembered, was where Kurtha had taken his story after David Montgomery's men had prematurely dumped him.

Now, while the *News of the World* was unsuccessfully trying to substantiate Monica's story, and thereby its own, by inducing Jeffrey to confirm it over the telephone, Jeffrey himself telephoned the editor, David Montgomery. While it was clear he neither knew that they were controlling Monica, nor that his telephone conversation with her had been recorded by the paper, he obviously knew something was up.

He began by routinely suggesting a lunch date during the Party Conference in mid-October. Jeffrey agreed to meet Montgomery and his new political editor, Grania Forbes, at the Royal Bath Hotel.

Jeffrey went on: 'David, you're not by any chance running a story about me this weekend, are you?'

Montgomery, with half his investigative staff busy controlling Monica, could hardly have replied in the affirmative.

'Only I just want to know,' Jeffrey said, 'so that I can go to the country free of worry.'

Montgomery's reaction was automatic. On Thursday 2 October Monica telephoned Jeffrey again; again, the *News of the World* tapes were running:

Monica: Is that Mr Archer?
Jeffrey: Speaking.
Monica: Yes, this is Debbie here.
Jeffrey: Oh yes.
Monica: I spoke to you last week.
Jeffrey: Yes, you did.
Monica: I've actually been staying with some friends in Manchester because I'm too scared to go to the house, because these reporters are there.

Once again, she was the hapless victim in the big bad world of powerful men. Jeffrey, who fancied himself as one of them, would surely not let her down. She reminded him, too, about a supposed incriminating 'picture' of him the *News of the World* had told her to mention:

> *Jeffrey: If anyone says anything to you, you stay very firm and say, 'I made a mistake. Now I've seen the picture more carefully, it wasn't him,' and that will be all right.*
> *Monica: But it was you, I've seen the picture, look . . .*
> *Jeffrey: I assure you, it was not me.*

Still she did not produce Kurtha's telephone number. Jeffrey pressed her, and she claimed she could not get into her bungalow to retrieve it. Nor, all of a sudden, could she remember Kurtha's name. The conversation was inconclusive, apart from the fact that Jeffrey now knew she had been offered money by reporters, and Monica had claimed she had rejected it:

> *Jeffrey: I think that's very good. I think you're a very honest and good person.*
> *Monica: Well, as soon as I can get the number I'll do what you said anyway.*
> *Jeffrey: And, in return, I'm afraid you'll have to say very firmly that you made a mistake. It certainly wasn't me and, uhm, don't tell them you've been in contact or there'll be even more trouble.*

Why did he simply not tell her to go away and then inform the police? There were well-established procedures for dealing with such problems. Nor, at this stage, would there have been many people willing to cast the first stone at him in Central Office or Westminster.

The answer must lie in Jeffrey's increasingly inflated idea of his own importance as a Conservative politician. He assumed that the fact of his every utterance being of such overpowering public interest, meant that the *News of the World* and other papers could not afford to ignore a story about him and a call-girl.

Now, he ignored the one irrefutable fact which an articled clerk, let alone Lord Mishcon, could have told him for nothing: *there was no story as long as he continued to deny it in word and deed*.

As the *News of the World* hoped, the stage was now set for a new Jeffrey Archer scandal. The setting, as it had been nearly twenty years earlier when Lady Osborne had heard about the dispute between Jeffrey Archer and Humphry Berkeley, was the annual Conservative Party Conference.

The Conference, held at the Royal Bath Hotel in Bournemouth, was dominated by three issues on and off the agenda:

– Security after the Brighton bomb two years earlier
– The imminent General Election
– The Deputy Chairman's sex life

Schoolboy cracks and investigative hacks abounded in unusual numbers. Instead of ignoring them, the target of both was visibly not amused. Even the lobby correspondents found him strained and tenser than usual. But it was at that lunch with David Montgomery and Grania Forbes, at which of course he was unaware of the real extent of the paper's involvement, that the Deputy Chairman's frustration began to boil over.

It was an extraordinary scene: the Deputy Chairman of the Party lunching to all outward intents and purposes in a routine fashion with the editor and political editor of the newspaper that was going to help ruin him. If they realised he had no intention of mentioning the two telephone calls from Monica, he had even less idea that they were in fact behind the calls in question.

They kicked off on safe enough ground. Who, asked Montgomery, were the key persons at Central Office when it came to organising the Prime Minister's style and presentation?

Jeffrey made various helpful remarks, not the least of which was that he was one of these persons. He personally had spent an hour with Mrs Thatcher the previous day. He added that he saw the Prime Minister on a fairly regular basis.

Montgomery listened appreciatively. Jeffrey now seemed suddenly rather keen to discuss certain scurrilous rumours about him currently circulating in Fleet Street.

'Margaret listens to me,' he told Montgomery. 'If I were to tell her that you were a thoroughly good chap, and that she should speak to you from time to time, she would do just that. But,' he added heavily, 'if I were to tell her you were a thoroughly disreputable fellow, and that she should have a word with Rupert Murdoch, she would also do it.'

Montgomery and Forbes listened in amazement. Other journalists joined the fray. Stewart Steven, the editor of the *Mail on Sunday*, pledged his support. Adam Raphael, then political editor of the *Observer*, also learned of the rumours circulating at the Conference. He despised cheque-book journalism and was generally regarded as one of the country's foremost political commentators. But even he would find himself unwillingly dragged into a legal battle featuring the *News of the World* and the *Star*.

Meanwhile, Jeffrey carried on his search for friendly newspaper editors, as if the future of the Conservative Party, the country, nay, the entire free world, was at stake. The idea that it was only his own future, and that it could now be measured not in months but weeks, does not seem to have occurred to him.

But to the minds of the anti-Archer faction at Conservative Central Office, who had harboured unkind thoughts ever since 'the novelist' had returned, there could only be good news that the future of the Deputy Chairman was under irreverent review. At the higher levels of Westminster, too, there were long memories of the youngest ever MP, the court jester who had somehow become court favourite. The apparent absence of support, and particularly of good advice, from his own Party was one factor in what happened next. But the key factor in his own downfall, as always, was Jeffrey.

On Thursday 23 October 1986, Monica called Jeffrey at Grantchester. History does not record if she first tried the London flat, and if he was unusually at the Old Vicarage in the hopes of avoiding her there. She had been away for two weeks, on holiday in Tunisia. If Jeffrey was beginning to wish she had stayed there, he gave no hint of it to her. But it was not a convenient time, and they agreed to talk again later that night.

Monica rang back at 10.55 p.m. As usual, the *News of the World* tapes were running:

> *Monica: Hi, did you . . .?*
> *Jeffrey: Yes, I did. I got a real grip of it today. Did you go to Tunisia on holiday?*
> *Monica: To Djerba. . . .*
> *Jeffrey: Do you, I mean do you have friends out there?*
> *Monica: I just took a holiday.*
> *Jeffrey: Well, I am sorry for what you are going through. They may still try to get you to talk but I've done two things today which will frighten them.*
> *Monica: What's that?*
> *Jeffrey: I can't tell you, but I can assure you it's been done.*
> *Monica: I just want these people off my back.*
> *Jeffrey: Well, that's what I worked on today.*
> *Monica: You're telling me that you've done something today, you're not telling me what. . . .*
> *Jeffrey: Well I've, I've spoken to two newspapers as well. . . .*

As well as what? The *News of the World* listeners woke up at this. But it was what they heard next that made them feel glad they were recording. History had already shown that

Jeffrey was susceptible to cleverly-worded telephone calls. But if they had not been able to replay this one later, they would not have believed their ears:

> *Jeffrey: Do you want to go abroad again?*

This was what they had been waiting for:

> *Monica: Go abroad again.*
> *Jeffrey: Uhm.*
> *Monica: It'll make things easier for me, of course.*
> *Jeffrey: What I'm saying is, if a friend of mine helped you . . .*
> *Monica: . . . a friend of yours . . .?*
> *Jeffrey: . . . helped you financially to go abroad again, would that interest you?*
> *Monica: Well, look, I'm not trying to hassle you.*
> *Jeffrey: Debbie, I realise that. What I'm saying is, would you go abroad if financially taken care of?*
> *Monica: Yes.*
> *Jeffrey: Would you be safe there?*
> *Monica: Yes.*
> *Jeffrey: And happy there?*
> *Monica: Yes.*
> *Jeffrey: How much money would that take?*
> *Monica: About three hundred for the flight, something like that, a bungalow and spending money while I was there.*

She was a prostitute. It was her living. She was very good at it. He did not disagree. She did not let him off. She wanted guarantees. Kurtha frightened her. Now she was the victim again, in the big, bad world of powerful men. If Jeffrey was bigger than them, he had to prove it:

> *Monica: All right, you say you're going to sort it out or you can deal with people.*
> *Jeffrey: Where will you be tomorrow?*
> *Monica: The station.*

216

Jeffrey: My friend would never find you . . .

Monica: I just feel scared . . .

Jeffrey: He'll just pass you an envelope and go away . . .

Monica: You must know somewhere in Victoria?

Jeffrey: Some part of Victoria station . . . the number, a platform on Victoria station would be easy.

Monica: A platform . . .

Jeffrey: Platform number three.

Monica: What, on the station or the underground?

Jeffrey: No, the station.

Monica: . . . the entrance.

Jeffrey: At eleven o'clock.

Monica: Well, how will he know me?

Jeffrey: Well, you'll be standing there.

Monica: I'll have a green . . .

Jeffrey: . . . leather suit?

Monica: Yeah.

Jeffrey: Now, how long do you think you can stay abroad?

Monica: Well, if you tell me, you know, you tell me what you want me to do. I'll stay there until you can tell me, you know, I can come home.

Jeffrey: Right. Well, if you'll ring me from abroad and tell me when you've got there safely . . . and when you ring on this 'phone [he told her] *please don't ever speak to anyone else.*

There was no story as long as he continued to deny it in word and deed. Monica called him back shortly afterwards. What, she asked, was his friend's name?

Jeffrey: Just call him David. He's just a close friend who is very safe. [He had already told her] *He's forty-five, grey-haired and a little overweight.*

It was a partly accurate description of Michael Stacpoole.

Stacpoole had already appeared in fictional shape as the proprietor of a modelling agency in *Not A Penny More, Not A Penny Less*. He was a similar character in real life, well

217

known in the Fleet Street watering-holes as a hype-artist, gossip merchant and friend of Jeffrey Archer. He was forty-five, grey-haired and a little overweight. Now, he was to be given a small but crucial walk-on part in the latest extravaganza from J. Archer Productions.

At eleven o'clock the next morning, a Friday, a bulky figure was to be seen approaching platform three of Victoria station. He was wearing a buff overcoat and carrying an envelope of the same colour. The envelope was stuffed with unused £50 notes. The figure was Stacpoole.

Stacpoole was to be seen by a number of persons. First there was the *News of the World* surveillance team, who had already wired up Monica with micro-cassette recorders and were now checking their cameras in a state of growing excitement.

Then there was a female commuter, wearing a green top. She smiled when Stacpoole approached her and shook her head. He had asked the wrong person.

Then there was Monica.

She was wearing a black, wet-look raincoat. She opened it to reveal the green leather suit. This time Stacpoole got it right.

He immediately went over to her.

'Hello,' he said, 'I'm David.'

'Did Mr Archer send you?' she said.

'Yes,' said Stacpoole. He handed her the envelope, and started to walk away.

'Hang on a minute,' said Monica.

She had been told to refuse the money, of course. Now, as Stacpoole watched, she opened the envelope and stared at the inch-thick wad of notes.

'I don't really want the money,' she told him, 'you can take it back. Tell him I'll ring him.'

Stacpoole took the envelope from her.

'Why don't we talk about this over coffee?' he said.

They walked to the nearby Grosvenor Hotel. In Edward's

Bar, the following conversation took place according to the court evidence:

First she told Stacpoole about Kurtha. 'He can't do anything to you,' said Stacpoole, 'have you been with him?'

'A couple of times,' said Monica, 'until he started pressuring me.'

'Where did you meet Mr Archer?'

'He says you are his friend,' she said, 'but he told me not to speak to anybody.'

'Tell me,' said Stacpoole, 'otherwise I can't help. I'm the one who had to make arrangements. Do you still work Shepherd Market?'

'I haven't worked since,' said Monica.

'So what's the money for?'

'To go away on holiday,' said Monica.

'Then why don't you do that?'

'I don't want to,' she said. 'I can't keep running, can I?'

She made as if to go. Stacpoole then recognised a *News of the World* man, watching them. Incredibly, he went over and had a drink with him.

'I'm here to do a favour for a very important political friend,' he confided heavily, 'he's having a spot of bother and he wanted my help to smooth it out.'

If the *News of the World*'s man sniggered, Stacpoole did not appear to notice. Instead, he ostentatiously got up and went to a telephone, where he could continue to be seen doing his very important favour. Who was he calling? Jeffrey? The speaking clock? A few minutes later, another character would be introduced into the drama.

Stacpoole, meanwhile, rejoined his newfound drinking companion.

'This is a pretty delicate job for me,' he confided, 'but I think I've managed to straighten things out.'

He pulled the wad of £50 notes half out of the pocket of his trousers.

'I'm being well paid,' he added, 'and all my expenses are being covered.'

The *News of the World*'s man kept a straight face while Stacpoole dug a deeper and deeper hole for himself. A few minutes after he had made his mysterious telephone call, the new character arrived. He was a young man in a suit. David Faber had not had such high jinks since his days as a member of the Assassins' Club.

Stacpoole joined the young man at the entrance to the bar, where they could be observed talking in low tones. Faber went away. Stacpoole then returned this time to Monica, who had not gone away after all. It was all very confusing. Once again, he pressed her to take the money.

'It will all blow over soon,' he told her, 'why don't you go?'

To make things even more confusing, Stacpoole then returned to the man from the *News of the World*.

'That man I was speaking to,' he hissed, referring to the twenty-five-year-old Faber, 'is a senior government official. *He's a very high civil servant.*' The *News of the World*'s man nodded politely, while Stacpoole went on: 'My friend's problems involve a man called Aziz Kurtha and someone else and it's been causing him a lot of anxiety.'

Finally, he admitted it. He was there to represent Jeffrey Archer. Not that they needed to know that, of course. 'I don't want any of this to come out,' were Stacpoole's immortal last words. 'I am not involved in this officially or unofficially.'

Then they all went their separate ways. Back at the *News of the World* a series of photographs was already in the fixing tray.

David Faber, the young man in the suit, had written to Jeffrey looking for a job and was invited to an interview in Jeffrey's tenth-floor apartment in Alembic House. The first question Jeffrey asked Faber was: 'Do you want to be an MP?'

'Yes,' said Faber.

The interview proceeded from there. It lasted half an hour

and Jeffrey grilled the young applicant. They parted amicably, and two or three days later Faber was informed that he could start on Monday.

Faber was paid not by Jeffrey, but by Central Office. He was a mixture of chauffeur and gofer, according to what was needed and how it suited Jeffrey. Jeffrey, when it suited him, would introduce Macmillan's grandson as 'my personal assistant'.

Faber would drive Jeffrey in the Daimler on three-day tours to marginal constituencies. He also drove Jeffrey back to Wellington School, where the latter was to present the prizes. Jeffrey had sworn he would never go back there unless invited to perform such a ceremony. He was in such a hurry to do so that Faber was booked for speeding on the M5. On the way back, Jeffrey was 'flushed' with his achievement.

Faber was sceptical, however, about Jeffrey's well-publicised claims to regular access to No. 10, Downing Street. Jeffrey certainly had weekly breakfasts at the Savoy with Mrs Thatcher's Political Secretary, Stephen Sherbourne. But his claim to regular meetings with the Prime Minister herself were in Faber's eyes highly exaggerated. In Faber's view, Jeffrey made no more than four or five visits to No. 10 during his entire term as Deputy Chairman.

Faber was in no doubt that Jeffrey wanted to be Chairman of the Conservative Party. Rumours of a rift, however, between Jeffrey and Tebbit were in his view exaggerated. Margaret Tebbit even used the Alembic House apartment to change a couple of times. Jeffrey had a good idea of his job and after the initial gaffes had looked set to survive as Deputy Chairman until the General Election.

Faber had found Jeffrey tense and snappy at the 1986 Party Conference, but attributed it to Jeffrey's apparent obsession with being on the conference platform whenever the Prime Minister was on it. He had been sent to the *Mirror* offices a couple of times with notes for Peter Jay; he had had no idea, however, that the Archer–Coghlan story was already current in Fleet Street, although he later heard that *Mirror* men Paul Foot and Bryan Rostron were reputedly preparing a 'major' Archer story.

In retrospect things had been a little strained at Alembic House, too, in Faber's eyes. On more than one occasion, he had answered the telephone in his capacity as personal assistant, only to hear Jeffrey take it hurriedly on the other line. But he had no inkling of what was behind the strange events of that infamous Friday.

When Michael Stacpoole kept his rendezvous with Monica on Victoria station, the day was beginning as normal for Faber. As he arrived at Alembic House at 9 a.m., Stacpoole was there with Jeffrey. Stacpoole was familiar to Faber, who regarded him as Jeffrey's court jester and all-purpose spare man at parties.

Stacpoole and Jeffrey left the flat together. Jeffrey had a speaking engagement in Lincoln and was driving himself that day – he was then going on to Grantchester. Faber and Angie Peppiatt (who had replaced Andrina Colquhoun as Jeffrey's other personal assistant) went on to Central Office. It was there that Faber received a telephone call – unusually – from Michael Stacpoole.

'I need to see you,' Stacpoole said, 'I've got a message for Jeffrey.'

'He's in Lincolnshire,' Faber replied.

'I need to see you now.'

'Where are you?' Faber asked him.

'The Grosvenor Hotel.'

'I can't come over to Park Lane,' said Faber, who was busy and assumed Stacpoole was referring to the Grosvenor House Hotel.

'No,' Stacpoole said, 'it's near Victoria.'

Alarm bells began to ring in Faber's mind. What on earth was Stacpoole playing at? He got into his red Honda and drove from Smith Square to Victoria. Only later did he realise he was photographed entering the hotel.

Stacpoole was in the bar. He came over immediately.

'We've got real problems, David. How much do you know about this?'

Faber, who knew nothing, listened as Stacpoole retailed a tremendous tale. 'That guy over there,' hissed the portly publicist, 'is from the *News of the World*. They're preparing a story about the Foreign Office and the death of Samora Machel. . . .'

Faber listened, and later it dawned on him that Stacpoole, still within view of the *News of the World*'s man, had to be seen to be telling him a dramatic tale of some kind, albeit not the true one.

Stacpoole's real message was clear. 'We've got to get hold of Jeffrey,' he told Faber.

Faber left the hotel, was again unwittingly photographed by the *News of the World*, and drove back to Smith Square. That afternoon, he tried and failed to get hold of Jeffrey.

That weekend he went to stay with friends in the country. One of the pleasant aspects of such weekends was the traditional browse through the Sunday papers. One of the less pleasant aspects of this one, for Faber, was seeing his grinning picture next to that of a prostitute, in the *News of the World* of 26 October, 1986:

. . . an anxious-looking man in a business suit . . . 25-year-old David Faber, grandson of former Tory premier Harold Macmillan . . . Archer's right-hand man . . . notorious reputation for high living while a student . . . wild drinking sprees . . .

While Faber's friends tried to calm him down, the twenty-five-year-old right-hand man to Jeffrey Archer tried once more to contact his employer. Again he was unsuccessful. Eventually he managed to speak to Central Office's Michael Dobbs, who advised him to stay at home until further notice.

The following Monday morning, Faber opened the front door of his flat near Sloane Square to find a reporter from the *Star* on his doorstep. He had still not heard from Jeffrey.

By Wednesday, after he had issued a stream of 'no

comments', the reporters had left him alone. Unaware that Jeffrey's belongings – including a large box of 'I'm a Deputy' badges – had already been ungracefully removed from Central Office, Faber telephoned him again at Grantchester.

This time, he received an answer.

'David, how are you?' Jeffrey sounded as if nothing untoward had happened, let alone that his and Faber's faces, with that of a prostitute, had been plastered all over the *News of the World*.

'I'll speak to you in a couple of days,' Jeffrey told him.

It was the last time they ever spoke as employee and employer; there would never be an explanation, an apology or even a standard expression of gratitude for a job well done, for Faber from Jeffrey Archer. Faber would not be called to the libel hearing. Unlike Jeffrey, he would, however, remain *persona grata* at Conservative Central Office, where he had wisely opened up his own channels of communication independent of his ex-employer.

The day after Stacpoole's and Faber's assignation, a Saturday, Jeffrey went to a rugby match. Mary was at the Old Vicarage when the first telephone call came through.

Central Office were desperately trying to get hold of Jeffrey. Where was he? It was extremely important. He had not been answering his car telephone.

Mary had no idea what was going on, except that it was urgent. When the Daimler arrived back at the Old Vicarage, she rushed out to tell him. Jeffrey was still on the car telephone after he had parked in the drive.

He rushed into the house, looking and sounding distraught. Eventually, he managed to tell her what he had just been told by Central Office. The *News of the World* were going to run a story about his paying off a prostitute. Mary did not take it well.

Nor, when Norman Tebbit telephoned her later that night, did Mrs Thatcher.

As the calls started from journalists, they had to move

from Mary's study telephone to the one in the kitchen, so that William and Jamie, home for half-term, should not hear what was being said.

So began the last night of Jeffrey's Deputy Chairmanship, with a weeping wife and two sons next door. As the calls came and went, he answered them all in person.

One of the first he made was to David Montgomery:

> *Jeffrey: I thought the least I should do before I ring the Prime Minister was ring you.*
> *Montgomery: Why don't you talk to the reporter and get an idea of just exactly what is being said? Because I have got a feeling that you will have been told a lot of things that will be rumour and speculation.*

It was an extraordinary reversal of roles, compared with the conversation that had taken place between them over lunch less than three weeks ago:

> *Jeffrey: I hope that is right, David.*
> *Montgomery: Can I get you the reporter?*
> *Jeffrey: Do you think this is a story on which I should resign?*
> *Montgomery: Well, honestly Jeffrey, you cannot ask me whether you should resign or something. I am not in your shoes. I am not the judge of that at all. It is not up to me to advise you in any way. I will speak to you after you have spoken to the reporter.*
> *Jeffrey: Thank you.*
> *Montgomery: Okay.*
> *Jeffrey: Can you ring quickly because my wife is here in tears, which is not making my life easy.*
> *Montgomery: Okay, Jeffrey.*

The kitchen telephone rang a few minutes later. It was Montgomery again; this time he had Lisners, the reporter who had recruited Monica in the Piccadilly Hotel, Manchester:

Montgomery: I have the reporter, John Lisners . . .

Jeffrey: Thank you.

Montgomery: . . . was working on the story. I am going to hand you over to him.

Jeffrey: Thank you. Will you be there, David?

Montgomery: I am afraid I have to go. The paper's at the height of production now, so if you could speak to him and I will talk to you later.

Jeffrey: And your name is?

Lisners: My name is John Lisners. L-I-S-N-E-R-S.

Jeffrey: Thank you, John.

Lisners: I am awfully sorry to have to say to you that we have a story that we are going to run in the paper tomorrow . . .

Lisners' tone was matter-of-fact, almost academic. As if, like one of Mary's colleagues, he was checking a footnote for literals:

Lisners: . . . and we would like your comments on some of the points I am going to put to you.

The essential point of the story is that you offered to pay money to a vice girl in return for her going out of the country and not mentioning the fact that she might have seen you at a previous occasion.

Jeffrey: That is not true.

Lisners: This girl apparently telephoned you on several occasions and asked you for your comments and help about matters on which she was very concerned.

One of these was the fact that she was being hassled by Mr Kurtha and she asked you for your advice.

You apparently told her to say that you had never seen her, not to mention that she had ever spoken to you and offered to help in whatever way you could. How does that affect you?

Jeffrey: That is not true either.

Lisners: That is not true? Is it true then that a girl phoned you who said her name was Debbie?

226

Jeffrey: Yes.

Lisners: Could you tell me what you said to her?

Jeffrey: On or off the record?

Lisners: On the record.

Jeffrey: I can say nothing.

Lisners: Fine. On record, is it true that you offered to pay a girl called Debbie, who telephoned you at your home, money to go away on holiday?

Jeffrey: Certainly not.

Lisners: Is it true that you asked this girl Debbie not to say that she has ever spoken to you, that she would not recognise you, that she had never seen you?

Jeffrey: No, that is not true either.

Lisners: Fine. As that is the main contention of the story – that you acted in a way which we would consider to be unusual for a man of your position, which was to offer money to a girl – I don't see how we can get much further.

    If you say that is a denial, I have to accept your denial.

Jeffrey then asked if they could go off the record. Lisners wanted to stay on:

Lisners: One further question I want to ask you is, did you send a friend of yours called Mr Stacpoole to pay her money in a brown envelope?

Jeffrey denied that he had done any such thing. Nor, he said, had he involved David Faber; nor had he sent Stacpoole to platform three at Victoria:

Jeffrey: No, you are just making it up now.

Lisners: I am not making it up, Mr Archer. I am sorry . . .

Jeffrey: Well, I shall say this to David and say it to you. I shall sue. I will win but you will ruin my career.

Lisners: Well, we won't ruin your career if you are innocent.

Jeffrey: No, you will, because it will take three years to get you to

*court . . . It will take three years to get you to court and by then
my career will be ruined.*

Lisners said he was sorry about that:

> *Jeffrey: I am sure you are.*
> *Lisners: I really am, no I really am.*
> *Jeffrey: I am sure you are.*
> *Lisners: I just feel that you have been very indiscreet in the way you
> have handled this matter and I am sorry. I think we have very
> good proof.*

Lisners, like many others, would never understand one thing:

> *Lisners: Can you tell me, on the record, why you spoke to her?*
> *Jeffrey: No, I can tell you off the record. I cannot tell you why.*

Jeffrey then spoke to David Montgomery again. Montgomery
maintained that their story was true. Jeffrey, who was still
unaware of the full extent of the *News of the World*'s involvement, told him that if the story was printed, he would
resign.

He had no quarrel with the paper, he told Montgomery.
He was not willing to spend three years suing them:

> *Jeffrey: I would resign and go amid, as you can imagine, the most
> amazing publicity. And it would be the end of me.*

He seemed to be talking straight from the heart:

> *Jeffrey: I could go back to writing. I can make a lot of money* [he
> told Montgomery, and added:] *It is very boring, but it is the end
> of what I really want to do in life.*

He was begging Montgomery now not to print the story.
Montgomery asked him for five minutes to consider it. But
Jeffrey was in the full flow of his own summing-up:

Let me say to you [he told Montgomery], *one thing and one thing clearly, so you know for the rest of your life. I believe I have an outside chance of being the Chairman of the party if this dies.*

I believe I have an outside chance of doing some work in my life that I would be proud of and I would like that privilege.

I realise [he went on], *I have made a fool of myself and I am telling you the truth about making a fool of myself. And in return what I might be able to do, for which I have never been paid as you well know.*

Jeffrey was throwing himself on the editor's mercy: 'I have been a fool,' he had told a newspaperman, twelve years earlier. But the *News of the World* was not the *Grimsby Evening Telegraph*, and Montgomery was not Pat Otter.

Fifteen long minutes later, the editor called again:

Montgomery: Jeffrey. It's David. Look, I am very sorry, but I cannot kill this story.

I have to go the way my conscience dictates and I have to print it because I believe it to be true.

And all I can do is offer you a platform to react to it in any way you wish.

Jeffrey: Norman [Tebbit] *has just called me and I have agreed to resign if you print.*

Montgomery: Yes. I have absolutely no choice as far as my own feelings are concerned.

I must go ahead and it is a very unfortunate episode indeed, for me as well as you.

It gives me no pleasure whatsoever but my people have stood up the story and I cannot resist that pressure.

Jeffrey: All right.

Montgomery: Rupert [Murdoch] *does know what is happening but, as always, he has not put any pressure on me one way or the other.*

He has left it entirely to me. And I have got a respect for that. Do you want to react?

Jeffrey: No.

Montgomery: Or shall we just leave it?

Jeffrey: No.
Montgomery: Okay, Jeffrey. Thank you. Bye.
Jeffrey: Bye.

Later, when Jeffrey had found out the true extent of the *News of the World*'s involvement in the affair that destroyed his outside chance of becoming Chairman of the party, he called Montgomery again. This time there was no mistaking his feelings:

I hope you live with that for the rest of your life when my resignation is announced.

I hope you smile for the rest of your life because you personally have achieved it.

Eighteen years earlier, he had thrown himself on another newspaper's mercy when a *Times* reporter had asked him about his dispute with Humphry Berkeley. The then would-be MP had put on the most amazing performance. Tears had come to his eyes, he had begged that the good names of his family and friends not be put at risk. He was only asking for a little back, he had said, of what he had spent his whole life giving: namely, charity.

The Times reporter had just managed to keep a grip on himself. The man who had played Puck then underwent a disturbing transformation, turning into a barking PE master: 'You'll be hearing,' he had snapped, 'from my solicitors!'

On that occasion, Jeffrey had settled with Berkeley on less than favourable terms, but managed to keep his political position. In the case of Montgomery and the *News of the World*, he would win the case but lose that position.

Both cases, however, would be distinguished by the same psychological characteristic. It was revealed only under extreme pressure, and was manifested as violent rage. It was the apparent inability to attribute to himself the ultimate responsibility for his own actions.

*

That night, he spoke to dozens of journalists apart from Lisners and Montgomery. If none of the others was as centrally involved, two would become unwilling participants in the subsequent libel hearing. They were *Sunday Today*'s Rupert Morris and Adam Raphael of the *Observer*.

Raphael had learned of the rumours going round during the Conservative Party Conference. His attention had been drawn to the unusual number of investigative reporters in Bournemouth by Sir Gordon Reece, Mrs Thatcher's former public relations adviser.

To Raphael, Jeffrey was a political acquaintance, no more, no less. Now, on the telephone to Grantchester, compared to Montgomery and Lisners, his was a not unsympathetic voice.

'How on earth,' Raphael asked him, 'did you get trapped like this?'

Jeffrey was clearly upset, and his answer was incoherent. 'How long have you known this woman?' said Raphael.

'I once met her very casually,' said Jeffrey, 'six months ago.'

'Where did you meet her?'

This time, Jeffrey did not reply. Raphael did not press him, but wrote their conversation down in his notebook.

The conversation was conducted off the record, because Jeffrey did not want the quotations attributed to him. He also told Raphael he would not let the Party down. Raphael would attribute this and other remarks to 'friends of Mr Archer' in his *Observer* article: it was a common journalistic convention.

Jeffrey said the same thing to Rupert Morris on the same terms. Neither journalist would think much more of it, until Jeffrey denied everything he had told them about meeting her in a prepared press statement only fifteen hours later.

Jeffrey's potentially damaging admission that he *had* met Monica before would result in both Morris and Raphael being subpoenaed at the subsequent libel hearing. It was an experience neither of them would enjoy.

That night, Mary asked Jeffrey: 'Did you sleep with her?'

'No,' said Jeffrey.

Early the next morning, he left for London. He was going to see Lord Mishcon.

Mishcon and Jeffrey then drafted the following statement:

I have never, repeat never, met Monica Coghlan, nor have ever had any association of any kind with a prostitute.

Some weeks ago I received a telephone call from a woman who gave the name of Debbie. She told me that she was a prostitute and that a 'client' of hers was letting it be known that we had met in Shepherd Market and that we had had an association.

I told her that this was absolutely false and that to my knowledge we had never met.

I subsequently received further telephone calls from her to the effect that the Press were pursuing her as a result of disclosures to them by her 'client' and that she did not know how to avoid the Press.

At this time her 'client' was insistent that we had in fact met.

Foolishly, as I now realise, I allowed myself to fall into what I can only call a trap in which a newspaper, in my view, played a reprehensible part.

In the belief that this woman genuinely wanted to be out of the way of the Press and realising that for my part any publicity of this kind would be extremely harmful to me and for which a libel action would be no adequate remedy, I offered to pay her money so that she could go abroad for a short period, and arranged for this money to be paid over to her.

For that lack of judgment and that alone I have tendered my resignation to the Prime Minister as Deputy Chairman of the Conservative Party.

Mishcon had ordered Jeffrey to keep his mouth shut.

Or, as he put it, 'I have advised him meanwhile not to make any further comment.'

The recipient of this advice could shortly afterwards be observed leaving his apartment in the windy, modern tower on the Albert Embankment. Norman Tebbit had already contacted the Prime Minister with the news of Jeffrey's resignation. He got into the Daimler and drove away without saying anything to anyone.

Meanwhile, back in Grantchester, Mary had started her morning by telling her two sons, fourteen and twelve, that their father was being publicly linked with a prostitute. Now they were getting ready for church. Mary, the choirmistress, stood on her front doorstep in a flowery dressing gown.

'My husband told me, and I believe him,' she told reporters, 'that he had never met this girl. There is no affair, neither technical nor sexual.'

She told them she felt only weariness and distaste. 'There's enough trouble in the world already,' she said, 'without having to make it up, without having to disturb families like mine on stories like this.'

Later they set off for church, only to return after a few minutes looking understandably embarrassed. Mary had forgotten it was the day the clocks went back. Perhaps in her mind too they had gone back to the summer of 1974 and the embarrassment of Jeffrey's involvement with Aquablast.

'I felt weak at the knees,' she had said of that occasion, 'but there was nothing else to do except carry on.'

It was exactly ten years since she had taken up the post at Newnham to support the family. It was now only three months after she had resigned from it, to return to a world that seemed stable again. Now, she was putting the same brave face on things.

'I hope I am ready for every eventuality, like a good Girl Guide,' she told the reporters outside the Old Vicarage.

By three o'clock that afternoon, the Daimler had returned to the Old Vicarage. Jeffrey and Mary posed briefly for photographs.

Jeffrey, who could not be described as a tall man, looked positively shrunken and wax-like. 'It's nice to be back with my family,' he told reporters.

Mary, close to tears, could only whisper, 'I am obviously very sad.'

A Matter of Judgment

The *News of the World* story was spread in lurid detail over five pages of text and photographs. As in all good tabloid newspapers, the substance of it could be instantly gleaned from the captions.

After

TORY BOSS

ARCHER

PAYS OFF

VICE GIRL

came

THE MONEY WILL BE IN THE PACKAGE ...

GO ABROAD QUICKLY

and

I'LL HAVE TO QUIT! TORY WHIZZKID FACES

WEEPING WIFE

The following day, Monday, the rest of Fleet Street followed it up. The different ways they did so, in some cases, were of equal interest to the bizarre story itself.

Jeffrey had already managed to persuade the editor of the *News of the World*'s sister paper in Murdoch's Wapping empire not to run the story. He had told Andrew Neil of the *Sunday Times* that there was a chance he would not have to resign if the story was restricted to the *News of the World*. Neil agreed. Later, he would tell viewers of the BBC's influential *Question Time* programme: 'It was not the kind of story I wished to see in the *Sunday Times*.'

On Monday, it was the turn of Sir David English's *Daily Mail*. In a longer and more informative piece than that of the *News of the World*, the Tory whizzkid was rapped over the knuckles for his naïveté, but credited with resigning 'as a matter of honour'.

Other papers suggested that Jeffrey was not a figure of importance in the Conservative Party, and that his resignation was a measure of his dispensability.

Meanwhile, reporters continued to cluster in the rain outside the Old Vicarage. Mary, William and Jeffrey handed out cups of tea. Jeffrey looked and sounded dreadful. He was even feeling responsible for the weather.

'I am sorry it is so cold,' he said, 'I am sorry about the rain. I just want to say we are not coming out again.'

Then he went inside. Mary stayed for a while and talked to the reporters. She agreed it would have been 'wise' if he had called the police.

'But then you know we all do foolish things under stress,' she said, 'particularly,' she added, 'when we choose to be unadvised.'

The Prime Minister sent a message of sympathy. So did the local vicar. Others were not so kind. The Conservative MP Peter Bruinvels declared, 'He has done the honourable thing and gone. As a Conservative Party we don't deal with prostitutes. We are a party of the highest morals and no deals must ever be done with people of dubious character.'

Three days later, it was unfortunately revealed that Bruinvels' fellow Conservative MP Harvey Proctor had been indulging in spanking games with young male prostitutes. In a quote recalling the days of Conservative Party sex scandals in the 1960s, Nina Lopez-Jones of the English Collective of Prostitutes announced, 'We have information which would shake the Government to its roots. We could put the finger,' she went on, apparently straight-faced, 'on some top Tory men tomorrow.'

She did not say if Monica was a member. Proctor would resign in disgrace. Bruinvels, who at best could be described as a political flyweight, would be dispatched along with his high morals into the political wilderness at the General Election.

Labour trade spokesman Peter Shore, too, had not been an admirer of the industrious Jeffrey: 'I think the greater surprise was his appointment rather than his expected resignation,' Shore said, flintily, 'and I can't see he will be greatly missed.'

Conservative Party Chairman, Norman Tebbit, had a soothing message for the Press: 'I very much regret the loss of Jeffrey Archer from our team at Central Office, although I know he will continue to be a firm supporter of the party and the Government.

'His energy and enthusiasm will be greatly missed at Central Office. I hope Jeffrey and his family will now be left alone by the press.'

The politician whose job Jeffrey had coveted was not taking any chances as the General Election approached. But now that the line was holding, there was some ribald laughter afforded at Jeffrey's expense.

But in other quarters of Central Office, there was genuine amazement. There were not many secrets kept at Smith Square. Generally, the rule was that you could tell how confidential a matter was supposed to be by the number of people who knew about it. It was an inverse rule; the more people who knew, the bigger the secret. Norman Tebbit and Michael Dobbs had apparently been in a minority.

Central Office staff were naturally regular *News of the World* readers. The first most of them knew about Jeffrey's little problem, however, was when they opened their papers that fateful Sunday morning. While some Central Office staff were telephoning each other all over London, others reread the story in astonishment. The next day, they found themselves equally amazed.

'I got into the office on Monday morning,' one would recall, later, 'and it was the old story. Did he jump, or was he pushed? And the general feeling was, he was pushed.'

For, behind the anodyne press statement, there was a ruthless closing of ranks. Norman Tebbit had his troublesome Deputy out of Smith Square before his feet had touched the ground. Out went the 'I'm a Deputy' badges. Out, too, went the expensive office furniture. Michael Dobbs put the Central Office furniture back. Peter Morrison took over Jeffrey's duties. He was rich, he was sound and he had good people to give him advice. It was business as usual, in the great Tory tradition. Even the former sprinter was unpleasantly surprised by the speed with which everyone seemed to have dropped him.

'The Cecil Parkinson thing,' said another, 'was an open and shut case. The problem with this business with Jeffrey, was that it was such an unbelievable sort of story.

'This mysterious Asian who appeared to have nothing to gain; the fact that it looked as if he had been set up by the paper; the whole thing smelled.

'People just didn't understand what was going on. And I honestly and truly believe that most people *still* don't understand what happened or how it all got started.'

Or, as another Central Office observer of 'the novelist' succinctly put it, 'I can understand why he offered the bird the money. I can quite understand him getting a load of jerks to go and hand out the money in a sort of bungled excerpt from one of his own novels.

'The problem is in the motives of the other people involved, which can only have been to destroy Archer as a person.'

In the shires, too, there was a mixture of incredulity and shock. Mrs Fitzwilliams was spending the weekend with her grandson at their Bayswater flat, when she heard it on the radio.

'I think we need some milk, Granny,' the eleven-year-old boy told her.

'Yes,' she said, 'and can you please get a *News of the World*?'

Roger Sharpley was another Lincolnshire acquaintance who had kept in touch since the day he was asked to read Jeffrey's early efforts at writing. Sharpley and his wife had a flat in Pimlico, from which he was accustomed to stroll on Sundays to the newsagent with their daughter. By coincidence, it was near the Albion Hotel. Sharpley normally bought the *Sunday Times* and *Sunday Telegraph*; but that day, like five million others, he spent 28p on a *News of the World*.

'I just couldn't believe it,' he said, later, 'I have always said there was no way he could have done it. I just don't understand,' he went on, 'why he handed over the money.'

Tim Cobb, Jeffrey's old employer at Dover College and witness to many of his subsequent adventures, did not take any Sunday papers ('they're all tripe').

'I'm a *Times* reader. I know what the *News of the World* stands for. The money is certainly possible, because he is such an impetuous fool! I can't imagine why he did it,' Cobb went on, adding: 'Surely everyone is brought up, if not by parents, to know that if anybody looks like blackmailing you, you stand your ground!'

Pat Otter did not take the *News of the World* on Sundays. His son heard about it on the golf course. 'He came in and said: "Have you heard about Jeffrey Archer?"'

Otter had not heard about Jeffrey Archer. He switched on the teletext and read all about the latest adventure of the best publicist he had ever met. This time, however, Jeffrey seemed to have slipped up.

'I think I experienced then,' Otter said, later, 'the same feelings as I experienced in 1974, as far as the money business went. As far as hanging out with the girl, I could not believe it. He never came across to me as a sexual person. A lot of the cynics I work with said, "He's guilty as hell," but I didn't think he was, to be honest. They didn't know him, either.'

Major-General Sir Gerald Duke was a *Sunday Telegraph* man. The distinguished ex-sapper did not normally take the

News of the World, but he had a great friend who was a keen 'News of the Screws' reader.

'When I read it, I thought, "Jeffrey's been a BF again . . . he's got himself into this fix and he's taken the wrong way of handling it." But I didn't believe the story.'

Nor did many others from Jeffrey's chequered past. Some of them now found themselves hounded by the tabloid press. Adrian Metcalfe found himself issuing a stream of 'no comments'. James Stredder, Bankie Bill's successor and Jeffrey's second headmaster at Wellington School, had his retirement made a misery by telephone calls from Fleet Street.

Certain persons from his more recent past, however, showed an even greater reluctance to talk to the press. This was in spite of their previously having been more than willing to do so. Unlike Jeffrey in Grantchester, neither Aziz Kurtha nor Monica Coghlan was available for comment at their homes in Kew and Rochdale. Nor did anybody seem to know where they had gone.

Others made brief and less than memorable appearances. Michael Stacpoole followed up his walk-on sensation at Victoria station with top billing on a breakfast television show. The portly publicist said he had picked up the buff envelope from Jeffrey earlier on the Friday, having spoken to him on the telephone the previous night.

Asked what he thought the reason was, he replied it was 'absolutely none of my business'.

What about the *News of the World*'s photographing the handover?

'Disgraceful,' he replied.

Jeffrey stayed at the Old Vicarage, cancelling engagements and trying to find some way of suing the *News of the World*.

It was not easy: the paper had apparently been careful not to suggest he had sex with Monica. Lord Mishcon told him to continue to be quiet. Scotland Yard considered the possibilities of a prosecution for blackmail, and announced there would first have to be an official complaint from Jeffrey. Jeffrey did not supply one. The police dropped the idea of an investigation.

But if Jeffrey was taking his solicitor's advice, others were talking in what was to be a costly fashion. That Friday, two reporters interviewed a well-built, former nightclub doorman from Rochdale. His name was Tony Smith and he was Monica Coghlan's nephew.

Smith proceeded to distract them from Monica's absence by regaling them with stories about himself, Monica and Jeffrey Archer. He seemed well-informed and the reporters listened attentively.

He told them how he and his wife had been watching television with Monica when Jeffrey's face appeared on the screen. Monica alleged she knew him. This was in early September, Smith added. In other words, she was claiming she and Jeffrey had met.

The reporters seemed rather interested in this. No doubt encouraged by their attention, Smith ploughed on. He was particularly articulate on the subject of the service Monica provided for her clients.

'One of them wanted to be dressed like Little Red Riding Hood, complete with suspenders,' he announced to the scribbling pencils. 'He had to be trussed up, and Monica would whip him on the floor of his room.

'People may not agree with her lifestyle,' Smith went on, 'she is a wonderful mother ... on-off affair with her son's father ... he's a black man ... blokes who are keen to dress up as women ... bondage ... never straight sex ... Mr Archer ...'

The reporters seemed pleased with this and money changed hands. It was one of the worst investments ever made by a British newspaper.

For the reporters were not from the *News of the World* but from its rival the *Star*. The next day, Saturday 1 November 1986, the *Star* splashed its front page with what its editor

Lloyd Turner no doubt thought would be a return salvo in the circulation battle:

Vice girl Monica talks about
Archer – the man she knew

POOR JEFFREY

This headline, and the story that followed, was to get Turner and the *Star* into terrible trouble. The following day's 'world exclusive' revelations by Monica in the *News of the World* had not only been poached by a rival, but the rival, in its indecent haste, had got the story disastrously wrong.

So far, no one had suggested in print that Jeffrey had had sex with Monica; only that he had paid her the money. Here, only six days after the *News of the World*'s damaging but apparently non-libellous story, was a possible libel. It was the opportunity for which Lord Mishcon and his men had been waiting.

What *had* Jeffrey done that night, after Richard and Caroline Cohen had left Le Caprice?

One thing he insisted he had *not* done was drive to the Albion Hotel for sex with a Rochdale-based prostitute.

An enquiry by the Conservative Party was told that on the night in question he had been to a meeting where about forty people were present. After that, he met Government Chief Whip John Wakeham. Then he drove another colleague home from Central Office. This kept him busy safely past the time he was alleged to have met Monica.

That winter, while the Conservative Party machine geared up for the imminent General Election, its fallen Deputy Chairman kept a low profile. He had been expressly forbidden by Tebbit from fulfilling any of his outstanding constituency engagements. The fact that there were over a hundred of them only made his frustration worse. He went back to what he had told David Montgomery he was bored with doing: namely writing.

He was reworking the play he had first written in 1979, the courtroom drama he had unsuccessfully sent to Otto Preminger and the producer of *The Mousetrap*. It was now called, somewhat ironically, *Beyond Reasonable Doubt*.

But if Central Office was officially out of bounds, there were other encouraging invitations.

On Christmas Day, the former Conservative Party Chairman Cecil Parkinson and his wife were invited to lunch with the Prime Minister and her family at Chequers. Parkinson, who had resigned after his affair with a secretary who subsequently had a child by him, was on the way back into favour. Then, on Boxing Day, it was the turn of the former Deputy Chairman. The Daimler bearing Mary and a smug-looking Jeffrey could be seen purring towards Mrs Thatcher's country retreat. This was definitely one political engagement Mary could classify as 'intellectually stimulating'.

Jeffrey's channel of communication to No. 10, Downing Street, maintained during his year as unpaid labourer in the shires, had not closed with his departure from Smith Square. The General Election was still imminent; it looked like taking place even earlier than expected. Mrs Thatcher had not needed to read the newspapers to know that her favourite had received hundreds of letters of support; she had written one of the first herself.

It came as no surprise, then, at the end of December 1986, that the ban on Jeffrey fulfilling those constituency engagements had been lifted. It was a measure of his standing with the First Among Equals.

He was to fulfil them in an unpaid, unofficial capacity, of course, as everyone within earshot would be reminded by Norman Tebbit. But there was no mistaking the message to the millions of thriller readers that comprised the bulk of the British Conservative electorate. Less than three months after they had puzzled over the unlikely tale of his resignation, their favourite, good old-fashioned storyteller was back.

It was the resumption of a free lesson in how to rally the faithful for the centralists, that the teacher had learned long ago, as MP for a constituency of eighty-nine villages and as a salesman who had hawked his books from Boise, Idaho, to Blackburn, Lancashire.

That January, the morose figure who had driven himself away from Alembic House a couple of months earlier was to be seen in the back seat of his chauffeur-driven Daimler, back where he wanted to be, in the company of a friendly journalist, on the way to address the faithful at the Norfolk Gardens Hotel, Bradford.

The ruins of the old industrial north was a penitential place to start, and he was uncharacteristically, visibly nervous: but after a couple of hundred handshakes and autographed books at a pound a time, he could be observed to relax a little. The standard speech did not work in Bradford, but it went down well the next day, in Pontefract. The women in flowery hats still loved him; and so did their daughters. It wasn't Archermania, but then it wasn't the Conservative Women's Conference.

The interest in Jeffrey's unofficial return to the hustings would reach greater heights when the date was set for his libel hearing against the *Star*. But his own, home-made fictional courtroom drama was already attracting backers. Marks & Spencer chief Lord Sieff, former Conservative Party Chairman Cecil Parkinson and journalist Godfrey Barker were among the 'angels' for *Beyond Reasonable Doubt*. The play, which was still undergoing the theatrical equivalent of the Archer-Owen-Cohen horse-under-the-picture refinement process, was tentatively scheduled to open in the provinces that summer.

That February, Mary too expanded her new freelance operations. The former Newnham don became 'scientific consultant' to the merchant bank Robert Fraser. The bank,

243

based in Albemarle Street a few doors down from where Mary had worked at the Royal Institution, had long been connected with the Archer family. Chairman of Directors Geoffrey Rippon had of course been a founder shareholder in the Archer Gallery; Director Colin Emson was Jeffrey's personal money manager.

Mary had also been courted for some time by the nature-loving life peer Lord Buxton of Alsa. Buxton was the Chairman of Anglia Television, whose own constituency included Grantchester, and Mary joined the board of Anglia that spring. As Director of the Fitzwilliam Museum Trust, she followed, albeit less controversially, in her husband's footsteps as a fund-raiser. The Fitzwilliam Museum's new gallery would be opened by Princess Margaret; its showpiece was a collection of fans formed by the late Leonard Messel.

Monica, by marked contrast, was not prospering. The thirty-five-year-old who had been a prostitute for half her life was to be seen peering at callers through the window of the back door of her bungalow in Rochdale. The front door was blocked by one of the few spoils of her long professional career: a red velvet sofa.

That March, Jeffrey won his battle to speed up the hearing of his libel case. 'I am prevented,' he said, in a sworn written statement, 'from any opportunity of resuming my political career.'

The statement was read by his counsel, Robert Alexander, QC. Alexander at fifty, was one of England's most formidable libel lawyers. His clients had included the Aga Khan, Kerry Packer and Cecil Parkinson. His cross-examination skills were legendary. His earning power was equally impressive; though he denied he made as much as £1 million a year, his fees regularly exceeded £50,000. His wife Maria was a former *Vogue* model turned barrister. In Jeffrey's tradition of hiring no one but the best, Alexander spelled firepower.

Mr Justice Boreham agreed. Although the libel action

would not normally have come to trial before the Christmas term of 1988, he said he would make an order for speedy trial. 'The circumstances,' he added, 'were very unusual.'

Express Newspapers, who owned the *Star*, did not agree. But there was little they could do about it. There was, however, no application on Jeffrey's part to speed up his other libel action, against the *News of the World*.

Both newspapers now fought back with whatever weapons they could find in their cuttings libraries and on the open market. On 12 April the *News of the World* returned fire on its front page:

ARCHER

CHEATED

it started, but then went on

IN TV

SHOW

The 'exclusive' story told how, a couple of years earlier, a fading TV quiz show had been in the habit of leaking questions in advance to panelists. The idea was to improve the standard of their answers and therefore its ratings.

Unusually for a front-page story on the *News of the World*, there was no prurient mention of sex, violence or anything else normally associated with that morally confused newspaper. The only thing that made the story, in their eyes if no one else's, was the fact that one of the panelists in question had been Jeffrey.

On 21 May the *Star* lobbed its own elderly grenade over the parapet and waited for the explosion. None came: not many people were interested in the story of how, after an adventure with bookmakers in the last days of Arrow, before he became a master storyteller, Jeffrey had been reported to Tattersall's Committee.

Meanwhile, with only two weeks to go before the General

Election, the self-appointed, Thatcher-approved, unpaid, unofficial, ex-Deputy Chairman and millionaire publicist *par excellence*, was charging round the country fulfilling his constituency engagements.

On the Isle of Wight, he descended by helicopter to speak for the Conservative candidate, Barry Fields. He addressed meetings, signed autographs, bantered with shopkeepers and fed the TV cameras. In Folkestone, he hijacked an Austrian band in lederhosen playing outside Marks & Spencer; wearing the bandleader's hat and waving his baton, he conducted them while the local MP played the trumpet. In Southend, he was to be seen speaking for Trade and Industry Secretary, Paul Channon: *'How quickly people forget . . . Britain under a Labour government . . . how we watched the economic success of the German nation and said to ourselves: "I thought WE won the war" . . . the days of the thirteenth Budget in four years . . . And what about the Alliance?'*

As the SDP and Dr Owen headed towards the political wilderness, the latter at least did so in the knowledge that he would be consoled there by his wife's percentage of Jeffrey's royalties.

Jeffrey shamelessly charmed, browbeat and autographed his way round the country. In Finchley for the Prime Minister, he was the soul of *gravitas*. But wherever he went, the message was fundamentally the same as it had been that day three years earlier, at the Winter Gardens, Cleethorpes: *'Exactly £427,727 overdrawn . . . 142 years to pay that off on a House of Commons salary . . . Look at me, I did . . . and so can you . . .'* – but only, of course, under a re-elected Conservative government.

Not that there was much alternative; in spite of a slick Labour publicity campaign that highlighted the Conservatives' traditional inadequacy in this respect, the Opposition once again trod on banana skins of its own making. On 11 June 1987 the divisions in the broad Left and the excesses of Labour local councils, with a divided opposition and a temperamentally conservative electorate, combined to return Mrs

Thatcher as Prime Minister of a Conservative Government for a third term running.

Mr and Mrs Archer took their family on holiday. On their return, Mary envisaged a quiet summer, dedicated in her case to the completion of her own long-overdue volume on the *Direct Conversion of Solar Energy*.

It would be a pleasant temporary return to academic life, with just her and her new Abyssinian kitten Archie, in the tiny study lined with books on inorganic chemistry, under a staircase in the Old Vicarage. Jeffrey could go off with his new play on its trial run round the provinces. The boys would be away at school; the housekeeper would keep house; the gardener would garden.

As usual, it was not to be. Archie fell ill and died of a virus. The book took even longer than expected; and Jeffrey's powerful friends Lord Mishcon and Robert Alexander, QC, agreed a date for his libel hearing against the *Star*.

It was to last considerably longer than the three days originally suggested, and would far outstrip his fictional courtroom effort in dramatic qualities of irony, suspense and rich characterisation.

Most of all, it would thrust Mary into the public eye in the way she had always feared and distrusted. But in doing so, it would not only reveal to the public the full extent of the steely will that had first shown itself in Louth and later in The Boltons. Also, it would reveal to her the extent of other emotions which she had bottled up for so long; and which now, as a good scientist, she would harness as energy and convert into power, to be exercised on behalf of her husband.

The Royal Courts of Justice in the Strand were an imposing backdrop for the latest episode in the bizarre life of Jeffrey Archer. On Monday 6 July 1987, in Court 13, the cast of Archer *v*. Express Newspapers began to assemble. All of them, in one way or another, were in costume.

The Honourable Mr Justice Caulfield was in charge. Sir Bernard Caulfield was one of the more colourful characters of a far from colourless English judiciary. He had also quite coincidentally been Deputy Chairman of the County of Lincoln quarter sessions during some of the years when the plaintiff was its MP.

Caulfield liked those present in his Court to feel they could relax, perhaps as he did himself. The seventy-three-year-old judge, a keen amateur jazz fan, had only recently been observed singing and playing the drums at an informal charity function.

Now, this hot summer's day, with the sun shining through the glass dome of the courtroom roof, he was concerned for the comfort of the eight male and four female jurors. He suggested the males 'discard' their ties and open their 'neckshirts'.

'The ladies,' he added, 'may take which course they think appropriate.'

Mary, sitting on a bench at the front of the court with her husband, did not appear to hear. She was dressed in a well-cut navy blue suit, pale blouse and dark bow at the neck. She looked for all the world like a promising young member of the legal profession. The inference, of course, was that no such person could possibly have the law anywhere else but on her side.

Jeffrey wore a grey pinstripe suit, blue and white striped shirt, and blue, white and red striped tie. The plaintiff, who was fond of telling his friends that they should never wear stripes on TV because they interfered with vision, looked somewhat less at home here than he did in the studio.

Behind them sat their QC, Alexander. At six feet six inches, he was nearly a foot taller than Jeffrey. He towered, too, over most of his legal friends and adversaries. The previous week he had defended the insider dealer Geoffrey Collier, keeping him out of prison and securing him a low fine.

Alexander opened the case by telling the jury how his

client's greatest aim was to get back into politics as soon as possible. After his resignation, he had denied ever meeting Miss Coghlan and had issued a statement both to that effect and to the effect that he admitted foolishly falling into a newspaper trap. The *Star* article in which it was inferred Monica had both met and had sex with Jeffrey was a libellous falsehood.

'That damage,' Alexander went on, 'was increased by the suggestion that the prostitute specialised in kinky sex.'

He eyed the jury.

'Mr Archer is a happily married man and his wife is sitting next to him in court today. He now puts his reputation, which is most precious to him and his family, in your hands,' he told them.

The court listened to the six tape recordings from September and October 1986 in which Jeffrey, unaware that the *News of the World* was listening, eventually agreed to pay money to the prostitute he said he had never met.

Mary listened too, as she could not help doing. For most of the time she sat motionless, with her eyes shut.

She opened them when Alexander took Jeffrey gently through his evidence in the witness box. The QC asked about their marriage.

'It is our 21st wedding anniversary on Saturday, sir,' said Jeffrey. 'I say this without any reservation. Mary was the most remarkable woman I knew when I was young and she remains that way now, sir.'

The most remarkable woman in the well-cut navy suit could no longer contain herself. Tears came to her eyes, as she looked at her husband.

Alexander took him and the jury through Jeffrey's CV: President of OUAC . . . three years on the GLC . . . MP for Louth, Lincolnshire . . . ran a small, fairly successful company . . . wanted to concentrate on political career . . . invested in a company which went bust . . . debts of £400,000 . . . determined never to go bankrupt . . . stigma . . . *Not A Penny More, Not A Penny Less* . . . sold to twenty-one

countries in a few weeks ... *Kane and Abel* ... delighted
... Tory Party Deputy Chairmanship ... no salary.

He did *not* go to Shepherd Market that night. He did *not*
pick up a prostitute. He did *not* go to the Albion Hotel. He
said he was having dinner that night at Le Caprice, with
Richard and Caroline Cohen.

After the Cohens had gone at around 10.45 p.m. he said
he talked at the bar for an hour with another person, a friend
who acted as his TV and film agent. His name was Terence
Baker.

After a brief interruption while Mr Baker went to the
lavatory and Jeffrey talked to other diners, he and Mr Baker
resumed their conversation. At about 12.45 a.m. he drove Mr
Baker home to Camberwell and then went home to Alembic
House.

This, then, was Jeffrey's alibi for the night in question.
The first day had been manageable, if busy, under
Alexander's guidance. Tomorrow would not be quite so
pleasant for Jeffrey.

On Tuesday 7 July, proceedings began and ended on a
light note, compared with the darkness in between. The
official press box only had room for eight reporters. The
Star's man was always first in the queue, but there were
twenty-seven others, nineteen of them without somewhere to
sit.

Mr Justice Caulfield obliged. While not actually sur-
rendering his own seat to the journalists who had already sat
in judgment on Jeffrey, he instituted some judicious furniture shifting. After a few minutes, four reporters had
joined him on the judge's bench, and others sat next to the
Star's lawyers.

The *Star*'s counsel, Michael Hill, QC, then proceeded to
make the plaintiff somewhat less than comfortable.

Hill, at fifty-two, was a contrast in style to the lofty
Alexander. He specialised in politely, almost regretfully,
allowing his victims to contradict themselves. Then he would
reveal the abrasive material of which he was made, and with

which he rubbed his victims' self-inflicted wounds until they bled all over the witness box. It was a very effective technique which Express Newspapers and *Star* editor Lloyd Turner were fervently hoping he would employ to maximum embarrassment in Jeffrey's case.

Jeffrey and Mary had arrived early in the blue chauffeur-driven Daimler. This time, Mary's white cotton dress and cherry blazer spelled honesty, sincerity and nothing more dangerous than one too many cucumber sandwiches eaten at a vicarage tea party.

Hill took Jeffrey through his evidence, which the barrister seemed to regard somewhat sceptically. How was it that suddenly Jeffrey could not recall when he first heard about the stories going round Fleet Street? Why did Jeffrey tell reporters he had not paid money to a prostitute?

Hill then referred to the tape in which Jeffrey had told the *News of the World*'s John Lisners that facts put to him 'on the record' about Monica were not true.

'I suggest,' Hill said coolly, 'that explanation was a piece of balderdash. Speaking on the record does not give you a licence to tell untruths, does it?'

'I gave a full explanation of that call in this court and I stand by it,' said Jeffrey.

Hill was unimpressed. 'Will you answer my question, please, Mr Archer. Speaking on the record does not give you a licence to tell untruths, does it?'

This time Jeffrey said nothing. Hill pursued with cold fury: 'Do you want me to say it again? Speaking on the record does not give you a licence to tell untruths, does it?'

This time, there was a long pause in the court. Eventually Jeffrey realised he was the only one who could break it.

'No sir,' he said, 'it does not.'

As Jeffrey became increasingly uncomfortable, Hill pursued this line of enquiry. Had Jeffrey not asked Michael Dobbs if the stories going round Fleet Street concerned a sexual relationship?

'I've no idea,' Jeffrey replied, 'it was months ago.'

'Yes,' Hill went on calmly, 'during which you have lied, and lied, and lied.'

'THAT,' Jeffrey stormed, 'IS GROTESQUELY UNTRUE.'

Eventually, Mr Justice Caulfield would ask the jury if they could stand another ten minutes of this 'injury time'. They laughed and said they could.

Jeffrey did not visibly share their amusement. Hill continued to take him, step by step, through his evidence. There was the irrational feeling that there was some personal battle between the two men. Hill's *Who's Who* entry listed his recreations as 'family, friends . . . and just living.' Also, he had been an undergraduate at Brasenose.

The third day began of a hearing which had only been expected to last three days. Hill accused Jeffrey of 'trying to wriggle yourself off the hook' by making speeches to the jury. He suggested Jeffrey was avoiding uncomfortable questions; Jeffrey denied this. After he had got Jeffrey to agree that Adam Raphael was a highly respected journalist, he then referred to the fact that Jeffrey had told both Adam Raphael and Rupert Morris that he had once met Monica, casually, six months earlier.

'What you said to them on that Saturday,' said Hill, 'was that you did meet Miss Coghlan once but that you had not slept with her.'

'Absolute bunkum,' said Jeffrey, 'and I will be happy to prove it.' His rage was beginning to manifest itself; he said Hill was being 'aggravating'.

Raphael had in fact been in constant touch with him for the three weeks before the hearing. He had warned him that, if forced to testify, he would have to repeat what Jeffrey had told him about having met Monica.

Hill pointed out that Jeffrey had given different alibis to some newspapers than he had given in court. Jeffrey denied it. He told Hill that when he had said he was at 'a meeting', he meant a meeting of forty or fifty people in a restaurant.

It was not until the fourth day that some relief would manifest itself, in the form of the most remarkable woman he knew, the pretty, dark-haired forty-two-year-old at present sitting with crisp dignity on the bench a few feet away from the witness box.

Thursday 9 July was the last day of Jeffrey's cross-examination by Mr Hill.

Jeffrey apologised for saying he had confused the dates on which he had first learned about the stories going round Fleet Street. Then he proceeded to deny every damaging aspect of the story Mr Hill put to him.

He had not approached, followed and had sex with Monica for the sum of £70 including 'extras'. He had not told her he was a used-car salesman.

He had not threatened the editor of the *News of the World* with the wrath of Mrs Thatcher. Nor had he made up the story about his having given a lift home to Terence Baker. Nor had he known whether or not Michael Stacpoole would be available before he, Jeffrey, described Stacpoole to her as the man who would meet her on platform three of Victoria station.

'You're telling this court, are you,' Hill inquired, 'that at the time you said, you had no idea whether Mr Stacpoole was going to be available or not?'

'One hundred percent yes,' said Jeffrey.

'That, Mr Archer, is a one hundred percent thumping lie.'

'No it is not, Mr Hill.'

'Stop being so polite to each other,' Mr Justice Caulfield said at one point, 'and get on with it.'

Mr Hill concluded his cross-examination. Jeffrey had told two reporters that he had met Miss Coghlan. He had given two other reporters entirely different accounts of what he was doing that evening. He had dishonestly misrepresented the matter to the jury. He had lied about the plan to send Monica on holiday to Tunisia, and he had solicited and paid her for sexual services.

Then he sat down.

Shortly before the court rose for the day, Mary took the oath.

She was wearing a blue and white summer dress. She gripped the side of the witness box.

'How old are you?' asked Alexander.

'Forty-two,' she said; her voice was barely audible.

'You should have said: "How young are you?" ' Mr Justice Caulfield interrupted, and frowned at the QC who had perpetrated such a searching question.

Then the judge turned to Mary. 'Relax, will you?' he told her. 'It may sound flippant, but try to feel at home in the witness box.'

'I wish I could, my lord,' she said.

Alexander was then allowed to go on questioning her. She told him how she was 'dumbfounded' when Jeffrey had told her of the story that was about to break in the *News of the World*.

'The thought of my husband consorting with a prostitute is preposterous,' she said, 'everyone who knows him, knows that far from approaching prostitutes, if one were to accost him, he'd run several miles in the opposite direction very fast.'

She described the events of that night at the Old Vicarage, as the calls started to come in first from Central Office, then from journalists. She said, in a breaking voice, that they had 'a very happy marriage'.

Alexander asked her how she thought Jeffrey had coped with the situation.

'I think he has withstood the outrageous barrage of events and comments with great fortitude,' she whispered, and at this point her voice seemed to disappear altogether. She broke down and wept.

The judge ordered an usher to help her down. Jeffrey dashed towards her, a clean white handkerchief in his hand. But she would not need it again. The fourth day of the hearing may have ended in tears, but the fifth would see a remarkable change in one of the many women who had wept in that witness box.

*

On Friday morning, she wore an elegant black and white silk dress and a defiant expression. The woman who had handed out cups of tea to them on her doorstep could no longer conceal her true feelings towards the overpaid reporters of Fleet Street.

'Mr Turner,' she leaned towards the *Star*'s editor, 'your paper cannot keep a consistent line from one week to the next. How about putting that in your next paper?'

Turner said nothing. He would say nothing throughout the hearing, a posture that did little to endear the balding bespectacled Australian to the jury.

Hill leapt to his feet. 'If you cannot keep silent . . .' he started, but she cut him off.

'I have long been silent, Mr Hill,' she retorted. Hill listened while she attacked him, in turn.

'I won't attempt the detailed, textual exegesis that seems to be the speciality of Mr Hill,' she said at one point, as if she were a don again, marking down a student's work with barely concealed pleasure. Hill had already shown his steel to a plaintiff who liked to be thought of as a Brasenose man; now he found himself countering the chill winds of a Newnham corridor.

'Don't be rude, madam,' he said at one point.

'Why not?' said Mary.

'Well, if you think it necessary to do so, then do so.'

'I do.' She stared at him icily.

Even Robert Alexander appeared to think she was going too far; but this was not an opinion shared by the seventy-three-year-old Liverpool University graduate on the judge's bench.

'Not to worry,' Mr Justice Caulfield told him, 'the jury may think Mrs Archer is looking after herself very well.'

The jury did not appear to disagree. Nor did Jeffrey. Mary had found a way of harnessing her emotions. Now, she set about using them in the most efficient way possible.

Hill had little luck with Terence Baker. Jeffrey's key alibi witness said he had met Jeffrey that night in Le Caprice; that they had talked until the small hours; and that Jeffrey had given him a lift home.

He said he had no record of their meeting and he had paid for his meal in cash.

Hill was unimpressed. He suggested Baker was not in Le Caprice that night.

'I was, sir,' said Baker.

Hill then announced he was calling his first witness for the defence. A theatrical murmur went round the courtroom. It was Monica Coghlan.

She came into the witness box and stared around at the packed court. She was wearing a light grey suit and a white silk blouse. She stared at the packed court until, in true theatrical style, her eyes rested on Mary.

The two women regarded each other with barely concealed contempt. Monica took the oath and Hill started to take her through her testimony.

She began nervously. She described her life as a prostitute in detail; how she commuted from Rochdale; how she regularly used the Albion Hotel; how she plied her trade in Shepherd Market.

She told how the man had approached her on the night in question; how he had disappeared to fetch his car; how she had gone with Kurtha in the meantime; how the man had reappeared; how Kurtha had told her it was Jeffrey Archer.

All the time she spoke, Mary stared at her. Then Hill asked Monica to point out the gentleman in question.

'That man sitting there,' she said.

'Point, please,' Hill said.

'The gentleman in the red tie,' she said, pointing with her forefinger at Jeffrey.

Mary's gaze began to waver. As Monica carried on with her story, Mary turned away and stared at her notebook. She started to scribble and went on doing so for much of Monica's time in the witness box. Was she too now indulging in a little textual exegesis? Mary stared at the ground as Monica stood down from the witness box, and did not look at her as she left the courtroom.

That Sunday, Rupert Brooke returned to the Old Vicarage, Grantchester. The poet had been reincarnated in the form of actor Mark Payton. The one-man show of Brooke's life took place on the lawn where he had read his poetry to D. H. Lawrence; the author of *Lady Chatterley's Lover* would no doubt have appreciated the irony in the timing.

Mary had helped organise the performance to raise money for the choir of which she was choirmistress. The Anglican accountant's daughter made a neat speech.

The event had been planned since Christmas, she said. 'But as you all know, I have been quite busy during the past week and I would like to take this opportunity to thank the teams from the village who have assembled the teas and catering for you to enjoy.'

She sat down next to her husband in the front row, Jeffrey appeared relaxed, in blazer and Panama hat of the sort more commonly seen at Lord's test matches. His own play would go into rehearsal shortly in rooms on the Chelsea Embankment. Meanwhile, the drama still had two more weeks to run in Court 13.

The second week of the hearing began with Monica continuing her testimony. She was noticeably tougher under fire. She insisted she had been paid £70 by Jeffrey for sex with her. She returned his glassy gaze without hesitation. She stood up for hours on end under cross-examination. Even Mary was observed to be sitting motionless, pencil unused, with her eyes closed.

Alexander's attempts to trap her with feigned friendliness were treated with like contempt. When he suggested she had taken 'a great deal of trouble' over her evidence, she retorted: 'Look, this happened, right? I didn't come looking for it.'

There were one or two moments of classic courtroom farce. She protested indignantly that her nephew Tony Smith had been fantasising, however, about the idea that most of her clients were keen on 'kinky sex'. 'Stockings and suspenders,' she said, leaning towards the press box, 'that's what most of my clients are into.

'I don't know what you mean by kinky sex,' she told the court, 'I have on a few occasions dressed up in a French maid's uniform or nurse's uniform.'

'What, what . . .' Mr Justice Caulfield sat bolt upright at this, 'somebody coughed and I want to get it down properly. Did she say matron's uniform?'

'Maid's uniform, my lord,' Hill said, helpfully.

'Oh.' The judge seemed relieved. 'I was a bit surprised at the matron myself.'

The next day, though, she seemed to be cracking under the pressure. Unlike Mary, she did not have the ability to withstand it. As Alexander bombarded her with questions about her lifestyle, she repeatedly broke down in tears. But she stuck to her story. She said it was Jeffrey; she had spent ten minutes lying on top of the man and looking into his eyes; she neither disliked men nor prostitution.

'Perhaps half the time,' she said, 'it keeps marriages together.'

Mr and Mrs Archer sat motionlessly together on the bench at the front of the courtroom.

The following day, Wednesday, she was back in the witness box. But after only five minutes, she seemed to lose control altogether to stronger forces. Alexander had accused her of lying in order to 'ruin a man for money'.

'Look,' she screamed, 'he's the liar!'

She had not been 'tricked' into believing the man with whom she had sex that night was Jeffrey Archer. She did not forget her clients.

'You might be big with words, okay,' she shouted at Alexander, 'I might be a prostitute. But I have never harmed anybody. Okay? I have just survived all my life.

'Why are you doing this to me?' she screamed at Jeffrey. 'Why are you doing this to your wife?'

By the time Alexander had finished, she was sobbing uncontrollably. Hill tried to console her, but she was past it. 'I've got nothing,' she said. 'I can't go back to this (prostitution) and carry on. He's got money. I've got nothing out of this.'

Monica eventually stood down after a total of sixteen hours and ten minutes in the witness box.

Adam Raphael appeared under subpoena as expected. Raphael had no time for the *Star* and nothing against Jeffrey. Now he repeated what he had warned Jeffrey he would have to say; that Jeffrey had told him he had met Monica previously, once, about six months before the *News of the World* broke the story.

'I fear,' he said, 'I did not make a mistake.'

Rupert Morris, too, told the court that Jeffrey had told him off the record that he had once met Monica.

Grania Forbes, the *News of the World*'s political editor, told the court that at the lunch she attended with her editor and Jeffrey at the Conservative Party Conference, Jeffrey had said that 'everybody had skeletons in their cupboard'.

Kurtha, too, appeared under subpoena on the stand and stuck to his story. He said he had been acting out of conviction.

'Mr Archer,' he told the court, 'was a very prominent figure who had very closely allied himself to the Conservative Party. That party had stated very plainly that it believed in Victorian values and the strict sanctity of the family. So his activity was total hypocrisy and against Party policy, and humbug. I believed it had to be exposed.'

Kurtha read out the rough draft of the anonymous article he had written and hoped would be published in *Private Eye*. But instead of his convictions, the self-confessed sins of the Pakistani solicitor were what would emerge from its pages.

'You knew this story would kill him,' Mr Justice Caulfield told the solicitor at one point. 'You know what I mean, destroy him.'

Kurtha knew what he meant.

David Montgomery took the stand and stuck to his story. Montgomery, now editor of *Today*, also confirmed among other things that he felt Jeffrey had been trying to threaten him during that lunch at the Party Conference.

Mary went back into the witness box to testify that her husband had excellent skin, with no spots or blemishes anywhere. The solar energy expert who avoided harmful sunbathing was therefore implying that his was not the rough, spotty skin with which Monica claimed to have spent ten minutes in intimate contact.

The next day, the *Daily Mirror* understandably could not resist the headline: 'THERE'S NO SPOTS ON MY JEFFREY.'

Mr Justice Caulfield adjourned the hearing until the following Monday. The summing up would then begin.

Meanwhile, he had some words of advice for the jurors. He told them they would be judges. 'And judges,' he added, 'should keep remote from people.'

On Monday 20 July, two weeks after the opening of a hearing that had been expected to last only three days, Michael Hill, QC, began the summing up for the defence.

It was to last until the following day, and was based on the premise that Jeffrey was a liar who believed that if he denied something loudly enough and often enough, then people would believe him.

In this particular case, they were expected to believe he had not paid £70 for sexual intercourse with a prostitute.

'What sort of fools,' Mr Hill asked the jury, 'does he take us to be?'

Robert Alexander, QC, began to sum up for Jeffrey by outlining the *Star*'s case in terms of doubtful testimony, unreliable motive and the overpowering need to sell newspapers.

Kurtha was not only colour-blind, a fact that had emerged in court, he was playing an 'evil' role.

Monica was a sad, disadvantaged person, but she was also an accomplished liar and actress. He reserved his special contempt, however, for the silent Lloyd Turner, whom he likened to a 'harlot'.

Jeffrey, by contrast, was 'a very happily married man with a strong family life. There is not a suggestion that Jeffrey Archer is a man who has had affairs or been with prostitutes before.'

He came to the question of damages.

'When you come to that figure,' Alexander addressed the jurors, 'we are asking you to award not a penny more but not a penny less. We are asking you to say that this is surely the most insulting, most wounding, most ruthless, the gravest libel of all times.

'We are asking you not to flinch because your verdict might have an extra benefit. It could ensure that neither the *Star* nor Mr Lloyd Turner ever put anyone through such a trumped up charge again.' Alexander told them their verdict would decide Jeffrey's reputation for the rest of his life. But there was more at stake than that.

'We have to consider,' he told them, 'whether there are any boundaries, any limits, as to what can be tolerated of the press.'

That Tuesday night, Mary, who dressed during Alexander's summing up in chaste white, went with her spotless husband to see *Les Liaisons Dangereuses*, a gripping drama about sexual misconduct in pre-revolutionary France. The next day, Mr Justice Caulfield too would begin his summing up.

On Wednesday afternoon, Mr Justice Caulfield began his summing up before ordering the jury to retire to consider its verdict in the case of Archer *v.* Express Newspapers.

The judge made the usual opening request for the eight men and four women to pay due attention.

'Just harken to me, please. Harkening means more than listening, and not in haste we are going to review the issues and the evidence in this very grave and serious trial.

'Jeffrey Archer, who sits before you, has by his own brain pulled himself from great debt to possibly considerable wealth in a few years. In material terms he can be described as rich. At this moment in reputation you may think he is a pauper, and if your verdict goes against him, you may think he is destined to endure the rest of his life as a social leper in a social workhouse for hypocrites. You can imagine how grave this trial is.'

Mr Justice Caulfield asked the jury to imagine a gravestone, with the words 'Poor Jeffrey' engraved on it. Underneath it, he went on, they might care to imagine the following names: 'The *Star* and its editor, who wish to acknowledge the co-operation of those who helped to erect it. "We acknowledge," it could read, "the co-operation of Monica Mary Coghlan, a well-known trader in Shepherd Market, and the co-operation of Aziz Kurtha, one of the many thousands of customers, satisfied customers, of Monica. A lawyer, a gambler and a writer of articles part-time. There are others, too, who have helped in this monument. Eddie Jones, Jo Fletcher, Gerry Brown and John Lisners, the protectors of Monica. Signed Lloyd Turner, editor, the Feast of All Saints 1986." That was the day of publication.

'Put that in imaginary form . . .'

Mr Justice Caulfield went on to repeat the allegations of the *Star* and warned them not to believe everything they read in the newspapers. He referred to Kurtha as the person who had identified Jeffrey and then warned them that mistaken identity was a common enough occurrence, especially in the dark.

Then he adjourned the hearing until the following morning.

On Friday, he resumed and finished his summing up. He drew the jury's attention to Jeffrey and Mary Archer.

'Remember,' he said, 'Mary Archer in the witness box.

Your vision of her probably will never disappear. Has she elegance? Has she fragrance? Would she have, without the strain of this trial, radiance?'

Had Mr Justice Caulfield read Jeffrey's fiction? Robert Alexander had already referred to *Not A Penny More, Not A Penny Less.* Had the judge, too, perhaps subconsciously absorbed the passage concerning the hero's wife, Mary?

Robin was relieved to be let off the hook until the morning. He clambered in beside his fragrant silk-clad wife and ran his finger hopefully down her vertebral column to her coccyx.

'You'll be lucky, at this time of night,' she mumbled.

No one would ever know. In a letter to this biographer, Norman A. Davies, Clerk to Mr Justice Caulfield, let it be known that His Lordship maintained silence on all matters concerning the discharge of his public duty.

His courtroom remark, meanwhile, would pass into popular legend.

Then he turned his attention to Jeffrey. Apart from his happy, full marriage, his interests were healthy and sporting. He had been President of Oxford University Athletic Club.

'Is he in need of cold, unloving, rubber-insulated sex in a seedy hotel round about quarter to one on a Tuesday morning, after an evening at the Caprice with his agent or editor?'

The judge tackled the scenario as put by the *Star*; was it likely that Jeffrey, even if he was in need of physical adventure, would seek it in that fashion?

For Kurtha, the judge had words which even he later described as 'cynical'. He referred to Kurtha's inability, because of his colour-blindness, to be certain of the colour of the car Jeffrey was allegedly driving. 'Aziz Kurtha has been,' he said, 'a TV presenter. Not being able to recognise red, green or brown, he is hardly likely, is he, to be the presenter of *Pot Black*, or a commentator at the Crucible Theatre in Sheffield?'

He stressed that Kurtha, as a solicitor, knew the nature of his oath and had emphasised he was telling the truth on the main issue.

Then he turned to Monica. Obviously, he told the jury, she had had a miserable life. He warned the jury not to let their opinion of her be clouded by pity; but nor should they doubt her sincerity on the basis alone that she wept and hurled accusations in the witness box. What they had to consider, said Mr Justice Caulfield, was her trustworthiness given the part played by the *News of the World*. He continued for some time to describe Monica and her life to the jury.

He concluded by asserting that Monica herself had described much of the *Star* article as 'sheer fantasy'. (In fact, Monica had said, 'The only true part of that story is that I went to bed with Jeffrey Archer and the rest is fantasy.')

Mr Justice Caulfield then described Jeffrey's career at Oxford, in politics and as an author. He ended with Jeffrey's reference to his wife and his happy marriage.

Then he told the jury to retire to consider their verdict. The case, 'as big a libel as has ever been tried this century' as he put it, was almost over.

Four hours and nineteen minutes later, the jury came back to the packed courtroom. It was 5.08 p.m. There were many more members of the public locked outside the doors, which were manned by security guards.

The jury foreman, a rotund gentleman in a suit and bow tie, stood to give the jury's verdict.

Jeffrey patted Mary on the thigh. 'Are you all right?' he mouthed at her.

'Yes,' she nodded and covered her face.

The foreman said they had reached a verdict; and it was unanimous. The unanimous verdict of the jury was that Jeffrey had been libelled.

What damages, then, did they recommend?

'£500,000,' the foreman replied smartly.

There was an absolutely stunned silence. Jeffrey looked

blank. Then pandemonium broke out. Jeffrey wanted to shake hands with the jury. Mary wanted to kiss Lord Mishcon. Then they both wanted to leave. In the continuing pandemonium they tried to make their way outside the court through a mob of photographers and newsmen. Mary told newsmen she was 'very delighted'. A security guard helped her into the Daimler.

'Move over, Mary!' Jeffrey barked and climbed in after her. The Daimler roared off, scattering TV cameramen.

Lloyd Turner muttered something about an appeal and beat a hasty retreat. The editor of the *Star* was followed by the rest of the press; unlike him, they still had an immediate future in Fleet Street.

David Montgomery went back to his job at *Today* after his bruising encounter with Robert Alexander, QC. But the *News of the World* had not heard the last of Jeffrey.

Alexander left the courtroom with his reputation and his bank balance enhanced. Of the estimated £670,000 costs of the hearing, Alexander's fees alone would account for around £150,000. Michael Hill, QC, who had given Jeffrey some uncomfortable moments in the witness box, received around £100,000. Lord Mishcon, for his second professional intervention in Jeffrey's chequered career, was likely to receive around £150,000. All these costs and more – the junior counsel, the *Star*'s solicitors, the transcripts, the transportation of witnesses – were now payable by Express Newspapers.

Other newspapers now capitalised on the *Star*'s disastrous investment. That night, only a couple of hours after the jury had returned their verdict, the *Mail on Sunday*'s Stewart Steven dispatched his protégée and favourite hackette, Susan Douglas, on a pre-arranged 'exclusive' assignment to the Old Vicarage, Grantchester.

Douglas's profile of Mary would be the front-page story for the *Mail*'s discriminating readers that Sunday: '*She could talk now, for it was all over. Yet the strain of the last nine months was telling on Mary Archer. . . . It was a remarkable interview . . .*'

The remarkable interview took place in Mary's study. Douglas asked Mary about her feelings and Mary told her a little in characteristically clinical and opaque terms. Jamie Archer appeared briefly with the cat and disappeared again. Unknown to them, and possibly himself, he had his own media appearance to make in the morning. Meanwhile, Douglas appeared to have been reading rather a lot of romantic fiction: *'We both let a silence fall. I wondered what was racing through that brilliant mind . . .'*

What indeed? Most likely it was the intellectually undemanding concept of a good night's sleep with the figure lurking upstairs. Jeffrey did not appear for the interview; he too had a performance to prepare for in the morning. Douglas and her photographer posed Mary in the kitchen and then sped back to Fleet Street.

The next morning, Mary rested that brilliant mind. Jeffrey, who had once declared jogging to be one of the twentieth-century farces, was now observed doing just that.

Dressed in his track-suit bottoms and his Achilles club sweater, the ex-OUAC President and Vincent's man cut a clean-living, family-minded *Chariots of Fire*-like figure, as he jogged through the Grantchester lanes with his son Jamie. They stopped briefly at the village pond, before jogging back to the Old Vicarage for a quiet family reunion with Mary and several dozen photographers.

That Sunday, the Archers, including Lola, went to church. Mary sang in the choir as usual. Afterwards, they walked back to the Old Vicarage through the ranks of the press to their twenty-first wedding anniversary party.

It was a splendid affair. A jazz band played popular hits such as 'Ain't Misbehavin'' and 'The Lady Is A Tramp'. The hundred or so guests ate smoked salmon and chocolate gateaux and strawberries and drank champagne and Pimm's on the fabled lawns of the Old Vicarage. They included Jeffrey's old assistant, David Mellor MP, Deborah and David Owen, Lord Chancellor Sir Michael Havers and ex-British Leyland head Sir Michael Edwardes. Mary had invited various friends from her Cambridge days. There were few faces from the upper ranks of the Conservative Party.

One or two favoured journalists were invited. The rest were, quite literally, in attendance; having waited outside the Old Vicarage to catch a glimpse of all these comings and goings, the motley courtiers were rewarded with a glass of surplus champagne.

Then they and all the guests went away again. The party was over. For his extraordinary misjudgment in trying to pay £2000 to a prostitute, Jeffrey was left with half a million pounds and a ruined political career. Mary's personal triumph in court meant she had temporarily overshadowed her husband; her achievement in the longer term was to have inspired new life in a backwater of the English language. As a result of Mr Justice Caulfield's courtroom remark the word 'fragrance' would enjoy renewed popular usage.

Her husband's behaviour, too, would not go without its linguistic epitaph. But it was a doubtful compliment. In the popular idiom, after the fashion of £25 being called 'a pony' and £100 'a ton', the sum of £2000 now became known as 'an Archer'.

After a Decent Interval

No sooner had the real-life courtroom drama closed, than the fictional follow-up opened in the provinces. The world première of Jeffrey's first stage play took place on 19 August 1987, at the Theatre Royal in Bath. In a last-minute attempt to spoil the suspense, an anonymous voice telephoned the theatre; in a thick Irish accent, it said there was a bomb in the building.

Nearly a thousand people were evacuated from the theatre. They stood for a hour or so in the pubs and streets while the building was searched. Lola had come from nearby Weston; Mary as usual attracted admiring looks; and Jeffrey signed autographs.

Eventually, the police let them all back in again.

Later, it would be regarded in some quarters as the dramatic highlight of the evening. *Beyond Reasonable Doubt* was revealed as a good, old-fashioned courtroom drama. The plot was straightforward: in the first half of the play Sir David Metcalfe, QC, leading barrister, Chairman of the Bar Council, was on trial for the murder of his wife. Did he or didn't he? Jeffrey was to be seen standing at the theatre entrance during the interval asking the audience this question.

In the second half, the play flashed back in time. While Sir David and his cronies regaled each other with legal anecdotes and quotations from Dylan Thomas over dinner, the truth quickly emerged. Lady Metcalfe was in fact dying of uncritical admiration for her husband. At the end of the play, some of the audience were ready to answer Jeffrey's question. Someone called: 'Author!' The spotlight swung round to his seat. But he was not there.

That night, the local reviewers sharpened their pencils:

'*Only the magic name of Jeffrey Archer could have got this play onto a professional stage,*' said the *Bristol Evening Post,* adding, '*the only tension is whether the cast will remember enough of their lines for it to make sense — not that most of them are worth remembering.*' The *Western Daily Press* thought it was '*just the kind of play you would find in a dim seaside rep in the Fifties*' but neglected to add that as the author was a native of Weston-super-Mare, this was hardly surprising.

None of this mattered, of course; the play was booked out for weeks. In a month, it would transfer to the West End of London. Meanwhile it continued merrily on its warm-up from Bath to Manchester and Brighton. Among the keener theatregoers at Bath was a young man in a blazer. He kept asking searching questions about the author. Alas, he was not from the Nobel Prize Committee; the presentable young man was a reporter from the *News of the World*.

A few days later, the *Star* announced it would not appeal against the libel judgment. Not long afterwards, the editor's seat became vacant. Lloyd Turner had paid heavily for his error of judgment; it was the one thing he had in common with Jeffrey.

Jeffrey, meanwhile, had decided what to do with the money he had won in damages. The announcement more or less coincided with the West End opening of *Beyond Reasonable Doubt*. The list of beneficiaries strongly suggested the influence of an academically-inclined Anglican accountant's daughter who was a keen gardener.

Ely Cathedral, Cambridgeshire, was thought to have received around £100,000. £50,000 went to Cheltenham Ladies' College, the exclusive establishment at which Mary had undoubtedly learned fragrance as well as physics and chemistry. The Kew Gardens Hurricane Fund was another deserving beneficiary, as was Newnham College, Cambridge.

Jeffrey's interests were also visible. Brasenose College, Oxford, the Sports Aid Foundation and the Royal Water-colour Society all received donations. So did a number of needy and disabled private individuals, one or two of whom had had Jeffrey's discreet financial help for years.

Jeffrey also agreed to write the captions for a book to be published to raise funds for the Sharon Allen Leukaemia Trust, whose Director was none other than Humphry Berkeley. Berkeley appeared to have come to some sort of understanding with Jeffrey; he had not even raised objections to Jeffrey's becoming Deputy Chairman of the Conservative Party.

Beyond Reasonable Doubt opened at the Queens Theatre, Shaftesbury Avenue on 22 September 1987. This time there were no bomb threats. The offstage cast of guests resembled an amalgamation of all Jeffrey's parties: Dr and Mrs Owen, Leon Brittan, David Mellor, Michael Caine, the Prime Minister's daughter Carol were all there. So were Michael Stacpoole and Monica. The latter was there at the behest of *Today* in the capacity of reviewer; its editor, David Montgomery, would extract this much revenge at Jeffrey's expense.

Monica, in spite of her extensive knowledge of the West End and her penchant for costumes, could not have been described as a keen theatregoer. She would sympathise with the accused barrister's wife.

Otherwise, her extensive review the following day would be summed up as follows: 'Just like a real court,' she said, 'the judge had all the best lines.'

Jeffrey, meanwhile, was denying the extraordinary notion that people would come to the play because of his recent real-life courtroom publicity. 'Absolute bunkum,' he barked at his Radio 4 interviewer, and even accused the interviewer of 'making it up'.

There was something about BBC Radio that brought out the rage in him; rage at being politely confronted with a truth he found uncomfortable. He rushed off to the post-performance party; it was at the Middle Temple Hall, where lawyers were called to the Bar.

It was also reputedly where Shakespeare's *Twelfth Night* received its first performance. Jeffrey, who had once played Puck and given some of his libel damages to the International Shakespeare Globe Centre, was not openly inviting comparison. Perhaps it was just as well. As David Mellor, the former assistant who had now far outstripped Jeffrey in the Conservative Party, said, 'He's not going to be another Shakespeare.'

The next day, the would-be Nobel Prizewinner was a little depressed at the reviews. The national newspapers had been no kinder than the local ones. The *Daily Telegraph* said it was *'mundane'*. The *Daily Mail* said it was *'very flat'*.

'We never get what we want in life,' the author told one journalist. 'I would swap all my wealth for a Nobel Prize and maybe many Nobel Prizewinners would swap their prizes for my riches.'

None of the reviews mattered. The publicity of his recent courtroom drama was of course what did. So did the fact, much derided by the local papers, of the play's outmoded innocence and well-played naïveté. It was exactly the kind of thing that appealed to the sizeable out-of-town audience who wanted to be sure of a safe soirée in the West End. They would come from the shires in their hundreds; anxious wives would crowd the foyer five minutes before the curtain went up, while their husbands tried to park the car. By October, they were booking for the following March. The earnings from his play as well as his books would see Jeffrey as well as David Owen through the political wilderness.

On 6 October 1987 the Conservative Party Conference opened in Blackpool. The night before, the former Deputy Chairman who had made such a hit at Blackpool in 1985 and begun to totter at Bournemouth in 1986, was to be seen in the box office of the Queens Theatre.

But on the day the Conference opened, he was a very long way indeed from London or Blackpool. This year, in the mutual congratulations that followed the third successive

Conservative electoral victory, there were to be no states-manlike nods and handclaps on his part towards fellow speakers on the political stage. There was not a hint, if there ever had been, of *gravitas*. He was back to being 'the novelist' again, in an aeroplane en route first for Japan and then America.

Mary, who still had not finished her own book, co-authored with Professor Jim Bolton of the University of Western Ontario, went with him and beyond to an electrochemistry conference in Hawaii.

That same month, the *News of the World* settled out of court for the sum of £50,000 damages and £30,000 costs, after they too had acknowledged libelling Jeffrey by inferring that he had had sex with Monica. The story of the £2000 he had attempted to pay her still stood, though, as it would do, forever.

But the Conservative Party's self-styled travelling salesman was soon back on the domestic political trail.

It was a situation that would be fully exploited by the Tories. Even people who had kept him at arm's length over the years were now willing to use his services in their constituencies. It was unlikely, that autumn and winter, that he realised the full extent to which he was now being ruthlessly used by the Party of which he had wanted to be Chairman.

That November, Jeffrey nailed his own manifesto to the wall in an implicit reference to the newly-vacant post of Chairman of the Conservative Party. Norman Tebbit had retired, and Jeffrey wasted no time in prescribing medicine for his successor. In a long article in the *Mail on Sunday*, whose editor Stewart Steven had been such a long-term Archer supporter, the former Deputy Chairman left the inescapable impression that he would welcome a return to the mainstream of British politics.

The new Chairman was Peter Brooke. Brooke, a former Treasury Minister and son of a former Conservative Home Secretary, made it rapidly and abundantly clear that there was no place for Jeffrey Archer at Smith Square while he was Chairman.

It was a conclusion, reluctant in some cases, shared widely at Conservative Central Office.

'Would *I* like Jeffrey to come back?' one Central Office employee who knew him well, would say. 'I have to look at it, and say, "Would it be in the best interests of the Party for Jeffrey to come back?" And I think at the moment it would not be in the best interests of the Party for Jeffrey to come back.

'And it's sad, because he's an original. He's a character, and there are few enough characters in politics. He's not the archetypal boring solicitor. The combination of conceit and this enormous ego; but with a certain charm and ability to get on well with people. I certainly can't think of anyone else like him, because I don't think that person exists.'

Another long-term inmate of Smith Square put it succinctly: 'I think he's a political animal and doesn't miss it any the less after a year in the cold. I think he perceived when he was made Deputy Chairman that it was a great comeback into political life and that he would go from strength to strength in politics. I think it must be a very bitter blow to him.

'To have the money, the success, everything ... and be denied what he really wanted it for.

'I think he's destroyed.'

That month, Mary failed by one vote to become the first elected woman member of the council of Lloyd's. She had been a 'name' since Jeffrey gave her that much-publicised £100,000 in 1977.

Jeffrey, too, had had his problems where Lloyd's were concerned. A letter of reference he wrote for Ian 'Goldfinger' Posgate, the flamboyant and controversial underwriter of whose syndicate he had been a member for years, had been leaked to the newspapers a year or two earlier.

Elsewhere, too, the once-proud name of Archer was now taken in vain. A Cambridge pizza restaurant, it was reported, had invented a dish characterised by lots of ham and a generally cheesy fragrance: it was called 'The Sword of Jeffrey Archer'.

Even the book for which he had agreed to write captions was dogged by problems. Some of Jeffrey's captions were politely judged to be inadequate. A freelance journalist had to be hurriedly hired to rewrite fifty of them for a fee of £500. When they were shown to Jeffrey, he complained that they were now too long and did not read like authentic Archer. The book was eventually published with the legend 'Text by Jeffrey Archer and others'.

On Boxing Day, Jeffrey and Mary were again to be seen arriving at Chequers. The 1988 New Year's Honours, however, came and went without reward for Archer, Jeffrey Howard. Peter Brooke, by contrast, became a Privy Councillor. Jeffrey would stay out in the cold.

He was older, grimmer, richer and yet to many eyes he was none the wiser. He did not seem to have learned the lessons a father might have taught him. Outside the High Court one day, when the libel hearing had been going well, he had emerged as usual with Mary into a scrum of pressmen. He had pressed forward, grinning, and left her behind.

When he turned round and realised what he had done, he underwent the characteristic transformation. Pushing them aside he barged back through the pressmen in whose attention he had just been basking, as if it were they and not he who had separated him from his wife. Aggressive chivalry had always been a familiar weapon in the Archer armoury. But in its application alone, it was no longer a substitute for a missing streak of humility.

In a way, he was history's marionette.

The Jeffrey Archer of the 1980s bore all the reborn, free-market characteristics of the Thatcher ethos and era . . . and its conclusion.

In the 1970s, he was the man who inflicted on himself, and then recovered from, his own recession.

The 1960s Jeffrey Archer was the ruthless whizzkid, who

both bypassed and exploited the conventional routes of ascent, in an age when people looked up to whizzkids.

The 1950s Jeffrey Archer was the soldier and policeman, who did not find the authority he craved, both in order that he might exercise it and be exercised by it.

The 1940s Jeffrey Archer: the child who was father to the man. The small boy, on the way home from school, boards the wrong train at Taunton Station. Realising he has done so as the train leaves, he pulls the communication cord. He goes unpunished – indeed, he is rewarded. It puts him into the newspapers. It gives him attention. It was one lesson he learned at an early age. He would go on boarding the wrong trains – and pulling the communication cords – all his life. But a grown-up must expect to pay the penalties.

Acknowledgements

The author would like to be able to thank Jeffrey Archer for his help and patience during the researches for this book. Unfortunately he is unable to do so. Mr Archer initially expressed his desire to grant an interview and encouraged various friends and associates to co-operate with the author. He subsequently postponed the interview on a number of occasions, the first because of a prior political commitment and the second due to the sudden and unfortunate illness of his wife, thereby urgently necessitating his presence in Grantchester. On a further occasion he was otherwise engaged in editing his new book.

It is therefore dedicated to him by default. *Nisi Dominus Frustra*.

The author wishes to thank the following for their help and patience with his researches for this book: Judy Bailey, Sir Brian Batsford, Edward Bayly, Alan Beck, Humphry Berkeley, George Black, Miss Jean Blackbourn, John Bryant, Tim Cobb, Eric and Ellen Curtis, Pat Davidson, Norman A. Davies, Natalie Downey, Major-General Sir Gerald Duke, KBE, DSO, Andy Edwards, the late John Ennals, Andrew Etchells, Julian Evans, Richard Exley, David Faber, Maureen Ferrier, Victor Finn, Major Clixby and Mrs Pauline Fitzwilliams, Freda Fox, Les Fox, Peter Gardiner, James Goodsman, Sarah Grahame, Jo Haesen, Elinor Hall, Marjorie Hurst, John Illman, Derek Ingram, Leonard Isaac, Ian Jack, Oliver James, Hilary Jones, Michael Kefford, Sir Leslie Kirkley, Aziz Kurtha, Nicholas Lloyd, Tom Maschler, Michael Maconochie, Colin McKenzie, Adrian Metcalfe, Bryan Morris, Penny Neary, Barnaby Newbolt, Pat Otter, Deborah Owen, Marie Packer, Geoffrey Parkhouse, Angie Peppiatt, the late Alexander Peterson, OBE, Maggie Pringle,

Private Eye, Hugh Pullan, Heidi Raj, Adam Raphael, Alex Rentoul, Dipty Shah, Henry Sharpley, Roger Sharpley, Dasha Shenkman, Victoria Smetherman, Cork Smith, Elizabeth Stamp, John St. J. Steadman, Edda Tasiemka, Henry Taylor, Philippa Taylor, MBE, Tim Taylor, Mary Rose Thompson, David Tilley, Olivia Timbs, Rosemary Unsworth, Jack Vincent, Elspeth Walder, Mrs J. M. Waters; and all those who for various reasons wish to remain anonymous, off the record, or on lobby terms.

The Author is grateful for permission to
quote from the following published sources:

In For A Penny

p. 1: *The Guardian* 21.7.73

Keen And Able

pp. 40–2: *The Daily Mail* 17.12.63

Charity Begins At Home

pp. 92–3: *The Grimsby Evening Telegraph* 15.10.69
p. 94: *The Observer* 16.11.69
pp. 94–5: *The Daily Telegraph* 17.11.69

The Class Of '69

pp. 110–11: *The Sunday Express* 22.11.70
pp. 125–6: *The Sunday Times* 3.6.73
pp. 126–7: *The Guardian* 21.7.73
p. 137: *The Grimsby Evening Telegraph* 23.8.74

The Prodigal Son

p. 204–5: *The Daily Telegraph* 16.7.87
pp. 228–30: *The Daily Telegraph* 8.7.87

A Matter Of Judgment

pp. 249–56 and 259–64: *The Daily Telegraph* 8.7.87–25.7.87
pp. 257–8: *The Sunday Telegraph* 12.7.87
p. 266: *The Mail on Sunday* 26.7.87

Index

MARLON BRANDO

David Shipman

He has been called *the* American actor; a blindingly intelligent man who invented 'method' acting and revolutionised his craft. He has also been accused of despising acting; 'mumbling', 'scratching' and 'itching' his way through films. While Elia Kazan thought he was a genius, Trevor Howard claimed that he had never met an actor who took so little pride in his work.

Marlon Brando rose to international fame in *A Streetcar Named Desire*, broke box-office records in *On the Waterfront*, rescued a flagging career in *The Godfather*, and scandalised the world with *Last Tango in Paris*. Yet he still remains an enigma – a Hollywood legend who refused to play the Hollywood game.

David Shipman traces Brando's career to the present day, providing new insights into the complex character who has provoked more anger and admiration than any actor of his generation. And he also follows Brando's extraordinary private life; a life marked by scandals involving children, wives and ex-wives – and his historic refusal to accept an Oscar for his most memorable role.

'Brilliant . . . a very straight-ahead account of the Great Adenoid. Shipman's great virtue is that he never goes soft on you; judgement and information come first and second, and adulation last'
Russell Davies, Observer

0 7474 0431 3   BIOGRAPHY   £3.50

RICHARD BURTON

My Brother

GRAHAM JENKINS

Richard Burton was one of the greatest actors of our age –
and one of the wildest. He is as famed for his reckless life
off-stage as for his brilliant and sensitive roles in
productions as varied as Antony and Cleopatra, Where
Eagles Dare, Under Milk Wood and Camelot.

Now Graham Jenkins gives the family-eye view of his
brother's turbulent and contradictory career: the brilliant
classic roles and the ham Hollywood moneyspinners; the
chequered relationship with Elizabeth Taylor and his three
other marriages; the public image of the jetsetting playboy;
the private passion for his family and for Wales – and the
battles with alcohol which finally killed him. Above all, this
intimate and controversial biography shines with the magic
of Richard Burton, flawed genius and enduring friend.

'The stories of wine, women and lusty song acquire a new
credibility from this close and apparently unembittered
source'
DAILY TELEGRAPH

0 7474 0351 1   BIOGRAPHY   £3.50

MONTY
THE MAN BEHIND THE LEGEND

NIGEL HAMILTON

'There are people who often think I am slightly
mad . . .'

He went into battle in World War I armed with a sword: he
emerged from World War II as 'the first soldier of Europe' and the
greatest British general since Nelson – with a reputation for being
vain, cantankerous, and more than a little strange.

A matchless tactician, Bernard Law Montgomery – later Viscount
Montgomery of Alamein – defeated Rommel in the desert,
masterminded the D-Day landings, and triumphed at the Battle of
Normandy – the greatest Allied victory of the war.

Yet what was he like? Was he, as Churchill called him, 'a little man
on the make', or was he the brilliant, difficult, yet considerate and
extremely lonely man held dear to friends and fellow-soldiers
alike?

MONTY: THE MAN BEHIND THE LEGEND paints a
comprehensive picture of Monty as soldier, diplomat, family-man
and friend. The definitive one-volume illustrated biography, it is
written by his official biographer and contains new and exclusive
material.

0 7474 0266 3   BIOGRAPHY   £3.99

CARY GRANT
A TOUCH OF ELEGANCE

WARREN G HARRIS

Cary Grant, adored throughout the world as the witty, debonair star of over seventy films, cultivated a screen image of ageless style which masked a private life of insecurity and tragedy.

Born in Bristol as Archie Leach, the man who would rise to play leading roles alongside such screen goddesses as Marlene Dietrich and Marilyn Monroe, was the son of an alcoholic clothes-presser and of a mother who disappeared suddenly when he was ten. Grant thought she'd abandoned him only to discover twenty years later that she'd been committed to a mental asylum. The trauma cast a shadow over the rest of his life.

In this fascinating and compelling biography Warren G Harris reveals all about Grant's five marriages, his affairs, his rapid ascent to stardom in Hollywood, his nervous breakdowns, his alleged bisexuality and his mid-life liberation through LSD therapy. It is a story of a life of magnificent achievement, of success mixed with despair, of stardom – of a man of incomparable charm, known as the 'epitome of elegance'.

0 7474 0202 7   BIOGRAPHY   £3.50

A selection of bestsellers from SPHERE

FICTION

LORDS OF THE AIR	Graham Masterton	£3.99 ☐
THE PALACE	Paul Erdman	£3.50 ☐
KALEIDOSCOPE	Danielle Steel	£3.50 ☐
AMTRAK WARS VOL. 4	Patrick Tilley	£3.50 ☐
TO SAIL BEYOND THE SUNSET	Robert A. Heinlein	£3.50 ☐

FILM AND TV TIE-IN

WILLOW	Wayland Drew	£2.99 ☐
BUSTER	Colin Shindler	£2.99 ☐
COMING TOGETHER	Alexandra Hine	£2.99 ☐
RUN FOR YOUR LIFE	Stuart Collins	£2.99 ☐
BLACK FOREST CLINIC	Peter Heim	£2.99 ☐

NON-FICTION

DETOUR	Cheryl Crane	£3.99 ☐
MARLON BRANDO	David Shipman	£3.50 ☐
MONTY: THE MAN BEHIND THE LEGEND	Nigel Hamilton	£3.99 ☐
BURTON: MY BROTHER	Graham Jenkins	£3.50 ☐
BARE-FACED MESSIAH	Russell Miller	£3.99 ☐
THE COCHIN CONNECTION	Alison and Brian Milgate	£3.50 ☐

All Sphere books are available at your local bookshop or newsagent, or can be ordered direct from the publisher. Just tick the titles you want and fill in the form below.

Name _____

Address _____

_____

Write to Sphere Books, Cash Sales Department, P.O. Box 11, Falmouth, Cornwall TR10 9EN

Please enclose a cheque or postal order to the value of the cover price plus:

UK: 60p for the first book, 25p for the second book and 15p for each additional book ordered to a maximum charge of £1.90.

OVERSEAS & EIRE: £1.25 for the first book, 75p for the second book and 28p for each subsequent title ordered.

BFPO: 60p for the first book, 25p for the second book plus 15p per copy for the next 7 books, thereafter 9p per book.

Sphere Books reserve the right to show new retail prices on covers which may differ from those previously advertised in the text elsewhere, and to increase postal rates in accordance with the P.O.